THE GUNPOWDER COAST
JOSEPH MACKINNON

I0537324

Guy Faux Book Company Ltd.
Toronto, Canada

For my parents.

THE GUNPOWDER COAST

"If socialism is a social necessity, then it would be human nature and not socialism which would have to readjust itself, if ever the two clashed."

—**Karl Kautsky**

PROLOGUE

The five of them sat in silence trying desperately to clear their lungs without alerting the Burrower drones skulking above. Sergeant Wesley Miller came up the rear covered in soot and soil, shaking his head. Using rudimentary sign language, he indicated that the rest of their squad didn't survive the cave in.

In the darkness ahead came a voice: "Enoch? Mehdi?"

Miller shook his head.

Not only did the cave in mean that they no longer had backup, they also no longer had anti-armour weaponry. Enoch and Mehdi, who made up the squad's bazooka team, were now engulfed in a flood of rock and clay. To clear the tunnel and to reach the centre of the red zone was already a Herculean effort; to do it with half the necessary trigger fingers and only small arms made the implausible virtually impossible.

They had travelled north of the English Democratic Socialist (EDS) air base in an attempt to avoid enemy Reduvius and Burrower drones, Goliath mechs, and the EDS cyborg units. This attempt was clearly no good; not for a lack of planning or bad strategy, but plain bad luck. Nevertheless, they remained committed to the mission. Besides, there was no going back; the eight good men the tunnel claimed were now mortar in a new back wall that made sure of it.

"We've got five, ten minutes, tops before they dig again," Miller said gloomily to anyone listening.

There was more thunder above. Silt rained down on them, nearly putting out Lieutenant Hugh McGregor's torch. He set the stave between his crooked knees and cupped his hands around the flame. As the enemy's machinery screeched and groaned—hungry for a few more regressive morsels—Hugh blew on the wick and whispered life back to their only light in the cramped, dark tunnel outside quarantined Lytham St. Annes. The light revealed who was still around, still kicking.

The geezer across from McGregor was a corporal from the decimated Independent Army named Nick Kemp. He was only beginning to realize the extent of his injuries, which he didn't make a fuss about although he probably should have. Like Atlas, Kemp had held the earth up, just long enough for the others to get through as the tunnel collapsed. While he too had made it through, the cascading stone and earth left their mark on him. His clavicle was broken. A shard of bone gored through his infrared camouflage. His

1

shoulder had caught the weight, but Kemp's face also took a beating. Were it not for his beard, his crushed, toothless jaw would likely have fallen to the floor or left to dangle. He wasn't going to make it far and he knew it. Although, and it may have been a trick of the light produced by McGregor's torch, Kemp didn't seem to mind. Unable to enunciate his prayers, he bowed his head and gurgled.

While Sergeant Miller tried to recharge his electric canopy— a plasmic shield that had already absorbed and deflected over a kilo of lead—Captain James Khatri, too tall to stand, went man to man with his spine curved like a question mark, and asked whether they were ready for one last drive. The fire danced in his determined eyes, which he passed on with every confirmation. Finally he set his heavy hand on McGregor's bowed shoulder. "They knew the risk."

"We better come to know their reward," answered McGregor.

They nodded in unison, fully aware of the demands on their remaining vigor.

Beside Kemp still gurgling away, a smaller, gaunt regular named Lenny Kaczynski was resetting broken fingers. He heard Kemp splashing about some sacred rhythms. He looked over to the source. "Good Lord!" he cried under his breath, concern diverted from his upturned fingers to the man next to him. "Eh, Cap'n…" He nudged Khatri and pulled McGregor's torch over to illuminate Kemp. "They've done up Nic'las pretty good."

Khatri pulled tunnel behind him and his injured man closer. He knelt down beside Kemp, and looked him over with a doctor's familiarity. "What're you going on about, Lenny?" He gently turned his patient's head. "Kemp looks good to me," he lied, nauseated by a passing glimpse into Kemp's throat. "Eh, Nicky boy? You'll be just fine." The Captain took the weight of Nick's plasma gun off of his crushed shoulder, and set it down between them. He stripped off and emptied his own bandolier, and used it as a sling to hold up Kemp's arm.

McGregor tried handing the torch off to Bob Dytryk who was oblivious to the bad news and busy feeding a fresh ammo belt into his machine gun, the red-hot barrel of which glowed in the dark. Instead, McGregor passed it off to Kaczynski. "Hold this, will yah?"

"Okay, Lieutenant. But it's the last time!" Kaczynski laughed morosely.

With his hands free, McGregor readjusted the order of grenades in his waist pouches. The priority went to his thermite and anti-personnel grenades, and that priority was reflected by their placement nearer his hip. "Wish I had a mickey for yah, Nick."

2

Completing Kemp's battlefield sling, Khatri shifted back and apprized his work. "Nah, he's good to go. *Eh?* Throw a few stitches in yah and you'll be sweet-talking the birds at Mises Tavern in no time."

McGregor brushed dirt off of an orange-striped electrostatic smoke grenade and slotted it away. "Notice Captain K said *sweet-talking* and not *sweet-looking*?"

Kemp's broken jaw couldn't stop him from smiling. His brows tented and his eyes wrinkled. He forgot his injuries—which shock had no small hand in helping with—and tried to reply. Though his tongue wagged, he couldn't produce any full words, but every one of his brothers knew what he was trying to say: *"All the girls in Underpool are pretty."* He wasn't wrong.

Captain Khatri pulled a bandage out of his satchel and tried to apply it to Kemp, but Kemp waved it away. Instead, the ghoulish-looking Corporal picked up his plasma gun, fought to his feet, and re-familiarized himself with his weapon, which was out of place in his left hand.

Using the bandage to secure the gun to Kemp's forearm, Khatri shuddered at the sound of Burrowers starting up again and clawing away in the tunnel behind them. "Those chickenshits..."

Seeing Nick Kemp bleeding on his feet with a new design for war, the rest of the lot firmed up. They readied their weapons and puffed their chests full of damp, rotten air.

Finished with playing doctor, Khatri picked up his automatic rifle, and grabbed the torch from Kaczynski. "I'm going to take a quick look up around the bend. All of you, be ready to go." He ran ahead to scout the way forward and the golden light went with him. Absent an explosion or a gunshot, the squad figured their luck was turning around. Once more, light gave the tunnel walls shape and colour, and the Captain returned, dragging his head along the ceiling. "Tunnel diverges. Keep right." He tucked the torch under his arm, and tried to establish true north using his map and compass.

Miller repeated the direction further down the line even though it was impossible to have missed it the first time around. "Keep right!"

"They must think we're headed northeast to sabotage the server towers," said Khatri, obsessing over his map of Lancashire County in North West England.

There was some confusion between Dytryk and Kaczynski, expressed in curt incoherent blasts of slobber.

"Lenny, need me to spell it out for you?" the Captain asked angrily.

Kaczynski shook his head and elbowed Dytryk. "Tosser..."

3

"Keep right! You all know where to go if they cut us up. You all know what to look for, yeah?"

McGregor didn't wait for the chorus and answered with conviction: "The painting called 'The Family' in St. Alban's Church."

Enemy cannons shook the tunnel and filled it with another fine cloud of dust.

Unfazed, Khatri continued: "The Family in St. Alban's! On Kilnhouse! Avoid the main roads, o-right?"

Dytryk answered for himself and everybody else. "Yes, Cap'n!"

"Now, once you have it—once you have *The Family*—you hightail to the coast and don't stop running. *North Promenade* is where you'll handoff to our carrier drone. You do that and you've saved all of us and given England a future." Repeating the plan may have been unnecessary granted the squad had studied maps and enemy readouts throughout the previous week, but the evening had already brought so much unexpected chaos that some additional clarity couldn't hurt.

"Where do we regroup afterwards?" asked Lance Corporal Peter Pitts, straining his husky voice so as not to alert the cyborg units above—mutilated Englishmen that Underpool's Rabbi Klotz named the Nephilim after the children of fallen angels.

The notion that any of them were getting further than the beach straightened each of the men's spines a little more, notwithstanding the low ceiling.

Remembering the most ambitious part of the plan he had given up on hours earlier, Khatri answered graciously: "There's a tidal bunker on Anne's Beach. Before you chase off the carrier drone, mark it up with our coordinates, o-right? Doherty will send a ride for us."

Kemp tried to speak, though ended up just spouting a torrent of blood. He went to wipe his face with his bandaged forearm, and winced with confusion at the feeling of everything so out of place and the inability to do anything about it.

Dytryk used his sleeve to stop Kemp's bleeding and piped up on his behalf, apparently indifferent to the interest of the steel beasts prowling about the surface with their ears to the ground: "Nic'las calls shotgun!"

Khatri grinned ear to ear. "Well, Nick—you're going to have to make use of that plasma gun first..."

McGregor didn't care for the playful repartee. Good men were dead. Those still alive owed it to those less fortunate to get the job done. He did a mute roll call then turned to Khatri. "We got

4

Miller, Kemp, Kaczynski, Dytryk, and Pitts. You plus me makes seven."

Khatri whispered directly into McGregor's ear so that his response couldn't spill over. "Six-and-a-half. Nick's falling to pieces."

Irked by the Captain's low expectations, McGregor bared his teeth and took a step back. "I'd put my faith in his left hand alone."

Khatri nodded apologetically to his second-in-command. "Then keep the faith." He raised his voice so all could hear. "O-right, you magnificent sons-of-bitches, let's crack on!"

Pitts took advantage of Dytryk's occupied hands and stuffed a brick of plastic explosives in his squad mate's breast pocket. "Just hold this for me, will yah? I'm already weighed low."

"D'I look like a mule, you ass?" Dytryk buzzed, cocking his gun.

"Clam up, the two of yahs!" ordered the Captain. He peered around the bend and snuffed out the torch.

Khatri tapped McGregor and McGregor tapped Miller and so on, and they formed a chain in the dark. Together, they made their way down the remainder of the tunnel, keeping right at the fork, and piled up where the earthen walls stopped and the concrete of the old sewer began. Purple twilight highlighted the tunnel's end. Pitts rotated to the front of the line, and used his cutter on the metal grate blocking the way out. As soon as he cut through, he returned to the rear and prepared his grenade launcher.

The Captain checked the area ahead. On the field behind the sewer entrance, Khatri could just make out the spiderlike silhouette of a Goliath drone wandering into the night. It left behind a crew of Nephilim who appeared short amidst the tall grass. Dressed in white armour with red joints, the Nephilim were sent down into the tunnel along with Burrower drones on direct orders from London to exterminate the Resistance team.

London wasn't just calling the shots; it was pulling all of the triggers at the disposal of the EDS Security Forces. An artificial intelligence supported by ten-thousand government agents directed all of the country's field assets, men and machine alike, with direct-to-brain orders, including those hunting Khatri's squad. As a result and by design, London's forces acted as one—as a selfless collective—which in their heyday meant they mobbed their foes like piranhas and flew together like starlings; graceful, synchronized, and deadly. However, the London's powerful central-mind had begun to degrade since the EDS formally come to power, or at the very least it had begun to underperform on account of bad resource-management and overloaded servers. This would not have been such

5

a setback had the Chinese, European, and English governments not already agreed to impose limits on their AI systems. Owing to this blessing of mismanagement, technological upheaval, and censorship, the Nephilim and drones assigned to kill the Resistance squad that night were slower to act. This meant that Captain Khatri and his men had some breathing room despite a noose everywhere waiting for them.

Khatri signaled to the squad: *MOVE*.

Miller and McGregor helped Kemp along. They joined the Captain in an old impact crater just off the side of the road.

"They're about to pick up our trail," warned the Captain, pointing out the last of the Nephilim disappearing into the grass.

While the rest of the unit made their way over to the crater one by one, Khatri scoped out their next steps. They were well inside the St. Anne's Red Zone, a quarantined area south of the Blackpool megalopolis whose lights strobed on the horizon. It was more or less abandoned; a well-protected wasteland containing whatever the government did not care to confiscate and the fires failed to consume. No one but the special police, the odd triad fixer, and EDS designates was permitted in or out of the red zone, which meant there would be no collateral damage—no innocents around looking to catch stray lead. The tunnel they had taken had gotten them past the main security walls; impenetrable and unclimbable slats of steel that looked like supersized razorblades. It also saved them from having to confront the Goliath mech whose journey north was still audible as a distinct sequence of crunches and thuds.

McGregor ambled over to the Captain. He mimicked his commanding officer's survey and grumbled at their lack of options. The road inches away from their noses bifurcated into another two roads, both of which had checkpoints where they split off. A dozen or so guardians milled about each of the checkpoints.

For cover, the EDS guardians had electric shields and anti-ballistic pylons. For fire support, they had a few mounted guns, although it was the Reduvius drone by the westernmost checkpoint that made McGregor especially uncomfortable. Its hind legs were fully extended and its front legs were bent as if it was bowing to the android ammunition-technician diligently resupplying its cannon feed. This Reduvius wasn't the same dog-like drone that had hunted them around the air base ahead of the Goliath mech, clear from its lack of plasmic scarring, but it was certainly of the same variety, and ready to continue where the other had left off.

6

Khatri and McGregor ducked to avoid being spotted by the eastern checkpoint's autonomous searchlight, and shared in a nervous chuckle.

"Oreet," said McGregor, risking a peek over the edge of the crater. "The residential strip between them there..." He indicated the derelict red-brick houses between the two checkpoints. "That's our way through."

The Captain nodded, and called up Dytryk and Pitts. "Bob, Peter; you're up. Don't engage unless spotted. Miller, keep an eye on our six."

As ordered, Dytryk and Pitts waited for the searchlight to pass, and sprinted across the road. Their jammers, advanced IR camouflage, and ID scramblers enabled them to pass undetected by the EDS' proximity sensors and facial-recognition aphids, and into an overgrown garden on the other side. Dytryk dropped the bipods on his heavy machine gun and took an east-facing position while Pitts watched for a reaction from the Reduvius to the west.

"Alright, Sergeant," Khatri said, switching focus with Miller, and taking aim at the tunnel entrance. "Go."

With a thumbs-up from Pitts, Kaczynski, Miller, and McGregor bolted over to the low-walled garden.

The front legs on the Reduvius stationed at the western checkpoint whined and extended to their fullest, raising the drone high above the street and revealing its gun-bedazzled underbelly.

"Damnit," said the Captain, holding Kemp back.

The drone nearly crushed the android technician that had topped it up, and cantered up the street towards the other checkpoint. Its weight not only shook the ground but Captain Khatri's insides as well. The Captain flattened Kemp and himself against the slope. A laminate against the wet grass with the drone towering above him, he prayed that his camouflage would trick the Reduvius' sensors. As he cycled the wishful mantra over in his mind, it occurred to him that Kemp's camouflage was compromised by bone. He looked over at the Corporal whose black, glossy blood reflected the white of the moon.

Kemp squinted back at the Captain. He waited for the drone to pass, and when it had he tried to speak, having already forgotten his unfortunate injuries. A tilt of the head was enough, however. He recognized he was a burden to his team. *Dead weight.* He was going to stay behind and watch the rear.

"On your feet now, Nicky," ordered the Captain, seeing the other five men ready for them across the road. "We've got to go!"

Kemp shook his head, and raised his plasma gun slightly.

7

Khatri gritted his teeth and shook angrily—not at Kemp or at Kemp's decision, but at this unfortunate situation they had been forced into. "O-right, Nicholas. I'll see you at home." He kissed Nick Kemp on the forehead, waited a beat for the searchlight to track past, and joined the rest of his squad.

McGregor pulled Khatri into the garden, sparing him from the searchlight that cut the air above his head like an executioner's blade. "What the hell's Kemp doing?"

Khatri looked gravely over at the Corporal's head, just visible over the lip of the impact crater. "He's not coming."

"All respect, Jim—*that's horse shit!*" McGregor tried to establish where along its pattern the searchlight was, and plotted his feet as if to run back over. "I'll get 'em."

"*All respect*, Hugh," said Captain Khatri, placing his hand in McGregor's way, "It's not your call."

McGregor brushed the Captain's hand away, and watched Corporal Nick Kemp reenter the sewer. "*Bloody hell.*" McGregor spun around, glared at Khatri, and then looked to the rest of the squad. "Hey guys, we gotta go!"

Khatri had figured Nick would have waited a while longer, but hadn't known how little time the Corporal had left to do what needed to be done.

"Move! Move! Move!" ordered McGregor and Khatri together, spurring the squad's advance on St. Alban's.

Muffled bangs and screams emanated from the sewer, drawing in the guardians posted up at the nearby checkpoints. Even the Reduvius drone powered over to investigate Kemp's tremendous last-stand.

Khatri's heart skipped a beat when the ruckus came to an end. He stopped to watch the Reduvius return to the western checkpoint, took a deep breath, and then carried on.

The squad trampled a dozen weed-choked gardens and cut through an entire fashion catalogue forsaken on clotheslines before finding the street one short of their destination.

Khatri and McGregor sleuthed ahead. What they found agitated them both greatly. It looked as if the neighbourhood had been emptied into the street and then set ablaze. Burnt-out husks of automobiles sat perched on melted tires out front of houses riddled with bullet holes and plasma singes. In the middle of the street there was a frozen parade of baby carriages. And everywhere there were piles of charred luggage.

"My mum used to live not far from here." Captain Khatri massaged his forehead, hoping to replace his vision with a memory from childhood. "Glad she didn't live to see it now."

"The 'burbs ought to be either glorified by romance and religion or else destroyed by firebrands from the earth," McGregor replied, quoting the yellowing pulp he had left behind in Underpool. He spat with disgust at the sight of this inglorious waterloo. "S'pose we settled on fire."

Khatri shrugged reflexively. "Yeah. I suppose we did." The shrug brought him back to reality. He smiled at his Lieutenant. "But just in case, stay on the lookout for the phoenix."

The Captain took cover by the steps out front of a house that was no more than four walls fencing in a mountain of rubble. There he consulted his map.

McGregor instructed the rest of the squad to catch their breath in the alley between this house and the next over. Once he had them settled, he moved up to study the opposing facades through his short-range scope.

As soon as McGregor had moved on, the men began debating the merits of the mission. It didn't take long for their voices to climb over one another in volume. Khatri turned his head around like an irritable owl and locked eyes with Sergeant Miller. Miller shushed Pitts and Dytryk as he got up, and stealthily made his way over to the stoop. "What's the play, Cap'n?"

Khatri double-checked the nearby street sign wrapped with ivy, and pointed down the way. "Alban's is just beyond those homes there. Get everybody over here and tell 'em to keep low."

Everyone huddled around Khatri except for McGregor who was still lying prone on the edge of the street—desperate to catch a stray guardian or Nephilim in his sights.

Khatri grabbed Lenny by the arm. "Kaczynski, you're with me. Dytryk, fix on that wreck there and watch the east. The rest of you: keep your eyes peeled."

Together with Kaczynski, Khatri navigated the low maze of carriages and piecemeal corpses, and made it to the other side of the street. They took a minute to see if they had been spotted, waved on the next group, and began to move up the sidewalk.

Pitts ran ahead of McGregor, who tried to recall him the second he saw it kneeling there— "Peter! Peter! Fall back!"

McGregor immediately opened fire—at *what*, Peter couldn't make out and McGregor couldn't put down. A moment earlier, it had looked like any other immolated penitent. But now, the onyx specter

9

was up off its knees and its mission was clear. It craned towards Pitts.

"Bobby! Light it up!" bellowed McGregor, feeding his gun another clip.

They had awoken a dormant Shepherd drone—a bipedal riot-control bot equipped with a crack baton and a machete. Its model was renowned for keeping the English flock from going astray during the Mob Rule. It brandished its blade, and chased Pitts through the rubbish.

Pitts knew he was being outrun. He turned with his launcher and fired a grenade at the Shepherd, but the round refused to explode at such close range. The drone leapt forward and shattered Pitt's launcher with its baton. Before Pitts could react, the drone's machete glided effortlessly through his arms and chest. His mangled body fell to the ground. Before he could muster a look of pain or surprise, the spectre slashed Pitts' head, frown to crown.

The Shepherd drone ran past Pitts' body, and leapt towards the Captain and Kaczynski. The squad's defensive fire did little more than throw the drone's shadow around the neighbourhood like a secondhand on a clock. The drone narrowly missed Lenny with its blade, yet managed to catch him on the upstroke with its broken bat, sending him flying back.

"C'mon you bastard!" Khatri roared as Kaczynski cartwheeled past him. He emptied his magazine into the faceless machine. Although his bullets couldn't penetrate the Shepherd's armour, the repeated action kept the drone back far enough to neutralize the erratic movements of its blade.

Dytryk contributed to the flow of molten lead focused on the drone, and hammered it into the front foyer of the nearest house. It instantly reemerged from a cloud of red clay, and lunged again at the Captain.

McGregor and Miller seized upon the distance Dytryk had given the Captain from his pursuer. They both stampeded across the lane, narrowly avoiding a collision with one another. McGregor threw a thermite grenade at the Shepherd's core. Before the grenade began to react, Miller thrust his staff into the ground at Khatri's feet. From the head of the staff bloomed Miller's plasmic shield, which protected them from the thermite's fiery reaction. The fire rapidly consumed the Shepherd's armour. The drone fell backwards, sparking and convulsing. It clanked its machete against the surrounding brick and cement as the thermite compromised its internal mechanisms. Miller discharged the plasmic shield, allowing

10

the Captain to close the distance and hit the Shepherd's fiery cavity with a few choice blasts from his rifle. The drone stopped moving.

Kaczynski limped over to watch his aggressor succumb to the might of flesh and will. "That confounded thing was tethered to their intranet," he said, checking the scrapes on his neck and arms. "They know we're here. They'll send more."

"Kaczynski's right. We need to keep moving." The Captain looked over to McGregor for affirmation. "*Lieutenant?*"

"We're not all accounted for," said McGregor, crouching by Pitts' side. McGregor knew for certain Peter Pitts was dead, but could not chance leaving the young man's brain intact for the enemy to needle.

The EDS was known to flip members of the English Resistance; to brainwash them, then employ them to carry out those tasks their own people were no longer mentally equipped to complete. Those Resistance members the EDS elected not to reboot as political slaves would instead be emulated on computers for nihilistic interrogators to deconstruct.

Pitts would suffer no such indignities. His pink oatmeal was fanned out on the asphalt. The Shepherd had deviated from standard practice and destroyed the man's brain, leaving McGregor to wonder if perhaps Resistance minds were no longer worth cannibalizing or there were no odd jobs left to be done.

"Pitts?" Khatri inquired.

"*He's not coming.*"

They hurried down the road without being accosted further, and cut across the field outside of St. Alban's. The number of bodies cluttered there was astounding—resultant of a massacre at least a decade old. No human attempt was made to conceal the fact. Bugs and birds, conversely, had done their part. Even the earth had tried to hide the EDS' callousness. Roses had grown through the divots in some of the skulls. Moss and grass had claimed other body parts entirely.

"A shame," said Khatri, careful at first not to trample the dead. Finding it impossible to land a step without shattering petrified bone, he quickly became indifferent and clacked away.

Outside the church rectory, the squad regrouped and McGregor pressed the Captain for answers. "It's in here, eh? It's come a long way from Rome."

The painting of which Hugh McGregor spoke—the same that had brought them here—was said to have been ancient, and although ancient, somehow capable of severing the neuro-

11

connection between a brain implant and the central authority, regardless of the legitimacy or beneficence of that authority.

"Only one way to know," answered Khatri, growing weary and concealing the fact that he pulled or broke something in the scrum with the Shepherd.

McGregor stopped him from entering and held him in place. "*She* said so?"

The squad encircled the Captain and the Lieutenant.

Exhaling and evaluating the angst carved into everyone's face, Khatri nodded. "St. Alban's was the location given her by the Vatican spy who brought it over. That was all the information he could give her, granted it was the last thing he said before the EDS dragged him to the gallows."

"Again, according to *her*."

Khatri nodded and sucked his bottom lip. "That's right, Hugh. *According to her*."

McGregor turned to Dytryk. "Set up on the far side of the field. Nothing gets in or out of this building except for us."

"Roger." Dytryk lugged his machine gun across the field of bone.

Unwilling to be further undermined by his Lieutenant, Khatri ordered Kaczynski to the front of the church to be on lookout. "You two," he said, indicating Miller and McGregor, "With me."

They entered the church.

St. Alban's was more a chapel than a church, although a church Khatri called it on account of what it withstood and the size of the parish left as carrion out on the green. Its windows were all smashed in. Its red carpet was browned by flooding, and there were dense gobs of mold in all of the corners. The altar was splintered and the crucifix behind it turned upside down. Hammers and sickles and other vulgarities were spray-painted on every imaginable surface so that the walls read like a lunatic's ledger.

"Where the hell is it?" barked the Captain, going pew by pew in desperate search of the prize.

McGregor flipped over a votive candle rack. Seething, he turned to Miller. "It's not here!"

Gunfire crackled outside.

"Who else knew about it besides her?" McGregor had written off the search, and motioned to jump into the fight outside. "Besides the spy?"

Still frantically digging through debris, Khatri shouted out his thought process in quick salvos: "Someone must have beaten us here. EDS could've picked it up and burned it..." He kicked a pew into

12

toothpicks. "If it's not here, then it could be anywhere!" He crouched down over some crusted hymnals, and pinched his brow. "No..." Khatri fired up in a state of fierce denial, and directed Miller to the sacristy. "Keep looking! It's got to be here. *It has to be!*" Betting on Miller's discovery, the Captain followed McGregor to the side door. He grabbed McGregor by the arm and confessed: "She said St. Alban's, Hugh."

"Buck up, man," McGregor replied, both for himself and for his Captain who had never before led him astray. "There's more than one way to—"

There was a cataclysmic thump outside. A powerful gust raked the outside of the church and razed the side door. A secondary, volcanic wind threw Miller and McGregor the width of the church. Glass, fire, and dirt blasted through the windows. Miller—who had just emerged from the sacristy empty-handed—was thrown back into the murk beyond the altar.

Red light filled the church and grew in intensity. There was a thrumming sound. A plasma bulb fired in. Time seemed to freeze. Miller, McGregor, and Khatri all saw the explosive, gelatinous ball ebb across the room. The moment it made contact with the front of the church, time caught up to the chaos and St. Alban's began to fold in on itself. Wood panels and tiles poured into the building while little fires coupled to become bigger fires and larger fires still.

Khatri scrambled to his feet, and pulled McGregor out of the way of a second bulb fired by the Reduvius drone outside. They made their way out the gaping hole punched through the front of the church by the last blast. They spotted Kaczynski right-away, dead and dripping from the front grate that he was forced through like cheese through a grater. Towering at the center of the field was the Reduvius drone from the checkpoint, one leg buckled and singed by Dytryk's borrowed explosives.

The doglike drone's main cannon creaked and grinded until it found its target through the flames: Sergeant Miller, trapped under a pile of Christian wreckage. The cannon turned red. Miller broke free, and ran up the nave. The Reduvius fired its bulb, which blew what remained of St. Alban's asunder. Miller narrowly escaped out the front despite a backdraft of superheated sand and glass. He stumbled, however, and dropped to the ground. On his hands and knees he looked up at the massive machine, preparing to fire once more, but something else drew its attention away.

The pkt-pkt-pkt of Dytryk's machine gun rang out. He peppered the sides of the Reduvius, destroying its infrared sensors and radar array. Dytryk cheated death the once and that was good

13

enough for him. As the Reduvius cannon swung around again and took aim, Dytryk fed his gun the rest of the belt and clicked empty. Seeing the plasma surge in the drone's cannon feed, he dropped his smoking gun, took to his feet, and reached for his pistol.

Welling with sadness and admiration, Khatri watched the Reduvius obliterate Bob Dytryk.

Miller, Khatri, and McGregor dashed across Kilnhouse Lane into the nearest structure not yet set ablaze—a two-storey brick house with white frames.

Overtop fresh corpses piled on old, the Reduvius lurched forward, firing molten bulbs into every house on the block. Supporting Nephilim followed in its tracks, keen on expunging nonconforming thought from their island. Whereas the drone hadn't seen the Resistance trio duck into one derelict and run to another on account of their IR camouflage, the Nephilim, who for the most part still had organic eyes, had a bead on them.

The Captain and his men ran up the street, into infernos and out of dust clouds, crisscrossing as if lacing a giant shoe. Nephilim bullets whirred through the air around them.

"Holy shit!" yelled McGregor, buzzed to deafness in one ear by a close-call.

Despite stopping several times to offer a lethal response to all the clamour the enemy was making, Miller kept pace with his Lieutenant and Captain. He was in a nasty flow state. Everything was reflex or unconscious adaptation. Without a real sense of direction, that was all he could do. "Where we headed?!"

"Damned if I know," the Captain answered over his shoulder. He kicked in a door on another gutted home, and led Miller into its bowels. The structure held together thanks to a few determined nails, tested by every stray bullet that chewed into its exterior.

McGregor muttered to himself out on the lawn: "The Promenade!" He pulled the pins on three grenades simultaneously. He threw the first—his last electrostatic smoke grenade—into the street to insinuate they would or had already crossed, and lobbed the other two—thermal grenades—into the yards opposite to further his deceit and the enemy's confusion. He waited for the nanoparticles from the smoke grenade to throw up their interference mask, and dipped into the house behind Miller. The grenades went off, one after the other, as he shut the door. "We're headed to the beach to hand off to the carrier drone. That's the plan."

Khatri raised his eyebrows in anticipation of some sort of elucidation.

14

"The knowledge that the painting is not here—we've got to send that home! For all Underpool knows, we simply couldn't retrieve it. They need to know it's not here."

Pigeon-sized Hunter drones sent by the EDS' central-security AI whizzed through the air above the house and swooped down into the neighbouring yards in search of a meaty target.

Khatri mulled over the Lieutenant's point while Miller pressed through the ramshackle house and checked the backyard. There was a pair of cellar doors, locked but rotten. Miller waited for the next swarm of Hunters to fly by, and limped out to check the lock. The wood had the firmity of cardboard. With one good kick, Miller had busted through. "In here!"

McGregor jabbed the Captain in the chest. "We're taking what we learned to the beach or else everyone died for nothing." He scanned the sky for threats, and scurried into the cellar. Khatri followed close behind.

The cellar was a glorified pantry beneath the house. There were two shelves loaded with cracked mason jars that at one time or another had contained jams and preserves. At the base of the steps there were four chairs and a pair of crutches. A chip in the wall opposite the steps revealed several layers of paint and mortar hinting at a storied history. The same cellar had likely offered comfort to those expecting another variety of statist bombs during the world war before last.

Khatri tried to shut the splintered doors, but the handle came off in his hand. He dropped it into Miller's lap, and sat down next to him. He figured that Miller would have had something to say and looked over hoping for a pithy riposte, but saw that the Sergeant was busy plucking jagged metal fragments out of his chest. "Damn, Wes!" Khatri pulled back Miller's jacket to better inspect his wounds.

"It's okay, Captain." Miller shrugged off Khatri's interest. "They didn't go deep. Even if they had, they probably would've missed my heart."

McGregor sneered. "Tell the truth, mate. You're heartless." He kicked the Captain's boot, and repeated his accusation.

"Nah." Miller yanked the last piece of shrapnel out of his chest, and buttoned his jacket up. "I got one. It just happens to be on the wrong side."

"Yeah, yeah." McGregor rolled his eyes.

"Dextrocardia. Meyer's got papers on it back in the 'Pool. I figured God flipped it to mess with my doctors. Now I'm thinking—"

15

Khatri spat foamy blood and laughed ahead of his own humour: "He spared you so you could talk us to death before the demsocks can have their way."

Garbled shouts nearby sent shivers down McGregor's spine. He gripped his gun tightly. "If we're going to the beach, we can't stay here long. Probably shouldn't have even stopped."

"Wes... Hugh..." The Captain was visibly running low on patience and bravado. He may have been sweating, but it looked more like his whole body was weeping. "We didn't get The Family painting today, but someone needs to." He pulled a pencil out of his breast pocket, put it in his mouth, and tore a corner off of his map. He flattened the paper and took down a note. "This goes in the carrier drone, yeah?"

"What's it say?" Miller asked, happy to let McGregor cool off.

"Note for my daughter or whoever's next in line to carry our cross." He handed Miller the note and the torn map.

Nephilim radio chatter grew closer as did the Reduvius' thunderous percussion.

McGregor smiled broadly and said: "Spare us the drama, King Khatri. The three of us are getting back *together*. We'll find The Family yet. *If the two of you'll be so kind as to get off yar asses!*"

The Captain and the Sergeant complied. The three of them dumped their gear to lighten their load, and the last of the fifteen men the Resistance sent south armed themselves for one last hurrah.

Khatri straightened up, which pained him immensely. "One good shot from that metal dog will snuff out the warning that'll save Underpool. We split up and reconvene on the beach." He ground his teeth, and stared daggers into McGregor awaiting disagreement, but there was none.

"Yes sir."

Even Miller was surprised by the Lieutenant's response. He would have preferred for them to have stuck together, but it was the Captain's decision.

Khatri scaled the steps out of the cellar and peeked out. "Must've been in another St. Alban's."

"Didn't realize it was a franchise," McGregor said with an impish smile. He took a few big breaths and steadied his hands. "Oreet. It's about that time..."

"Remember now: don't let get the demsocks get ahold of your noggins," Miller said, checking the charge on his plasmic shield. "Especially since you'll need 'em to buy me a drink at Mises Tavern."

Khatri shook Miller's hand and then McGregor's. Knitting both brow and lip, he looked out into the night with eagerness. "Take

16

heart, lads. Fear no evil. His rod and the staff precede us in the dark..." He vaulted out of the cellar.

ONE

Ten years later...

It was still only misting, not yet raining proper, but the creeping autumn wind that replaced the maritime breeze had gone cold and threw the damp sideways. Hundreds of thousands of teeth chattered, which collectively could have been mistaken by one with the memory file handy for a drunkard playing spoons.

Chilled to the bone, Alek Neuhaus instinctively tucked his arms into his shirt. He had forgotten that there was a prohibition on doing so in or around the Department of Information and Historical Accuracy (DIHA); that it was just another insignificant liberty sacrificed on the People's behalf for security—to prevent more Lancastrians from smuggling in weapons to off themselves or department officials.

One of the guardians keeping citizens in line for the DIHA singled Alek out with his megaphone: "Arms out and at your sides!"

Alek quickly yanked his arms out and bowed his head. As soon as the guardian began hollering at someone else in line, Alek stuck his hands in his pockets, which for whatever reason *was* permissible. Weapons could just as easily find their way into a person's pockets, though EDS rules like their social conventions didn't need to make sense.

In his left pocket, Alek's fingers found a hard two dimensional plane. *No!* It was piece of paper folded twice, both times very neatly. All three folds were identical. Someone had made them with care and without a robot's help, paper being banned and anathema to steel hands. Alek looked around to make sure his discovery hadn't been witnessed by any of the officials nearby, and then unfolded the piece of paper. For all his trying, Alek couldn't think of anyone who might write to him. Laundry services must have neglected to empty the pockets before sending up his pants. He hunched over more than he had already been so that the drizzle wouldn't blot out the note or weaken the paper. The note read:

"I should apologize. I have been feeling awfully low lately. I thought it was the weather, but we're indoors the whole time, so that shouldn't matter. Something is off, and I've been taking it out on you. I believe you when you tell me it'll be alright. I know we'll get away some day. The waiting has just torn me to ribbons, and every time we talk about it, the prospect of that day being tomorrow seems even more ludicrous. Maybe we should just focus on the work until it's time. You'll have to put up with my sulking, but I put up with your jokes, and that's an even trade. What I don't find funny is you threatening to download my older version. We haven't anything to lose but each other. I just ask you don't risk it, especially over nostalgia for who I was. ANYHOW! Bricks, I have to go. They want me to correct the brainframe on the Shepherd drone series. Please leave my sphere to charge. There's some whisky in the hole. Love you."

Melancholy swept over Alek. He felt bad for the author while simultaneously envying them. They had someone they cared about—someone who tracked sidelong, realizing the other as an individual and as a social agent. He balled up the letter. It was contraband to begin with and now it was a reminder that he was alone, the same as everyone else ahead and behind him in line. He motioned to eat it, seeing one of the guardians peep up from his ever-repopulating attendance sheet, but decided just to drop it and heel it into a rainy mush, indistinguishable from the muddy pavement.

Alek saw ahead that the line was barely moving, and when it did, it seemed to move in the wrong direction. This was ruinous given the worsening weather and the pressing sense that he had someplace else he needed to be. The letter had made mention of work—that it should be the subject of focus—and this call for responsibility arrested him. The trouble was that he was unable to recall exactly *where* his services were concurrently needed or *what* they might entail. His thoughts were scattered. The past, present, and future seemed to converge. On this the thirteenth day of the cycle, Alek was agitated both in the spirit and in the flesh.

The DIHA was a horrid building; a grey, windowless monolith sat where the Imperial Hotel once stood on the west end of town. It loomed above Alek and judged him in advance of the other state-appointed judges waiting for their turns inside. Its size didn't furnish the building with its unmistakable menace, as the DIHA was dwarfed relative to the housing complexes that shadowed Blackpool's pedestrian streets. It was one of several mandatory destinations for all citizens in Lancashire County, barring those who had graduated in trust and equity value past the point of needing to prove their devotion to the People and to the Supreme Council's forward vision—referred to by their junior comrades as *senior trustworthees*. The DIHA's real menace derived from the fact that it was routinely the last place where thousands of Britons were ever seen alive.

19

On the front ramp leading up to the DIHA, Alek warred with his foggy thoughts, every word and meme of which would inevitably become public record. He couldn't let himself hate the situation because it would be self-incriminating, and he was already low on calories. He certainly couldn't realize his loathing for the falsity of the city or for the phantom sight his implant gave him, hiding reality under a cracked virtual veneer. He turned his thoughts to the cause of his hate, desperate to defer the vile emotion. They would be listening, after all. Anger derives from weakness, but what had weakened him? Anxiety, he thought. It's the job. *I just have to find the joy in it again.* An EDS campaign banner furled and fanned above the archway. It caught Alek's eye and confirmed his thesis. "The Problem Starts With Me." *Damn.* There it was; the agitation again. Alek counted his breaths, flooding his head with a most exculpatory mantra: *Power to the forest, not to lone trees; for the rogue wood stands against community.*

Despite all of the confusion, Alek's section was finally summoned inside. Metronomic grunts and cries coming from the mouth of the processing bay alerted him to the threat of an imminent thrashing. Two gunmetal security droids stationed opposite one another on either sides of the incoming line swatted citizens along with their steely hands, which could very well have been replaced with cats-o'nine-tails without making them any less inhumane.

Alek shuffled past the soulless soldiers on an angle, shoulder-first. While he successfully evaded their anthropomorphic hands, he overlooked the possibility of more molestation past the threshold. As soon as he cleared the entrance to the processing bay, a Personal Progress technician snagged Alek's arm.

"Anot'er t'ick head," said the technician disdainfully. He tattooed Alek's wrist with a heavy shoulder-mounted biograph device, and then sought out additional *thick heads* further down the line.

Envy's colour isn't green. It is red, like the smears along the DIHA's main hallway; like the burnt skin around the insertion marks and temporary ink deposits constituting Alek's latest biographical stamp. Alek gripped his forearm, cursing the technician—knowing full-well he had been singled out for having angered the agent's red-eyed monster. The resultant itch was so terrible he might have hacked off his arm had he the means available to him. The tattoo, tantamount to ten thousand tiny Braille together telling the story of Alek's life as a CBLOCK neuralnet machinist, was the kind administered to those so-called thick heads that the deputies outside had silently flagged. Older brain implants were harder to scan,

20

especially if buried beneath scar tissue and dense muscle like Alek's. That those in charge couldn't simply reform or update their scanners seemed foolish to him, even with his brain power limited to basic functions. This whole stamping affair demanded the daily oversight of dozens of chip-trained trustworthees and hundreds of hours of the People's joyous labour, which might have been better spent distributing the food that routinely failed to turn up in CBLOCK32's pantry.

"Numps," Alek said under his breath. As soon as this word cleared teeth, he realized that he had compromised himself. He quickly clutched his mouth, hoping the utterance didn't pass for violence. Everyone around him was so focused on clearing the heavily-armed security droids at the doors that no one had noticed Alek's transgression. Although he successfully swallowed the expression, the sentiment remained. The same governmental bloating and unchecked depreciation that maligned the whole English Democratic Socialist project was on display from the bottom to the top. But what did Alek know? Not only was this question above his station, but a low priority, granted he didn't know a great deal. For starters, he had no memory of precisely how he had gone through an entire thirteen-day cycle with not so much as an inkling as to whether he had condemned himself with similar outbursts. Nevertheless, he knew where he presently stood—at the mercy of a handful of numps inside the DIHA—and that was enough.

The sound of galloping horses drew Alek's gaze rearward, through the DIHA front doors, and outside. His blockish head failed to swivel on his thick neck as if the two were fused together and riveted to his broad shoulders, so his entire body turned to satisfy his curiosity. Instead of a stampede, he saw that the autumn drizzle that had turned his felt shoes a darker shade of brown had become a torrential downpour. He pitied the thousands trampled by the watery hooves. Nature clearly did not share the English Democratic Socialists' devotion to equity.

"No dillydallying!" screamed one of the guardians monitoring the procession. Unlike the other security operatives limited to their armored black uniforms, she wore an exoskeletal brace and was stilted above the line on heavy pneumatic legs. Were it not for the fact that everybody inside the DIHA but those operating on the sidelines had their mental dampeners greatly amplified, this warning may have otherwise alerted someone in line to the possibility of dallying—perhaps even *dilly*ing. But there was nothing of the sort as far as the eye could see. Even the cautioners' colleagues didn't see the inherent humor in the warning as they too were more or less

21

diligently queued up on the side, ready to go back home to their quiet bachelor apartments and daily nutritional supplements.

The whole place ran like clockwork but no one knew the time. Alek had no idea what it was to dillydally, though with his luck, he was surely guilty of it. He hurried along and hid his face from the five-metre-tall guardian whose metal feet continued to pummel the floor.

The guardian's face was just as hidden as Alek wanted his own to be. Like the rest of her ilk, this armored goon wore a mask composed of two visors fitted to a ballistic helmet. These masks were mandated by the government and intended to prevent guardians from being recognized as individuals with privileges disparate from those they policed. The masks, therefore, concealed their identities, and in so doing prevented the inequality of contrast. They also did a good job of terrifying the citizenry on account of the way that they hid the guardians' eyes. Those would-be-executioners might as well have been looking at Alek the entire time, a job officially assigned to the historians and EDS surveillance teams.

Deeper inside the DIHA, Alek came upon a circus of robotics and higher-order technicians. Here the line was broken up into a scrum loud with incoherent questions and incoherent answers. Drone-mounted cameras scrutinized each citizen and registered them for the penultimate stage of their weekly synchronization. Citizens were then funneled through a single full-body scanner that forced them all back into a uniform line.

Depending on one's trustvalue, citizen unity ranking, and assigned discipline, synchronization took place on a different day of the thirteen-day cycle twenty-eight times a year. For Alek and the majority of his neighbours from CBLOCK32, their experiential review and mental adjustments always fell on the thirteenth day of the work week. Forgone a God demanding a day of rest and any meaningful work to seek respite from, the thirteenth day in the thirteen-day cycle was no more of a weekday or a weekend than any other. There was no way around it; the walls were too thick to claw through and the guardians too numerous to pay off. A better alternative might have existed, but with his cognitive dampeners doing their job, Alek wasn't able to think one up.

While waiting for registration, Alek and CBLOCK32's inhabitants were deloused and re-chipped. To someone with a spotty memory, the flow and brevity of this preparatory process made it appear easy, even painless. The truth that Alek had to relearn each time was that the technicians had simply disguised their butchery under the veil of simplicity.

22

The stamp on his wrist didn't convey the requisite details about his experience and past behavior, so the higher-order technician hassling Alek was forced to scan his implant. This, too, proved difficult. Unable to penetrate the scar tissue at the side of Alek's head, an even higher-order technician appeared with a microdrill, gripped Alek's neck, and created the portal to his implant necessary for his upcoming examination. If Alek had cried or resisted, the drill would have certainly made it the last time.

Trickling blood and grinding his teeth, Alek wondered what the interloping matte-black Defence Department drone hovering over him would conclude after scanning his antiquated muscles, boxer nose, and furtive glances. Was he a model citizen? Was his physical strength a subliminal assault on the emotional security of his comrades? Had he given away a prejudicial consideration with an unkind look? Perhaps someone had heard him use the derogatory term "numps." He also wondered how many times before had he pondered these same questions.

In lieu of a bullet, Alek knew that he was registered and cleared to proceed. Whether or not his synchronization would be successful was another story, which would be written by members of the Culture Committee past the turnstiles marking the end of a mile-long hallway.

The hallway, narrow and streaked with fingernail scratches, was lined on one side by dozens of masked and armored guardians who kept the peace with their cudgels and electric clubs. Unlike the smooth metal wall behind the guardians—textured at seven-metre intervals by both English and Continental posters claiming, "With great labor, we will fulfill the plan!"—the wall opposite had featureless doors every nine metres along the way. There was no hope for someone forced from the line and through those doors, especially if the order was issued from one of the commissioners patrolling the catwalk that hanged low over the lineup. After all, anything that required a commissioner to take a break from scouting the procession underfoot for underage "delicacies" or regressives warranted the utmost severity in terms of punitive justice.

Alek was sure not to make eye contact with any of the guardians or commissioners—not to individuate amongst the People's Body. Although he couldn't distinctly remember any previous encounter with the guardians' clubs, his muscles and creaky joints knew better. Any fleeting glance to the right produced in him a quick and uncontrollable tremor. He instead focused on his feet as well as on remaining conscious. This latter effort was especially trying on account of his pounding headache.

The technicians had inserted new mental dampeners into his brain, leaving his occipital-implant sites swollen and Alek with nothing for the pain. The throbbing alone had a dumbing effect, but when coupled with the mental dampeners once again keeping Alek's faculties busy, his aptitude on the level, and his ambitions grounded, there was little room left inside for a soul or personality. The state's technology retarded him to the point where he was more or less equal to all of those with his trustvalue rating. Lucky for him too as any difference would be found out and remedied as soon as the historians responsible for scrutinizing a citizen's every thought, word, and action, made their recommendations.

In terms of costume, everybody in line was dressed similarly. Most citizens wore their regulation felt slip-on shoes, white or off-white underwear, track pants, and a sleeveless shirt. Some had lost their shoes, pants, or knickers along the way, which the EDS refused to replace. The punishment for such an infraction would usually be deferred to the offending party's respective immune system, but if during their review a historian deemed it to have been intentional, the ragamuffin in question might find herself fertilizing one of the People's forests. Others, particularly those with prosthetics or cybernetic components, were permitted to wear their custom-fitted shirts and shorts, unless they belonged to a technologically-privileged category, in which case they were forced down the way naked.

The elderly woman in front of Alek, whose garments did a poor job of concealing her greying intimates, was not presently in violation of any EDS protocol; however, judging from all of the scarring on her back, thighs, and legs, she had a forgotten history of subversion.

Each mesa of the woman's scar tissue likely corresponded to a subversive tattoo she was forced to forget and to memories the EDS likely disposed of years earlier. While her memories of the days of resistance were all gone, in the past week, she had certainly re-made up her mind about the government. She quietly ranted and raved as she trudged forward, indifferent to how her protest was reflected in the dark visors of the guardians, all anxiously waiting for an opportunity to break from their row to cave in her head. Her murmurs were just loud enough to be audible to Alek but to no one else. "Taking our kin behind the blocks to hollow them out...Doing the Pingos' dirty work, all of yahs. You nunces! You capitulators!" The curses and accusations flowed out of her naturally, although judging by the confused expression wrinkling her face, she wasn't in control of her verbal content. If anything, she could only affect its

24

outgoing volume. It was as if her past selves were striving to have their say ahead of the next experience examination and memory wipe.

Alek tried his best not to process whatever the woman was rattling on about. Internalizing any of her anti-EDS slurs might mean his own re-education or worse. Anticipating this precise moment to come up in his experiential review and certain not to contravene EDS protocol, Alek leaned forward and whispered: "Comrade, those you criticize belong to the People's Body."

The woman turned around and shrieked: "Oh piss off yah coward!"

"That one there!" yelled one of the commissioners indulging in prohibited smoke and drink up on the catwalk. He lowered one of the two onyx masks to get a system-ID via its heads-up-display, and then directed the attention of the guardian immediately below him to the irate woman. "Take 47-3004 off the line."

Alek stiffened while the old woman turned to the sound of the order. She threw two fingers into the air and screamed again: "Cowards and rapists!"

The guardian first ordered to act struck the woman across the back of the head with his club, and pressed her up against the steel wall to the left of the line.

To the tune of hundreds of anxious gasps and murmurs, a second guardian broke from formation, produced a pistol, and pressed it against the woman's bloody temple. "Treason?" he asked his colleague holding the woman up, voice garbled by his helmet.

"Treason," answered the other guardian.

The second guardian shot the woman without further hesitation.

Alek recoiled in tandem with the smoking gun and nearly fell over. He would have fallen too, had the person behind him in line not instinctively caught him and pushed him upright. While Alek found his footing, the old woman slumped to the ground, trailing dark blood and grey matter on the steel wall.

Smoke poured out of the commissioner's helmet. He ashed his cigarette on the brutal result below, flicked his visor back up, and progressed down the catwalk.

The gun-toting guardian took aim at Alek. "You putting those words in 'er head, were yah?"

Alek closed his eyes. A vivacious image of a smiling young woman entered into and then dominated his thoughts. The image became clearer and clearer until the young woman's face seemed to burn into the front of his skull. Her face faded as Alek came to the

25

realization that he was still alive—alerted to this fact by the guardians' laughter.

"It's not nap time yet, comrade. Now 'elp me with this one 'ere," said the guardian, pointing to the body with his pistol, which he proudly holstered.

The other wiped his club clean and returned to his spot along the row of guardians.

Alek lifted the old woman by her shoulders and the guardian seized her legs. One of the doors along the left side opened to a dark room crowded with motionless body parts and tufts of hair.

"Over here," said the guardian, nodding towards the chamber. With Alek's help, he tossed the corpse onto the pile, which cried under the added weight.

Swallowing down vomitus slurry and impressed by the look of relief on the dead woman's face, Alek tried to reenter the line. His every attempt was thwarted however; all of the Alek-sized gaps were quickly and intentionally closed. He tried to elbow his way in, but the guardian-turned-executioner behind him pulled him to the side. "Back of the line."

Despite not having been allotted the requisite amount of calories necessary for this unexpected exertion or the extra wait (he had already been docked nutrients for having a physique that greatly exceeded his female peers', thus prompting inequality), Alek knew not to argue. After all, were he to have, he would likely be pulled apart, atom by atom, for treason or toxicity or individuating or whatever the thought crime *du jour* happened to be. *The body that does not act in complete synch does not survive, and any attempt to desynchronize the body is an attack on the collective.*

As he trudged towards the rear of his section, Alek scrutinized the sallow and sullen faces of his neighbours, none of whom could possibly imagine the dead woman's solace. Instead, the gunshot had awoken the panic in their technologically-repressed past selves and forced their machine-like compliance. Those who were taller arched their backs to make themselves shorter while those who were shorter tried their best to reach average height. No one wished to stand out. No one wished to be considered in the singular. With exception to the citizens' wheezes and black-lung rattles, the only ones in the hall making a commotion were the commissioners and the guardians.

Recognizing Alek a few paces before he set outside in search of the fabled end-of-the-line, Howard Tisdale, dean of CBLOCK32, yanked him over. "Comrade Neuhaus, where do you think you're going?"

26

Alek bowed at the waist. "Citizen Commander Tisdale—hello!" Catching his breath, Alek looked back towards the turnstiles. "The People's guardians found a regressive and told me to go to the back of the line." Alek scratched the gaping divots at the back of his head. "I figure they meant the *very back*."

"There is no back-of-the-line unless you're a time traveler." Howard grabbed Alek's shoulders, and turned him around to face the front. "This will do." Howard, similarly bald but permitted both by his trustvalue rating and unity rank to wear a luxurious moustache, leaned forward so Alek could feel the warmth of his breath on his neck. "There is a rumor going around that the Lancashire Lethe is using our residences as a base of operations. You know anything about that?"

Though not obligated to answer—certainly not in the Information Department's main queue—Alek responded: "A lethe?"

Howard grimaced. "A spirit of forgetfulness. You know—the scrubbers who erase guilty citizens' memories before the historians can pick through them for guilt."

"Doesn't the DIHA erase memories?"

"That's not the point, Neuhaus! And no; not always. Our honourable comrades up ahead only erase bad ideas and criminal memories. If they were erasing everything, we wouldn't have the words or the understanding to have this conversation now."

Wary of the guardians scrutinizing the line and sure not to be ejected from it once more, Alek tried speaking without moving his lips. "Makes sense, Citizen Commander Tisdale."

"Last night, they found a councilperson who'd somehow managed to hide an entire cycle's-worth of memories, but whose neighbour's memories exposed the difference. Guardians cracked 'em open. Could tell, based on his implant, what illegal devices interfaced with him. They were even able to figure out where and when those devices had last been charged."

Alek was genuinely impressed. "No kidding."

Sympathetically shuffling his eyebrows, Howard lost himself in the scandalous tale. "Yes! No joke at all. They really are quite good at their jobs. Based on the time and the wattage, they were able to determine that the illegal devices were charged days earlier in our own CBLOCK32."

"That'd mean the Lethe lives among us?" Completing even the simplest sentence required an immense effort on Alek's part because of his mental dampeners. The pain, worsened by his cranial swelling, was excruciating.

"It's a possibility, Neuhaus. We'll know soon enough."

27

TWO

The Head Water, like the other marinas in Blackpool, was crowded with derelict ships all chained together, groaning and useless. Overhead, the half-sunken fleet's aerial replacements scorched the night sky with their jets. Of course the airships constituting the Lancashire commitment to the EDS Trade and Security Wing were out of reach of Stephen Nowak's Molotov cocktails, but he didn't overthink the futility of trying. The mickey he just polished off probably had something to do with his brashness; that and the fact that this was an important anniversary he had hoped to honor with one form of action or another.

The day was marked on Stephen's calendar as well as his heart. Ten years earlier, his dream of a successful counter-revolution died along with the last of his kin. It was his older brother Michael's idea to make it to the coast and then to one day reach what remained of America. With their kid brother John, Stephen and Michael fled CDS-occupied Poland for England, which at the time had begun to realize the Mandarins' utopian vision, but was still home to a massive resistance movement. Stephen and his brothers were lucky enough to escape the Massacre of Silesia. Luck always runs out though. John's ran out in Normandy where he was identified as a Christian and, although only a lad aged six, lynched by virtuous demsocks. The Nowaks' luck was then tried and bested north of London. Michael, a liberal torchbearer with Promethean promise, killed a guardian who had turned up a citizen's mental dampeners and raped her repeatedly for days on end. Michael had his bloody good deed repaid in kicks to the face at the center of a mob of passionate revolutionaries. A twelve-year-old Stephen, choked by tears and hiding in a trash heap at the time, saw the light of liberty snuffed out for good.

On this, that special anniversary, Stephen recognized his good fortune: he was still able to taunt the darkness with bottles of flaming petrol. Thanks to Brigadier Wesley Miller, he didn't have his every thought and action micromanaged by a machine or by an EDS official. Thanks to Wesley Miller—the man making all the noise in one of the neighbouring boats—Stephen had begun to understand how it all happened.

The EDS had been clever from the start. They knew that to keep citizens abiding laws that didn't necessarily make sense and to have them following in lockstep without asking questions, they had to make them completely dependent on the central government. In exchange for a guaranteed minimum income, Britons readily accepted advanced linguistic policing and centrally-planned mobility. These government initiatives were a means to an undisclosed end. In pursuit of that end, the EDS eventually implemented old American technology following the example of the Socialists in Europe and China. They had done the same after the dissolution of the infamous Outland Corporation whose corporate empire had spanned the reaches of the solar system.

Every English and European citizen had a BiAnima neural implant drilled into their head, which was wirelessly tethered to a second brain via the government intranet. To access any government service or utility one needed an implant. It all seemed so efficient and sustainable. After all, it was in every Briton's interest for it to succeed. With private enterprise and nongovernmental services eradicated, refusal of implantation meant erasure or starvation.

EDS implants ensured other forms of dependence the population hadn't anticipated. The Democratic Socialists, referred to by doomed Resistance fighters and subversives alike as "demsocks", intentionally overloaded English brains with meaningless and artless swathes of data—more than any organic brain could handle. This made them dependent upon the storage and processing power of their new cloud-based secondary brains. These secondary brains were housed in well-protected server towers out of reach of governed flesh. If a citizen ever entertained subversive thoughts or was found guilty of breaching one of the innumerable new social conventions, they would be re-educated or sent to a labor camp. With their minds under government control, their very thoughts could be reworked to induce a change of heart. If a citizen ever broke out and lost contact with their second brain, *that was it*; they would become a pilotless chucklehead.

The untouchables who dodged the implantation might as well have been ghosts. They were invisible in society; unregistered, unscannable, and therefore incapable of receiving any regulated good or service. If captured, they would be normalized or euthanized.

Some of the untouchables who resided in the watery subterrane beneath Blackpool—called Underpool by its inhabitants—were refugees who had fled the Continental Democratic Socialists in France or Spain or Ireland, only to confront the same foe by another name on English shores. Others had escaped from the purge of England's rural hamlets at the beginning of the Labour Revolution (not to be confused for the later 'Mob Rule'),

29

around the same time the government started scanning and profiling the minds of minimum-incomers and those with "anomalous intelligence." Wes and those who came to be known topside as *regressives* belonged to another camp—to those members of the British Armed Forces who had fought a brutal war against the state and lost. In their retreat from the Battle for Manchester, they collected survivors like Stephen and took them to Underpool.

So far as old-world normalcy went, Underpool was the closest you could find in Europe in the way of meat-and-chemical man.

In Underpool, contentment was come by honestly; not passively by wire or by implant, but willfully and through real interaction. Sex and debate; food, drink, and smoke—its inhabitants were free to damn or redeem themselves, ruin their lungs or strengthen their muscles, grow fat or die rake thin. And even if they wanted to appeal to neural tech to pacify their existential or basest needs, they couldn't.

Active implants were prohibited. Not only were they viewed both in religious and secular circles as constituting the mark of the oppressor, they were a sure-fire way of alerting the enemy to the last English outpost because of their wireless link to the government servers.

This prohibition concerning active transplants didn't extend to the inert hardware itself, since not all of those who lived in the tunnels constituting Underpool had escaped implantation. Stephen's neighbor in Underpool, an EDS-naturalized northerner named Mirek Dubchek, had gone through the full prick and prod. After his family unit had been disbanded and midway through his neural wipe, Mirek yanked his implant and killed the state physicians overseeing the procedure. How he escaped with spinal fluid leaking from his implant site remained a mystery to everyone including himself, but he pulled it off. Could very well have become a sputtering, directionless clump of cells after yanking the cord, but he figured he was going to go down fighting.

Mirek was fortunate enough to have unplugged in the early days of the EDS' regime. They had not yet begun uploading incoherent data to citizens' brains to keep them reliant on off-board cortices, meaning his organic brain was still doing all the heavy lifting. While out scavenging, Wes Miller found Mirek bleeding out under the South Pier the night he unplugged, and brought him to Underpool where he was immediately embraced and feasted as another prodigal son.

30

On this anniversary, Stephen watched his fire hiss as it hit the water. When he was younger he wanted to exact an eye for an eye or eight for the family he lost. Time and experience convinced him that revenge wasn't enough. It wouldn't bring about the change he needed to justify being the last Nowak alive, and he knew full well the kind of change necessary required a saint's patience and a tyrant's callousness.

In Blackpool, Underpool's unfree twin, citizens' thoughts were invaded. Their impulses were regulated. One couldn't start a family, and if he managed to procreate, guardians would abduct his children. His intelligence was normalized. He was employed by the state, but made to do custodial or menial tasks that robots would otherwise be wasted on. And he was kept alive by a strict regimen of tasteless edible pastes. Out in the wild, a Briton was free—not from fear or violence or pain or doubt—but to chart the most meaningful path to the grave. How a tyrannical saint could convince a generation of sleepers to risk comfort for liberty Stephen had no idea.

Whereas Stephen followed Wes' lead and schemed ways to liberate his countrymen, Mirek perseverated on the country's complicity. He hated every man and woman who peacefully accepted their implant and an artificially-clear mind. *How could so many people surrender so many liberties so quickly?* In times of war, it might be understandable, but England more or less flipped before the Sino-American War had begun in full. The change wasn't hastened by fear, as such changes often are, but by the British establishment's greed, laziness, and loathing for the common man, and by the common man's misplaced trust in his government. Unlike Stephen, Mirek solely blamed the generation that preceded his own for trading in their freedom for free stuff. He blamed it for permitting the state to turn from a referee in a game made scoreless by leftist design into a despotic parent overseeing a family that it would ultimately lock away; a parent whose children it wouldn't raise to maturity, but would keep instead as chemically-content dependents. Unlike Stephen, Mirek would have thrown all of his Molotov cocktails in the other direction.

"Ay, Stephen!" yelled Brigadier Wesley Miller, a middle-aged black Englishman scrambling out of one of the rusted boats they had yet to mark as fully stripped for parts—the Serf's Up. When Stephen failed to reply right away, Wes yelled again, careful not to reach the kind of volume that might draw unwanted attention. "Quit your firebrandy and help me out with this one...C'mon! Don't have much time before the swarm comes back for another scan, unless they've already spotted your bottles." It wasn't the massive military ships

31

above that Wes feared. If one of the EDS' countless killer-drone swarms that assured against escape and liberation registered the threat of Stephen's fire, the two of them would be mulched and left as trophies for the tide to claim.

Staring hopelessly at the remaining incendiaries crewed about his mildewed boots, Stephen sighed. Although a lad aged twenty-two, Stephen's white-blonde hair and sunken eyes made him look less like a capable scavenger's apprentice and more like the victim of a wasting disease. "It'll just be more of the same, Wes. Gospel, Torah, Liberty Manifestos, porn..."

Wes patted soot off of his tattered velvet blazer and wiped his brow. "Mind your tone. I think I've really found something worthwhile this time 'round. Now get over here, and give me a hand."

Stephen doubted that there was anything of value still to be found on the coast, especially after the English regime dropped massive nets out at sea to keep autonomous American submarines and literature from making it to shore. The only treasure of any use to the Resistance would be found in the red zones sealed off throughout the country—regions where the English Democratic Socialists preserved or at least deferred the destruction of old-world artifacts. These quarantined areas were usually taken advantage of by high-ranking bureaucrats in the government; places reserved for councilors and commissars to party in, and where they could live out their debauched fantasies without recourse from EDS historians and guardians. The red zones, deemed inequality's mausoleums by Lancashire's former Commissar Amir Dorz, were also notoriously difficult for the hoi polloi to enter, making whatever scrap the Atlantic rejected the regressive's best bet despite the infrequency of useful finds.

"Alright. Gimme a sec," Stephen said, crouching over his incendiaries and carefully pouring the petrol back into his can. Despite the inevitable return of the EDS drone swarm—out looking for scallywags and recidivists—Stephen didn't feel particularly rushed. He did, however, feel a responsibility to keep whatever fuel he wasn't going to toss Poseidon's way. After all, Congress—the anti-EDS leadership that helped organize the subterranean English Resistance to which Wes and Stephen belonged—depended upon thrift and rationing, especially going into the winter months.

Tired of Stephen's tardiness, Wes threw his hands up, huffed, and disappeared below deck. After some muffled cussing, a metal groan emanated from the hatched stairwell. Wes reemerged ass-first, pulling a heavy case up the rotted steps. "I 'unno. It's locked up

32

good. Guaranteed it's not more tackle." Puffing his cheeks and bubbling at the lips, Wes continued tugging, but the chest was snagged on a step. "Sailor's booty, perhaps," Wes said, trying to unmoor the case with a kick.

The suggestion of treasure sent Stephen leaping from ship to ship with his petrol can, chancing an encounter with the briny waters sucking at the barnacled fleet. "Hold your horses."

"Could be an EMP unit. Boy, that'd be lovely, eh? Take out the kill patrols and watch the sun rise without anyone doing our heads in."

Stephen landed hard on the Serf's Up. Ignoring a split knee just asking for tetanus, he put his can down and helped Wes surface the case, about the size of a coffin and heavy enough to be holding a massacre. Together they wiped the steel clean, revealing an Independence Party insignia. A look of mortification twisted Stephen's face. "Damn it, Wes. Put it back. It's probably boobytrapped."

"Don't be a little prat." Wes ran his finger along the grooves in the insignia. His eyes widened. He took out his RF bug-detector and scanned the case. Four green lights on this little wand indicated the case was clean. It might still have been boobytrapped, but no one nearby would hear the bang. Wes put away the detector and tried to lift the lid. Unable to do so, he sought out the latch and found a padlock. "Hand me your blade."

Stephen backed away and shook his head. "Nah. That's trouble. And you should know better."

Wes may not have known better, but he knew enough. The Independents were one prong of the populist revolt that failed to prevent the great national reshuffle following the armistice between the Communist Chinese and the American-Russian Alliance. Unlike other resistance groups, their movement was ideologically incoherent. Liberals, conservatives, anarchists, and Christian distributists, all rallied and died side by side in the streets of Manchester, Preston, and Blackburn. Their only unifiers were a common barracks and an antipathy for the newly-formed Democratic Socialist government. A few of the old folks holed up in Underpool had fought with the Independents before it was whittled down to *the Resistance*, Wes included. Whereas other old fogeys might have known better, Wes simply knew that if he wanted change, he could rely on no one else to achieve it.

"Go home, Stephen. Let a man alone to do what needs doing." Wes stepped over the case and seized Stephen's electroblade from his satchel. His look of disappointment quickly gave way to one of intense curiosity. He cut through the padlock with the red glowing blade. Noticing Stephen hadn't retreated as ordered, Wes bid him over silently. "On the count of three." On three, they pried the lid off. A bloom of dust had them both coughing, but the contents had them trembling with excitement. "No bloody way!"

"Jesus!" yelled Stephen, reeling back. "Who on God's green Earth leaves something like this behind?"

Together with Stephen, Wes gazed at the chest full of micro-neutron-warheads nestled in black foam. The sleek black cones were the kind fired by the second-generation Russian Tyulpan mortars. They could alternatively be fired by smaller 120mm mortars if the gunners didn't mind bubbled skin and cancer.

Wes' watery eyes reflected the glow of the EDS jets and stabilizers above so that he had a dozen twinkles extra to his own. "No one." He shook his head with amazement. "Captain Khatri ordered these direct from Kiev before he was killed in St. Anne's. Had a gunpowder plot all his own in case we couldn't find the..." Wes gulped.

"I don't think gunpowder is what makes these things go bang." Stephen looked at the various warning labels and cautionary stickers plastered all over the inside of the lid. "Ever see one of these go off?"

"Out east. A beautiful sight, I tell yah." Wes smoothed out a crease in one of the radioactive stickers. "For those of us who didn't immediately go blind anyhow."

Stephen deflated. "You know what Congress is going to say— *what this will force General McGregor to do.*" In the years since their failed attempt to acquire The Family painting, McGregor had become the head of the Resistance.

"I sure do."

"He'll fire them at something symbolic, as if anyone is still paying attention; as if a couple bodies and a flaming building will suddenly remind little Englanders that we're the good guys."

Wes pursed his lips and nodded.

"We'll get a bloody stain in the Blackpool city square and our guts spread in some demsock garden."

Stephen's fatalism struck a chord. Wes stood tall. "You want me to shut it up and put it back?!" He jabbed Stephen with his thumb. "Eh, Stevie boy? They won't win us the war outright so they're not worth using at all, is that it? The great Churchill doesn't want to trouble himself with symbolism? You'd rather shoot at the Moon than blow a hole in the same bastards you've been so keen to lip off about?" Indifferent to the drone swarm drawing nearer and nearer,

34

Wes thundered: "All that shit talking. Years of white hot spit. One of these would take out one of their brain-storage towers. Two would level an entire re-education complex or the baby-killers. That's not symbolism. That's action. And you know what? It wouldn't hurt you or me to make our action a little more symbolic, especially if the symbol turns out to be a dozen mushroom clouds."

Stephen looked around paranoically and shut the lid on the explosives. "This is different. We take out a brain bank, and then what?"

"We take out another!"

Stephen squared his jaw and yelled his counterpoint. "That'd kill millions of innocent people, you knobend—millions of people who can be weaned off of the EDS teat slowly, but who'll die if you pop it out of their mouth in a hurry and then jam a nuke down their throats. What's the good in that?" Stephen pointed to the label adhered to all of the mortar shells. "What's the good in radioactivating—*ah guddamnit*—what's the good in blowing up the people we want to save? Besides, you'd be doing the EDS screws a favor. They want fewer people anyway because the Chinese want the land under them. That's why the EDS made everybody neuters and controls all the in'n'out."

"Calm down, Stevie boy." Wes slowed and smoothed his speech as if he was trying to put his apprentice to sleep. "Doesn't have to be the towers. There're a ton of other targets, and I doubt you'll have a pansy argument for leaving every single one of them standing."

The conversation seemed to age Stephen. His eyes receded further under his Cro-Magnon brow. "I want to hit them, Wes. But we've got to hit something they can't rebuild. Something that hurts the EDS, not the English under their boots. If these bombs don't lead to freedom, then *I don't know...*" Stephen had tied his mind into knots. He felt as if a fog had him, and for the first time, Wes was unable to show him the way out.

"The rest of England, Europe, and Africa are full of slaves who would do anything for this chance. *This?*" Wes pointed to the case. "This is the 'NO' we offer them the next time they try to fill our heads with noise and tell us to kneel smiling." Wes leaned in. "I'm going to let you in on a little secret, alright? You keep your trap shut?"

"Of course, Wes."

"General McGregor squeezed a high-ranking bureaucrat for intel on the new EDS commissar running defense northwest of London. McGregor and Congress are convinced that this commissar

35

has new tech that's going to radically change things. While we're pulling punches, those pricks've put bricks in their gloves."

"What kind of technology?"

"I 'unno. You know that runner from Piccadilly? The one with the snaggle tooth always singing songs at Mises Tavern, trying to impress Mirek's little girlfriend? He said it had something to do with memory and those innocent millions you're keen to save. At a certain point, you're going to have to recognize them for what they are: *traitors*. They're traitors who stand between the Resistance and freedom."

Stephen realized that he and Mirek both had picked up most of their rhetoric from Wes, depending on his different moods. Trouble was Wes had far more practice than the two of them combined. Stephen's edge was his optimism; a trait neither Mirek nor his mentor went for, except after a few pints. "So we have to save them now is what you're saying."

Wes splayed his fingers out on the lid. He gazed skeptically at his mentee. "Once they are in your head, there's no more room for you. I'm no hollow man." He reopened the case and looked covetously at the warheads. "I'm a free man. *What about you*?" Wes glared at Stephen with tender dismay. "I tell you what: we'll split these fifty-fifty. You now have the tools to do what you've got to. But if what you decide to do is nothing or simply to throw them into the pond, well—then I'll know I've wasted my time these last few years. And your brothers? *Michael especially*...They'd be bloody ashamed." He ran his finger along the mortars. "Me? I'm putting my share in the DIHA or the English Broadcast Station and buying Blackpool a day without a scan or an upload."

Unconvinced that a day without the historians reading his countrymen's minds or the state propagandists filling them would amount to anything long-term, Stephen began spitballing, keen on delivering Wes a real alternative—not just to impress the man, but to make the best out of an explosive situation. "We've got to think bigger. With these, we can take out far more than a complex or a tower."

"What then?"

Stephen violently rubbed the week-old bristle on his shaved crown. "Just hold on."

"To your hand? Old son, I tell you with love in my heart: you're not cut out for this. The damp has gone to your brain."

"The Americans!"

Stephen's international appeal barely registered with Wes, who had gone back to tallying warheads and regretting the years he

36

spent training Stephen how to fight as he'd been taught when he was in the Royal Marines. "Huh?" he muttered.

"A day with a clear head isn't worth the heat. But if you dropped these on the Yanks, then maybe they'd intervene."

Wes grabbed one of the warheads and carried it portside. He stared out at the sea and at the blinking red lights on the drone patrol in the distance making its way back down the coast. "The demsocks are lying about how the war turned out. They lie about the Pingos having won and what they left in the Americas. It isn't all radiated dust. There's an empire out there still; one that's diverted its attention away from us and focused on the heavens. That said, the demsocks got one thing right. The Americans are done bothering with the world. The Russians too." He pointed the warhead west like some possessed compass needle. "It's been over twenty years and not a peep from old Uncle Sam." There was a profound sadness with which Wes rejected Stephen's suggestion, as if he had fallen in and out of love with the idea and was left with impotent bitterness. He nodded in the direction of Underpool. "Now head back to the labyrinth and let me do what needs doing."

"Don't you remember?" asked Stephen heatedly. "You should because you're the one who told me. The war ended with the Armistice. We just need to violate it. If we blow up something in the Americas, they'll throw whatever peace they've agreed to out the window. They'll have to break quarantine. They'll look at what's been done to us. Shit, Wes—maybe they will invade."

Wes turned around slowly, and spoke even slower: "No, mate. *You* don't understand. They won't rush to judgment. Supposing Kip still knows what he's talking about, the Chinese have floating fortresses in the Mediterranean. You got them Brazilian subs in the Caribbean. Continental suborbitals are dying to break through the politosphere and disrupt the Martian trade route. The Yanks will press the Pingos for an explanation, and we'll be offered up as a sacrifice, and for once, that'd be the right thing. No, a few thuds won't make the Americans mad or the Resistance sympathetic. It'll just make us monsters."

Stephen shook with anger. He indicated the warhead in Wes' hands. "Even if these produce smaller bangs than the ones they dropped back when you were a kid, it'll at least get the attention of someone who's willing to do something. England's gone to shit."

Wes gestured to Stephen with the mortar shell. "Watch it, boy."

"If there is blood left in American veins, it'll power the will to wipe the EDS off the map."

"Hah!" Wes returned the bomb to his foam mold.

"Crackin' 'em off in Blackpool will prompt reprisals. If you're lucky, you'll clear a slave's head for a day. Me? I'll get us a Republican occupation." Stephen stumbled back on legs numb from the drink and excitement.

"If you've listened to a word I've ever told yah and retained an iota, you'd be better than that. We're not terrorists. You don't spill American blood as a means of securing American support."

"Then we steal a Pingo jet; rig it to blow. It doesn't have to hurt someone just so long as it detonates over American soil."

Wes knelt by the case, and turned the warheads on top so their warning labels all faced up. As he rotated the last to match, he began to laugh. "God-damn, mate." Wes once again surveyed their good fortune and ground his molars. "Maybe you're not a total milksop like Mirek's always saying..."

Stephen felt betrayed. He and Mirek weren't cordial, but they were stand-ins for everything the other had lost. "Mirek's wouldn't know courage if it clubbed him over the head."

Wes raised his eyebrows and nodded. "Truth is, old son, I don't have it in me to stay firm between the tide and the demsocks. I've got to fight inland or let the sea take me. And if they're rolling out more mental controls, then we truly will be the last of our kind. We will be all alone."

"I know, Wes." Stephen tossed his satchel into the Independent case and shut the lid. "It's wearing on all of us." He playfully elbowed his elder in the gut. "Bet we both look like these boats inside."

Chuckling at the notion of being corroded and useless, Wes rolled up his sleeves and took one end of the case. "We'll keep the truth of what's inside secret for now, at least until we figure out what to do. If there's a smidgeon of proof the Americans might say boo, I may consider helping you lure them to Lanky shoals. But where they are concerned, it has to be nonlethal—purely *symbolic.*"

Stephen beamed at the possibility of rekindling a decades-old international conflict. He quickly grew sullen realizing Wes was being facetious.

"Absent that proof, I'm happy to act symbolically at home."

"Alright, Wes."

"Don't tell Congress right away or they'll squander these on dents like you said. And definitely don't say anything to Mirek. You know how he gets..."

"Yeah, sure thing." Stephen took his end and together they lifted the case off of the Serf's Up. "Mirek would trade these in for

38

airtime, anyhow. That pillock's a dozen addictions walking around in a human sleeve." Stephen regretted putting Mirek down the second he finished saying so. Not too many addicts kill their pusher and go cold turkey, especially not when cold turkey guarantees a life spent half-frozen on the outs.

Wes looked ready to chastise Stephen, but saw he was already punishing himself. To say nothing would kill the boy's trust, though. Stephen had to know that Wes had his boys' back, regardless of who had knives out for them. "Could have been you, don't forget."

Between the weight of the case blistering the edges of his palms and the notion that he could have been stuffed full of EDS implants, Stephen felt the fiber of his very being stretched to the point of breaking. His mind cycled through revisionist histories, torturing himself with Mirek's yesterdays, until he adjusted his hands and remembered what was in the case. "You figure we have a shot at making this work?"

Wes struggled to smile between wheezes. "By the weight alone, I can tell you we have several."

THREE

The express train from London had been crackling above its magnetic strip in Blackpool North Station for some time, but the new commissar just appointed to oversee Lancashire had refused to disembark. Although the dozens of bureaucrats and security officials waiting at attention for him on the platform were no doubt chagrinned, especially with torrents of dirty rain pouring onto them through cracks in the glass ceiling, they would say nothing—offer no word of complaint—for they knew what the Commissar knew: *no one was in rush to go anywhere.* For a citizen to be in a rush meant they had prioritized some other task over the current task assigned them, yet there in the caboose sat the taskmaster cleaning his knife. No, the decision to prioritize something else wasn't up to the Commissar's underlings. It was up to the People whose collective will was mediated by the Supreme Council and its appointees. As an appointee confirmed by Home Defence Minister Andy Corven, the Commissar was the head of the Lancashire body; equal, rhetorically, with the People, but also grossly unequal. He could have stalled all movement in the entire region had it pleased him. He could have had entire CBLOCKs liquidated. Luckily for production and for morale he wasn't so capricious. Although taking his time meant that those on the platform would have to wait, the Commissar was doing so in service of the greater good—of Lancashire's greater need for security. While he wiped his blade and picked at the grooves along its serrated edge, his mind wandered in virtual realms.

With the help of AI historians and personnel files given him by the Home Defence Department, Commissar Jagjit Hassan was deciding precisely who amongst his predecessor's surviving advisors would stay in their positions and who wouldn't be so fortunate. Jagjit had to make up for lost time and needed only the most obedient, sleek-headed individuals who would act without hesitation. This was essential if he was to live up to the Supreme Council's expectations and to his own—to those ambitions he long-contemplated while stuck in the hospital.

A terrorist attack in the south had nearly killed him; broke his back and left him with third-degree burns across his stomach and scarring elsewhere. Socialist medicine had saved him as it routinely saved many with his rank and status in the regime—yet another reason he felt indebted and was now willing to take the extra time to repay the state with decisive action.

40

Once he made his personnel selections and was certain his blade could not be made any cleaner, he tucked away the weapon and stood up. Jagjit was a large man with a heavy beard; an affectation permitted only to those with his lofty trustvalue. When it came to masculine-hair prohibitions, a moustache was for regional bumpkins; a goatee for department heads, assuming there was no equality complaint from female coworkers. Muttonchops were strictly forbidden—only colonialists and capitalists wore muttonchops, and they had no place in an enlightened society or its jails. From the edge of his beard to the crow's feet fanning out from his eyes and towards the black hair pulled taut away from his temples, Jagjit had a trail of pockmarks that framed his menace, blazed by a plasma rifle's exhaust.

He peered through the slats on the window closest to him and counted at least sixty people waiting eagerly for dismissal—to make the soggy walk back to their barracks or to their assigned bureaus. Jagjit sighed. Micromanaging regional digestion and placation was humdrum, though he would have to do it if he wanted also to execute the task he had prioritized for himself: the location of a cyber weapon of mass destruction.

Home Defence Minister Corven deemed Jagjit "Uniquely fit to locate and secure the weapon" before regressives could use it against the People. It was all he could think about in the hospital and later in the rehabilitation clinic. Mood enhancers and virtual congresses ceased to satisfy him. In many ways, his obsession had individualized him, putting him at odds with the collective. Nature had, however, rewarded him with a good overseer: Corven knew that some such subversion would be required to combat the subversives and to end terrorism once and for all. But before he could satisfy his obsession, he had to deal with the demands on the office of the commissar.

Two guards stood patiently outside the door between the caboose and the next compartment. The Commissar knocked gently, indicating that he was ready. One of the guards opened the door while the other secured passage to the exit.

"Comrade Commissar," said the guard holding the door. "Was your ride peaceful?"

"Very," Jagjit said unconvincingly. "Call ahead to my cavalcade. I won't be long now."

Although the order was directed to just the one guard, both saluted and answered, "Yes, Comrade Commissar."

A ramp extended from the train to the platform. Jagjit crossed it and maintained his momentum past the row of wet faces

41

turned towards the train. Salutes fired up as he passed. In return, Jagjit nodded solemnly.

At the end of the row, a bovine woman stepped forward, and turned to greet Jagjit. "Commissar! So glad to see that London has sent us a commissar worthy of its project to whom Lancashire will in turn prove itself worthy." She too offered up a salute.

Recognizing the woman from his research, Jagjit returned the salute and shook her hand. "Comrade Deputy Commissar Fik!" Releasing her hand, he gestured for her to join him in his procession inside the station.

Two guards in the row similarly broke formation and joined Fik to whom they had been assigned as security attachés.

"I hope your ride was peaceful," said Fik, wordlessly ordering her guards back aways for the sake of privacy.

First the guard on the train, now his second-in-command—this sudden obsession with peace troubled Jagjit. It was inconsistent with the Supreme Council's call for perpetual revolution. After all, there were inequalities at home that had yet to be rectified and still external pressures preventing the country and the world from fully realizing their utopian vision. The notion that peace could be reached or felt in the interim was treasonous. Nevertheless, he tried to smile for Fik's sake. He would correct or report her another time. "Yes. My predecessor's cabinet—what remains of it?"

Fik rolled up her sleeve exposing a manacle with a small screen. She engaged the device, and it threw up a hologram shaped like a carousel whereon dozens of faces turned, most of which had been greyed-out. "All but four have been re-educated. The four have been sent to an idle camp in Lancaster." Though most in the country were still unaware, work camps had by and large been done away with by machines and by the work committees that wouldn't permit competition. Instead, most prisoners exempted from capital punishment were dumped off in warehouses with their dampeners turned up as high as possible. Their processing power could still be utilized by the EDS, and it was helpful to always keep a few volunteers in the wings in case a job that neither machine nor state official could or would do came around. Fik held her arm out in front of the Commissar for him to double-check her math.

Jagjit turned the carousel to see if he recognized any of the regional ministers who had been turned into fertilizer. "Excellent work. The People's well-being is clearly in good hands." He gently pushed Fik's arm out of the way, and she pulled her sleeve back down. "Over the next several days, we'll be readying the Patch Over. The technology is ready, but there's a great deal of red tape we still have to cut. In the meantime, see that my prisoners on the train are brought to the Council House at once. I need them for a demonstration I have planned this afternoon."

"Yes, Comrade Commissar." Fik intuited a summons for the prisoners via the secret police.

Together, along with their entourage of timid guards, Jagjit and Fik entered the train station's main building—a large room with a bronze statue of seven faceless men and women at its centre. Each of the bronze figures either held high a hammer or a diagnostic wand in their left hand, which they pressed together in the air between them, a few metres shy of the red and black EDS banners suspended from the mosaicked ceiling depicting geometric patterns that had no discernible meaning. There was writing on some of the banners, crowded by the meaningless shapes: "From Each According to Xir Ability, to Each According to Xir Needs!"; "One Class, No Struggle"; and "Unity by Force!" The lettered variant of the EDS logo was sewn into others, with the 'E' containing the 'D' and the 'S' and its middle arm bisecting both.

Below the slogans and calls to action, there were hundreds of benches, forever bare as few citizens were permitted to leave their region and the few that could never had to wait.

Despite the lack of traffic and use, the ticket booths that ran along one side of the room were fully staffed. Black-hatted men and women stood ready to process mobility requests and to rubber-stamp transit papers. These government employees watched the Commissar with satisfaction—rare was it that passengers passed through, and it was even rarer a sight to see someone from London.

Outside of the station, Jagjit provided Fik with a dozen trivial jobs to keep her busy. He did not want his deputy stepping on his toes or proving herself ready to take his position so soon into his command.

"Comrade Commissar, if there is anything else, I'll keep my neural line open to you at all times."

"Thank you, Deputy Commissar Fik." Jagjit spotted his limo pull up along with its security complement. "I look forward to working with you." As soon as he turned to make his way over to his ride, Jagjit demanded a full mental evaluation of Fik. He was resolved to demote her pending any detectable ambition to improve her station.

FOUR

It took an hour for Alek to re-reach the dead regressive's bloodstain along the hall, and another three hours to reach the Department of Information and Historical Accuracy's synchronization clinic. Inside, he sat reclined and cuffed on a sweat-soused swivel surgery chair. The cubicle was enclosed by padded green walls. As the padding failed to muffle any of the surrounding screams, it was more than likely intended to block errant signals and microwaves. Several machines buzzed and hummed in a semi-circle around the chair, most of which were in one way or another connected to Alek's neural-implant via his occipital ports. Wires weren't used for their nostalgic flair; rather, they were heavily relied upon during synchronization because they provided the DIHA raw data without running the risk of loss or interruption.

An historian, dressed in a plain white jumper and big yellow goggles, checked Alek's wires. The man plugging and unplugging neural links seemed indifferent to his body odour—his stench was almost as great an affront to his patient as the whole matter of cranial penetration. Satisfied that all of the wires were in place and having properly transformed Alek into a marionette, the historian checked his AI companion's conclusions on a duotone monitor.

"Hmmm. Curious! Yes, ahem. Number 47-6792...That you?" asked the historian.

"Yes, comrade."

Alek's number pulsed on the monitor above a loading graphic that promised his file would soon be up. Finally, the number was replaced by a name. "Alek Neuhaus. CBLOCK32," said the historian. He opened a virtual notebook on his tablet and turned to a fresh page, which he filled with presumptuous scribbles. "Ah-hah!" he said, as if epiphanic. "Your privilege is off the charts in several categories. Doesn't seem your dampener intensity reflects these disparities. We'll have to do something about that, won't we?"

The threat of an even worse headache nearly drove Alek to tears. "Yes, comrade."

"Now!" The historian turned counter-clockwise on his backless chair, and adjusted the wires jammed into Alek's head as well as the wireless cortical pad on his forehead. "I am going to say a number of words that you will repeat." He unknotted one of the cables. "Ready?"

44

Alek tried to nod, but the cranial grips kept him still. Instead, he nervously answered, "Ready."

The historian opened a holographic model of Alek's brain, illustrating all neural activity and well-established circuits with a medley of colours and metatags. "Regressive."

"Regressive."

There was no particular excitement on Alek's neural map apart from a slight flare-up indicating basic recognition of the word but no emotional attachment. The rapidity of the connection suggested that certain association circuits had been well-insulated with myelin, although that could very well have been the product of years of synchronizations all prompting Alek to react to the very same vocabulary.

With disinterest, the historian made a short note in his notebook and continued. "Independent."

"Independent," Alek replied, trying not to twitch despite his watering eyes and cramping neck.

"The Family."

"Uh, the family."

The historian made a note of Alek's hesitation and correlating neural flare-up.

"Blackpool."

"Blackpool."

"Underpool."

"Underpool."

"Lethe."

Alek shifted uneasily in his seat. Why the word bothered him so much, he wasn't sure. Had Tisdale used the word in line to skew Alek's results? If so, then why? Was the dean himself a subversive? Wherever the truth lay, the historian seemed to have a general idea.

The historian replayed Alek's reaction on the holographic brain scan, and tagged all those places in his subject's brain where there was a radical shift in the color combinations and luminosity. After running the reaction through for the fifth time, he filled the top sheet of his notepad with heavy-handed scribbles and glared at Alek. "Are you undermining the People's Body?"

"*Lethe,*" Alek responded.

"Too late." The historian exited the cubicle and returned with his supervisor, dressed all in black and wearing a face-concealing visor. "It's not a full incrim, yet there's a verifiable emotional response," he explained to his overseer. "Also got some back and forth in response to 'The Family'; more so in response to 'family'."

45

Cupping her chin with latex fingers, the supervisor hemmed and hawed. "Pre-levelling class, origin, education, and upbringing?"

The historian consulted his notes and held up Alek's intersectionality and trustvalue ratings for his supervisor to inspect.

"Might as well give it one more try. If he reoffends, then it's off to the field for—" She checked Alek's case file. "*Comrade Neuhaus.* Target the impressions that flare when the subversive's codename is mentioned."

"I don't want to leave Blackpool! I haven't done anything wrong!" bleated Alek, unable to properly glimpse those discussing his fate. In his panic, Alek kicked off his felt shoes. "I don't know anyone or anything that goes by the name!"

The supervisor left the historian to complete his task. "Alright, '92. Once more: *Lethe.*"

"Lethe!" Alek replied enthusiastically. As soon as he finished saying the word, his thoughts turned to static and his inner voice retreated, leaving nothing but incoherent noise.

They dragged Alek barefooted out of the DIHA, and sat him on an open lorry destined for his home, CBLOCK32.

Someone told another: "Keep a close eye on this Neuhaus fellah. Suspend his laundry service a full cycle."

Left at the mercy of the cold and the rain, neither of which he could feel, Alek nodded back off to sleep.

When the lorry lurched forward, the jerking awoke him somewhere between thoughts, and a good thing too; he would have drowned as his mouth had collected enough rainwater to collapse a lung. He spat, snapped his mouth closed, and hunched forward.

The mental voice that returned to Alek was alien; it didn't recognize itself let alone all of the memories and emotions it now had access to. Reacquainting himself with his ego, Alek salivated and blinked dumbly at the sight of the Information Department shrinking on the horizon behind him. Those huddled around him on the juddering transport were also having a tough time recalibrating. Didn't matter at all to the EDS if these bleary-eyed citizens pulled through, just so long as they offered the state their brains' computing power until the end.

As the lorry eased into station below the towering CBLOCK32 housing complex, Alek regained awareness of his headache and some of his more recent experiences. They hadn't erased him entirely; that he could be sure of.

The burly receiver at the door helped the vegetables off of the transport, and passed them to ushers who either took them to

46

the elevator or to the first-floor restrooms (depending on how much vomit and excrement they had produced on the ride home).

Alek's legs were wobbly, but he dismissed the usher assigned to help him. "I'm alright, thanks."

Incredulous, the usher took a step back half-expecting Alek to go arse-over-tea-kettle. "Do you know where you're going, mate?"

After vainly trying to remember his apartment number, Alek shook his head and some sputum free.

"Let me see," said the usher, consulting the registry on his implanted computer. "47-6792...Ninety two, ninety two...Ah! Neuhaus, yeah? You're on the fiftieth floor. Room 5006."

"Thank you."

"All for the good of the People's Body." The usher pushed Alek through the doors, and bellowed back to the crowd of invalids, "Who's next?"

<u>FIVE</u>

"Alright, kid. Just keep your mouth shut," said Wesley, losing feeling in his hands on account of the case. Their feet sank in the sand, making the expedition home especially exhausting. He nodded to Stephen as soon as he could get his attention, and they put the case down. Fifteen metres off was the southernmost entrance to Underpool. You couldn't tell on account of the new holograms in place deceiving passersby into seeing only a windswept knoll and a seaweed-stricken beachhead. Wes waved to the apparition, and then picked up his end of the case. "Alright, here's goes everything."

Stephen was silent. He was no stranger to the Resistance Special Forces defending the entrance, but it was Wes they respected. Wes didn't need an ID because he was one of the originals; his face would open any Resistance door in the country. Besides, he had carried back so much uninteresting loot over the years that no one even bothered anymore asking him what he had found. Stephen, meanwhile, was still a kid to the lot of them. He was afraid they might open the box just to toy with him even with Wes's musk hiding the smell of that very fear.

The two of them permeated the hologram. Inside the tetragonal projection there were at least a dozen Special Forces soldiers and about just as many Centurion combat drones. The men were as beaten up as the machines, only there was far more gear oil in reserve than blood.

A round-headed northerner with red hair rushed out to shake Wes' hand. It took him a moment to realize there would be no reciprocation, and patted Wes on the shoulder. "Ay mate. You lads find some buried treasure?"

"Crown jewels, Thomas!" joked Wes, fighting to keep balance at the lip of the tunnel that sloped to a thirty degree incline.

Thomas chuckled and gestured to Stephen, raising his voice for the sake of his brothers in uniform. "Don't listen to a word this guy says until the bullets start flying."

"Hear, hear!" confirmed a metal-faced man holding onto his machinegun as if it was a snake trying to escape.

"When that time comes, the same becomes the loud-speaker of the Almighty." Thomas opened the tunnel door and waved in the scavengers.

48

Wes used the tunnel's acoustics to carry back some smack: "Keep your blaspheming to that outer darkness with the gnashing and the weeping."

Before the heavy steel tunnel doors rolled back into place behind Stephen and Wes, they could hear Thomas's rejoinder: "And keep all the soft-voiced virgins inside!"

The warm brassy sound of Mirek's acoustic guitar echoed in the tunnel ahead of Stephen and Wes. While hardly pleasing to the ear, the repetitive riffs were as good a sign as any that their Luddite base was safe for the time being.

"That boy needs to quit rinsing that ear poison, and find a rhythm and a melody that doesn't make me wanna do my face in," said Wes, desperately trying not to drop the case or slam it against the hall's narrow sides.

"Careful, Wes," Stephen replied, looking over his shoulder as he walked backwards with his reversed headlamp illuminating a narrowing passage, graffiti-d concrete, and heavy metal doors along the way. "He might just end up writing you a love song."

Stephen led the way for two reasons. They were headed down a slight incline so as to avoid Blackpool's demsock-controlled guts, so his longer legs meant the case would remain level and easier to carry. And no one besides himself and maybe Mirek knew this tract of tunnel better. After all, Stephen's room—a concrete box a kilometer off the beaches and hundreds of metres beneath the CBLOCK's pilings—wasn't more than twenty paces away, two rooms past Mirek's. Although not as luxurious as some of the original regressive congressmen's lodgings, Wes' included, it was as good as home.

His nine-by-eleven-meter cell had been the pantry off a fortified subbasement built by an Arab construction firm whose name was stenciled here and there. The Gibran Group's work, which redefined the Blackpool skyline in the early '40s, had been altogether erased from the face of the earth by iconoclasts of various totalitarian stripes. Beneath the surface, however, they left behind nearly two kilometers of tunnels and a dozen rooms, all of which they had built to withstand the inhospitalities of time and decay. Since municipal authorities both before and after the EDS takeover would no doubt have axed the proposal to build such a complex in the first place, bureaucratic resentment for the industrious and the independent being what it is, the Gibran Group built their subbasement in secret. So, years later, when the EDS razed the upper floors and paved them over, the screws had no idea that they were

49

securing property underfoot for the Resistance tunnelers who would one day find the safe house and join it to their larger system. With exception to the Resistance settlements in the Three Counties System—an interconnected series of limestone tunnels spanning over eighty kilometers beneath Lancashire—the Gibran bunker was by far the best engineered.

"Alright, old son," Wes said to Stephen, setting the munitions case down midway along the hall. He stretched and shook loose some golden beads of sweat onto the concrete floor. "Check the way. See that it's clear."

Stephen laughed. "I always forget you're an ancient..."

"Go guarantee the way, yah pissant."

Stephen mimicked Wes' stretch, and hurried down to ensure safe passage. He passed Mirek's room, which boomed with an eerie chord progression, and then peered into his own. Past the tattered curtain that served as his door, he saw that the room was just as he left it, except for his overflowing garbage bin, which appeared to be moving. For a moment, he figured his eyes were playing tricks on him, but then Stephen realized that maggots had found his waste. *Damn things would find a corpse on the Moon.*

Pasted to the wall above Stephen's festering bin were promotional photographs of American might and tech in space, which similarly came to life under his lamplight. Featured prominently were infrared photos of the American colony on Europa along with images of the Outland Corporation's bases on Titan and Io. The fantasy of space travel was offset by the lists of names on the wall opposite, signifying all of the people Stephen had met or had wished to have met who couldn't even escape England, including the names of Gibrans.

"Oy, Steve!" Wes' voice ricocheted down the hall.

Stephen, transfixed on the Saturnian vision, stumbled back into the hall and returned to Wes.

"You takin' a nap, you lazy slug?"

Stephen lifted his end of the case. "Quit your 'plaining and help me before your joints turn to dust. Way's clear..."

Wes smiled. "Keep crackin' wise and I'll crack you, Stevie boy."

They grumbled at one another some more and lugged the case into Stephen's room. Stephen pulled the curtain over the doorway, set his hands on his hips, and looked proudly at his flat. Now, in addition to the cot in one corner and the chesterfield in another, the room boasted several-mushroom-clouds'-worth of ordinance set at its center. *True military chic.*

"Damn, it reeks in here!" Wes pinched his nose and looked around the room until he located the source of the stench. "When's the last time you took out your bin?"

Stephen ignored the nagging and studied the insignia on the case.

Shaking his head, Wes spotted Stephen's stash of whiskies, stored under a discoloured map of Lancashire with one corner torn off. He ignored several half-drunken bottles he himself had scavenged from a sunken Chinese leisure vessel and procured an unopen one. "Unless you get good at flapping those arms for effect," he said, wrestling with the cap on the bottle, "You're going to have to find another way across the Atlantic for your plan to work." Wes took a swig, handed the bottle to Stephen, and tottered away from the explosives case in pursuit of the comforts afforded by Stephen's raggedy chesterfield. "And it will have to be airborne," he said, easing onto the split cushions. "There are more demsock patrol boats than there are fish out there."

Stephen took off his headlamp and stared blankly into its brilliance. "That art dealer selling the chief's old propaganda has a bird..."

"Her name is Cassandra," said a gravelly voice outside the room.

Wes pulled a gun from his waistband Stephen didn't know existed, dropped onto one knee, and took aim at the doorway. "Freeze!"

Mirek pressed his face through a gap in the curtain and yelped at the sight of Wes' gun. He recoiled from the gap. "It's me, mate! Wesley! It's me!"

"Reckless plonker!" roared Wes, holstering his weapon.

Mirek entered Stephen's room with his hands out in front of him as if readying to catch a speeding bullet.

"You can't pipe in unannounced," said Wes, getting back up very slowly. "Gonna give me a heart-attack for sure."

Stephen angrily scrutinized Mirek's tombstone teeth and jaundiced skin. Even though it didn't affect his tone, Stephen's anger quickly turned to pity. "Yeah! Get stuffed, Mirek."

"Come on, brother Steve. Heard the two of yah go on by. I just came by to lend a hand. Also heard yah mention t'art merchant Cassandra."

Stephen crossed his arms. "You have to mind your own business."

Mirek ambled over to Stephen. In the lamplight, his tattoos seemed to move up and down his wiry orangutan arms, still shaking

51

after his brush with death. "Well, if it's *your* business, you should already know she's in tomorrow with her latest. Buys art off red zone scavs and EDS two-facers and gives 'em tech to make war or tech to make off."

Stephen resentfully handed the bottle over to Mirek. "That so?"

Wes preempted further questions out of Stephen with a stern look, and pointed to Mirek. "Now's not the time, Merry. I'll catch you up come low tide."

Tapping the munitions case with the toe of his boot, Mirek scratched his chin and flashed a Cheshire cat smile. "Anything good? If it's rations, you go'n tell me straight away. If I have to eat one more smoothhound, my stomach will turn."

"You'll be the first to know, Mirek." Wes' disposition quickly turned from murderous to paternal. "Now don't make me tell you twice."

"Alright, pops." Mirek capped the bottle and passed it off to Wes. "Don't let me interrupt your in'mate afterhours."

Stephen flipped Mirek the bird.

Snarling and muttering to himself, Mirek disappeared into the darkness beyond.

"Good Lord…" Wes massaged his muddled thoughts. "Never a second alone in this godforsaken sewer. If it's not rats, it's you delinquent kids."

"Do you think he knows?"

"Quiet!" Wes secured Stephen's curtains. "The General and Congress won't go for the America trip unless you draft an ironclad plan. Certainly won't let either of us pinch Cassandra's ship, especially after what she's done for the Resistance."

"Oh yeah? What's she ever done for us?"

"I don't know her very well, though my best mate trusted her something fierce. That's enough for me. And besides, hers is probably an unmarked private vessel and you need a Chinese military cruiser or better to get past the border."

"I'll think of something."

Wes slipped halfway through the curtain. He turned and said solemnly: "See that you do. If you don't, then by this time tomorrow, my guess is that old Hugh MacGregor will hand these out like batons in the Resistance's last relay race."

SIX

Commissar Jagjit Hassan stood rigid before a round table seating forty-nine security councilors, all of whom purportedly represented the People's interests within their assigned divisions in Lancashire County. In his scarred right hand was a glass full of tonic water, which seemed to weigh him forward. He took a sip and eyed the councilors one by one, each time defying a riposte. He set his glass down with a thud, mistaking it for the gavel he believed he had by now earned. Even the armed guardians stationed around the room's periphery went silent in advance of Jagjit's speech. "Comrades," he said disdainfully, "I understand that the agenda you prepared to tackle today concerned the re-education centers; that there was, by accident or perhaps malice, curricula that detailed alternate ethical models and posited there was more than one way to be a good citizen. The re-educators will be re-educated with the understanding that the Party is partial only to the truest philosophy enshrined in our manifesto: the collective is the *only* ends worth protecting. Morality lies in its preservation and maximization."

The councilperson from East Lancaster—who had prepared a report on this crime with several pages of painstakingly detailed conclusions—seemed distraught, folding his arms and tucking his cleft chin into his chest. All others found this executive declaration agreeable.

"All in favour?" Jagjit didn't need a consensus. The steps towards correction were already underway. After feigning to count hands, virtually all of which were raised, he continued: "Today, we will instead discuss the implementation of an important new measure mandated by the Home Defence Department, but first one note on my predecessor's unforgiveable crimes against the state and the People. For all of Commissar Dorz's inherited privilege, he hadn't a single ounce of humility. Our young alliance needs new blood unspoiled by old-world contaminates and fresh perspectives unfixed to the doctrines of yesterday. The world can only be healed through ceaseless revolution..."

An anxious cheer went around the table.

"And through revolutionary updates." Jagjit breathed heavily and stroked the greys in his beard. "We will not humor reformist rhetoric—the kind that pushes the Mental Union further into the future, into unattainability. We must commit all of our resources to the renewed revolution underway. Dear comrades, to ensure that the

Mental Union embraces only the best of humanity before perfecting the species, we must take a half-step forward. I am referring to what Doctor Worthing, one of our most esteemed scientists, calls the Patch Over. Although those of you with friends in the English Broadcast Station may have already caught wind of it, I imagine some of you will be hearing this for the first time. At the end of the next cycle, we will be severing every citizen's direct connection to their thoughts and memories. You see, it is those circuits and modules that avoid detection that lead offenders we've temporarily cured back down the road to treason and hate. Therefore, with technology designed by one whose own mind was shaped by it, we no longer simply store mental runoff in our reservoirs, but the whole of English thought and experience. There it will be impossible to hide and easy to assimilate once we join together as one national consciousness. As you could imagine, the Patch Over is an excellent trial run for the global Mental Union. It will be something more: it will be the most effective crime-prevention tool ever conceived. All infractions and imperfections can be immediately resolved. Just imagine! We can shutter our synchronization clinics and devote all of our energies to completing the realm where our Mental Union will dwell: *Kunlun!"*

Kunlun was the name the Chinese communists had given to the vault into which they intended to upload their minds. It was named after the mythic mountains where their ancestors' gods dwelled.

"The Patch Over," continued the Commissar, "is the way to improve the *gleichschaltung* of all minds and the method of our humanity's perfection."

A chipper adolescent dressed in the colours of the Education Ministry's youth brigade went around the table handing each councilor a copy of a dotgram, which would activate in their minds' eyes all the data that Jagjit and the enlightened vanguards of the English Democratic Socialist regime wished them to know. The various councilors mulled over the dossier that the dotgram conveyed to their implants and softly questioned its conclusions.

"As you can see," Jagjit continued, "The EDS continues to commit immense resources to the elimination of regressive strongholds in England, Europe, Northern Africa, and in Southeast Asia. Our comrades on the Continent have faced serious challenges posed by rising rates of subversive thought and defection in the south and eastern provinces, particularly in their former Polish, Czech, Hungarian, and Italian settlements. And do not think that the Russians are entirely to blame. Here at home, we have a similar problem, particularly in our northern CBLOCKs and on the west

54

coast. Whether the fault of genetic programming, inherited toxicity, or environmental deformation, we have been unable to seriously curb recidivism. Every single one of the reoffenders under my predecessor's original purview in Bedfordshire was rehabilitated by the very best of our peers at the Department of Information and Historical Accuracy. Each had their memory wiped repeatedly. Their secondary brains were flushed with the cultural experience designed by our gracious peers at Noospherics. And yet..." Jagjit leaned on the table and glowered, studying his colleagues' uneasy expressions. "Every person seemingly rehabilitated and reintegrated into society chose again to subvert our laws and the will of the People, costing the EDS a great deal of grief."

"The poisoned generations will soon be no more," interjected a cotton-mouthed councilor whose nameplate indicated he was Comrade Bradley Miliband of Manchester. He drew from his cigarette, and elbowed the youth brigadier as the boy passed by on his way back into the hall. "Once London allocates the children of tomorrow to replace them, we'll be fully cut off from our loathsome past." Like most of his peers, Bradley believed the Mental Union to be some goal post that the Supreme Council would move every so often to keep up the revolutionary spirit and hone the bureaucracy's focus. Children, not nirvana, seemed as always to be the country's future, even if they were a rare sighting, with the exception to the mascot youth brigadiers. "Now, *Jag*, the issue at hand—"

Jagjit leered at the elder member, ensconced in cigarette smoke and an air of self-importance. He waited for the youth brigadier to leave the room. Once the door closed, Jagjit seemed to grow in stature. He abandoned his diplomatic tone. "The issue is not that some of the more privileged among us feel so empowered as to interrupt without using our state-given titles, *Councilor Miliband*, though I am sure our historians might think otherwise."

The old councilor coughed, and then looked anxiously at his other peers for support that didn't come. He dashed out his cigarette and lifted himself out of his chair with wobbly arms while apologizing under his breath. However, a sharp voice froze him in position.

"Commissar Hassan, forgive the esteemed gentleperson from Manchester," boomed Major Poyraz Vola, a tall Turkish man in a green jumpsuit with red epaulettes. He approached the table from the far side of the room where his masked underlings—the guardians appointed to protect each of the councilors—stood, vigilantly watching the proceedings. Poyraz's baton clacked against the table. "After the Southport incident, I impressed upon your

55

predecessor and Councilor Miliband the extent to which this has gone from a manageable pattern of minority self-destruction to an outright crisis."

Councilor Bradley Miliband reseated himself and tried to catch his breath, which had evacuated along with his hopes of returning home after the meeting.

"And this notion that our scientists can succeed in an area where they've repeatedly failed," continued Poyraz, "is dubious, not to mention possibly reckless, given the enemy's ability to detect our reprogramming and to help subversives reintegrate their past selves."

"Major Vola," said Jagjit sternly. "Much of your lived experience is undoubtedly out of my reach and is therefore as vital as it is unique, but..."

Poyraz set his hand on the headrest of the nearest chair, driving its occupant forward, and smiled. "Comrade Commissar, *I do believe* in your abilities unlike those of your predecessors, and I think your instincts are better cultivated. Carrying on without reform is out of the question. And I welcome the Patch Over. But in advance of its execution—you said one cycle, yes?—I believe we should execute every single reoffender and apprehend anyone who does not deserve a clear conscience. A strong show of force before a concerted show of brilliance will surely secure for Lancashire the respect of Regional Commander Xi Weihan."

The very mention of Xi Weihan, the Chinese military overseer in England, seemed to chill the air in the room.

Councilor Sharon Kay, a lumpfish of an old woman whose toothless scowl seemed to be structured entirely around her pronounced nose, cut into the hush with a nasal whistle. "Gentlepeople, I must volunteer my feelings on this matter and speak my truth." Sharon adjusted her collar. "On innumerable occasions, the People and their government have attempted to inoculate themselves against the sicknesses of individualism and liberalism. These attempts are foolhardy! If the Mental Union is imminent and with it guaranteed the perfection of the species, as you've said Commissar, then there is no reason to rush to rehabilitate those who will not make the grade." Sharon began to cough, and indicated with a panicked point that she needed water.

While the guardian assigned to Sharon hurried to her side through the remnant of Bradley's smoke and helped alleviate her respiratory episode, Jagjit spoke up. "Comrade Kay, thanks to the Patch Over, all will make the grade. Esteemed Councilors of Lancashire; Major Vola; guardians, and comrades all." He held his

56

hands out in a signatory embrace while waving away Councilor Kay's elitism. "Beijing and Brussels will follow suit. The Patch Over is first being tested in Lancashire County, but soon it will run its course throughout the rest of England and the world round. So far as this new technology is concerned, *Councilor Kay*, we have learned valuable lessons from the failures of previous administrations and their efforts. In fact—and you are the first councilors to learn this— we have finalized the technology!"

"This is all a sideshow," Sharon replied. "If the technology is ready to unify human thought, then why bother waiting any longer? Once we have the island's population in full neural synch, outliers will be easily dispatched with. The sickness within the greater body will be instantly purged." She coughed again, but this time edged words out between phlegmy bursts. "The more we focus on the minutia, the more we lose track of the mission."

Jagjit shook his head. "We may now finally be ready to upload ourselves as one into Kunlun, though Kunlun is not yet ready for us. Earmark your objections and peel your eyes. I think it's time for a simple demonstration." He snapped his fingers. "I hope your mental equalizers will permit you to see it for what it is."

The four guardians standing watch on either side of the room's heavy oak doors opened them and guided a group of ten men and women inside. Those seated around the table began to mumble and whisper, confused by the sudden intrusion.

"We have before us eleven recidivists on a new narrative pathway," said Jagjit.

"Ten recidivists," Bradley corrected the Commissar, satisfied with a quick count.

Jagjit raised his eyebrows. "All *eleven* have had the totality of their minds transmigrated to our servers. Before, they were susceptible to influence. Now that their consciousness is code, we can make any and all alterations. Without their organic brain registering these changes as alien or remotely implemented, they are unable to reverse them. In fact, they don't even recognize anything as different." Jagjit reached down to grab his briefcase from beneath his seat, and set it on the table. He hastily opened it and produced a tablet. On the tablet, he scrolled through several pages of reports, and located a page with eleven faces all annotated and hyperlinked to massive personnel files. "After the Patch Over, if I were to depress an offender emotionally, remove his inhibition, and focus his will according to ours, we might see something like this." Jagjit tapped a button, and five of the ten recidivists who had been ushered in began to tear at their faces.

57

The guardians idling at the rear of the room raised their weapons, but Jagjit silently ordered them to hold their fire and stand their ground.

The guardians and the councilors watched in horror as the recidivists pulled skin from muscle and muscle from bone. In a matter of seconds, the five ordered to kill themselves crumpled to the ground, dead or dying. The remaining five, permitted by the Commissar some self-awareness, were absolutely mortified. Nevertheless, they remained totally still, hoping they might impress their captors with their stoicism and escape unscathed. Despite their hopes, their bodies recognized the direness of the situation. The smell of urine hung in the air.

"Commissar Hassan!" shrieked Councilor Sharon Kay. "This is very triggering! We should not be subjected to this kind of aggressive display."

"Only immune to the sight of fetal excisions, eh, Sharon?" whispered Councilor Bradley Miliband. Realizing that his remark had caught Jagjit's attention, Bradley slapped the table. "This kind of impulse control, if not unprecedented, is certainly finer tuned than what's been proven on the Continent. We won't even need security forces if the population will self-police."

Jagjit smiled at Bradley. "*Indeed.* What is truly novel about this technology—even if it is simply a stopgap measure—is that the offboard, inorganic mind can still direct the body, but only through EDS mediation. We can freeze an offender before he attempts a crime. We can regulate temperament, meaning happier, healthier citizens. We can read thoughts in real time." Jagjit pointed at the haggard recidivist standing at the center of the surviving five. "Watch, comrades. See and hear proof of this technology's efficacy!" Jagjit prepared to read the subversive thoughts that were instantaneously transcribed and published on his tablet, though the thoughts didn't belong to the recidivist he had indicated with a point. The internal monologue belonged to someone else; to someone who silently thought to himself, "*Jesus Christ!*" and had his exclamation read aloud by Jagjit.

All of the forty-nine councilors appeared startled. Was the Commissar testing their allegiance? Testing their resolve to uphold and execute EDS protocol? One yelled, "Problematic!"

Jagjit ignored the anger and confusion about the invocation of a prohibited word referencing an EDS opponent and a banned religion. He continued to read atonally off of his tablet. "*He's wasting everybody's time with this technobabble.*"

58

The haggard recidivist's eyes widened. He looked around despairingly.

"Murdering regressive scum—pure theater! He wants another promotion so badly that he'll throw us all into the fire like kindling just to warm Weihan's backside," Jagjit read aloud, scrolling through the live updates on his tablet.

"Have you lost your mind, Commissar Hassan?" asked Sharon, dabbing spittle off of her mouth with a napkin.

Without returning her stare, Jagjit smiled at the recidivist in the doorway. "No. I have gained insight into another."

Bradley covered his gaping mouth with a knobby hand and jerked back in terror.

"He's reading the bigots' thoughts in real time," said Poyraz, smirking mischievously at the petrified recidivist standing in the doorway.

"But that's not—that's mine! It's not possible..." Jagjit continued reading, beginning to enjoy himself. *"But how? I know myself—unless... No! No!"* Jagjit let out an ominous laugh.

The haggard recidivist pushed his fellow prisoners aside, and tried to rush into the hall. Just as he made it past the threshold, he stopped. He turned around with a blank expression on his face, and took his post alongside the other prisoners.

Although the recidivist was now more or less comatose, Jagjit continued reading criminal thought, prompting nearly everyone in the room to wonder whose thoughts were actually being read. It could have been anyone!

"How is this possible? I've been a loyal servant of the People's Will!" Jagjit grinned at his peers and at the deer-eyed recidivist. He made his way around the table, but stopped behind Councilor Bradley Miliband. He peered down at his tablet and read aloud one more neural update: *"Good gracious. It can't be..."* Jagjit set the tablet down in front of Bradley for him to inspect, and placed his hand between Bradley's shoulder blades. Tears joined the streams of sweat running down Bradley's face. "The Patch Over will be successful," said Jagjit. "This I know only because *it has been* successful. We can wipe bad memories permanently, comrades. We can also generate good memories—we can grant absolution. What better way to demonstrate the perfection of this technology, our complete self-control, and our charitable disposition than to give a blank slate to a former enemy who has worked hard to regain the People's trust by eliminating the very last of the recidivists, regressives, and fascists?"

59

"Well, Commissar Hassan, that's very impressive," said Bradley, caving under the weight of Jagjit's hand. "In fact—"

"Spare us, Councilor," said Jagjit angrily. "I know what you're going to say, and it's not worth the time or the effort. You're my proof—one of many, in fact."

Indignation, shock, and doubt were expressed by a cacophonic and successional offering of gasps around the table.

"B-but I escaped a regressive prison! They tried to flip me, but they didn't have it in them!" shouted Bradley.

Jagjit focused on Bradley's balding crown. "Councilor Miliband here was a colonel in the Independent Army. Killed over one hundred of our people in several heinous acts of terrorism. Destroyed a great deal of our social and political infrastructure in the name of the very freedoms that brought our species rape, genocide, inequality, and irrationality..."

A young woman with a Chinese-communist-style tonsure stood and recited an old Party slogan: "Freedom is domination by the first unshackled!" In unison with a baritone-voiced guardian whose keenness was muffled though not masked, she continued the idiom: "Rights are the keys to universal liberation!"

Bradley shook uncontrollably and tried to stand. He was so troubled, he didn't know whether to join in chorus with the zealots to rebuff his accuser or to flee, but it didn't matter. Jagjit firmly held him down.

"Bradley Miliband is one of our first success stories, comrades."

The room settled down and all went silent. The eyes and ears of the council were trained on the accused. Everyone became a de-facto juror.

"Two years at his post. Not a major doubt or a subversive thought in all that time. *Councilor Bradley Miliband* is an exemplar of Democratic Socialist values. So too can all of our problematic citizens become exemplars in advance of the Mental Union." Jagjit whispered into Bradley's ear: "Better an exemplar than a briquette..." Smiling for the benefit of the panicked councilors, undoubtedly pondering whether their lives were similarly fabrications—if their realities were as manufactured as the consent and happiness of those they lorded over in their respective regions—Jagjit returned to his seat.

"Hang the fascist!" cried the baritone zealot. His demand was met by supportive finger snaps.

Bradley began to sob. Those seated adjacent to him shifted as far away as room along the table permitted.

60

"Even you, most equitable and fair councilors of Lancashire, were unable to determine Councilor Miliband's innocence or guilt. *We have* the technology. *We have* the human assets in place. *We have* won the war on regressive terror. They just don't know it yet."

Bradley began to slap his gnarled hands together. Without Jagjit's hand keeping him moored to his seat, he stood up clapping, mainly out of confusion and fear. Poyraz joined in, and whistled for good measure. Sharon and the other councilors similarly stood up to acknowledge Jagjit's accomplishment. To the sound of uproarious applause, the remaining recidivists cried quietly while their felt slip-on shoes soaked up blood and excrement by the doorway.

After savoring the adulation, Jagjit quieted the room and had his colleagues sit back down. "Comrades, the Patch Over will be our last great victory as ourselves. I thank you for your faith in the operation moving forward and in the Home Defence Department. The Supreme Council and our allies in the CDS and in the PRC will know that the glorious end began in Lancashire!"

"I am glad to have been—" started Bradley.

"Guardians, we have a regressive in our midst," said Poyraz, waving his baton in the air.

"I am cured of my past evils! I've been awarded a blank slate!" howled Bradley. Despite his age, he managed to throw his chair back and wagged a finger at Jagjit. "You reek of old-world zeal, *Jag!*"

Jagjit nodded knowingly to the guardians who seized Bradley by his arms and shoulders. "Even an exemplar must be made an example. The mercy of a blank slate will be doled out to another regressive. Your cure is out in the city quare."

Bradley was dragged out into the hall. His geriatric wails grew distant until they were no more. The silence cued action. The remaining forty-eight councilors busied themselves with questions and schemes on the basis of the new paradigm ushered in by Jagjit's prophesized technology.

A skeletal young councilor named Jennifer Dunkel, likely denied the sufficient allotment of calories on account of her striking natural beauty, posed a curious question: "There is no doubting the capability, given what we have seen already. My concern is really quite an obvious one: besides Councilor Miliband, who belongs to your trial group? And when will you make the list of names and aliases known?"

"It is not up to me when or whether to declassify those names," replied Jagjit, swirling around the remaining tonic in his glass.

Keen on a meaty answer to fill her hunger, Jennifer pressed the issue: "London Central, then?"

Jagjit nodded. "Our esteemed Home Defense Minister Corven reserves the right *to* and the secrecy *of* the list. In fact, I was only made aware of Miliband's dual allegiance before setting out for Blackpool for the purposes of this project; his and a few others."

"Thank you, Commissar Hassan," responded Jennifer.

Eyeing one recidivist in particular, Jagjit walked over to the doorway with his tablet in hand. "On second thought, I *will* name another to whom we'll deny absolution. I'm sure Minister Corven would favour our transparency." Jagjit lifted the chin of a large-pored gaffer standing amongst the remaining recidivists. "Rather, I'll have him identify himself. State your name for the record."

The gaffer filled his chest with air and indignation, and snarled at Jagjit. "My name is Kip Wilder and I hope you all burn."

Jagjit typed furiously onto his tablet. Kip firmed up. His eyes glazed over. His body was no longer his to control. It was now appropriated flesh belonging to the EDS.

"Councilor Dunkel," said Jagjit with an air of satisfaction. "Moving forward, we won't have to spill another jot of blood in the service of national security. The guilty will self-identify and their minds will be wiped, from abstract thought right down to reptilian governance."

Kip Wilder stopped breathing. He dropped to the ground. He flopped side to side and convulsed, but this was not his brain's doing; his muscles were reacting to the evacuation of his consciousness.

Major Poyraz Vola pricked up and grinned.

"That will be all," replied Jagjit, spreading his attention to the entire room. "I look forward to seeing you at the Patch Over ceremony." He returned to his seat.

The recidivists were marched out while the dead were carted away. Jennifer and her fellow councilors followed, emptying the room along with their security attaches. Councilor Kay meanwhile approached Jagjit, who was busy reorganizing his briefcase. "Fantastic work, Commissar Hassan."

"Hmm," he replied, distracted by the crossed-out faces blinking on his tablet. "Oh yes. Careful, Kay. It's always a collective effort. Don't individuate lest you tear the body apart."

Deaf to her superior's tangential concern, Sharon sought the answer her peers were too terrified to seek for themselves: "Miliband had high-enough security clearance to communicate with the enemy across the Atlantic."

"Fortunately he did not succeed in doing so or even make the attempt."

"Yes, Commissar Hassan. I understand and am grateful. But as I too have been cleared to deal with classified information, I think it necessary for the good of the People to demand confirmation that I am who I am; that I, Sharon Kay, am not an enemy of the English Democratic Socialist state."

Jagjit chuckled, closed his briefcase, and took Sharon's hand. "You are a great councilor; every bit as dedicated to the cause of progress as one would suspect. Have faith in the revolution and in your love for it."

Although older than dirt, Sharon failed to produce mud as she cried happy tears. "Thank you, Commissar Hassan!"

"No need to thank me, Councilor Kay. As always, it is a pleasure working with you and for those you represent."

Sharon withdrew her hand and dried her eyes. "I thank you anyway." She prepared to leave, but stopped mid-turn, nagged by self-doubt. "How *would* one know?"

"I beg your pardon?"

"How would one know if they were who they thought they were? How would I have known? I mean, without your confirmation?"

Jagjit sighed, and drank the dregs of his bitter drink. He stared past Sharon, seriously contemplating the question. "That's what makes this technology so wonderful, Councilor Kay. That's what makes it a triumph of the People's Will. You wouldn't. And neither would I."

SEVEN

Alek's apartment didn't feel like his own. Nothing about it reminded him of who he was or the kind of person he meant for himself to be. Even if he could remember something about his home of thirteen years, the EDS' mental dampeners prevented him from connecting the dots.

He closed the front door behind him and leaned back against it, sighing away some of his fear and frustration. Fortunately, his CBLOCK sector had power for the moment, so he could see much of the mess he had left for himself. With the door closed and out of the way of the hooks on the wall beside it, Alek also glimpsed several hints concerning his identity. A wrench, a tool belt, and some diagnostic wands that he had borrowed from the common chest, all hung from the hooks. He brushed his knuckles against the wrench's cold steel. Despite the hint at his past activity, Alek was still fuzzy about who he was and what he did. A tradesman? A plumber? A repair-droid's assistant? He intuited on his implant and prepared to query the system for whatever job title the EDS had conferred on him by way of lottery and trust, but the ache in his lower back reminded him of his assigned duties, first with wordless pain and then a fleeting memory of long nights on CBLOCK rooftops correcting sunburnt satellite dishes. He was CBLOCK32's special attachment, on loan from the Noospherics Department; a glorified mechanic they called a neuralnet machinist. His role was making sure that the state maintained cognitive control over his neighbours. Even though the worst of the pain in his back subsided, chased away in part by the cold of the door pressed against him, Alek somehow felt worse. He felt ashamed.

He stumbled into his kitchen. There was a kettle on its side on the stovetop. He righted it, filled it with water, and turned it on. Satisfied with this minor accomplishment, he set to work on his next, and searched the cabinets for a cup. The synchronization had left him dry-mouthed and tired. Tea was as close as he could get to a proper stimulant without risking a life-sentence. Peering into the cabinets, he saw that the only cup without a chip or a crack was at the very back. He groaned as he reached for it, and groaned again as he pulled it out. Inside the cup was a note, which read: "Consult the tea leaves to determine your fortune."

The writing was in Alek's hand—block letters like one might find left by an EDS Road and Safety stencil. Alek rolled his eyes.

64

"Don't tell me I'm some sort of superstitious twat..." He grabbed his tin of tea, and spooned some dry leaves into a rusted infuser. As he dug up the shredded leaf, his spoon clinked against something deeper in the tin. "What's this, now?" He set down the spoon, and sought out the treasure with trembling fingers. It was a small black object, no bigger than a pocketknife. A fine wire was coiled around it like the snake around the rod of Asclepius.

Taped to the black gizmo underneath the wire was another note that read: "Plug me in." Muscle memory showed him how. He pressed a small button on the side of the device and his apartment disintegrated around him.

"More chalk on the board," said Monica Neuhaus, rubbing her tired eyes. The previous night had taken its toll. She had to erase an entire parish's memory of their underground Sunday Mass.

Alek pulled up his chair and dropped his elbow patches on the desk. The monitor in front of him relayed the proof of the chalky sign via a live CCTV feed. A "C" followed by a ten-digit number was printed in chalk on a red brick wall. Anyone who wanted to solicit Alek and Monica's services had to find one of their hacked EDS surveillance cameras hidden in plain sight around Blackpool. When that particular camera went live, indicated by a green light both on-location and in the Neuhauses' apartment, the prospective client would mark their citizen registration number in chalk. Monica and Alek could search the number and determine on the basis of risk and reward whether they would take the client. Although Blackpool now had a population of over five-million souls, the Neuhauses nevertheless recognized most of their clients. The chalk ritual was still important, though; their memory-scrubbing service was a secret well-kept by citizens and EDS officials alike, but ever-rising demand required them to remain vigilant. "Who needs wiping?" Alek asked his wife.

Monica entered the number into her tablet and a chin-heavy face appeared in the holofield. "Janet Croft. Blackpool-Preston CBLOCK18. She's a junior in the Department of Agriculture."

"Needs to forget she has put aside some ration jelly, no doubt."

Nodding, Monica converted the holofield into a wall projection. The last three months of Janet Croft's schedule were superimposed onto the Neuhauses' kitchen wall. The name of every bureaucrat Croft met alongside their affiliations streamed down one side, while every geo-tagged location she visited was plotted on a map. "She's on the three-cycle synch. Earned the warden's trust selling out subversives with regressive ties."

Alek sighed. "Forget it. She's not worth the risk."

Monica red-flagged Janet Croft's file and rejected her appeal, sealing the stranger's fate. Like a urine test, if one couldn't buy a clean sample, they were in deep trouble. Only, in the case of Croft, trouble meant more than losing her job; it likely meant death.

Unperturbed by her husband's hasty judgment, Monica pulled up live footage of another red brick wall graffitied with white chalk.

Alek got up with cup in hand, kissed Monica on the cheek in passing, and poured himself some more tea. The chalked letter "G" ahead of another long number printed on the brick caught his eye. "Out of our depth, but worth a gander."

Scott Townley's file was already on Monica's lap. She filled the holofield with his specifics. "Works for Reclamation. Appointed by Commissar Dorz himself."

Gaping at Townley's hardened, Slavic face, Alek concluded aloud: "EDS prick. Useful because of what he knows. Dangerous because of what he remembers. He's not forgetting jelly. He's washing away blood."

"He's gotta be worth his weight in mobility chits." Mobility cards permitted citizens to leave their CBLOCK and travel between regions. Their distribution was strictly regulated, although the higher-rated chits were rarely questioned at the checkpoints littered throughout England.

The Neuhauses looked at one another's partial form edging through the holofield. Monica clasped Alek's hands and smiled. Alek pressed his lips through the projection to her knuckles. "Well then," he said, reclining and finishing his tea. "*Fine*. Tell Danika we'll be taking a ride to Townley's place in Queenstown." An EDS guardian named Danika Frye had become their getaway driver after finding herself owing both Neuhauses a fairly hefty favour, which she paid back in mileage. "She'll ask for a bigger take, but with this job we'll be able to afford it."

Before zipping up his duffel bag full of old Outland implant-readers and memex wipes, Alek double-checked the magazine on his handgun. The theater of it amused him—brandishing a threat he had never made good on.

While their scrubbing gear charged, Monica hid her tablet under her drawer's false bottom. "Alek, my dear, you've got your memex put away?"

"With the leaves. How about yours? That it there?"

66

"No. It's in its usual spot."

Alek closed his bag, and set it by the door. "In your sock drawer?"

"I told you! It's not good for either of us to know where we keep them. Besides, I don't want you uploading me. We'll have nothing left to talk about."

"Only the future," Alek said, nosing up to Monica and raising his palms. She laughed away her concern and seized the waltz. They graced the kitchen with an intimate and well-rehearsed dance, and hummed variations of the same illegal tune. "Que será, será..."

Approaching the bittersweet end of the song, Monica's posture caved. "What future?" She broke off and finished preparing her kit.

"Good Lord," Alek said, exasperated. "We've been over this."

Monica's eyes glazed over as she unknotted the quintessential tool of their trade, a neural net capable of reading and mapping out memorial associations in the mind. It was her creation, her design. Nobody east of New York shared her knack for neuraltech or memory salvage. "Talking about dreams doesn't make them real. It just makes reality that much harder to bear."

Alek tongued his molars and retreated from his wife's melancholy, seeking refuge in the kitchen cul-de-sac. Even with his head bracketed by open cupboard doors, Monica's point nevertheless found him. First, her honesty angered him. Then it emboldened him. "A couple more jobs, Moni. Four, maybe five big payouts...With enough crypto, we can get the right mobility cards. With the right mobility cards, we can go north. From Skye, we can connect with the—"

"Stop." Monica set the neural net down and looked forlornly out the window at the CBLOCK across the way. "I love the dream. Honestly, Alek, it usually warms me on days like today. I want a little cabin in the woods. I want to start a family. I want to thank God without having my gratitude drilled out. I want to leave Blackpool so badly, but I know, I just know, the guilt is going to eat me up."

"What guilt? We've helped out. We've done our part. *Just one more and we're out.*"

"One, twenty, thirty-thousand..." Monica reset the floorboards concealing their stash of crypto chits and lockboxes. "There's what? Two-hundred million Britons out there. All opened up and checked on weekly. What is that? Ten trillion wipes? Who is going to give people peace when we're gone?"

Alek closed the kitchen cupboards, and sauntered over to embrace his wife. Even though she was cold and rigid, he kissed her

67

nevertheless. She pulled away, but he maintained contact. "Oh, come on. There's always someone."

Unenergetically swatting her husband's advances, Monica replied: "No. There's not. And no one will remember that there was a way to enjoy a little bit of freedom or lethes to make it so."

Growing frustrated, especially with a big job to do, Alek shut down emotionally and attempted to throw as many solutions at the wall as he could in hopes something might stick. "I can teach Geoffrey." Their old neighbor Geoff Littlefield was a fixer. He had been downgraded by the government and sent to the city limits after the screws discovered he had a dog. Despite being on the outs and borderline suicidal without his furry friend, he still sent a great deal of business their way and could locate most black-market items.

"Geoffrey was a moron even before they implanted him!" Monica shouted. She didn't mean it. Geoff was actually quite intelligent, which was truly unnatural granted he still had his mental dampeners running fulltime. The pain the dampeners would deluge him with every time an idea occurred to him was his drug of choice. Geoff was probably the only bloke on the island whose kink improved his intellectual faculties.

"Don't be an ass! Geoff's been good to us." Alek's face went blank, and contorted around a new idea. His eyes lit up as it hit his lips. "If you're worried the guilt will follow us to the States, then we can do a targeted wipe. We can forget all about this nightmare and move on."

Monica turned bright red. "Alek Cornelius Neuhaus—ever heard of him?" She turned and jabbed Alek in the chest. "Big guy. Likes to brawl. In fact, he fought the demsocks in the early days of the Labour Revolution and even harder during Mob Rule. Fought the new regime before *and* after it stuck metal in his head."

"Enough of that, Moni." He placed her hand on his chest. "He's here. But he's only got one last fight in him—the one that'll get us the hell out of this commie dump."

The red in Monica's face faded, and she burst into tears.

Alek threw his arms around her and enveloped her in bruised muscle. "I love you, sweet pea." Alek made enough room so that he could dry the tears from her cheeks. "But I have no love left in me for all those twats who surrendered their freedoms without a fight. The Chinese and the Continentals didn't invade. The EDS was democratically elected. Fifty-one percent sealed the deal. They did this to themselves. They did this to *us*. Don't let them hold your happiness hostage."

"What about the kids? The nation's children all trapped in London? Indoctrinated. Engineered. What will happen to them?"

"What about *our* kids? Don't you want little Neuhauses milling about?" Alek stroked Monica's shoulder. "Charity starts at home. Hope starts with the individual."

Monica sank into Alek's heft, and rubbed her nose dry on his sleeve. She buried a noncommittal smile and a muffled response in the crotch of his arm. "Charlie and Elizabeth."

Alek was giddy with relief after seeing Monica chin-up. "Liza for short."

"Liz!" Monica blurted, pushing Alek back playfully.

"Liz and Charlie will grow up free. And who knows? Maybe their generation will repair the damage that ours has done."

"Maybe."

Alek gasped as he came to. He sat on the cold kitchen floor amidst scattered tea leaves with a cable dangling from the back of his head. He unplugged it, and wrapped it around his little black memex. The external memory drive had synchronized with his implant and bridged the chasm between his present and past selves. It had restored all of the memories he had to hide from the English Democratic Socialists' hunter AIs and historians. He wished he and Monica would have just kept dancing.

His headache had dissipated, and for that he had his wife to thank. She in turn might have thanked her uncle, Cedric Warmington.

Cedric Warmington made a small fortune selling lude virtual scenarios to clerics and businessmen in the Ottoman Federation. Unlike other experience-gatherers who kowtowed to the emperor, Cedric saw an opportunity to monopolize on the devious demands going unsupplied. He devised a way of circumnavigating the sharia neural censors that would inevitably produce painful responses in the implanted whenever blasphemous or sinful images were encountered. Sufficed to say, his bypass pleased many Turks, including the emperor's youngest son.

Warmington did not teach his method to Monica in any conventional way. In his customary fashion, he sent her the relevant experience file. In the privacy of her parents' apartment, she relived his discovery and assimilated his understanding. When the EDS forcefully made her an engineer at what later became the Noospherics Department, Monica recognized the applications of Warmington's bypass right away. After all, the EDS' mental

69

dampeners consisted of the same hardware, and the state-feared complex thought was more or less blasphemy.

This override meant mental freedom for her and Alek. Danika Frye too. They weren't useful idiots. On the contrary, when the government had dumbed down the citizenry to make everyone easier to manage and to utilize their processing power for affairs of the state (save for those who had proven themselves and rode promotions into relative clarity), the EDS had unwittingly made those with the Warmington fix supermen.

Although he had now overcome the dulling pain, Alek did not feel particularly super. He had relived a nightmarish thirty-three years in just under five minutes. This was emotionally jarring, as would be expected, but cathartic too. He was solaced to have himself back. It felt like a cramped and arthritic hand had been permitted to relax for the first time in ages.

He pulled himself up and realized he was once again soaked, but this time with warm water. The kettle had boiled over. The countertop had a shimmering gloss as a result, and on the floor there were two rivulets racing towards the drain at the center of the room. Unfazed, as he had been waterlogged since the wee hours of the morning, Alek wrung out a tuft of his shirt, and resumed his tea-making. The routine of it helped him reacquaint his mind with his body. He stood there by the kettle, trying his best to piece together his final memories of his life with Monica. He knew that the demsocks shot her and that she wasn't coming back. He knew that it was his fault, at least in part, and that he would never again be whole.

The night it happened flashed before his eyes—the night they took her away from him. Although emotionally potent, this memory did not strike him as vivacious or as immediate as those that had been delivered him via his memex. No, this was a loosely-linked series of moments he had to piece together as would an old-world historian or any other storyteller. Granted the memory's cast and lasting import, Alek was certain to get it right.

After packing their gear, Alek and Monica had made it to Scott Townley's CBLOCK in Queenstown with the help of Danika, whose guardian van served as an all-access pass throughout Lancashire. Upon arriving at Queenstown Plaza, now Lancashire's CBLOCK02, Alek and Monica split up because the only thing more suspicious than a greasy interloper is a pair of greasy interlopers walking hand-in-hand. It seemed as if the very moment they split up, everything began to unravel.

70

On his way to impair the security system, Alek tripped a crowd scanner. The individual whose identity he was temporarily stealing had been too close and was scanned in the same surveillance sweep as him. The double-confirmation tipped off a DSSP agent who in turn made Alek in the lobby and gave chase. That should have been it; that should have been enough reason to call off the job, but Alek had convinced Monica it was the last one they would ever do, which was all the justification she needed to carry on while her husband ran like a mad man.

Despite the fact that his pursuer called in a Shepherd drone, Alek had somehow managed to lose his tail and make it back to Queenstown Plaza unbloodied. The DSSP had likely figured he wouldn't have dared return to the scene of his first sighting, or perhaps they had been called elsewhere on a more pressing security concern. Either way, Alek made it inside, and raced up to Townley's floor.

The hallway outside of Townley's was packed with guardians and special police. Alek avoiding being seen and pressed into the first apartment with an unlocked door, knocking out the occupant without a second thought. He watched helplessly from the stranger's doorway.

Some med bots had Monica strapped down to a stretcher. Her head was bleeding profusely from what looked like a bullet wound. Her hair was matted down and had flecks of flesh strewn about it. While the bots carted Monica's body out, passing Alek on the way, Alek heard Townley lying his face off to the DSSP agents gathered around; telling some tall tale about being attacked in his sleep. How he had procured a gun despite the ban or why he had been targeted apparently were questions that didn't need answers because the solution he arrived at would have been the same as the one his comrades would have come up with one department over.

Alek could have and should have shot Townley then and there. Had he, maybe Monica would have heard the second shot and passed knowing she had been avenged. But no, Alek spent the night hiding in the apartment belonging to the stranger.

In the time he had spent alone since the ambush, Alek had become a different man. That is what he convinced himself of anyway—that he would kill anybody to save the innocent. Problem was, he no longer knew of anybody on the island who was still innocent, so his gained fortitude was wasted not to mention left untested.

71

As Alek tried to separate fact from emotion in three decades of disjointed memories, the kettle blew its ceremonial trumpet. Only then did he realize his occipital implant site was bleeding.

Once he had prepared the infuser and devoured his daily-allotted eMeal brick the kitchen distribution pipe spat out, he began to set up his gear, most of which he had concealed behind false walls or under warped floorboards. Alek's bandaged head disappeared below the floorboards. He berated himself as he rummaged through lock boxes in search of the various gadgets that would complete a scrubbing kit. "Where'd you put it, you damned fool?!"

As he untangled wires, he ignored the various baubles that cluttered the space, every one of which reminded him of Monica. He tried to repress his emotional response and may have succeeded, but in the last lockbox, he found one of her socks. She had been using it to clean something or other and hadn't thought to put it away or throw it out. Alek laughed. "Moni, you slob…" He rose from the floor with the lockbox in hand and set it down on the desk. There was nothing besides the sock inside it, and yet it seemed horribly full. Alek stared at it while his chest heaved. He reopened the box, seized the sock, and trudged over to the bedroom.

He mournfully opened the third drawer from the top, and neatly tucked it away with the other unmatched orphans. Just as he had suspected, it was there, nestled between her ankle socks: *Monica's memex*. That little black box might as well have been a coffin.

Cradling his wife's backup, full of every memory, thought, and consideration that had ever passed through her mind except for her surprise and pain at the end, and waiting for comfort that might never come, Alek wept. His eyes were too shocked to tear up on account of echoes of the EDS synchronization still wreaking havoc on his limbic system. The only outward evidence of his despair was the sob permitted past his cracked enamel. Shaking himself numb, he firmed his upper lip, put Monica's memex away, and shut the drawer. "Damn the EDS."

72

EIGHT

There was no point in hiding the nuclear mortars, especially when the attempt would draw more interest that what already existed. Stephen threw a blanket over the case and shut the curtain behind him. He was going to find a way to America and, as with all good adventures he had embarked on, the Underpool market was the best place to start. The Resistance had shot down enough Chinese drones and jets that there should at least be something flyable parked in one of their various lockups. That's what he told himself, anyway.

He heard snoring when he passed Mirek's room, so loud that it overwhelmed even the sound of Underpool's drainage pumps keeping the subterrane dry. *Good*, thought Stephen. Had Mirek supposed the case Stephen and Wes lugged in contained anything worthwhile, he would have hounded both of them day and night for answers, sleep be damned. *Yes*, Stephen thought, progressing onward. The case would be safe, at least until he locked down some form of transportation.

Stephen had written Mirek off prematurely, however. Something popped underneath his boots. Glass! *The sunnuvabitch put glass down as a rudimentary warning system*. No nightmare could stand before Mirek and his prey. The punk charged out of his room, eyes all munged up by sleep. He skidded across the hall, and then charged again to catch up with Stephen. "Hold up, now! Hold yar horses, Stevie!"

"You dingus..." Stephen tapped the toe of his boot, sprinkling shards free from his heel. "What if I pattered out barefoot?"

The twenty steps from his door to Stephen's heels were enough to throw Mirek's diaphragm into palpitations. "Aw, damn it. I feel winter in my chest already." He keeled over, caught his breath, and then lifted himself on his spread legs. "Yah haven't seen Wesley, now have yah, bruv?"

Stephen steeled his face and denied Mirek the slightest bit of caring. "Not since the witching hour." He pressed on, cracking more of the glass shards.

Mirek lunged forward and grabbed Stephen by the arm. Stephen turned angrily, but Mirek preempted trouble by smiling and speaking softly: "Listen, I'm not another dribbler you can cut out of big happenings and the like. I carry my weight. Might only be eleven stone, but I carry it. Every day. Scavenge, defend, kill, clean—I do it all, Stevie."

73

Stephen threw Mirek's hand back, and balled his fists. He had no intention of throwing a punch, not with Mirek's chances of shattering so damned high. Still, his knuckles turned white while his cheeks turned red.

"You don't gotta tell me what's in yar box. Damn me if I'm not spit shaking to get in on the action."

"Seriously, mate. Bug off."

"I can tell that what yahs found has changed yah. I need a change too, Stevie. Don't leave me in the dark."

America and the prospect of roping it into a just war seemed to slink further and further away. Stephen hadn't even made it to market and the whole scheme already seemed pointless. Nevertheless, to protect that infinitesimal possibility of salvation, Stephen would do anything. Problem was that the right thing was unclear.

It would have been easier to lie to Mirek—to tell him the case was full of flour or petrol—but Stephen finally saw what he previously figured Wes had only imagined. There was a kind of spark in Mirek that Stephen hadn't seen around these parts for years, not since he watched it kicked out of his brother. There wasn't a word for it, for the way Mirek's eyes shone in the murk of the tunnel. Stephen saw past his neighbour's meat right through to Michael's bones rattling off his favourite saying: "At spes infracta." *Bent but not broken*. Whatever lay ahead, if faced alone, Stephen could snap. But faced with a friend beside him? With a brother at arms? Nothing could break them. That said, Stephen didn't want to come off as a suck in accepting him outright. "Listen up, you tosser…"

Mirek snarled.

"Fine!"

Unaccustomed to any kind of acceptance, good or bad, Mirek didn't know what to do with Stephen's reply. He pushed Stephen and stumbled backwards. "The hell d'yah mean, 'fine'?"

"*You're in*. You've always been in." Stephen spread his shoulders and fanned his hands. "I s'pose we're a team down here." He was not only convincing Mirek but himself as well. Stephen was drunk on hope, and he had always been a sentimental drunk.

As much as the sentiment felt strange for Mirek to hear, it felt just as strange for Stephen rolling off the tongue like it did. But he was desperate and all of a sudden Mirek's unfiltered stream of bad ideas seemed like the only creative juices flowing subgrade.

"Relax bruv. I don't need a marriage cert'icate, I just wanna know what's in the bloody box."

"You got to keep your big mouth sealed."

Mirek bit his upper lip and flared his nostrils. "Alright. Fine." He set his shoulders back and clasped his breast. "On my heart and soul, I swear it."

Stephen looked up and down the hall then back to Mirek. "We've got bombs. We've got a lot of bombs."

Mirek dropped his oath. "Bullshit."

"And we're going to use 'em where they'll do the most damage. But I need an airship. And it can't be that Yank Cassandra's. Needs to be an enemy ship."

"Oh, well, Stevie." Mirek spat and brandished his fuzzy yellow smile. He adjusted his pants while he peered around for potential eavesdroppers that Stephen may have overlooked. "You be careful now, lying with your glass jaw just so, because I might be 'clined to believe yah."

Stephen grabbed Mirek forcefully by the collar and dragged him down the hall to his flat. Mirek barely resisted, and even if he had, Stephen had twice his muscle mass.

"Go on! See for yourself!" Stephen shouted.

Mirek was dumbfounded before he even pulled the blanket off of the case. "You got 'em on your salvage?"

Stephen nodded.

Mirek yanked the blanket and pried the lid open just enough to confirm his neighbour's tale. He dropped to his knees like a penitent pilgrim. "I can't be happier with you, Stevie." He looked up to Stephen with a look of pure joy. "You best take off runnin', cause I'm going to lay my lips on yah!" A look of hunger and excitement firmed up his happy visage. Just as quickly, he broke down into hysterics. Laughing, Mirek fell onto his back. "Steve! Help me up before I catch whatever you have."

Stephen tried desperately to deny himself the excitement, especially after the first flush of hope had giddied him, but something about Mirek's laugh unmoored whatever was holding him steady. He too broke into bursts of laughter. He hadn't felt so good in ages and had someone at last to share it with. Wes' honorable pragmatism made it too real to enjoy. Mirek, conversely, saw it for what it was: a box full of promise.

Recovering the case with the blanket, Mirek looked up to Stephen. "Cassandra's ship would be an easy git, though."

Stephen sighed. "I'm headed to the market to find out if anyone has leads on an airship. If I don't, Congress will decide what to do with 'em."

As much as Mirek wanted to please General McGregor and the Congress, he didn't want to hand off the glory right away. "Screw that! We can find a bird, no problem! Besides, there's nothing in the market in the way of wings."

Pacing across the flat, still reeking of garbage, Stephen reconsidered heading to the market and thought up ways to utilize his forbidden-ally's skillset. "But where? They don't exactly leave Dreadnoughts sitting around with t'keys in 'em."

"When's the last time you spoke to old man Carrella? Everyone's always saying he's got everything you could ask for in his lockup." This was hearsay; Mirek had heard about Carrella's morbid curiosity shop from Stephen, though never made it so far as Preston in his own travels.

"Carlo?" Stephen stopped to think. Carlo Carrella was an English arms dealer who had somehow gotten through the Mob Rule without officially choosing a side or having an EDS implant jammed into his head. If he was to pick a side, Stephen liked to think that Carrella would have chosen the Resistance, mainly because his head was full of too much of his own organic tech to make room for an EDS off-switch. He was not, however, forced to choose a side. European and Chinese *innovators* with party ties had made it worth his while to keep producing gizmos they could later scale up, and this demand was only justified by the persistence of their enemies in the Resistance that he similarly kitted. Was it not for the demsocks' inability to trust their own AI systems to create the weapons and systems they depended upon—that is without the AI hijacking their perpetual revolution—they likely would have snuffed Carrella out. Fortunately, they were forever in short supply of trust and would never risk letting a rogue AI pointing out all of the inefficiencies and pathologies in their socialist worldview. "I saw him a few months back. Went with Wes and Zeke. Traded Carrella plasma vents for a drainage pump. Damned lunatic tried to take Wes' gallbladder."

"But he had planes, yeah? Jets or the like?"

Stephen bowed his head and racked his brain, trying desperately to remember as much as he could about Carrella's compound. It was on the edge of the Preston Red Zone, a short walk from the unlawful demsock black market that had been permitted to exist on account of the Chinese demand and English diplomacy. The compound had been an underground carpark, which Carrella transformed into a laboratory and warehouse. Street-level, above the parking lot, stood the remains of a shopping centre, strategically dynamited to allow aerial units in and out of the compound. Stephen rocked back and forth, trying to recreate the scene in his mind. They weren't allowed into Carrella's laboratory, although Stephen had seen snippets of it as they passed through a labyrinth of tarps and

76

scrap-metal barricades. He recalled seeing some thrusters attended to by little helper drones; that there were batteries littered around the place; and, *YES!* There was a large, arrow-headed vehicle covered with a white sheet whose landing gear was visible. "I think so, yeah. I don't know if it can fly or if there were others like it. No idea if they were Chinese."

"That's as good a start as you're bound to find anywhere else in this hole."

"How the hell do we get to Preston? Forget the demsocks guarding the way and the red zone patrols waiting for us. The triads are posted there making sure no Englishman interferes with Pingo business."

"What'd Wes say?"

"About Carlo Carrella?"

Ironing out the blanket, Mirek's head fired up. "No, yah muppet. Your plan!"

"He thought my plan was crazy and that I shouldn't mention it to *anybody.*"

Mirek turned around and beamed. "Great! We *are* crazy. What's the plan then, bruv?"

Stephen sat on his chesterfield and rubbed his forehead. "Forget it, man. Preston's a long shot."

"I didn't ask you about Preston. I asked you about the confounded plan."

Surprised by his neighbour's focus, Stephen sat upright and gripped the arm of the couch. "Well...I figure we blow a few of them up over American soil. Nobody needs to die, you see, but the Yanks need to see them go off. That's essential. Has to be an enemy ship that drops 'em too. Would be ideal if the 'sploding ship was Chinese. Either way, I think our best bet is violating the Armistice. The Yanks will punch back and free us in the process."

The plan was either lost on Mirek or so beyond the pale that it failed to register as anything more than idle banter. Mirek lifted the blanket and lid, and peered at the mortars again. "I 'unno. Maybe Wes is right. I'm all for crazy, but wasting these o'er the puddle sounds like..." He racked his brain for a synonym, but came up short. "A shameful waste. Wouldn't it be easier just blowing up the Pingos and saying it was the Americans?"

"They'd know right away that it was us. 'Member back when the Liverpool Monarchists blew up the Birkenhead cypulchre?"

"What? The brain bank? Yeah. They built a new one and pu'up a wall."

77

"So if we drop every one of these on an EDS project, all we'll get are more walls and more special police raids, yeah?"

Mirek had drunkenly debated Stephen enough times to see a trap a breath away. "Then drop 'em on the baby-makers. Drop 'em on their breeding centres. Hell mate, I still say drop 'em bombs on the Pingos offshore. But don't think GI Joe will cross the puddle because you re-bombed US shores."

"Alright. You win, Mirek. Take that blanket off. We'll bring these to the General and see what he—"

Mirek stalled Stephen's surrender with a point, and hit Underpool's contrarian-in-residence with an alternative. "If your plan is crazy, then Carrella is our man. Wes is always talking about 'em Pingo ships blustering about the red zone in Preston—you know; the big ships that look like they crawled out of the sea. Carlo Carrella can probably pull one down for us if he doesn't have one handy."

Stephen rose slowly from his perch on the chesterfield. There was something to Mirek's suggestion, but so far, all he could see were red flags. "The new Flyde tunnel caved in a few weeks back. Even though Colonel Phan was able to hack the Reduvius drones and the Burrowers the EDS sent in, there're probably still a couple strays behind all the rubble. We won't make it east past Clifton."

Mirek directed Stephen's attention to the map of Lancashire gummed to the wall near the whisky bottles. "Tunnel's down, yeah. But if we could catch a ride with someone..." He pointed out the road. It was outside the Blackpool perimeter wall, but still under EDS control, meaning patrols and checkpoints. Face compressed by grave thoughts, Mirek yanked the map down and pocketed it.

"Oi! Oi!" shouted several deep-voiced men in unison out in the hall.

The shouting outside shook Mirek and Stephen to their cores. Stephen silently instructed Mirek to sit on the munitions case, and peeked past the curtain. Torches lit the faces of a dozen men and women marching up the way, hitting each door they passed and yelling, "Intelligence brief! Thirty minutes. Intelligence brief!"

Stephen retreated to the chesterfield, scratching at the excitement in his chest. "Who the hell did you tell, Merry?"

Slack-jawed and every-bit-as-bewildered as his neighbor, Mirek shrugged and shook his head. "No'ne, bruv. I swear it." He held onto the sides of the case when he sat on it so that it looked like he was keeping some sort of monster from breaking out. "Y'only just told me now."

"Right," said Stephen, peeking through the holes in his curtain. "But did you tell anyone Wes and I pulled a crate in?"

Mirek clowned his lips and shook his head.

"Then what's the brief for, d'you figure?"

Underpool intelligence briefings usually took place before or after a skirmish. To counter speculation and gossip, Congress always made them open to anyone who cared to hear the latest about the war effort, whether or not soldiers were needed or ever to return. If the Resistance wasn't up-to-date about their brothers' most recent activities, how were they to know the importance of their involvement in the next?

The most recent briefing dealt with the last-in from Dublin. Shrapnel-scarred and badly burnt, the Paddies reported the destruction of the resistance ferry that had kept some dreams of a successful diaspora alive. These dreams were dashed when the Continental Democratic Socialists, in cahoots with the EDS, flipped a high-ranking Resistance fighter. After days of torture, he gave up the whereabouts of Father Flemming and his neo-Jacobite commandos who had managed to transmit security keys for Irish airspace to the English Resistance. With great sorrow and a few of them dying from their wounds, the last of Underpool's sister outpost at Saint Columba had eulogized the Irish Resistance.

Regardless of whether this latest intelligence briefing was going to be another community obituary or a preamble to Stephen's exile or execution, the two of them knew that they had to be there. That was one of the rules Wes came up with that had stuck: *assume responsibility as soon as you're able.*

The hallway mob rattled Stephen's cage as they passed, and sparked him to action. "Mirek, this is on me. I told Wes to wait, not to tell Congress right away. I didn't mean to drag you into it. You tell them whatever you need to."

Offended by Stephen's haste at assuming blame and cutting him out of responsibility, Mirek took to his feet and squared his shoulders. "Back off. You don't have a monop'ly on guilt, mate. We haven't done anything wrong, either. Just waiting on our strength to carry this shit to the General."

The anxiety sitting beneath Stephen's breastplate dissipated. He looked at Mirek with new eyes. "Yeah, that's right." Stephen grabbed his ball cap. "But let me do the talking."

Their animal subtext overtook the conversation. Mirek shook Stephen's hand. "Sure thing."

79

Mirek lead them out and down the hall. As soon as they reached the glass shards, they both looked at each other and froze. "Probably should bring the bombs, eh mate?"

Stephen backpedaled to the doorway, "Aye, maybe we should."

"We'll hand 'em over if General McGregor mentions 'em, how 'bout that?"

Stephen reentered his flat, threw the covering off of the case and took one end. "And if he doesn't mention 'em, we won't have to stand."

Mirek stood on the other end of the case, but didn't make any attempt to lift it—so puzzled was he by Stephen's meaning that any other exertion be it mental or physical would have been calamitous. "Stand trial yah mean?"

Slapping the case, Stephen grinned. "No. I mean we've got a portable bench!"

"Ah good! My guts always hurt when I've gotta stand too long." Mirek crouched down to get a hold on the case, and stood up straight, cartilage cracking all the way.

"Lift with your knees, Merry!"

"Me knees don't have fingers, yah numpty. I'm lifting with my hands!"

"Go on then! Throw your back! But don't expect any sympathy."

Mirek cursed under his breath, but focused his resentment on the case as opposed to Stephen.

They scraped out and into the hall, Mirek first. As they moseyed along, sullenness beset them both. Even if they weren't in trouble, there was always something troubling to learn at an intelligence brief.

"Maybe they've found us out," said Mirek, pressing his silhouetted profile to his shoulder, "And thunk it a righteous idea! Maybe they've found us a jet!"

NINE

Waiting for Commissar Hassan in the lobby of the Blackpool Council House was a tall young man with pointed shoulders, one Councilor Dustin Reiter. Reiter rushed to intercept Jagjit before he managed to cross the marbled EDS insignia at the center of the foyer. "Commissar!" he bleated.

Two guardians stationed outside the elevator saw the commotion and sprinted over. Without so much as a warning, they both strong-armed Reiter against a pillar.

"You making an attempt on the boss?" said one, pressing his helmet against Reiter's forehead while fumbling with his handcuffs and his captive's hands.

"Comrade Commissar Hassan!" yelled Reiter. His one hand was cuffed, but he managed to throw up his free hand through the tangle of armoured limbs and EDS branding. Waving frenetically, he yelled the Commissar's name again.

Jagjit did not recognize the man from the meeting. Perhaps his eyes were one of the sets that didn't stand out in defiance. Jagjit did however recognize the station signified by the man's badge; a councilor from Cleveleys. He stopped and rattled his briefcase authoritatively. "It's okay, constables! The councilor has my ear."

The guardians released Reiter and uncuffed his hand. Reiter straightened out his shirt, ruffled in his suppression, righted his belt, and squeezed his reddened wrist. "Bloody masqueraders," he whispered to the guardians. Raising his voice, he addressed Jagjit: "Thank you, Commissar Hassan."

Jagjit continued walking and presumed the councilor to follow. Without raising his voice, he addressed the space beside him where the young man should already have been. "Councilor Reit, is it?"

"Councilor Reiter, Comrade Commissar." Reiter caught up but left his breath behind.

"Reiter, what can I do for you?"

Reiter pulled out a dotgram as meaningless without implant integration as a blank sheet of paper, and pointed at it with conviction. "Commissar Dorz—uh, *your predecessor*—knew of several likely entry points into the Resistance complexes along the coast."

Jagjit smiled and stopped at the threshold. He turned with interest to Reiter and folded his arms. "Did he now?"

81

Reiter held the dotgram with both hands and shook it with excitement. "I believe there is no reason not to task a full fighting force to eliminate the last remaining threat to cohesion and democracy. Four or five swarms could clear the entire regressive nexus. A platoon of DSSP officers could confirm their results."

With his arms still crossed, Jagjit tapped his toe and nodded. He recognized the danger in Reiter's ambition. Fully aware of the fact that no ambition can be realized without aggression, Jagjit wondered what the man was after and who he was ready to knock off to succeed. His smile vanished and he looked up at the councilor. "My predecessor was extravagant. His interest in revisionist histories made him a dilettante. His secret appreciation for hateful artifacts made him a traitor."

Reiter beamed. He folded his dotgram and stood at attention as if readying to receive some grand and historical order.

"And yet he knew the joy of labour. He knew that the guarantee of work must be protected, especially if the work advanced the Supreme Council's vision."

The young man who had a moment ago so badly wanted the Commissar's attention now looked like he would do anything to avoid it.

Jagjit yanked the dotgram out of Reiter's hands and stuffed it into his pocket. "Councilor Reiter, it is really important that you realize the extent to which the regressives are impotent; the extent to which the terrorist McGregor is history's bastard who, along with other feral children, tends to a sand castle while oblivious to the rising tide. To my knowledge, they haven't successfully attacked the People or our infrastructure in months. They *will* be destroyed and that destruction will be facilitated by the Patch Over. To pre-empt the Patch Over is to presume it to be ineffective."

Focusing on the feet barely shoring up his two trembling legs, Reiter stammered: "But comrade..."

"And if we rush our final victory, we won't fully understand it; we won't know what to attribute to force of arms or to technological genius, thus robbing all labourers of their results." Jagjit set his hand down on Reiter's shoulder, the perceived weight of which seemed to pain the young man. "Think in terms of the good of the People, not the threat of a few condemned individuals. For us to properly unite the species and to heal the Earth, we have to always prioritize the collective. Do you understand?"

Reiter took a step back and managed something of a bow. He audibly returned a throat full of vomit back to sender. Sucking his teeth clean, he answered: "Yes, Comrade Commissar."

Giving the young man an out and making way for his own, Jagjit chippered his tone. "When the time is right, we will revisit your strategy for purging Lancashire of hate."

As Jagjit pressed through the door and out of the Council House, he heard Reiter yell out his thanks, mired by the jargon of officialdom.

Outside, a dozen laborers stood in front of the Blackpool Council Building. They had put up a heavplast cast and were tapping at it mindlessly with hammers. Jagjit looked at them with disdain. *Joy of labour.* What a joke, he thought to himself. He took little joy from his work with the Commissariat. The enemy was at least honest in this regard, recognizing that one sacrificed joy, as well as his time and energy, in exchange for self-esteem and monetary reward. Self-esteem was guaranteed by the EDS' virtual comfort data-packets, and in England there was no legitimate market of value. These mindless hammerers clacking away to no avail may have been joyful, but it had nothing to do with their labour. The job, like most on the island, was a distraction. Idle hands crafted the revolution and idle minds would ensure that it rotting fruits were preserved.

"Good day, Commissar!" said one of the fudgels without missing a beat.

"Comrades, excellent work! Such diligence!" Jagjit checked the time. "Your joy inspires my own!"

Jagjit's sleek, black driverless limousine pulled up at the base of the steps below the Council House. Jagjit ignored the hammerers' salutes and got into the limo hastily, glad to escape another useless conversation as well as Blackpool's maritime stench. He sat on the car's back bench, and looked out the window and up at the tall black building housing Lancashire's brain trust.

Reiter and Vola's enthusiasm he could forgive. Sharon's questions about the list and her identity, however, continued to irk him. He would have preferred to have accused her of having been on the list. In fact, he would have liked to accuse the whole council of having been janissaries of one sort or another—enemies masked as the People's representatives.

Two defense drones de-cloaked and took position above the limo, one just ahead, and one behind. A voice boomed over the limo's intercom. "Oy, Jag!"

Off to the side and fifteen metres off the ground, an antler-like ship equipped with several machine guns and rocket launchers also de-cloaked. It bobbed on a magnetic cushion while its stabilizer jets burned the sea salt in the air. Visible inside the cockpit was an

83

obese man with a metal plate fused to his forehead and jaw. He waved down to Jagjit.

"Allister," Jagjit replied. It prickled his skin to hear an underling use his first name so casually, but Allister Jowett had earned the right. Allister had tipped Jagjit off about the unorthodox interests and behavior of his predecessor Dorz, the former commissar overseeing security and noospherics in Lancashire. Jagjit could not remember wanting anything as badly as knocking off the old man and taking his place. With Allister's help, he did just that. "How're we looking?"

"Clear skies. No rumblings from the depths. Will see you through to, uh—*where we headed, Comm'sar?*"

"Run a wide circuit. I want to see the mess they've left me to clean up."

"Aye." A cloud comprised of tiny surveillance aphids escaped from a compartment beneath Allister's ship and spread out in all directions in search of data to satiate Jagjit's curiosity. Allister's gunship kicked up dust around the limo, and in a flash, was high above the ground and coordinating the security of the Commissar's convoy.

Jagjit settled in and draped his arms on the back-bench headrest. He silently intuited an instruction to the limo computer, which deluged the engine with charge. Uncurling one finger and indicating the road ahead, the Commissar reiterated his order, this time aloud: "Roll out." And with that, the limo sped off along with its drone accompaniment.

Since family units were a thing of the past and most of the basic animal needs anybody could want were provided to them in their CBLOCKs, there was little need for the citizenry to be up and about. What cars were on the road were most likely moving government employees or prisoners along, everyone pre-cleared by the central mobility authority. Every so often, a train of lorries would pass full of citizens en route to the DIHA. For the most part though, there was little or no traffic. This of course made Allister's job awfully easy. And all of those who didn't belong to the aforementioned groups—headed to Lancashire's eco-sanctuaries, English Democratic Socialist Party museums, or to the other destinations that the more inflexible on the Supreme Council deemed "dilettante daytrips"—had such high trustvalue ratings that they might as well have worked for the EDS' top brass, meaning it was a rarity to have Allister use his cannons.

A guardian patrol van approached Jagjit's driverless on the left. Law enforcement vehicles were the only mode of non-military transportation that could be piloted by a human rather than by a machine. This particular van was certainly under the reins of a human, as its movements lacked an AI's precision. Jagjit glimpsed inside the van as it passed his limo. The guardian responsible for driving so imperfectly—Danika Frye according to the intel pulled in Jagjit's quick optic scan—seemed engaged in conversation with two specters aback the van. Whoever she was talking to were neither prisoners, clear from the empty detainee rack, nor another pair of guardians. The two man-sized shades kneeling at the back of the van may as well have been ghosts; the AI historians and security archivists working overtime for Jagjit produced no hits, nothing at all. As the limousine took the corner, the guardian patrol van continued straightaway.

Jagjit mentally unlocked his implant and intuited a command to the AI hunters and historians ready to do his bidding: "*Danika Frye*. I want a full analysis and experience-report within the hour." Once a requisition receipt was provided him by an auto-mate at the Department of Cultural Equity, Jagjit rolled down his window and took a breath of the air he found so repugnant. The stench prompted him to wonder about the kind of person who would accept a lifetime suffocated by it. Any sensible socialist would make a ruckus over the olfactory inequality. That no one, not even the councilors, would bring it up must have meant they were either used to it or certain that they would not have to get used to it. The latter of the two outlooks belonged to social climbers that could not be trusted. "And I want a full personality evaluation for the following people," Jagjit ordered the Cultural Equity auto-mate on the other end of the line, "Dustin Reiter, Poyraz Vola, and Sharon Kay." His implant's interface made a note of three additional Cultural Equity receipts. As his hotly-anticipated Patch Over had yet to totally sever the English people's connection with the past, the past continued to threaten the common good with old-world perversions.

In this new world, a human being is born a blank slate, a *tabula rasa*, and it is society that writes much if not all of her story. A bad society produces evil stories. Reiter, Vola, and Kay lived in a good society and helped make it better, but there was something off about their narratives; something very old world about their arcs.

Reiter's ambition proved him to be an egotist, at odds with the collective will.

Major Poyraz Vola's aggression was permitted by his guardian-specific mental dampeners, but he seemed to enjoy it—the violence and the pain he exacted from his victims. According to his peer review, Poyraz would often find himself sexually aroused both during and after torturing regressives. His performance of male toxicity made him simultaneously unpredictable and manipulable, which put the larger community at risk.

Sharon Kay was more of a reformer than she was a revolutionary. Months before Jagjit was reassigned to Lancashire, he attended a closed-door meeting with the Home Defence Minister, to which Sharon had also been invited—she had been Corven's confidant during the Mob Rule. Sharon then objected to the Supreme Council's proposed Mental Union, at the time only just recently declassified. Americans had toyed with collectivist technology that permitted various minds to merge. Of course, the technology was never properly utilized; first, because the Americans decided to destroy it; second, there was no mass appeal on account of American individualism; and third, that same individualism forced the collective into types or archetypes as opposed to a single entity, unlike the EDS' goal of a single mental union. Kay believed that an equitable and equal society constituted by the various peoples of the world was the ideal, and that the merging of minds and the complete subordination of the flesh resulting from the Mental Union was tantamount to extinction, at the very least genocide. She was forgiven then for not understanding the reasons why the Mental Union was the most compassionate solution—why it alone could save the dying Earth, only after all minds were merged and all opposition was eradicated.

Jagjit feared what he might learn about his subordinates and peers. He cared very little that they might be spies or subversives. There was a simple solution meted out to enemies of the state. What concerned him was that the more he learned, the more he might prove his presuppositions to be lacking. If his instincts were off, then how was he to perform his duties as required? How could he be certain that he had not misled Corven and the lead scientist responsible for the Patch Over, Dr. Worthing, and doomed Lancashire with a lethal update?

More and more the question of first principles nagged at him. His hands trembled, though he chalked it up to the limo's inhumane handling. What was the difference between a false understanding and a falser self? Jagjit trembled at the possibilities. He knew who he was; that he was who he purported and was meant to be. However, his own murky history prompted questions he did not want the answers to, mainly because they could prove his faith in the mission wanting.

Before the EDS broke up England's couples and families citing research showing that parental units undermined the will of

86

the People, poisoned young minds with old-fashioned ideas, and created cognitive inequalities through unevenly-distributed domestic instruction, Jagjit himself had a partner and the voided marriage certificate to prove it. Given his trust and equity value, his memories of those days weren't wiped or obfuscated. This was apparently true of most of the EDS' commissars for they were true believers from the start, and therefore deserved access to their earliest passions. But the woman who had been his wife he could not for the life of him comprehend wedding or loving—and not simply because the kind of monogamous devotion supposedly involved was the ultimate form of discrimination, which to him was now unconscionable. She wasn't, as the indoctrinaires from bygone generations might have deemed, *his type*. And while his memories were clear, his gut betrayed him.

Not only did he not recognize the married man from his memories, but the childlessness of that relation also. After all, he felt a paternal calling to faceless sons and daughters that that loveless relation never produced; to little phantasms that looked like him and played on his back while he read problematic literature. It could all be explained away, thought Jagjit, familiar with the unquestioned science on the subject. The false impressions of paternal responsibility and parentage were a trick played on him by the most primordial elements of his brain. That the marriage was loveless was a retroactive realization given his present understanding of true love, as exemplified by the EDS in its relationship with the People. The lifestyle he could never have imagined pursuing belonged to that of a lesser man who had not yet come into his own, rescued late in life by Minister Corven. Ultimately, he reassured himself, the top brass trusted him and that meant he could be certain of himself and his memories, at least for now. Assurances aside, he demanded certainty. Jagjit intuited one more demand over the intranet to which he had direct access via his implant: "I also want Cultural Equity to create a classified personality evaluation for Jagjit Hassan."

A low pulsing sound caught his attention just as the last receipt arrived from the department. The green light on the communications panel at the center of the limo strobed, indicating an incoming transmission. Jagjit adjusted his jacket, and opened the call window. "Home Defence Minister Corven, good afternoon."

87

TEN

Hundreds of 150-storey pentagrammic housing complexes dominated the coastline, staged in quads going all the way inland to Bradford. Although the interiors of these CBLOCKs differed depending on their zoning and on the trustvalue of their inhabitants—the more valued of whom received better lodging, improved services, and greater mobility—every unit in every one of the CBLOCKs had the same view of the EDS' grey utopia. Alek shuddered at the view and recoiled from his fogged-up window.

Apart from their end-of-cycle synchronization at the Department of Information and Historical Accuracy and garbage day (when citizens had to separate all of their waste in front of security officials), most Blackpoolians' movement was restricted to these vertical towns or city blocks. The CBLOCKs had everything they might need, modelled with Charles Fourier's self-contained phalansteres in mind. They had gyms (which largely went unused on account of the likelihood of exercise fostering physical inequalities), food services tubed to every living unit, well-policed laundromats, clinics, and labour appointment offices. The obstacles to going outdoors weren't bemoaned or contested because any desire on the part of the populace to go out for a jaunt was satisfied by a virtually-managed dopamine drip and the understanding that unnecessary movement led to unwanted pollution.

Those who came and went as the government pleased were those assigned duties elsewhere. After all, there were still jobs that needed doing, machines that needed fine-tuning, and government offices demanding of breathy mannequins. Thanks to these exceptions, there existed the possibility, albeit a risky one, for a citizen to run a side-hustle when out and about. It was upon two such exceptions that Alek and Monica Neuhaus founded their illicit business.

Even with Monica most likely dead, Alek told himself that he had to keep working. For starters, the food and services his government guaranteed him were mismanaged and misallocated with the kind of caprice only a corrupt system could consistently manage. It wasn't simply a matter of survival though, as the black market job he had created for himself with his late wife fed a spiritual hunger.

Lancashire's subversives depended upon Alek to hide the persistence of their truer selves, and he depended upon their money.

88

With enough money, he could realize Monica's dream: escape to the Americas. Of course, he only wanted to go if she came with him, which was now impossible. It would be easier for him to put his gun in his mouth and go with her. On the other hand, there was no chance she had gone to Hell, so if he took what belonged to God they would be apart forevermore.

Alek did have a dream of his own, one in which Monica wasn't dead. He had heard of stranger things. His driver Danika Frye had told him about one of her guardian friends getting clipped in the head by Resistance snipers and surviving. Then again, the state valued their foot soldiers, at least enough for a bioprint and a quick tissue reconstruction. If they valued Monica, it was only for the information she had in her head about her clientele or about her technology. Despite the hard reset she designed to defragment all of her memories upon capture, the demsocks would probably still have gotten something out of her, and they certainly would not have been nice about it. For Alek's dream to work, Monica had to be alive, but for Monica to be alive—and this reality he ignored—she would almost certainly be in perpetual pain. He kept kicking the can along, kept pretending that Monica had passed painlessly, and continued pretending that the world still had one more happy ending for him.

The first order of the day was for Alek to participate in the compulsory condemnation of a fabricated personality that had committed some form of hateful act. Alek knew the loathsome caricatures not to have been based on anyone living—to have been invented—because Danika had told him so. None of the names were on file with the police and there were never any charges or convictions recorded. Before sitting down to eat breakfast, he received a reminder to join in on the virtual kangaroo trial and to vote on the offenders' level of guilt and sentencing. Innocence was never an option. This practice kept most citizens feeling involved and risk averse. (What good is direct democracy if the mob hasn't the power to usurp life in increments, sometimes small, and sometimes in its entirety?) One supposed provocateur had cooperated with American survivors and sought to undermine majority rule on the island. The votes were quickly tallied and the avatar was read his sentence: re-education of the highest order. Even with the danger simulated, the proceeding was still deeply unsettling, especially when everyone voted for the maximum sentence.

By the time he condemned a phantasm to be phased out at Blackpool City Hall and finished his breakfast, Alek had already selected a client. Although there were numerous requests from the Fish Bowl, the CBLOCK whose inhabitants—formerly Britain's

89

conservative intelligentsia—were permitted only to have a day's memory before having them wiped, he decided to play it safe and select a regular patron. The dirty mind demanding a wipe belonged to Margaret Green, a councilor sent over from Cultural Equity to the Department of Reclamations to help oversee a red-zone cleanup. Alek and Monica had done her dozens of times before, going back to the first days of their burgeoning business. Why, wondered Alek, would Green need a scrub this time?

Red zones were those areas of the country that hadn't been redeveloped since the Mob Rule. They were off-limits as they frequently contained art, graven images, religious paraphernalia, books, false histories, and capitalist miscellany. As a Cultural Equity minister, Green was responsible for rolling into a quarantined red zone and overseeing its total destruction. Unbeknownst to regulars in the EDS, their bosses—commissars, councilors, ministers and senior officials alike—would frequently take their time and enjoy their stay in the red zones, but this was so common a practice, few were innocent and no one was levying accusations. What did she need to hide that her superiors weren't already keen to overlook?

Alek studied Green's schedule. Nothing seemed out of sorts, which meant that she was likely playing it safe. Perhaps she had humored an unkind thought about the Supreme Council or contemplated life without coercions consistently applied by ethically-inconsistent zealots. That or she may have turned confiscated items into a profit and failed to cut any of her colleagues in.

Those *the People* appointed to Reclamations and Cultural Equity to erase yesteryear's culture of inequality were well-known for stealing and killing to make a profit. Staring through Green's round and heavily-lashed eyes, Alek decided that he would charge her in illegal crypto, mobility chits, and in the supposedly-outmoded pound sterling; the latter to satisfy Danika, his driver, to ensure the mission's success.

Alek went over to the mismatched tile in the recreation corner of the apartment. He flipped the tile. A square opening popped out of the wall. The wallpaper's age had hidden the creases. Alek leaned against the wall and ferreted out his handgun, a heavplast custom he had printed before they confiscated all the presses and dropped the net. With the gun in his hand, he didn't feel as vulnerable or as crushed. The latter sensation was the worst of the two. There was no recourse left to a wronged citizen but violence. Stroking the cold metal didn't make him feel powerful, but for a moment he didn't feel so powerless.

90

Now armed and psyched to go, Alek shut off his monitor and tidied up his kitchen. Having been denied laundry services on account of the note from Monica he had carelessly forgotten in his pants pocket, which had aroused some suspicion, he hadn't gotten back his machinist uniform. Instead, he put on a pair of work boots, his track pants, and an old leather jacket. There was nothing wrong with him wearing EDS-approved track pants, but the jacket might have been grounds for punitive action in the lower-grade trust zones. Uptown, on the other hand, it would make for a fitting costume. Trustworthees often flouted their status by wearing antiquated and prohibited garments. They played off their furs and leathers as irony—as mockery of the dead.

Snug in his tanned-leather jacket, Alek pulled an envelope out of his desk. He put his memex inside the envelope and sealed it shut. Unlike on synchronization day, whenever he was out on jobs, he no longer risked leaving his memex in the teacup in the kitchen. After all, if Alek was ever captured, the state would search his apartment and find it, and have both a virtual Alek and an embodied Alek to torture. And so he pocketed the envelope to stash with a friend.

Mulling over the risk of meddling with a dirty Cultural Equity councilor at a time when London was cracking down on "cancers of the People's Body", he zipped up his duffel bag. He opened his door to leave but froze. Something begged his attention—just what he wasn't sure. It wasn't *a what* but *a who*: *Monica*. Her absence reminded him of what he had left of her, what he couldn't leave behind. It occurred to him, accessing a memory impressed upon him between wipes and searches, that he had destroyed her last note to him. He keeled over and clutched his breast. He smacked himself to end the slideshow of images of what he had done to the note— turning it to mud under his foot. Desperate for a connection to Monica, Alek rushed into his bedroom and grabbed Monica's memex from her sock drawer. As his hands enveloped the little black device, he stopped panting. He didn't have a portrait of her or a home video or a gravestone, but he had her incarnate memories. Very carefully, he placed them in his pocket. Repressing the images of the crumpled letter, he surveyed the apartment for anything else he may have forgotten, and then hurried out.

Alek passed several open doors. He stopped glancing inside as every incumbent was more or less doing the same thing: seated with their eyes glazed over, tuned into the EDS intranet's feel-good channel. At the end of the next hall of openings there was a closed door. Alek marched with purpose. He was going to check in on his neighbour, a brilliant seamstress named Evaun Reed.

Evaun Reed had a black-market business all her own, one that provided Blackpoolians with unsanctioned garments. Her side-hustle ran in direct competition with the Tailors and Garment Workers Unit's hideous auto-designed and printed productions, and was therefore treasonous. Evaun would no doubt be digging ditches or filling one were her talents not sought by party officials who ensured that her subversive memories were overlooked on synchronization day. Any flagrant display of colour in CBLOCK32 was more than likely her doing.

Alek saw that Evaun's door was partially ajar as he closed in. He immediately feared the worst. Evaun must finally have been summoned and sentenced. He pressed the door open wider and heard the sound of a metallic stream, no, a sewing machine! "Eva?" he inquired, loud enough to rule out the need for a knock.

"Alexander!" Evaun answered in her sweet, sing-songy voice. "Come in, come in. Just stitching for Dean Tisdale."

Tisdale, like his immediate superiors, felt strongly about the Supreme Council's commitment to ensuring joy in labour. The obvious joy Evaun yielded from the days she spent pedaling behind her machine absolved her, in his eyes, of the obvious crime of competition.

Alek wandered into the room. It was so full of dyes and coloured threads that it could easily pass for a fallen rainbow. Ducking twine and ribbons, he made his way to Evaun, who was sat behind a metal office desk. The desk was missing two of its legs and was propped up with cinder blocks, which flaked ash onto the floor every time the machine juddered.

"How are you, my dear?" said Alek, eyeing the spool spin and the needle bob.

Evaun finished hemming a pant leg, and turned off the machine. She smiled fondly at Alek, and then relit a half-smoked cigarette. "Behind! Always behind..." She wiped the sweat off of her forehead, and feigned to wave away smoke she had yet to produce. "I could work sunrise to sundown for a life cycle and still not meet demand. You're not looking for a job by any chance, are you? My last apprentice was phased out in city central."

Alek grimaced and handed Evaun the sealed envelope containing his memex. He could count on her to keep its contents secret owing to her special relationship with those micromanaging her DIHA synchs. "If I come back wonky, not acting like myself, you mind slipping me this?"

92

Evaun stood, grabbed the envelope and stuffed it into a folder full of similar envelopes in her desk's lowest drawer. "Trouble is, you're always wonky."

In complete agreement, Alek smiled and nodded. He took Monica's memex out of his pocket. He would have given it to Evaun as well, but in the infinitesimally small chance he might encounter Monica's resurrected body out on the job, he would never forgive himself for not having the means to give her back her soul. Alek bent down to grab a loose thread off the floor. He ran it through a small hole in the top of the memex, tied it off, and hung it around his neck.

Evaun looked with trepidation at the black device strung over Alek's chest. She had access to enough memorial cycles to know what it was. "Forever on your heart and in your heart, eh Alexander?"

"Always."

A sudden seriousness gripped the seamstress. Her fingers curled and she folded her arms. "I forgot...I am so sorry, Alek. I forgot."

Alek set his bag down and approached Evaun's desk. "You forgot what?"

"I'm sorry...I meant to tell you. My memory isn't what it was. I made inquiries. I asked about her. I asked them about your Monica." Evaun knew a scarf aficionado who had aged into an intermediate overseer's position at the primary re-education facility for Lancashire. Alek had asked Evaun inquire whether or not his wife had survived.

"And?"

"She was never brought in."

Alek's shoulders slumped. The yarn rainbow turned to a wicked kaleidoscope around him. He faltered, but managed to right himself with another hollow rationalization.

Evaun's face lit up despite Alek's grief. She placed her hands down on either sides of the sewing machine to buttress the words that came next. "Finbunlk is rather fond of me, so I pressed him further. He understood that she meant a great deal to me. I told him she had been the best seamstress in England. Anyway, he consulted the devaluation archives. Had the sufficient access to pull up her file."

"And?!" Alek tented his hands over Evaun's.

"There was no devaluation notice. A medical resource notice indicates that she was checked into a high-security clinic. The rest of her file was redacted."

"Redacted?"

"Deleted. Someone wiped it out. Finbunlk said he only sees full narrative redactions in the case of terrorists or discards from the councils' assorted harems." Evaun found the pleat in the pants she had just finished and folded them. Hanging them on the rudimentary horizontal beam behind her desk, she sighed. "Good news, Alexander, no?"

Alek pinched the bridge of his nose and chortled. "She's alive? She's alive!"

Evaun scrutinized the memex dangling from Alek's neck. She slowly ambled over, and kissed Alek on both cheeks. Her soft lips made him feel once more and in so doing brought all of his suppressed pain to the surface. Tucking the necklace behind Alek's shirt, she replied, "It is possible. The only thing we can be certain of is that she didn't perish that night." Evaun and Alek didn't need to utter the unthinkable and likely scenario: that Monica lived long enough to wish that she had died. Seeing the creeping horror paralyze Alek's face, top to bottom, Evaun squeezed Alek's arms. "You'll be alright."

Alek clasped Monica's memex through his shirt. "Always am, Eva!" He sniffled and then noisily cleared his nose. "Thank you for asking. I owe you one."

Evaun released Alek and returned to her chair. "Let me cash that favor in right away, then. Wherever you're going and whoever you're helping, I want you to keep your wits about you. Be smart, if that's possible. And *be safe!*"

Correcting the strap on his duffel bag, which had curled on his shoulder, Alek chinned-up. "Safety is for the herd. Adventure belongs to the strays."

Evaun shook her head. "That's one theory; at odds with the established science on the subject. But today I'm going to presume them all wrong and Alek Neuhaus the expert. Whatever the price of success is, it's not worth your life. You now owe it to me to come back in one piece."

Alek flashed his teeth and inwardly debated Evaun, arguing against a strawman unable to respond: *If success is Monica's freedom and the price is death, I'd pay it every second of every day for all eternity.* "I'll try."

"You damned well better." Evaun turned on the sewing machine. Once again the sound of a metal river flooded the room. Feeding it some tatters, she said without looking up: "Your sense of humour is a rarity in these parts." She was serious. Alek had made her cheeks hurt with naughty jokes more times than she could count; certainly enough to have given her a few laugh lines.

94

Desperate to evidence her claim with something humorous, Alek scoured his mind for puns and jokes. All he could pull from the archives was less of a joke and more of an innocent statement of fact. "Why can't we get a minute to ourselves?"

Tapping the sewing machine's foot pedal with a rhythmic riddle all her own, Evaun raised her eyebrows.

"Because the minutes aren't hours."

Evaun halted her operation and looked up at Alek with a look of incredulity. A moment of silence passed between them, and they both broke into laughter. "Get out of here before I report you to the Ministry of Forbidden Quips."

"Thank you, Eva." Alek blew Evaun a kiss and left her to her work.

"Safe, Alexander!" she shouted after him. "There are many new faces in the government and the streets are full of the secret police. It's a dangerous time for a stray."

Stopped in the doorframe, Alek looked back and smiled. "But ever so fashionable!"

Alek produced his counterfeit waiver for CBLOCK32's mobility officers on the ground floor via his implant. The waiver indicated that Noospherics had summoned him for a job uptown. Since Alek was a familiar face and his waivers were usually legitimate, the officers—one an extremely short man and his partner a man nearly two-meters tall—didn't give him the gears. They even neglected to enter the waiver into their system. They did however hassle him about his jacket, which he neglected to stow in his duffel bag until he had made it outside as per his custom. The jacket, a hand-me-down from the old days, wasn't regulation. The fact that it was made from animal product was justification enough to lock Alek up.

"Gonna have to dock yah points for looking sharp, Neuhaus," said the tall officer. He had been standing by the security panel at the side-street door, but was drawn over by the exotic texture of Alek's leather. He pulled at Alek's jacket sleeve and ran his finger along the shoulder seam. "Gonna have to confi'cate the coat too."

The shorter officer waddled over and tugged at the jacket's side seam. "Douggie, he's wearing livestock. The gall!"

Alek pulled up his collar and flashed an insincere smile. "Y'ever fix a repeater on a rooftop with the night wind on yah? No? Well, it'll give me chills. Chills enough to put me out for a count and to force Noospherics to have to train someone else. Experience upload won't do the trick, either. And in the time it takes to replace me while I'm upstairs coughing up a lung, the People will have

95

suffered—all because you focused on the one as opposed to the many. Call my unit boss, comrades. I apologize in advance if she gives you a hard time."

The mobility officers looked at each other. The taller officer raised himself on the tips of his toes, searching for the ranking officer—most likely Citizen Commander Tisdale. Granted the lobby was sparsely populated, his exaggerated concern was more for posterity. He dropped back onto his heels impressed with a look of uneasiness. "Akay, well...Don't bring i'back when yah return, chills or no. Will have to penalize yah if yah leave anyone feeling envy." He punched in his code and the door creaked open.

"Cheers, mate," Alek said, side-stepping the shorter officer who was keen to keep feeling the leather. He waited impatiently for the door to open at Tweedle Dum's discretion. The second there was enough to room to slink through, Alek did so. He was not willing to chance the mobility officers having a change of mind or finding their superior officer.

"Wait, t'ere! Says a note of caution. Yah been slipping subversive notes, ha'e yah now, eh?"

The question lingered behind Alek and he wasted no time getting past giving an answer. The guards had already incriminated themselves once. Applying the law now would just draw attention to their previous lawlessness.

It occurred to Alek as CBLOCK32's heavy doors clanked closed that it was a damned good thing it was the beginning of a new cycle. By virtue of their position in the social democratic pyramid, Tweedle Dum and Tweedle Dee had a great deal of social capital. Day-in, day-out they conversed with everyone in the place by necessity. They may have had no power, but they certainly had plenty of recognition. To prevent them from taking bribes or forming subversive relationships, the government had Dee and Dum's short-term memories wiped the same day that the rest of CBLOCK32's personnel had their domes inspected over at the DIHA, which just happened to be that day. This meant Dee and Dum wouldn't remember all the other times this cycle they had chastised Alek for wearing his jacket; for going off late with an improper waiver; for treating them both like they had shit for brains. It was approaching the end of cycle where they would become a problem—when they would remember how miserable their existences were and how their job was about ensuring immobility, not the other way around. Timing is everything.

With the street dwarfed by concrete and glass monstrosities, it didn't feel much like being outside; more like being in a darker,

96

colder inside, be it with a higher ceiling. A gust of wind tested Alek's balance, and he laughed hollowly. Although he had been talking out his posterior to Tweedle Dum and Tweedle Dee about the cold, he turned out to be right. First he was right about Monica not dying the night they shot her, and now this? A front off the Irish Sea making for a blustery night in Lancashire could only mean that Alek Neuhaus was a regular Blackpool prophet.

CBLOCK32's prophet looked down the lane and saw red light dancing on a puddle where an alley met the road. He headed over, flattened himself against the corner, and leaned around just enough for a visual confirmation.

Down the alley, Danika sat in her guardian van studying a small holographic map above the dashboard and plotting out her route. The brake lights on the van were responsible for the alley's slaughterhouse red. There was little competition in the way of light; this sector had already enjoyed its power period. The central authority excused such timed and regional power outages as an environmental policy, when in fact it was just another method of controlling the public. For Danika, lie or not, the darkness meant a relaxation of the rules on the whole. She could take off her modular helmet and let her milk-snake dreads breathe. She closed the hologram and gripped the steering wheel. "C'mon, c'mon."

Although more relaxed than usual, Danika made sure to follow the protocol she and Alek had set for their late-night treks. The van's mirrors were turned inward. She sat facing forward, ensuring predictable blindsides so she wouldn't unwittingly ID Alek or notice the rear door opening and shutting. This was as much about protecting Alek as it was about protecting herself. If found complicit in a black-market deal, a guardian faced a far greater penalty than a normal citizen; they would be interrogated and then strung up for all of those with city-square access to see.

Alek studied the van from afar. Monica used to scan the van to ensure it hadn't been bugged. Alek wasn't so cautious. He looked the van over with enhanced vision from afar. Certain that there weren't DSSP officers laying in ambush, Alek sprinted to the rear of the van and jostled in.

Dan put her helmet back on after hearing the rear door lock. She recited their code-phrase indicating all was well: "The fewer regressives, the better." Without a word from Alek, they rolled into the murk of Old Roan.

The Lethe, as Alek had come to be known, needed Dan for the success of every wipe, and her fee reflected this fact. A guardian appointed by the People—in this case, the EDS superior councilmen

97

living high off the hog in London—was better a friend than an enemy as Alek's closest friend Geoff Littlefield also learned in his semi-frequent dealings with her. As an enemy, she could have more than a subversive's soul. Thankfully, Danika wasn't interested in souls; just cash, crypto, and the maintenance of the Warmington bypass Monica had given her.

Danika had Margaret Green's address, courtesy of an anonymous tip made by Alek suggesting that someone in the target building had downloaded prohibited material. This tip made it possible for Danika to avoid appearing too proactive. As far as her captain at the Criminal Investigations Department was concerned, she was just following up on one of Green's neighbours, and rightly so—if he had prohibited material, it might well be inconsequential, but it might alternatively be a monarchist poem or a prayer card or blueprints for a scrubbing kit. If one of the latter two, nipping such resistance in the bud would be grounds for the promotion currently out of Danika's reach on account of her barely-adequate trustvalue points.

It was impossible to know if the moon was out, for the shadowed faces of the CBLOCKs encroaching on the road dominated the sky. There was not a single light on in any of the windows that blurred by, no sign of rebellion.

The van slowed for a salute at the checkpoint between trust regions. The difference between the regions was immediately and glaringly apparent. Here, open spaces, parkland, and trees substituted in for the concrete barricades raised throughout coastal Blackpool.

Danika whistled two tones and adjusted her seat, signaling that they were close.

ELEVEN

Instead of cutting through the Underpool market to get to the grotto where the intelligence briefing was being held, Mirek led Stephen around the long way. Since they had borrowed a wheel barrow to transport the mortars and still had ample time, Stephen didn't whinge about the detour. He figured that they had gone through the old subway tunnels and past the desalinators, Mogg's fish farm, and the Williams Sisters' tobacco patch, to avoid the crowds and their questions. But as soon as he saw the kerosene lamp outside of Mises Tavern, Stephen realized he misjudged his neighbour. He set the wheelbarrow down on its legs and held Mirek back. "You creature of habit! What's going through that head of yours?"

"*Just one*," pleaded Mirek. He peered into the noisy tavern. "We've got ten minutes and the grotto's only jus' down the way."

"Yah could have had a dram at my place!"

Mirek nodded thoughtlessly, focus trained instead on *who* was holed up inside. As much as he was a creature of habit, Mirek was also something of a romantic. Fiona, the love of his life, tutored children from all over the labyrinth at a table near the bar six days a week. Mises Tavern was well-lit, which made it a great place for learning despite the occasional scuffle and intoxicated rant. On days where he wasn't working, Mirek would wait for Fiona to finish her tutorials and then walk her home. He hoped to one day become something more than an escort.

Stephen looked at the winding tunnel ahead and grumbled. "I don't want to miss a word, Merry."

Mirek groaned and slapped the side of the wheel barrow. "What is a republican without a visit to the pub?"

Shaking his head in disproval, Stephen drove the mortars past the stalagmites that framed the tavern's entrance, and parked it just inside a room hewn into wet limestone. It always appeared wet, even if there wasn't a leak in any of the various drainage pipes that snaked in and out of various floors, walls, and ceilings.

Despite the tavern looking like an emptied-out cave at the bottom of the sea, the owner, Teresa Kaczynski, had gussied it up. There were old windows hung on the walls with coloured LEDs behind them simulating daylight, which made patrons feel a little less claustrophobic

"Last call!" yelled Teresa. She might as well have been mayor of Underpool. She knew everybody's name and vice. Impending doom had most Resistance members fixing their souls for judgment, so their preferred vices ultimately came down to whisky or shine.

Mirek adjusted his shirt and wet the bristles on his head with a licked finger. "How I look, Stevie?"

A yellow smile at a table near the door caught Stephen's attention. Brandon Dove, one of the old airmen who had spent his youth flying medical supplies over to the embattled French Resistance, sat with a jug of moonshine, blathering to the half-conscious woman hunched over beside him. "Just fine," replied Stephen. He turned to Mirek with his eyes still fixed on Dove, but Mirek was already off, calling on Teresa for a glass of blindness and to run the clock should Fiona show up as everyone shoved out.

Stephen double-checked the case, and nervously approached Dove, who looked about ready to have his stomach pumped. He pointed to an empty chair across from the old lush. "Mind if I join you for a slug?"

"What the hell, mown? Cannah see us here having a private chat?" Dove did his best to train both eyes on Stephen. The woman beside him snored heavily.

"Commodore, sir..."

Dove finished his drink and set his fists on the table, nearly toppling over his jug in the process. "What's t'matter with yah? You lookin' t'punch dust?"

Doing his best to steady his shaking leg, Stephen pushed in the chair denied him and stood at the edge of the table. "We're headed to Preston in search of a Chinese ship. Going to do a bomb-and-run for the General. Was just wondering if you knew of any alternatives—places with Chinese ships; maybe something closer with fewer watchful eyes on it."

Dove smirked. The idea that younger folk still wanted to put their freedom to good use pleased him greatly. "That I canno do. Besides, if I had me a pair o'wings, doncha think I'd be airborne o'er London Town and setting fires right about now?"

Stephen sighed and prepared to thank the old man and leave.

Looking to the barfly beside him, clearly not holding up her side of the conversation, Dove waved Stephen over. His breath smelled like turpentine. "W'all heard tell of this Yankee Doo-Dandy woman givin' us a boost there and here. Should ask 'er. Word's she's bringing Congress a weapon of—a weapon of—" Brandon hiccupped and kneed the table.

Stephen caught the Commodore and helped him settle back onto his stool.

"Weapon of mass destruction. I tells yah, boy, I tell yah, it's a pack of lies. A bill o' bad goods Lost me my sister's son, Peter." His face compressed around his self-correction. "A bad bill o' goods. Be no different now. That great hope ours, James Kha-kha-katri, died shewing it false ten years ago." He wiped his mouth clean and lubricated his gossip with more shine. "James, our fearless cap'n, was goin to give us the life-affirming Family Icon but it's no'er to be seen."

The woman beside the Commodore sat up and lifted her glass. "James! Killer K!"

A pair of teetotalers taking advantage of the bar's light for their knitting reached for their waters and similarly toasted the name James Khatri. Before long, just about everyone in the tavern had raised their glasses and relished in the melancholy that the name evoked; everyone except Fiona who still had not shown up.

Mirek waved to Stephen. It hadn't been five minutes and the northern punk had already lost his balance. Stephen quietly thanked the Commodore, pulled Mirek away from the bar, and cajoled him out of Mises. He went back for the wheel barrow, and blocked Mirek from reentering the pub.

"Just one more, Stevie. Didn't yah hear? Teresa's closing up shop. Congress is getting all of t'civvies into the Sanctu'ry. What's all that about then?"

Stephen saw through Mirek's concern and bumped him with the mortars. "Fiona is probably already at the briefing. Let's get a move on."

Mirek put a hand on the case to simulate helping it along. "I can only hope."

"Hoping is well and good, Merry, but you're going to have to tell her how you really feel eventually."

"Shows what yah know 'bout me! Fiona and I are like this..." He intertwined two fingers. "Just not official or written into the book, yah know?" Mirek gave up on helping balance the barrow, and strummed his fingertips along the metal grid which kept the stone walls from caving in. "Her mum's a Grundy; thinks Fiona should find 'erself a gallant knight."

Stephen shook his head sympathetically. "Well, Gawain, you'll turn the tide in this war, and Grundy'll change her tact."

"Probably." Once again Mirek took Stephen's speculation as scripture.

They took turns pushing the mortars—past the nurseries and the medical station, past the water pump control room, past the ladders to the lower floors, and past the aquifer. Stephen could

101

already hear the first of many booming orators work up excitement about what even the staunchest optimist would call a bitter end.

"Picture it, Stevie boy. Heavy knock at the Sanctuary gate. Who's there? Us and Wes. I've got me guitar. Fiona's all waterworks thinking I died in America. No, no, fair lady; it is I, your Merry in the flesh."

Stephen rolled his eyes.

"And I'll seal the deal by playing her my new song."

"Who? Grundy or Fiona?"

Mirek threw his intertwined fingers into the air.

Steven co-opted his neighbour's daydream and imagined returning from a successful mission. There wouldn't be anybody waiting for him. His valor and strife was less for the living and more for the dead. As this realization began to sour his mood, he focused on Mirek's dramatic return. "Play her something melodic. Girls like Fiona Marsh don't like the punk vibe."

"Well, guys like me don't like girls who don't like punk!"

They both laughed their way down the hall until the yellow glow of the grotto's two-hundred-pound candelabra engulfed them. Two soldiers shouldering rifles with bayonets fixed blocked the way.

"Stephen Nowak and Mirek Dubchek here for the briefing," said Stephen with a hint of attitude.

The soldiers looked at each other with concern. One backed into the grotto and signaled another. A heavyset man barreled over and gently pushed Stephen aside. He seized the handles on the wheelbarrow, and drove it towards the rear of the grotto.

"Oi! What're you doing?!" Stephen shouted.

"Easy there, Private," said the doorman. He indicated another door at the back of the grotto. "Your wheelbarrow and your explanation will be waiting for you in the radio room."

Mirek looked forlornly at Stephen and said nothing.

"Well then," Stephen said, rubbing the back of his head. "After you, Merry."

Together they ambled into the radio room. The room was lit by Tiffany lamps, which painted the ceiling in a mosaic of greens, yellows, and reds. It smelt of pinewood. CB radios with Turing scramblers were set on tables on either side of the room with headsets resting where wiremen normally sat around the clock getting updates and giving orders to Resistance field assets.

Wes stood at the center of the room beside General McGregor with the wheelbarrow before them.

The heavyset man who had carted the wheelbarrow inside gripped his lower back "What's in there? Weighs a bloody tonne!"

102

"That's enough, Sergeant McIntosh," said General McGregor, eying the case.

A searing sense of angst filled Stephen. He wanted to scream at Wesley. He wanted to tell him to go to Hell, to suck on a stovepipe, et cetera. But he kept his mouth shut, knowing better than to jeopardize good will or self-incriminate, especially given the fact that down in Underpool, one was innocent until proven guilty.

"Heya lads," said Wes, arms crossed and face averted from McGregor's piercing stare.

"Wha's the fuss?" said Mirek, eyes darting from the mortar crate to Wes and back again.

Stephen turned to Wes. "I thought we were going to tell the General together."

McGregor spoke up. "The South Gate's scanners went haywire after you and Brigadier Miller brought the mortars inside. The radioactivity registered on our scanners; prompted the security detail responsible to start asking questions."

Stephen stiffened. He emulated his brothers' pre-death stoicism and calm. He squared his jaw, raised his chin, and accepted his fate, fear be damned. "I accept full responsibility, sir."

McGregor laughed and winked at Wes. "That's good, son. Every man and every woman is free if and only if they do the same."

Stephen grimaced at Wes.

Mirek interjected, "We got a line on a Chinese ship in Preston." He was satisfied with giving his neighbour's plan some heft. He looked over to Stephen for affirmation but didn't get any.

McGregor prioritized his replies. "American satellites would determine the origin of the doomed flight in an instant. They would know right away that it wasn't an official launch, and would laser it out of the sky fifty miles before it made landfall. Worse than the problem of wasting the treasure you've found: our American allies would turn on us and sever whatever tenuous connection we have left." He cracked his knuckles. "And if we hit local civilian targets here at home, that's about all you'll hear discussed on the English Broadcast Station, day in, day out. You'll hear renewed calls for the discovery and destruction of all surviving Christians, Jews, monarchists, republicans, liberals, and Westerners. Before or after this regional decerebration they've got planned and are calling the Patch Over, there won't be a man or woman alive sympathetic to the Resistance." McGregor turned his attention specifically to Stephen.

"General, sir," said Stephen, feeling lightheaded. "What about the EDS solar fields? Can't we take out their power? Y'know," he smiled impishly, "Leave 'em powerless?"

103

McGregor shook his head. "The old Chinese Belt and Road power corridor gives them access to unlimited reserves."

Piling on with another suggestion, Wes added: "I was just telling Hugh that we can take out the force field pylons in Ireland—give the Yanks an open window if they're looking to get in."

"*Ireland*," McGregor said thoughtfully. He leaned against one of the desks along the side. "Pylons are useless props. First, t'American fleet is equipped with plasmic cutters. Second, those ships that don't come from the mainland—those that come from outer-orbit—will bypass Ireland altogether. Force fields aren't a problem. *Detection is.* If the Pingos and the demsocks see the Americans coming, they're going set up a perimeter and hold hostage whoever they don't kill on the coast. I agree with you boys: we need the help. But the help needs the element of surprise." His face hardened with new resolve. "Your instinct was dead on, Wes, but I have a better target in mind."

There was a knock on the door. The two soldiers standing guard on the inside shared looks of suspicion. One took aim at the door, while the other opened it a crack to determine who sought entry. They stepped back to let in a giant amputee with a saw for a hand.

"Morning, gentlemen," said the man, looking to every wary face but the one whose attention he sought.

McGregor waved him over.

Though the saw-handed man tried to whisper, the acoustics in the room permitted all to overhear: "The EDS are sending test data-packets out to citizens now. They're getting ready for the Patch Over."

"Our field agents said that we had two weeks."

"Sorry sir. Not looking that way. Likely going to take place tomorrow morning."

"Thank you, Lieutenant," said McGregor. He clicked his teeth together, shook his head, and kicked over a chair. "Shit!" he roared. Forgetting himself and the men watching him, he reached into his pocket, yanked out several pages full of notes, and tore them to shreds. "Guess we'll have to improvise." He took a deep breath, and seeing the shadows of other men on the wall, turned slowly. "No more time for daydreaming. We've got to set our dominoes. Miller, how many mortars do we have?"

"Ten," Wes answered back, lightning fast. He opened the case for McGregor to see what they were dealing with.

"Good find, *the three of you.*" McGregor summoned Sergeant McIntosh back over. "Take 'em to the stage."

104

As McIntosh casually pivoted the wheelbarrow, everyone cringed.

"Easy there, Sergeant. Don't want to turn our hallowed hall into a microwave."

"Yes sir," he replied.

"Lads," said McGregor, eying Stephen and Mirek. "I appreciate you bringing the mortars to our attention and to the grotto, saving Sergeant McIntosh a trip and Underpool a firestorm. Go on. Find yourself some real estate inside the hall." The General turned out the lights, and ushered Stephen towards the grotto. "Miller and I are first going to have a word."

On his way into the great hall, Stephen overheard the General inform Wes behind him: "Doherty has located The Family."

"Yeah? I'll believe it when I see it."

"When you see it, it'll be a matter of knowing."

"Well," said Miller, unable to hide the incredulity warbling his voice. "Where was it?"

"Back when *we* were looking? In St. Alban's," replied McGregor.

"Piss off! I looked everywhere. I know for certain it wasn't in there."

"*St. Alban's in Blackburn.*"

"We hit the wrong church? *Blackburn?* Not St. Anne's? That's no small detail."

"Khatri would be over the moon as would the rest of the lads. Anyhow, we're working on getting our hands on it, and when we do..."

TWELVE

Minister Corven's face entered into the limosine's holographic viewing window, which barely fit his chiseled jaw and slicked-back curls. He was a man just entering the final quarter of his life—the first three-quarters of which he spent purging the party and the country of social traitors—although it was hard to tell given the youthful characteristics afforded him by the stem cells extracted from liquidated generations. "How did it go?"

"Exactly as you said it would, Home Defence Minister."

"I have yet to assimilate the minutes, but I will take your word for it."

Jagjit tried to conceal the sense of pride that fortified his upright posture.

"I have just received a progress report regarding steps taken in Beijing towards the Mental Union. Coalition engineers have finished armouring and sealing the Kunlun container, its batteries, and the bunker where humanity's past and the world's future will be stored. Additionally, we also have the DNA of all species of flora and fauna catalogued and stowed away. Altogether a work of craftpersonship from what I've been told; impenetrable and immoveable. We'll be immortalized in steel."

The Supreme Council and their comrades in Europe and in China had committed to engineering a restorative doomsday. The idea was to collectivize humanity into a singular, loving and harmonious mind and to embody that mind in a machine. That machine would be contained and safeguarded in an indestructible shelter, which would withstand the next stage of the grand plan: a great firestorm and plague that would wipe away the human stain from the rest of the planet. The entire planet would be reclaimed for nature and restored absent the resource-hungry humanoids of old. Even if flesh-bound humans survived on Mars, Ganymede, Titan, or Io, they could and would not return for fear of contracting the plague that will have made the planet volatile for hundreds of generations, after which time the transcendental Mental Union would re-emerge as a benevolent mechanical custodian of the commons, wanting of nothing and protective of all.

"This progress means we are well ahead of schedule; years ahead, as a matter of fact. We may arrive at our goal in twenty-cycles'-time."

106

Jagjit had viewed the Mental Union as he did any other proposal the government had put forth: intended to win for the proposing parties bigger soft budgets, more power, and short-term increases in labour efficiencies owing to the incentivizing excitement of a fresh new goal. It never occurred to him that this particular plan might actually work or that it might happen in his lifetime. Had the possibility occurred to him earlier, he would not have worked so hard these past few years. Why waste time trying to distinguish oneself believing that sooner or later all would be consolidated without distinction?

"I can't emphasize how important that Patch Over of yours is to Kunlun's completion." Corven nodded in agreement with himself. "It really is a feather in the leadership's cap. We are now the essential architects of the new world. And I must say: Dr. Mallory Worthing, notwithstanding who she was before her mental reset, has truly proven herself deserving of collectivization."

Jagjit had been assigned to oversee the Patch Over's development two years earlier. At the time, it wasn't a project most officials took seriously—including the scientists tasked to see it through. They had repeatedly failed to produce any results, but were nevertheless rewarded with greater and greater resource-expropriation power. About a year into its wasteful and much-criticized development, Dr. Worthing joined the team. It was her input, her programming, and her general expertise that made the Patch Over tenable. It was her past, however, which undermined her genius and in Jagjit's view compromised the project. Corven had spared Jagjit the details, yet indicated she had been a subversive, guilty of thousands of crimes. She was handpicked because of her seemingly innate expertise, for her proclivity to succeed in the field where the EDS' own trustworthees had proven themselves to have been exceptionally unexceptional. Many subversives who hadn't been mentally engineered in the same way as other citizens not only had the skills (which anyone with an implant could download) but the creative wherewithal to use them to great effect.

Even though Jagjit knew why the Supreme Council was flipping enemy forces with the help of the DIHA to work for the betterment of the People, he couldn't bring himself to appreciate the result. He found himself as unable to trust Dr. Worthing as he was unable to understand her thinking on the project, and this dual inability left him feeling naked, especially now with praise being doled out. He glanced out the car window at a city brightened by the rain, and back at Corven with determination. "By day four of the next cycle, the Doctor and I will be ready to initiate the Patch Over," said

107

Jagjit dispassionately, hoping to enunciate the right words in the right order that would bring about the end of the call. He still had yet to familiarize himself with his newly given powers of command and hadn't even set foot in the Commissar's Mansion.

"You don't understand, Hassan. You are ready now."

"Defence Minister?"

"*The time table has changed*. We cannot dally any longer. The Patch Over must be carried out this cycle in the northwest; tomorrow evening at the latest. The time originally designated for Lancashire will now be the time around which London itself will undergo this transformation, given thirteen days from the time you Patch Over in Lancashire will be sufficient to work out any possible bugs that may have been overlooked."

"As you wish, Defence Minister." Jagjit felt as though he was running short on air when in fact he had simply run out of the time he thought was guaranteed. "I had just anticipated having a greater interval to prepare the region and to assure against any possible interference by the regressives."

"Ah yes; *interference*...Even with Paris lending us organic server support, we are still maxing out all available processing power. Centralizing our data and cutting down on the costs associated with synchronizations and re-historicizations will free us up to be ready to execute the final stage of our transformation in adherence to the Kyoto Timeline."

Jagjit felt crushed. The future was telescoping closer and closer, much faster than he had anticipated. And arguably worse: that future might make room for Dr. Worthing. Although his resentment would have been best centered on the Home Defence Minister or the Supreme Council for rushing the inevitable, those inhuman inquisitors parsing through his thoughts might flag him as a traitor and just like that he would end up as plant food. Instead, he honed in on his insecurities and found a substitute for all his animosity: Dr. Worthing. *That know-it-all.*

Corven waved to someone or something off-screen and mouthed the words, "Coffee. No—*almond milk*." Nodding once more in agreement with himself, the taskmaster's master raised a curled finger and spoke carefully: "Yes, we'll run the Patch Over in Lancashire tomorrow morning and then throughout the whole of England next cycle. Once more the world will follow our lead." He breathed deeply and caught his reflection in the rear window of Jagjit's limo. He manipulated his jaw so that his creeping jowls couldn't be seen. Recalling the matter of interference, Corven glowered. "It is, in part, the threat of regressive interference that has spurred the Supreme Council to expedite the Patch Over. Just today the DSSP intercepted word that elements among the regressive forces, sensing their own demise, have not only revived their search for *your* cyber weapon of mass destruction but have potentially found it."

Jagjit tensed. He knew precisely the nature of the weapon of which Corven spoke—a memetic virus; the DDOS painting commonly referred to as "The Family." In fact, long before the Patch Over had even been conceived, Corven handpicked Jagjit to track down the painting, thinking that it might have been in London. Of course it wasn't, though that didn't stop the Home Defence Department from squandering oodles of time, supplies, and peoplepower. Once the Patch Over became Corven's priority, Jagjit's search was put on the back-burner. "Where is it? *Underpool?* I'll seize it at once, Home Defence Minister." Tapping the dotgram Reiter gave him, now bulging in his pocket, Jagjit replied confidently: "I have a map of the new entry points to the regressive labyrinth. I can organize a raid for tonight."

Corven hawed. "It's been tried. Several times in fact. Your predecessor expensed eight-cycles-worth of regional production on nine failed sieges. That's why we have that map in the first place. Classified too, *by the way.* Have whoever gave it to you shot."

Jagjit stroked his beard and mentally rescinded his request for Reiter's personnel file. In an hour's time, it would be permanently deleted. "Yes, Minister."

"Besides, The Family painting isn't there—otherwise they would have used it already, and moreover, a battle on the eve of the Patch Over will give the Supreme Council cause to doubt me and our project." Studying Jagjit's body language, Corven leaned forward. "Hassan? Is everything alright? Should I begin finding someone with a stomach to do what the People need done?"

Jagjit felt like he was spinning—as if his mind had lost its body and was floating along with the limousine, losing a grip on the physical world, senses fading. He wasn't sure whether what upset him most was the prospect of failure, of letting the regressives get their grubby hands on the painting, or of Kunlun—that evolutionary slingshot into an unknown deindividualized future. Panic set in. He looked for control and rediscovered it in violence. He decided then that Dr. Mallory Worthing would not see the result of her programming—the perfected version of the software that would liberate the English people of their pasts. She was neither worthy of collectivization nor of redemption. Redemption was an old-world concept anyway. It boiled Jagjit's blood. Sins could not be forgotten.

109

He would kill Dr. Worthing the next evening or as soon as the EDS got what they needed out of her. Jagjit sanctified his oath and satiated Corven's apprehension: "I am ready and willing." He took a deep breath. "It is simply a matter of the air here. It's wretched; tainted by what lies over the Atlantic."

Pricking back up with enthusiasm and lightness, Corven set Jagjit's priorities: "Waste no time in Underpool. The continued existence of that horrible place may in fact aid us in tracking down this cyber weapon of mass destruction. After all, it is helpful knowing where the enemy will return once he has acquired what it is that we cannot abide him having." His eyes glazed over momentarily. "And we have an inkling of where the enemy may seek to return *from*. I have sent several personnel files to your exocortex."

A colorful display of names and images flit over Jagjit's eye, and in an instant he had assimilated all of the information, some details more comprehensively than others. "The Reclamations Department?"

"Our friends in the east have noted a sudden uptick in black market interest with regards to a cyber weapon. I believe it to be The Family painting. After all, if what you and others have said about it is true, it is the only cyber weapon that has a chance of success against our collective. Enemy chatter from the coast indicates that McGregor's Congress is of the same mind."

Jagjit balled his hands into fists. "What does Reclamations have to do with it?"

"Consult the files. The Department of Reclamations is in the business of reclaiming things lost and forbidden. I do not want to divide your focus to the detriment of the Patch Over any more than I want to run the risk of its ruin by some confounded painting, so I'm sending Doctor Worthing over to the English Broadcast Station in Blackpool to prepare it now. While she makes her final touches, I want you to find out if anything lost or forbidden has been found and left unreported. I want everyone responsible devalued. Afterwards, you will head to the English Broadcast Station and execute the People's Will."

"If this cyber weapon is used before we implement the Patch Over..."

Corven's frown made his cheeks bulge and bracketed his cold eyes. "I trust you to see to it that it won't. This may all just be hysteria. Nevertheless, we must keep our wits about us. Though you have just under a day, I want a full and thorough investigation. Get the painting if it exists, and eliminate anyone who sought to steal, sell, or buy it."

110

Jagjit saved the data from Corven's briefing. Even though much in the files was redacted, it was clear that the DSSP knew what he had discerned already: that the cyber weapon in question was no trivial matter as it threatened not only the efficacy of the Patch Over but the entire English Democratic Socialist project's survival. "It is my duty and my privilege..."

"And to reward your service to the People, you will personally oversee the Patch Over's implementation. Yours will be the voice broadcast to every mind in that part of the nation—the voice that narrates their last moments as citizens of the old and first moments as citizens of the nearly-new. It will also be the last taunt heard by that insufferable regressive horde on the coast. Yes, Hassan—you will turn the lights on for an entire generation of people cramped in the shade cast by yesteryear's monuments to greed."

"I appreciate the opportunity." Although this gesture and the recognition it entailed made Jagjit despise Mallory Worthing a little less, he remained committed to her ruin.

"Once again, Dr. Worthing should arrive later this afternoon with the latest build of the program along with its resonance sphere. I have instructed her to assist you in developing possible contingencies in the event that the weapon has been found by the enemy. Security and salvation, Hassan. Call me when the job is done." Corven's face disappeared along with the holographic window.

Jagjit intuited new directions to the car's computer via his implant. "Take me to Reclamations immediately."

111

THIRTEEN

The excitement Alek used to feel when out on jobs was sapped. Then again, he wasn't helping star-crossed lovers, martyrs, or renegades. He was helping a traitor. With Danika's help, he was propping up a card-carrying member of the very regime he despised—the same that had taken Monica away from him; if not permanently, then certainly for longer than he could handle. As they drew nearer their destination in Danika's van, Alek felt more and more nauseous.

Green's CBLOCK06 had all of its lights on when they rolled up. As per their custom, Danika got out of the van and sauntered inside 06 without looking back. Alek crept out of the van, swallowed his bile, and trailed her at a distance.

Four heavily-armored Praetorian drones stood outside the main doors to CBLOCK06 armed with rotary cannons and sword staffs. Were it not for Monica's clever engineering, both drones would have eviscerated Alek without hesitation. Fortunately, Alek had his wife's dislocation program running beneath his skin. Although the sight of gunmetal and the EDS logo on the killer machines still made him nervous, he had already come too close to have been deemed a threat. The dislocation program was working. Now, when scanned by an AI, a killbot, or an overhead drone, Alek's implant would provide the stolen personnel file and biometrics lifted from a nearby citizen. Only someone with a memory of that specific citizen, including the victim of Alek's crime, would be able to call him out for being a phony. Alternatively, if the same biometrics were scanned twice in different locales, the jig would be up—both positive IDs would lead to arrests.

Alek held his breath as he passed between the drones. His assumed persona was apparently above harassment. Made sense; this building was full of government officials all with additional privileges and rights. Judging by their freedom of mobility, their collective trustvalue was off the charts.

The instant Alek crossed the threshold into 06, he took a sharp right. He avoided a crowd of party members and kept close to the wall, hoping to eventually find a way upstairs. Gargantuan statues of androgynous revolutionaries with blunted features were set back against the wall, forcing Alek into the crowd every three metres. The same statues served a function besides endangering Alek. They doubled as pillars and held up the mezzanine balcony above, which looked like a cage for pale-eyed public officials.

Despite the number of people present above and around, the room was relatively quiet. Many of the officials relied upon limbic implants to regulate their movement and to avoid environmental danger while their minds transcended their flesh and mingled with those of their cohorts in virtual realms. Why they needed to leave their rooms or their beds was a question for scientists hanged long ago for the crime of producing facts deemed too hateful. Alek figured that the virtual realm cheated the neocortex but not that part of the reptilian brain that could sense the presence of another, meaning these chuckleheads were congregated merely to deceive their most primitive senses into believing they weren't alone in their dreams. Truth was that they were as alone in their dreams as they were in the lobby; so distracted by their pursuit for pleasure and positive feedback that none of them saw one another. Alek shook his head disapprovingly at the tone-deaf blather of the Peoples' new aristocracy.

Still under the guise of one of the true believers nearby, Alek hid his face as he passed the building's dean, who was disinterestedly watching the English Broadcast Station on a wall-mounted screen. The talking heads on England's state-run news channel read directly from the Supreme Council's press releases. They mentioned radioactive winds from Russia dissipating before they reached the CDS' easternmost citizen-housing complexes; noted the anniversary of England's liberation from fascism; and provided a reminder about remaining vigilant with concerns to religiosity, nonconformist thought, and hate speech. Lancashire's new commissar, Jagjit Hassan, appeared on the screen. The Commissar was taking pre-authorized questions from so-called journalists in London Central Train Station. Hassan promised to clean house once he arrived in Blackpool, beginning with allies of his compromised predecessor, Amir Dorz. Beside the Commissar throughout his press conference was a woman wearing a low-rimmed cap with her hair pinned back. Alek stopped in his tracks. His legs felt like concrete. His blood ran cold. The woman beside Hassan looked a great deal like Monica. *No it couldn't be.* Alek walked right up to the screen, blocking the dean's view.

"Oy, share the view, will yah?" The dean pushed Alek to the side, thankfully so transfixed on the news that he didn't notice the discrepancy between Alek and the tenant he was digitally imitating. "See there? That's the pride of Lancashire: Dr. Worthing herself." The dean looked to Alek, but not at Alek, and smiled. "Regionalism is toxic, I realize, but that's the brain behind the Patch Over, no matter what people say about the Commissar's involvement."

113

The news feed cut to a clip of Dorz' execution. Alek's eyes couldn't have grown any wider. They were red-rimmed and shot. He looked at the dean, then back at the EBS program. He mumbled to himself: "I'm losing it," and retraced his deviating steps back to the path he had mentally plotted at the outset.

An obese woman fattened on ideological possession and drunk on virtual life walked straight into Alek as he intercepted his old pathway through the crowd. She regained her senses and stuttered after him some broken accusation of aggression. Failing to get a rise or an apology out of Alek, she waddled to the dean in pursuit of justice. "He assaulted me!" she shrieked, pointing every which way. She was as dense as the crowd, which boded well for Alek.

Alek had no intention of hanging around to be kicked about by some kangaroo court. He cracked open his bag just enough to get ahold of his gun. Setting it under his belt, he threw the bag over his shoulder, and found the closest staircase. The security scanner on the door to the stairs cleared him for entry and flashed him with a green light, supposing him to be whoever his dislocation program invoked. The flash of light was so bright that it momentarily left Alek blind. As his vision returned to him, he thought he could see Monica standing at the top of the first flight of stairs. Alek growled and blinked away the apparition, and began climbing the steps. The news from Evaun—that Monica might still be alive—challenged all of his presuppositions. It was a strange feeling hating hope's return.

Looking up at the engraved number twelve, Alek growled once more and clomped up the remaining steps. The door to the twelfth floor would only open for one of its residents. Alek's alter ego lived on the seventeenth floor, which would have been a problem had Alek been a weakling like those whose subsistence diet consisted solely of what the state decided would keep them alive, and exercise was limited to what would only keep their hearts beating. He kicked the door so hard that it nearly came off its heavy hinges. The pneumatic mechanism above the door that kept it from slamming whined even louder than Alek's hoofing. He quickly activated his ocular implant and scanned the hallway.

At the end of the featureless white hall lined on either side by numberless doors, Alek saw Green's right away, marked in invisible ink with a giant "X". He could make out the "X" because he had ensured his implant was sensitive to the colour spectrum that he and Monica insisted their clients use. "Bingo."

There were loud footsteps booming below. It wasn't out of the ordinary for a building with thousands of occupants to see those

114

very occupants using the stairs, but any social encounter could be Alek's last. He peered once more down the hall, and switched his vision to pick up electronic signals. It was just as he figured: the hallway was littered with cameras and sensors. Instead of giving security a sense of who was getting an unauthorized visit, Alek pulled an infrared flare from his bag and rolled it down the hall. It fizzed and pulsed, blinding the government's artificial eyes. With the footsteps behind him now louder and growing more rapid, Alek sprinted down the hallway.

He overheard snippets of unlawful conversations emanating from the various sealed rooms. The patter of his own feet had a silencing effect, one that left the apartments dead silent as he rushed by. Only the DSSP came by in the night, and they never left emptyhanded.

Green's apartment was unlocked. Alek slipped in and shut the door just as the door to the stairwell finally clicked shut on the opposite end of the floor. Monica would have chastised him for taking unnecessary risks. He felt her disappointment like a latent sneeze sitting between his eyes. He shook Monica's disappointment free, locked his neck, and fell into his routine. "Alright, what've we here?"

The apartment was at least three times the size of Alek's own. While it had the same barren walls—a problem of iconoclasm remedied by augmented reality—that is where the similarities ended. The floor was polished hardwood. It had a full kitchen, sink, stove, and all. There were several eMeal bricks beside a printer capable of transforming them into shapes reminiscent of old-world dishes, and for dishes, Green had a cabinet full of fine China. Like the apartment, the windows were also much larger. She had done well for herself. The last time Alek had her for a client, she lived in a grubby central unit with windows forever scaffolded. It had still been in a high-trustvalue zone, but the place was nowhere as nice as this.

In front of Green's floor-to-ceiling living room window was a bureau desk. On top of it there was a neat stack of dotgrams and a bottle of schnapps. Even though the label had been peeled off the bottle, it was nevertheless a major crime to possess an alcoholic drink in the first place (even though the officials at the Ministry of Transportation and Cultural Equity were always pickled and managed to get a free pass). But it wasn't there for Green's consumption; had it been, she would have almost certainly hidden it for later discovery. No, it was for someone else entirely. Green used to leave a bottle, sometimes two, for the Lethes. Alek didn't trust

115

himself when it came to the drink, so it was Monica who would indulge. The bottle stood as a reminder to Alek that only he felt Monica's absence. The rest of the world had forgotten or never made a point of noticing her disappearance in the first place.

The desk chair was a fanback with felt arm rests. Green had pulled it out and to the side just enough to reveal what was sitting on it: an attaché case. The case contained the prize Alek really cared about.

Alek clipped his debugging wand to his belt and produced his pistol. He sleuthed around the living room. The wand was silent. The room was clear, *thank God*.

The bedroom door just past the kitchen was ajar as requested. He peeked inside. Margaret Green lay in her bed with a breathable black hood over her head. Alek tucked his gun away and rummaged through his bag for an anesthetic. Dead set against discovery, he readied the syringe, and after checking the debugging wand for another all-clear, stormed into the bedroom and injected Green. There was little resistance nor would there have been; she had actually been asleep—a rarity for customers granted their exposure to possible malice. Then again, she had no reason not to trust the person who had saved her countless times before.

After setting his duffel bag down beside his sleeping client and neatly laying his gear on her imperceptibly rising and falling chest, Alek hurried back into the living room. He placed the case on the bureau desk and dragged the chair over to the apartment door. He wedged the headrest under the doorknob. Satisfied with having created at least one obstacle for his faceless pursuers, he unclipped the debugging wand from his belt and scanned the case for bugs or tracking devices, and once again was happy to learn from three green lights on the device that everything was hunky-dory. "Okay, Maggie. D'you got what I asked for?" he mumbled to himself as he unlatched the case. Inside were different denominations of outmoded currency, including the pound sterling Danika coveted for no other reason that the paper's weight and the accursed faces printed thereon. There were also the mobility chits he requested, and...Alek caved over. Amidst the chits and cash, there was a photograph of Monica dressed up in an EDS tunic. On the photograph, Green had written in bold letters: "I AM SORRY."

Alek saw red. His ears burned hot. His nostrils flared and became fixed so that he looked like a bullish gorilla. The first thought that came to mind was not nearly as murderous as those that followed. His gun was cocked in his hand before he had even decided on using it. He pressed off the barrel of his gun to get back to his feet.

116

Tears he did not know were there broke from his face. He charged into the bedroom, put a pillow over Green's hooded head, pressed the gun to where her face was underneath—*but not for much longer*—and squeezed the trigger, just not all the way. His hand shook. Then his full body shook. It wasn't fear or cowardice that stayed his hand. He needed to know who Margaret Green was to him; who she was to Monica; why she was sorry and for what. And why the bottle of schnapps?! More than anything, he needed to know whether that had been Monica on the news—whether she was alive, as Evaun had suggested, or indeed dead.

Green was out cold. She would be until the early morning. Alek removed the pillow and her hood, revealing a grey-haired woman pushing fifty. Her eyelids were purple, probably from having spent too much time at her desk by the window without proper lighting. *If you can't tell me what happened, you can just show me.*

Alek opened his duffel bag and pulled out the neural net. He attached it to the gear resting on Green's chest. He pressed the little suction cups belonging to the neural net to Green's forehead and temples, and wrapped the brace around the back of her head, indifferent to how it yanked at her hair. Had she not implicated herself in having something to do with Monica's capture, Alek would have set his wipe drive to "TWO CYCLES" and cabled it to her occipital port. Instead of clearing his customer's guilty conscience, he pulled a data converter out of his bag, plugged one cord into Green's head and the other directly into his own. Unlike the synchronization clinic back at the DIHA, Alek's converter could lift repressed or hidden data. Green was an open book only he was able to read. He set the experiential transfer to "TWO YEARS", took a deep breath, and lay down beside his comatose customer with the gun still in his hand. "Alright bitch," he grumbled. "Spill the beans." He quickly lost sensation in his fingers and toes, and before registering any further desensitization, was subsumed by Green's past.

After writhing through an aggressive assimilation of trillions of points of data, Alek turned stiff. The converter emulated and translated Green's memories into parsable data; the same data that would have otherwise been downloaded by the DIHA at the end of her cycle. This data was carried over to Alek, where it was automatically broadcast and stored in his secondary brain under careless management by the EDS at their Blackpool cypulchre. This simplified data then synchronized with his organic brain, where the key impressions were left like fresh footprints in snow just a centimeter behind his forehead. Those same footprints blazed new

117

pathways in Alek's neocortex, confusing whatever paths he had created himself.

It was immediately apparent that Green wasn't a believer in the demsock cause, though she left enough evidence to the contrary to fool the AI historians. She was an opportunist; one who played their game well enough, earning for herself the praise of her comrades at the Ministry of Cultural Equity. While she wasn't ideologically possessed, her hands were as dirty as the rest. Hundreds of men, women, and children had gone to their deaths as the result of the inquiries she had made and the discoveries she had logged when overseeing reclamations in the country's numerous red zones. What had driven her to subvert the state? What did she want to forget?

The drudgery of a life spent doing the Supreme Council's bidding was no obstacle to Alek's pursuit of the truth. Into her consciousness he shadowed her, haunted her, and followed her; into her yoga courses, her meetings with Commissar Dorz, her half-remembered dreams and nightmares. Anywhere she had been, mentally or physically, so too Alek went.

Alek came across one hot summer afternoon where Green was called to the site of a beached Chinese naval drone. Inside there was a manifesto detailing the Mental Union. Of course any Chinese literature had to be tagged and archived at Reclamations. Before she did so, she read it in its entirety. As she had found comfort and security in her role at the ministry, the manifesto's suggestion that it was all for naught greatly troubled her. According to the manifesto, on year twenty-five, all citizens belonging to the Socialist Alliance would have their minds and experiences mashed together to create a singular human consciousness; one that could withstand and overcome the evils of the West and restore the planet to health. Although no stranger to groupthink, Green loved herself more than anything or anybody else in the world. She couldn't come to terms with losing what she cared about most. For several cycles after finding the manifesto, she somehow hid her apprehension, all the while looking for opportunities to escape what she believed more and more to be a certain and loathsome fate.

Green had overheard her colleagues discussing a vacant desk on the thirtieth floor of the Ministry of Cultural Equity. A staffer had gone missing. While people went missing every day, usually taken the night before by the DSSP, this particular absence was far more controversial. Several investigations were launched into the man's disappearance. Word through the grapevine was that he had sold a high-value artifact for safe passage to the Americas. This memory

118

had been wiped by the DIHA, so Alek's reconstruction was patchy—enough to remind him not only of himself as a distinct entity in this trip down her memory lane but of the mission at hand. Detached from Green's experience on account of its surreality, Alek paid close attention to her interdepartmental communications, clearly more than her superiors had.

One cycle before Monica was shot, Green caught a hot tip from a colleague at the Ministry of Cultural Equity. Apparently, there was an irrefutable offer for a specific painting that the EDS had confiscated from a red zone in Blackburn. The same colleague had hatched a plan with a friend of his, some senior official from the Department of Reclamations. They committed to selling the painting off to a foreigner—an American promising money, dirt on their respective political opponents in the EDS, and ways out of the country. They roped Green in with the promise of a promotion and a two-tier trustvalue upgrade. All she had to do was requisition the painting for departmental review and then swap the painting with another. It was essential she swap them because otherwise they would never see another opportunity to snatch it. The interdepartmental security AIs would see the sudden interest in a specific work as a possible risk. The painting would be seized by Reclamations and vaulted. Meanwhile, the real painting would be brought to Cultural Equity where it would temporarily remain in Green's care. So Green swapped the paintings as promised. The coveted painting was a huge oil portrait of a wrinkled old technocrat bearing special significance to the Socialist Alliance. Why her co-conspirators called it "The Family" she had no idea. She was unable to migrate the painting to Cultural Equity right away, so she hid the painting in plain sight—on a wall somewhere in the Department of Reclamations—and then hurried home, in desperate need of a clear conscience before the inevitable cross-examination by the security AIs. She left a trail of breadcrumbs for herself to find her way back to the painting with which she could escape the Mental Union and other calamities.

Alek lost himself in Green's plan. He too had heard about a certain painting of value, though had figured it for wild speculation or at the very least wishful thinking. So far as he knew, the painting wasn't of interest to the Americans. It was the Resistance that wanted it, and they wanted it badly.

Some of Green's unattended memories seemed to die, particularly those that had no significance and found no associations with Alek. The whereabouts of the coveted painting, however, became all he could focus on.

119

Muffled voices in the hallway shook Alek free of his rigor. Head full of Green's lived propaganda, Alek yanked out the occipital cable and rushed to the bathroom to splash water into his face along with a modicum of mental stability. Scrutinizing his haggard mug in the mirror, he tried separating himself from Green. Their disparate dispositions made this a rather simple exercise.

Upon assigning guilt to its respective owners and isolating his own voice in the psychic cacophony resultant of the transfer, Alek's eyes widened around the realization of what he had just learned. There was so much more he had learned but still did not know consciously. He returned to Green and sat on the end of the bed. He set his elbows on his knees and made a cradle for his face using his fingers. More and more, the truth came to him concerning Green's apology and what happened to Monica.

Scott Townley. He was the one who ambushed them; the one who shot Monica. Green knew Townley well. Her trust in the man deteriorated within Alek's mind. It was Townley who put Green onto finding the painting and it was Green who put Townley onto Alek and Monica. Their plan hinged upon clear consciences and leaving behind no witnesses.

Alek smacked himself. An image of the American art dealer flashed through his mind. *Cassandra Doherty*: a tall blonde woman with soft features. An actual American! Alek wasn't too surprised there was still something of it left—the United States, that is; nuked into oblivion by China according to the EDS' scant tracts on global history as of the year zero.

They were in cahoots, Townley and Green; both trying to secure for themselves fortune or liberty by way of a trade with Doherty. But why would Townley shoot Monica? If she had done her job, he wouldn't have remembered her. And when instead he shot her— without her absolution—he would have had to have his mind scanned as soon as his victim was carted away. He must have figured Monica for a secret agent: one who might turn them in or extort them with the memories she had allegedly wiped from Green's mind. Whatever Townley's motivation to murder, for Townley's murdering Alek only needed the one.

Lording above Green, Alek contemplated what to do with her. He wondered why she would admit guilt. Then of course, her reasoning occurred to him: she hadn't known, at least not until she saw the former Lethe on the EBS parading around with the new commissar. The bottle of schnapps, then, was a taunt? Alek had no recollection of Green's reasoning there. Perhaps it was as simple as her thinking he might need the drink after learning the truth about

120

his wife. No, thought Alek. It was just more carelessness on her part. She was careless in recommending the Lethes' services to a stranger, and she was careless in asking for help once more, knowing full well that Alek would know the extent to which she really didn't care.

He couldn't bring himself to fill her head with lead, but decided to empty her brain altogether. Instead of wiping a week or two of her experience, Alek wiped her entire history. He scrubbed her entire past. It wasn't murder per se; he killed her identity but left her the means to start again. Although, in all likelihood, the EDS would figure out something was amiss with their empty-headed servant and finish the job.

"You're not sorry, I'm not sorry. Nobody's sorry," Alek said before folding the hood Green had been wearing. He pocketed her end of the bargain and went out the way he came, making sure to grab his infrared flare on his way to the stairs.

Danika was patiently waiting out front, both for Alek and her cut. Alek climbed in the back.

As soon as the doors were closed, Alek broke Danika's cardinal rule and began to speak: "I need to ask you something."

Danika turned around, stunned by Alek's disregard for their code. "What d'yah think you're doing?"

"Scott Townley." Alek climbed into the front of the van and attempted to interface with the computer embedded in the dashboard. "I need to know where he is."

Nodding, as if considering the name, Danika gently pushed Alek back, reached over, and grabbed her gun from the glove compartment. She took aim at Alek. "No. You need to get out of my van."

Alek raised his hands slowly. "You're having a laugh."

Danika scowled and wrapped the trigger.

"The hell's the matter with yah? It's just a quick query. I'll wipe you as promised. Nothing to get fussed about."

"We said no talking, and you come in here running your gab, telling me what to do. Gonna get me and Lisa killed."

Alek chuckled, head full of Green's apocalyptic outlook. "I wasn't tellin', I'm asking! And if you're worried about dying, then I've got some bad news for you..."

"Get out of my van, Alek. Leave me my cut and get out."

Alek looked out the window. The weaponized drones would undoubtedly pay attention this time around. "Ah, c'mon. I'm supposed to walk home? I'll catch a cold. And who'll wipe you?"

"I'll manage."

121

Alek didn't take Danika's threat seriously and lowered his hands. "Sure you will, as I'm sure you'll manage to dodge the Mental Union."

Danika pushed a button on the dash and the rear doors opened. "Out!"

"You've heard of the Mental Union, have yah?" asked Alek, preparing to get out. "They are going to stick everyone's minds in a bloody dumpster underground—yours and Lisa's included, assuming they want to keep you in the first place." Alek gulped, realizing Danika was in fact serious. He felt the cold of his own gun pressed up against his skin, but felt disinclined from reaching for it. Though Danika was being a dick, it was entirely possible that he had indeed compromised her by talking, that the van was bugged or that AI historians had managed to glom onto her immediate senses. That said, without Alek and the mind wipe he had promised, she was as good as dog meat. No one else in the region would wipe a guardian's mind, and his good friend Geoff Littlefield would refuse on principle. Instead of violence, Alek sought to calm his co-conspirator with more of Green's insights. "Bunch of childless pricks in Beijing, Brussels, and London figure the best thing for humanity is to wipe it out and lord over humanity version two-point-oh."

"You're not the first man to lie at gunpoint."

"I'm not lying." Alek got out of the van and clasped his hands atop his head. Desperately he chattered on: "I know who shot Moni. And I know why."

Danika put her hand over the button to close the rear doors.

"They were worried she knew about their plan to escape what's coming *and what's coming won't spare your daughter.*"

Unconvinced but well aware that it was unwise to have a debate out front of a trustworthee city block, Danika holstered her weapon. "You're a real tosser, Alek Neuhaus." She looked at the city map, at the route back to CBLOCK32, and sighed. "Get in." She hit the button to close the doors, u-turned, and accelerated, throwing Alek against one side.

"Easy now, Danika! You don't want to break the neural net!"

"What is coming?! And who told you that bunk about the Mental Union?"

Alek picked himself up off the floor, and leveraged himself against the back of Danika's seat. "Green and her friends in Cultural Equity and the Department of Reclamations—they're all trying to get the hell out of England. They're scared, Danika. They are going to keep us virtual and get rid of our meat. Then they're going to mix our virtual selves together."

122

"The top brass have us scheduled for an update, the morning after next. You don't think that's when they'll do it?" Danika hugged the steering wheel close, looking out for blockades or the odd nosy Reduvius drone while her mind raced through worst-case scenarios.

"I mean, it's probably related."

"Shit. If true, I've got to get Lisa out." Danika's daughter was already living a ghostly existence—although she wasn't implanted, she had assumed the identity of a missing person. With no implant and an emulator capable of faking only topical scans, Lisa was more or less confined to quarters. "Where are the trustworthees all headed? I mean, where does one go?" Danika began to panic as the lower-trustvalue CBLOCKs began to block out the sky once more. "How does one leave this place?"

Alek crawled to the center of the van so that he could see Danika as well as the curves in the road ahead that had been making him carsick when unanticipated. "Monica would tell you to take her to Underpool."

Danika scowled at Alek in the mirror. "Frying pan or fire? *Great.* See, this is why people went offworld. Earth's out of places where you can be left alone."

"Listen, Danika." Alek couldn't tell if his sudden calm was his or Green's, or whether it was just a matter of seeing where the van was going. "This Townley guy—he's the one who shot Moni. I'm going to ask him where he's planning on going. And that's where you'll take Lisa."

"How'd he figure he'd get out?"

"With a—" Alek stopped himself. The idea that a painting could double as a key out of this prison seemed absurd, notwithstanding the conviction of those other prisoners dead set on smuggling it for reward or profit. "With a highly-valued item."

"And you plan on getting that highly-valued item?"

The truth was that Alek only really wanted to choke the life out of Scott Townley. A painting wouldn't bring Monica back, but if she wasn't dead after all, perhaps it could set her free. "Yes, mum."

Keeping an eye on Alek in her rear-view mirror, Danika punched in the name. The query turned up two search results. The Scott Townley with the higher trustvalue was located in CBLOCK04 and reported daily to the Department of Reclamations in Blackpool.

Alek clamored to the front of the van once more. "That's him," he said, memorizing the details. He peeled back a few hundred pounds for himself and gave Danika the rest—certainly more than her share. "Don't know what it's good for granted markets need people and people are about to swiftly become a thing of the past."

123

Danika tucked it away. "I guess our no-talking rule is null and void, huh."

Unwilling to test the good will his soothsaying had garnered by being a smart ass, Alek kept quiet.

Too anxious to deal with the prospect of mental collectivization and drive, Danika appealed to her passenger for a distraction. "Who'd ever have thought that all it'd take for Alek Neuhaus to shut up would be doomsday?"

"Were you really going to leave me out there for the wolves?"

After a pregnant pause Danika, looked to Alek and smiled. They both burst out laughing. Danika wiped her eyes dry and replied: "I probably would have circled back for you. They would've caught me using your memories. Now you tell me something: you're not pulling my leg about this Mental Union shit?"

Alek shook his head and focused on the mountainous silhouettes encroaching on the road, striving to repress the thought of Monica dressed up as a demsock.

"You think we stand a chance of making it out of here?"

"Maybe with a little help from our friends."

FOURTEEN

At least twelve-hundred men, women, and children had gathered inside the grotto, with more pouring in from the back and side entrances, all adding to a sea of greasy hair and tattered clothes. The candelabra suspended above them by a heavy anchor rope provided the majority of the light in the limestone hall, the striated walls of which seemed to pulsate. Around the periphery were benches for mothers with infants and the elderly. Church pews provided seating for about half of those already present, while everyone else stood wherever they could find space. At the front of the hall was a raised stage, and at the center of the stage was a podium behind which stood Rabbi Klotz, a tall, rawboned man with a long white beard.

The Rabbi collected his notes, having just given his statements in full. Although near the end he had spoken in the abstract about wisdom and perseverance, most of his talk concerned the sort of political system they might adopt once the Resistance knocked out the EDS. Since any Briton with ties to the monarchy had been liquidated, barring the odd duke and the odder duchess now either imprisoned in London or working with the Resistance, there was little likelihood that they could revivify a constitutional monarchy, one connected to the old anyhow. He stressed the danger in attempting another parliamentary democracy, citing several instances including the English example where a super majority dissolved the democracy that had conferred it power. Instead, he argued, they needed a constitutional republic with a separation of powers such that the majority could not tyrannize the minority, and that the resultant premier, president, or prime minister could never take on the kind of unchecked authority those offices enjoyed in past systems. It was a hopeful talk in that Klotz, by virtue of speaking of a new government, presumed victory in the coming days and weeks, and presumed further that the liberated masses might still be able to stomach rules and rulers after what had been done to them in recent years.

Cardinal Nechtan took the ramshackle stage after two men helped Rabbi Klotz down and over to his seat. Tonsured like a warrior monk, cheeks reddened by the cold air gusting through the cavernous hall, and dressed in a hand-stitched purple cassock, Nechtan ended each sentence with a shake of his pastoral staff, not one word of which Stephen or Mirek could catch on account of the

125

noisy throng that kept chirping "Amens!" and "Hear, hear!" However, as soon as Mass began, the hall grew quiet.

The faithful stood before the Cardinal and followed along in the missals that had been smuggled over from the Holy See in Kentucky. Former Anglicans were just as engaged, historical and theological differences now long forgotten. After all, their archbishop's office had been adopted as an agency of the government and had since endorsed the EDS regime. Together with members of the ancient Christian faith of England and the Orthodox escaped from Eastern Europe, they stood for the reading from the Gospel of John, which expounded on the variety of love forbidden aboveground. Everyone else waited respectfully for General Hugh McGregor to begin the intelligence briefing, which was still a few minutes off granted he was deeply involved in the ritual, hands intertwined and pointed to the Infinite from whom he desperately wanted forgiveness—not for what he had done, but for what he planned to do.

As all the seats and standing room had not yet been filled with the last of the Resistance, Nechtan took liberties with the time allotted him. His homily was brief relative to his usual elaborations on just war, but not to be outdone by Klotz's call to arms. "Christ tells us in today's reading that we are no longer slaves. Although called to do God's bidding—which is to love one another and to love God—we are not *His* slaves, but His children; invited, not ordered; called, not coerced. Only a free man can choose to accept an invitation. A slave can only obey and must hurry else he be beaten or destroyed. Of his earthly master the slave knows only the order and the whip. But of our Father, we know only His love and Intention, detailed by the Son who died to save us from whatever prisons we have or will come to know. The Father's Son tells us today not to let our temporal slavery trouble us if it seems inescapable, but only because it is escapable."

Bitter murmurs and whispering rose like radio static above the crowd.

Nechtan's brow appeared to pinch his eyes. "But we are also told that if we can gain our freedom, we must do so."

There was agreement from all denominations. Their armoured garments clattered and their metals clinked.

"Brothers and sisters, we have one last opportunity to seize our earthly freedom, to remind the world that we, scarred friends of Christ and bloodied children of the Most High—we free peoples of the West—rebuke the mastery of nihilistic brutes who demand our full and undivided allegiance; those who offer threats in lieu of invitations." Nechtan struck with his staff the rickety planks

126

underfoot that elevated him above the crowd. "Outside of this, England's last remaining holy place, our kin know only one master, and he loves them not. He has cut out their free will. He has usurped their powers of procreation. He has offered animal comfort as a fleeting prize for sacrificing curiosity and imagination, choice, individuality, and understanding. He has conquered their hearts and bodies both. The Devil remembers neither Michael's sword nor the power of Truth because he has chosen to live in the present without any connection to the past; solaced by the understanding that he and his worshippers in London, Brussels, and Beijing are unopposed. But the great liar has deceived himself, failing to recognize the faith of the free men and women gathered here today, ready to lift the Archangel's blade and strike our generation's tormenter. My friends, brothers and sisters in Christ, sons and daughters of Abraham, ye defiant men and women of Underpool—you are here and so you are free. Hundreds of millions are not so fortunate; chained in prisons dark. In a few minutes, Hugh will instruct us how to mount our blessed last stand and we will have a choice: to fight or to flee. I would fear a coward's grave over a martyr's charge as it would be a satanic effort to do nothing and to let our friends serve the Devil for the rest of their days. And so I invite you to put your freedom to work..." Nechtan's eyes teared up as he surveyed the room. He pulled a note from his sleeve, and ran his finger down the page. "I received notice from one of our friends across the Atlantic that the Holy Father has dedicated today's Mass and every Mass into next month to our success. The Holy Catholic Church prays for us along with believers of other faiths and traditions, including the Dalai Lama in the Republic of Canada and Imam Tawhidi in Minnesota. Though they may not have the words or the freedom to use them, the world under the Devil's spell also prays for us. May God bless us and keep us. And may St. Michael watch over us in these early hours of strife and pain."

After the room recited the creed that would get anyone above grade a death sentence, a young Indian woman dressed in fatigues, with a shaved head and a botched implant scar on her temple, emerged from the crowd, genuflected, and took the stage beside the Cardinal. He gave her a kind nod and she turned to address the room. "We pray for the repose of the souls."

Those-in-the-know bowed their heads in solemn reflection.

"Including," continued the young woman, "Our fallen in Ireland and on the Continent. For the Duke of Norfolk who remained true to the cause of freedom. For our Ethiopian and Nigerian brothers and sisters in their time of need. And for my father."

"Hear! Hear!" roused a rustic voice from aback the crowd.

"Thank you, Major Khatri," responded the Cardinal.

Major Zoya Khatri, daughter of the Resistance's beloved Captain James Khatri felled in St. Anne's ten years before, smiled politely, but her eyes did not wrinkle. Her heart was broken and her sincerity was sapped. She reentered the crowd.

After receiving the Eucharist along with dozens of other contemplative soldiers, McGregor escorted Nechtan to his seat beside Klotz. He shook hands with everyone in the front row and prepared himself to address the room.

Stephen led his neighbour through the mob of anxious Underpoolians and located Wes.

"Yah better not have missed Communion, I tell you what," Wes said, crossing himself. He saw that Stephen was still wearing his ball cap, yanked it off of him, and jammed it into his gut. "Show a little respect."

Stephen had an excuse ready, but Wes denied him the opportunity. He hushed Stephen, and instructed him and Mirek to face the front.

Colonel Shelly Phan, a square woman with a short brunette bob nowhere near touching her muscular shoulders, intercepted the General. She showed him a checked list, and received his approval. He pointed to the wheelbarrow and whispered something that made her beam. Shaking her face clean of delight, she took the stage and rocked the podium.

A mousy private broke through the crowd, and set a holographic camera and a projection sphere at Shelly's feet. Once both were set up and the camera was sending the live and encrypted feed to the other Resistance units in England, the private reclaimed her anonymity amongst the crowd.

"Good mornin'. Now listen up, Underpool." Shelly flattened her crinkled checklist. "I've taken stock, and I know that some of you haven't disclosed your carry, but ne'er mind Poolian secrecy. So far as we're concerned down here, we're sittin' on: thirty-six exosuits; twenty-nine mortars plus the General's latest acquisitions; two-barrels-full of EMP grenades; a flat of plasma rifles down three from the index given previous on account of Hannah's heroics..."

A heavily-bandaged woman with gauze taped over one eye waved cartoonishly to Shelly. She had successfully destroyed a prisoner transport north of Blackpool and rescued those inside destined for a crematory. The room erupted into cheers and whistles. "Eh, Hannah! Hannah! Hannah the Horrible!"

Shelly waited for the clapping to subside, and then threw her hands out as if to take credit for the preceding silence. "That's about enough of that. Thanks to our friends north of Hadrian's, we've got another ten sets of 'dustrial cutting tools. The rest are the basics you've all come to expect. Couple of 'em stabilized machine guns, seventy rifles, and a sidearm for every man." She folded her checklist and stowed it in her breast pocket. "How about you fellas down south? What are the men of Harlech bringing to the party?"

Shelly, the podium, and the entire stage were enveloped in a dark holographic sphere. The sphere quickly took on a medley of colours, and then finally formulated into a three-dimensional projection of the Welsh Resistance's outpost in Maentrog. Unlike Underpool's cavernous grotto, the Welshmen's war room was set inside a stable. Behind their designated armourer was a Dutch door with its upper-half ajar. The morning light that cut through the doorway gilded Commander Lewis.

"G'afternoon Colonel," said Lewis, the blonde-headed giant whose neck seemed too big a pedestal for his head.

"Commander Lewis," Shelly replied, invisible within the live projection.

"It seems you have us bested in terms of assortment, but I always say: guns win confidence, men win wars." Lewis pointed somewhere off-camera. "We have got over sixty-thousand cartridges of 7.62, two-hundred rifles, and about ten plasmic shields. Only problem is we're down to a platoon, so we have more than we need."

McGregor sat off-stage with his arms crossed, just outside of the area of the projection field. He leaned forward, elbows carving into his knees. "Good. Very good." He stood up abruptly. "They've got guns, we've got guns. Thank you, Commander Lewis." He approached the stage and turned the projection sphere off, exposing Shelly. "We've all got what we need. To our Hebridean and Mank allies, I presume you similarly have enough to kill your fair share."

"Yup," responded the Manchester armourer over the broadcast.

"Sure do," said another in a robust, baritone voice.

While McGregor settled behind the podium, Shelly dismounted the stage, and joined the Cardinal and the Rabbi in the front row. She frowned as she took her position, disappointed that she didn't have a breakdown of their allies' inventory to compare against. After all, how else would she have known who had done the best job if the results from the competition were kept secret?

The rest of those gathered in the grotto were growing antsy, including Stephen and Mirek.

129

"Oreet. Thank you, your Eminence," said McGregor, smiling at Cardinal Nechtan. He looked one face over and nodded to Rabbi Klotz. "Thank you, Rabbi." He continued to scan the room for particular faces. "Thank you, Major Khatri. And *thank you*, Colonel Phan." McGregor put a page of notes down before him on the splintered podium. He briefly looked his notes over, giving the room an opportunity to settle. When finally there was total silence, he erupted: "Underpool?! What are you still doing here?! I thought that the Europeans told you to surrender! I thought the Chinese told you to surrender! I thought the EDS told you all to surrender! How could it be that you're still here?"

The crowd went wild. Given their uncertainty about the exact purpose of the intelligence briefing as well as the early calls going around the undercity for nonmilitants to head to the Sanctuary, everyone seized on this opportunity for a release. Some screamed obscenities at the three socialist powers the General had invoked, while most laughed and hollered incoherently.

"Oh!" continued the General, smiling jauntily. "That's right! Underpoolians don't know what it is to surrender. They sacrifice comfort for freedom as opposed to freedom for comfort. That's why they fight—why we've fought for as long as I can remember. Some of you—many of you—know nothing but *the fight*. For over twenty-five years we have stood our ground. And in that time, I have seen the best of humanity tested and proven. I have seen charity, faith, and hope combat greed, nihilism, and despair. I have seen broken bodies move mountains and dying men defy gloom. Although there are among you some who wore the badge of England's saints with me opposing the Mob Rule, most who had coloured chests have come and gone. These medals," he said in a gruff voice, pointing to the so-called fruit salad on his breast, "were pinned to me by dead men commemorating actions taken in wars long-forgotten; actions taken in service of a country that squandered any advantage won in blood." McGregor unpinned the medals from his jacket and placed them down on the podium. "We are not restoring the nation that took its own life along with tens of millions of its own citizens. We are on the verge of creating a renewed nation *for* and *of* free men and women. Like the Rabbi said: a system of checks and balances designed to forever protect individual liberty. His Eminence was correct in saying that you do not have to be here. I am glad that you are, but to anyone who's afeard of engaging with the unknown, I *invite* you to leave immediately. There will be no penalty and no ill will towards you. The new world won't coerce your obedience, unlike the demsocks who depend upon cowards in order to maintain control."

130

He took a step back and gave those with uncertainties a chance to excuse themselves.

Mirek elbowed Stephen. "Yah alright? Feel like stickin' around?"

Wes smacked Mirek. "Quiet, you two!"

Embarrassed but still unable to contain himself, Mirek pressed his lips close to Stephen's ear. "Bruv, you figure we'll be the ones to bomb the General's target?"

Stephen stared daggers into Mirek. "If you keep talking, we're bound to miss the answer."

While there was undoubtedly a handful of people who feigned to mull over the open invitation to leave, no one did. Perhaps the realization finally sunk in that the subaltern life wasn't sustainable and that life under EDS rule was worse than death.

Absent some great exodus, one of the elderly nurses at the back of the room lowered the newborn in her arms and shouted: "Cut to it, McGregor!"

The General spied her through the tangle of hair and bodies, and smiled. He saw courage and irritation beaming back at him, steeled and affixed to the concrete floor. "Oreet, oreet," said McGregor. "I'll tell it to yah straight."

"Please do, Gen'ral!" clamored a young man in the fifth row. "Longer we wait, colder goes t'homecoming feast and warmer goes Teresa's ales."

The General became stern. "Your interruption keeps us waiting, Private Yaxley! Quiet now, the lot of you!"

Seeing that Wes had returned his attention to the podium along with the rest of the volunteer army, Stephen turned the tables and pestered Mirek: "You realize you promised the General a bird in Preston?"

"You told me you saw one parked at Carrella's—back in the day when you and Wes traded with him. If he knows what's good for him, Carlo Carrella will come through for the Resistance, I'm telling yah."

Stephen turned pale. "What are you basing that on? We don't even know if he's still in Preston!"

Mirek shrugged his shoulders. "Unless Commodore Dove gives yah the keys to his blimp or the General charters Cassandra's puddle jumper, the Preston tinkerer's our best bet."

Stephen shook his head, and tried to focus on the General's speech.

Grinning ear to ear, elated over the importance of his connection and the importance that connection gave him, Mirek

131

whispered again to Stephen: "Maybe a mickey of yar whisky would grease his gears a great deal."

"Carrella? Fine." Stephen nodded, gently brushed Mirek back, and turned his good ear to the General.

"Well, Nurse Hobson and *Private Yaxley*," said McGregor. "I don't think it'll distress either of you to know that the demsocks have new tech. We had it on good authority that they were going to roll it out at the end of their next cycle, but they've rescheduled it for tomorrow morning. This new tech will make resetting and restoring an implanted mind impossible. That means we will be unable to convert another lost soul. Earlier, I spoke with our friends in Liverpool, Iona, Inverness, and Glasgow. They're ready to support those units we've just touched based with in Wales and Manchester. As there won't be another shot at liberation, it's now or never. We have a possible ace up our sleeves if our American friend comes through for us one last time. If she is unable to produce an antidote to the EDS' latest poison in the next twenty-two hours, we must rely upon kinetic resistance." McGregor pointed at a pencil-necked lieutenant holding a pre-programmed projection sphere. The officer carried the sphere over, turned to the crowd, set the sphere down, and turned it on. A detailed three-dimensional map of Lancashire rolled out, hiding the General and the wall behind him.

Wes' face was twisted. McGregor's plan didn't factor in his find. He turned to Stephen. "So you told Mirek, eh? Bet that didn't take long."

"And *you* told the General," Stephen seethed.

"You wankers..." If the stakes weren't so high, Wes would probably have laughed. Instead, he tensed his jaw. "I told nobody nothing...They found out and I pulled your big fat head out of a noose. I must say: was good thinking on your part to bring the mortars to the grotto, otherwise people might have figured us for traitors. Now, can you track down a Pingo ship or what?"

"We're gonna get it after the meeting," answered Mirek.

Stephen massaged his forehead. "What's the target?"

Wes shrugged and pointed to McGregor.

"The new tech the demsocks have they call the Patch Over. It's a systems patch of sorts that will eliminate organic memory storage. All of England will be remotely saved; at the disposal and under the total control of the EDS. Our agents say that they've rolled out the programming in advance and have been hitting civvies's virtual brains with the preparatory data packets for days, but for activation they need to provide a visual code. The only way for them to do that properly is in-person or by lossless video inputs, which

132

means they'll do it here." The General indicated the English Broadcasting Station headquarters in Blackpool on the map. "Now, it is Providence that Brigadier Miller and his men discovered old Tyulpan nuclear mortars on the coast..."

Shelly threw her checklist on the ground. "Nuclear? Oh, that's what you meant by special? Something worth mentioning, *eh General*?!"

Extra to Shelly's displeasure with being found out of the loop, this announcement produced a great deal of excitement in the grotto.

"Five teams will each take two mortars," continued McGregor. "I will notify the corresponding officers who will in turn notify their teams. Until it is hit, your primary target is the EBS building. It must be destroyed before the Patch Over, which they plan to carry out just after sunrise, around the time they do their usual roll-call. Once their media building is dust, we'll hit the politburo, the DIHA, the Ministry of Social Justice, the Department for Internal Affairs, as well as the committee houses in Blackpool, Preston, Manchester, Sheffield, Leeds, and Scunthorpe. We are going to blackout the west coast and then work our way east. The success of this part of our plan rests not on the height of the stack of bodies we pile—I should hope to avoid killing our countrymen under the EDS' spell the best we can—but on the chaos we create. If the chaos is great enough, I'm told we might expect support from the Americans, who will be able to synchronize the minds and memories stored in EDS cypulchres, and protect them from deletion. If not—if we are alone—then we remind the enemy why a little bit of aggression and toxicity can come in handy from time to time. Oreet?"

Everyone in the room yelled back, "Oreet"—most of them unconsciously mimicking the General's accent.

McGregor looked around. "Major Khatri?"

Khatri's arm fired up in the crowd while all other arms slumped down. "Yes sir?!"

"You will lead one of our nuclear units, but you will not be headed for the EBS. Instead, you will coordinate an aerial assault on the continental demsock's advanced-warning station off the west coast of Ireland. There's an island named Tearaght, which has one of the few technological marvels the Chinese didn't pinch from us— used to detect any and all intercontinental movement. They'll see you coming. Fortunately, the last of the Irish Resistance sent security codes our way. They are only good the once, so don't transmit until prompted. These codes will let you pass into CDS airspace, at least for a while. You'll still need to fly in disguised as a friend, so either in an EDS, CDS, or Chinese vessel. As of last autumn, we've had no

133

wings, but our own privates Dubchek and Nowak have a line on an enemy ship in Preston. Isn't that right, lads?"

Stephen turned bright red and answered in the affirmative. Once the General's attention was lifted from him, he nudged Mirek. "Right?"

Crooking a smile, Mirek nodded unconvincingly.

"With the station destroyed," continued McGregor, "The charge of the last brigade may find reinforcement from the New World. Major Khatri, I'm sure you can figure out your next steps with the help of the privates just mentioned."

"Yes sir!"

McGregor cleared his throat and prepared to delineate his plan for those who would remain in Underpool, but a sudden jolt of intrigue cut through the room. Whispers and conversation divided the crowd, making space for a stunning blonde woman. She had on tall black boots, black pants, a green-vested blouse, and a sun visor, the rim of which sloped low over her face. Her trust that the crowd wouldn't react poorly to her presence certainly outweighed the general trust that she wasn't a double agent. Despite the gossip and defamatory murmurs, she strode confidently over to the stage.

Stephen stood up on the tips of his toes to get a glimpse of what was causing the commotion. He saw only partial glimpses of her until she took the stage, at which point there was no mistaking her identity. *Cassandra Doherty.*

Wes lightened up a bit and elbowed Stephen. "Looks like America came to us."

Cassandra Doherty shook McGregor's hand, and waved to the crowd, which still did not know what to make of her—after all, there were still many who blamed her for the loss of their beloved Captain Khatri. She covered a whisper to the General, whose excitement immediately faded. He shook a dour look of defeat, and gestured to the podium and for her to take it.

"Great to see you all in such good spirits," she said staidly.

"Get stuffed!" was the answer from the crowd.

Raising her eyebrows and sure not to waste any more time with pleasantries, Cassandra got down to business. "On my way in, I heard General McGregor mention an ace—a trump card *if you will.* The enemy believes that an infamous cyber weapon is lost, but I have confirmed its existence now for a second time. It is a painting called The Family. Our experts have indicated that this paining is ancient; that it was first discovered in Syria and later gifted to the Vatican by the Patriarch of the Russian Orthodox Church after the reunion of the Christian churches. It has been alleged that the painting was used

134

once in a pivotal battle between the Americans and the Chinese; that it worked on account of some sort of code embedded in the painting itself that messes with surveillance tech and implants alike. What we know for certain is that it was smuggled out of Europe before Rome fell to the Continental Democratic Socialists; that it is now in the possession of the EDS, downtown Blackpool, *though they do not know it."*

Angry and disappointed voices quarreled before her, demanding she produce evidence. "Oh yeah, yah muppet?! We're going to kill 'em Pingos with lady luck's conviction and a *pretty picture?!"* This comment elicited miserable laughter from a portion of the crowd—the kind of forced bird song you might hear at a crank's funeral.

"You'd need a powerful family to destroy the demsocks!" shouted another.

Cassandra took a step back from the podium to let the dissenters exhaust themselves.

Even the General took issue with what Doherty had said. He whispered to her: "Sounds like a trap."

Cassandra shook her head and indicated that she would elaborate.

One heckler chimed in, this time with a fair question: "If it's ancient, how's it effective against modern technology?"

"Yah shouldn't've come back!" bellowed an elderly gentleman seated behind the Rabbi—a relative of Bob Dytryk, killed years earlier in pursuit of The Family painting.

Another rebel screamed: "Lot o'good an ace will do in the enemy's hand, McGregor! Tell this warbler to head back to the safety of her perch!"

Panic and furor swept over the room.

McGregor shouted in his deepest voice: "Enough!" He brought Cassandra back to the podium, and stared her down. "Where in Blackpool?"

"I made a public offer even a trustworthee couldn't refuse. Top bureaucrats at the Ministry of Cultural Equity and the Department of Reclamations accepted. In exchange for amnesty overseas or offworld, they have agreed to hand it over—The Family painting, I mean." Cassandra smiled coyly as people debated giving EDS officials anything besides a thrashing. "Don't worry, we'll dump their bodies over the bay..."

McGregor winked at the crowd, pleased he was not the only one who had thrown out the rule book.

135

"In any event, our business partners have gotten ahold of the painting."

Cardinal Nechtan stood up after intercepting a whispered question from behind him. "Whose partners?!"

Cassandra sighed. She pursed her lips and rapped her fingers on the podium. "*Your Eminence*...After a very long hiatus, the American government has ratified the work my team and I are doing over here."

"Answer the question! Who are *you* with?"

McGregor looked to Cassandra and Cassandra reciprocated. They both shrugged away the secrecy that someone somewhere down the line had demanded they maintain.

"The Central Intelligence Agency," Cassandra answered proudly.

There was quiet in the Great Hall. Any Underpoolian who had visited Meyer's bookshop in the North Tunnel had at one time or another caught a lecture about American history as it pertained to Great Britain. Those who listened closely or long enough had learned about the CIA—how, in its first fifty years, it had frequently staged anti-democratic coups worldwide, emboldened tyrants, and haphazardly redrew borders, in part as a means of combatting communism. But everyone including the undercity's illiterati knew how the CIA, in its later years—leading up to and immediately following the Unholy War—had made tremendous efforts to combat Chinese incursions into the Americas and Africa, and had managed to keep Gibraltar free until the Armistice. If a Resistance fighter did not admire the work the CIA did in that time of choosing, he at least respected the effort.

With her audience stunned, Cassandra continued: "The only problem is that Lancashire's new Commissar Hassan, whom some of you might recognize, has recently been tasked with finding The Family painting. We must get to it first."

McGregor shook his head angrily.

"Our business partners are in too deep to forsake the deal they've made with us and at the same time too exposed to fulfill their end..."

Nurse Hobson covered the ears of the child in her lap and shouted: "*Where* is the bloody thing?!"

Cassandra looked sheepishly to the crowd whose members were hanging on her every word and syllable. "In the Department of Reclamations. All we need to draw my country's support is a sign that the tide could change. You and I—all of us—need something big.

136

The Family painting will do the trick. Now," she said, clearing her throat. "I'm going to need a few volunteers."

The room fell deadly silent, even more so than the pin-drop quiet that followed Cassandra's earlier admission. Everyone was willing to follow McGregor to victory or death, but Cassandra? *An American?* It was out of the question, clear from the unchallenged airspace above all of the heads in the crowd.

Wes pressed Stephen back, and ensured Mirek's twitches couldn't be confused for him volunteering. "Listen up, lads," he whispered to them. "I know all about this Family painting. Some kind of DDOS print; messes with implants and screws up EDS tech. S'what got old Khatri ganked and my leg bowed. Old news to you, I know. Anyhow, *it's real.* And if Doherty can get her hands on it—if *we* can get *our* hands on it—then the Resistance stands a real chance..." He looked at Stephen with sober intensity. "A chance at making more than dents and the like." Wes grabbed both of the young men by their shoulders and pulled them into an impromptu huddle. "I'd feel a whole lot better having two aces up our sleeves rather than just the one." He double-checked that everyone around was still focused on Cassandra or on avoiding selection. "You two help out Zoya. Get the job done and make me proud." Wes turned and raised his hand.

"Wes!" Mirek tried to pull Wes' hand down. "Mate, you gotta stick with us!" It was too late.

McGregor smiled earnestly. "Brigadier Miller! Ready to see to some unfinished business?"

"You're damn right."

Another hand fired up, this time belonging to Dax Tomar, another veteran keen on settling an old score. He had burns all over one side of his face and a bandage covering his one temple. "I don't mind chaperoning!"

Looking across the room at his old friend, Wes answered back with a response almost melodic: "Three's company; *bad, bad* company!"

As Cassandra counted the two and only raised arms in the room, Mirek trembled, shaken by the realization that he might not see Wesley again. Seeing this, Wes patted him on the back, and ordered Stephen: "Take care of your brother for me."

Eyes one blink away from breaking into tears, Stephen kept his head perfectly still. He hated change. Change always meant misery and loneliness. The life to which he had grown accustomed was barely a life at all, and yet he had made the best of it with Wesley's help. Despite there being no choice in the matter, he was

137

sad to put it behind him—Wesley, Underpool, Mises Tavern, the sea. He considered protesting but answered instead: "Yes sir."

FIFTEEN

Geoffrey Littlefield may not have met Monica's standards for a viable replacement—to continue doing the work that she had earned a notable reputation for in Lancashire—but he was still Alek's best bet for answers concerning England's black-market dealings and best friend to boot. Once Alek had shared key insights into Margaret Green's experience with Danika and had hidden his scrubbing equipment, he took the stairs up twenty storeys and rapped on Geoff's door.

"Who the hell is it?" Geoff roared from the other side. Without a peep hole, he had no real way of knowing whether or not his time had finally come.

"Open up. It's me."

The door swung open to reveal an orderly apartment without any sign of having been lived in. This mirage quickly disintegrated. Holographic projection spheres mounted in the corners of the room flickered off, revealing the room's true, underlying reality. The apartment had the same layout as Alek's and every other unit in the CBLOCK, though it was hard to tell under all the dotgrams, papers, and soiled garments strewn about the place. There were several packed bags and a few other bags in process of being stuffed full of gear. Geoff was the last thing in the room to appear, standing just off to the side and holstering an oversized six shooter.

Geoff had on a pair of long johns. His hairy belly jutted over the elastic waistband on his underwear. "Good lord, Neuhaus. You look like shit."

Alek gestured to enter.

"Yes, yes. Come in."

"That's a nice trick." Alek counted the projection spheres. There were enough to simulate any locale with the kind of detail and scope that could cheat the inner ear and a skeptic's disassociation. "When d'you put those in?"

"Huh?" Geoff looked around the room. "Oh yeah! Few cycles back. Didn't want to keep cleaning up for inspections. Needed a way to hide my lifestyle. And it doesn't hurt that they also spare me a look out them windows. Not a big fan of heights, *as you know*. Anything to ground me is always welcome, real or illusory..." Geoff saw Alek looking for a clear place to stand beside the doorway. "Ah, of course! Real sorry about the mess," he said, pretending to organize amidst

139

the chaos. "I've just been trying to find my journal. *For want of a horseshoe nail!*"

Alek shut the door behind him. He didn't bother looking out Geoff's windows. They had the same view he woke up with and fell asleep to every day for the past several years. Geoff's projectors would have done well to remedy the vista. "Well...How's it going?"

Geoff carefully navigated the mess, a great deal of which was comprised of memory drives. Sidelong to his other business ventures, Geoff Littlefield was both a connoisseur and purveyor of rare memories. Trustworthees and Britons with access to memory-wiping services such as those offered by Alek would often pay to experience second-hand places and things forbidden (for being bourgeois or hateful) or extinct (made so for having been bourgeois or hateful). Curiously, the most popular memories were those with dramatic value—stories told and written by persons with connections to the pre-EDS days.

Geoff grabbed a tin cup. He uncorked a bottle of shower moonshine, filled the cup, and handed it to Alek. It was too early in the morning for tea, which meant it was not too late for a nightcap. He found his own cup and topped it up. "Things have been going a little sideways these past couple days."

"You could say that again." Alek gripped the cup and cleared some rags from the nearest chair. He sat down slowly, feeling an internal weight that any sudden movement might weaponize. "That's actually why I'm here."

"It's why you should be anywhere but here. I've been listening to quite a lot of EDS chatter coming over the pirated lines. There're a number of state officials looking to spend everything they've stolen from the People to secure safety nets for themselves. Black market is red hot. Everyone from the—*oh there you are!*" Geoff stormed across the room and plucked his notebook free from a makeshift shelf. "Everyone from the Deputy Commissar on down to them Underpoolians is worried about the changes London is rolling out."

"The Mental Union, yah mean?" Alek not only had his memory to consult, but Green's as well. His brain's sorting function was working overtime.

Geoff wrapped a piece of twine around his notebook and set it on a side table where he wouldn't lose track of it again. Far more relaxed now that he had his collected thoughts in plain view, he righted a chair and sat down opposite Alek. "Haven't heard anything about a union. There's a cognitive-systems upgrade coming that some are wont to call a patch."

140

Danika had mentioned a patch-over, no doubt linked to the Mental Union.

"Some big scientist they roped in came up with a way to give everyone a proper blank slate and migrate their entire minds into EDS custody. They're going to start rolling it out. Spoke direct with a lady who was on a committee overseeing the Harmony Festival. As soon as everyone gets wiped—" Geoff checked the time. "Not this morning, but tomorrow morning, they're going to execute all of the subversives out front of City Hall. It'll be the New Order's first collective memory."

Alek nearly choked. "Shit. So it's not just the guardians getting *upgraded*?"

Geoff shrugged. "That's what everyone's sayin'. Festival kicks off on day three. They've got the workshops printing out banners and decomposable confetti 'round the clock."

"Harmony Festival, eh?"

Geoff rubbed his legs. "Yup. Like the demsock's solidarity cycle, only with a bigger parade. I tell yah, Neuhaus, it all sounds like oblivion. End of the road for those in your business, eh? No memories and no inclination to run afoul of the law."

Alek was overwhelmed. He knew how bad the Mental Union was from Margaret Green's own fear, and that fear was predicated on the misbelief that it was still at least twenty cycles off. Between Danika's suspicion and Geoff's speculation, it was clear there wasn't much time to throw a wrench in the gears. Alek nodded while trying to wrap his head around the proposed technology—how the state could fully hijack people's minds without killing them or turning the country into a vegetable stir fry.

"End of the road for mine, anyway. I've got to get the hell out of here. Going to squeeze these plonkers for everything they've got; maybe get an outgoing security chit and be clear of this mess. Brazil, maybe? God, I hope they're not still commies." Geoff saw that he was depressing Alek or at the very least overloading his concern. "Oh well, the boom before the eternal bust. So to what do I owe the honor of this visit? The great Lethe is going to bless me with forgetfulness?"

Alek shifted uneasily in his seat and scratched his occipital implant sites. "Did a job last night." He jerked forward. "This blank slate nonsense—what are you going to do about it?"

"Pardon?"

"You've got to have figured out a way around it—some sort of mental block to counter the *Patch Over*?"

"I do and I don't, depending on how you look at it. There's no more getting by as a subversive; no more passing as a citizen, if you

141

take my meaning. I've heard a lot of talk about technology that'd overload the government systems while synching you with some satellite or the like, so that your mind is untouchable and forever yours but..." Geoff made a crude gesture. "Talk is cheap, eh. Only costly when the screws overhear yah."

Monitoring his breathing to avoid succumbing to panic, Alek sat like a Buddha with his hands clasped in his lap. "You didn't answer my question."

"I don't have a block or a reroute. I've just got a way to go fully organic: a cortical loader. You and I can do it, because we've got Monica's tech blocking the excess data that the demsocks fill everyone else's heads with. Can't scale it up though, as it's a little more tricky with normies. Yah see, it can eliminate redundancies, but the genius of the EDS' useless data is that it's indistinguishable from real memory. Even if we could get around that, the screws would clue into the brain drain, and figure out a way to prevent people from withdrawing their minds from the brain banks."

Clutching the sides of his head, Alek grunted. "So unless we found a way to get England's data out of the cypulchres without the state hampering the withdrawal or deleting important data on their end, your cortical loader is the only way to cut free?"

"If by cypulchres, you mean their brain banks, then yeah. Anything stored in 'em the demsocks will be able to delete, copy, or mess with."

"Alright. To hell with it." Alek realized that he could no longer risk having any part of his mind under EDS control, even if that meant excommunication from the state and its services. He reached into his jacket and pulled out a wad of cash. "I got two hundred pounds for you to do it now."

Geoff twinkled his fingers and pursed his lips. "Oh, Neuhaus!" he said in an affected voice. "Do I look like some kind of tart?"

Alek slackened and smiled. He slapped Geoff's knee. "Thanks, mate."

Geoff grabbed the cash and pretended to count it. The transaction was a formality at this point, especially with the black market's value system about to undergo a massive realignment. He dug through another pile of laundry and metal, and found his cortical loader. It was no larger than a thumb, but was capable of mapping a brain and targeting particular circuits for organic data pulses. "Jam this into yah head." He held the device out to Alek. When Alek didn't grab it right away, Geoff got up and plugged the device into Alek's freshly-reopened implant site. He seized Alek's moonshine and gulped it down. "Won't hurt you any. It's just going to synch with your exo-cortex and pull any data you don't already have down organically. Like I said, damned thing even eliminates redundancies. If you're lucky, yah might be smarter as a result." Geoff patted Alek on the shoulder and whispered for only his own benefit. "Probably not though."

Geoff said it wouldn't hurt, although the sudden intake of memory was certainly discombobulating. Alek swayed to and fro, face running through varied expressions. "Jesus, what have you done to me?"

"It's okay, mate." Geoff pulled his chair closer to Alek and held him steady. "It'll be over in a minute. Just remember, you're offline moving forward. Can't go back to the DIHA. Can't go to work. Can't be scanned by a guardian. You're persona non grata."

"Reclamations..." Alek began to salivate. He saw his life in still frames. Each frame encapsulated a moment, but was taken out of sequence and overlaid as if Alek was snapping along in a jumbled flip book comprised of marked-up transparencies.

While babysitting the bad trip, Geoff tried to make small talk. "Did a job, you say? Whereabouts?"

"Yeah." Cross-eyed, Alek worked on keeping his head up despite the little node beaming a lifetime back into his brain. "06. Trustworthee. Pulled some experience firsthand."

Geoff's eyebrows stooped over his pink eyelids. "Heh. How's pulling jobs without the missus?"

One still frame froze atop all others. Though other memories distilled down to thumbnail images effaced it, discoloured it, and monstrofied its subjects, it was nevertheless powerful. In it, Alek saw Monica. She wore a white gown that Evaun had made for her out onto the rooftop of CBLOCK32. She sat near the transmitter array, bathed in its green light. It was then and there, years earlier, that Alek realized life was still worth living. That was the first of many nights together that they serenaded each other and danced slowly, tirelessly, without feeling trapped or horribly disembodied. They laughed and experimented with different melodies. It had been ages since they had heard them or had the courage to sing them. After finding one that they both enjoyed, they managed harmonies and swayed about in the moonlight. The image disappeared. Alek braced himself for a fistfight or tears, and he wasn't particularly one for leakage.

Noticing Alek's agitation, Geoff leaned forward. "Sorry mate. My mouth moves before my brain's started sometimes."

"No, it's..." Alek unknotted his fists and clutched the memex pendent above his heart. "It's just different now. No fun left in it to be sure." Alek looked around for his moonshine. His vision was clear again, which helped him see that his drink had been drunk. Whatever work Geoff's device was still up to was subliminal. "Anyway, this client worked for the Ministry of Cultural Equity. She got mixed up with some lughead from Reclamations named Townley. Scott Townley. They found a painting in Blackburn that the EDS wanted desperately, but that some foreign buyers wanted even more, the latter in exchange for South American amnesty. D'ya catch wind about such a sale? Anyone talking about some kind of painting?"

Geoff didn't need to respond. He perked up right away and vaulted out of his chair. He rushed into the kitchen, opened one of the lower cupboards, and yanked out a Harpocrate jammer, the shape and size of an old car battery. Swearing under his breath, he lugged it over, and set it down at Alek's feet.

"What's this all about?" asked Alek, shifting his feet away from the jammer.

With a finger pressed to his lips, Geoff turned on the machine. "Don't worry. Won't interfere with the cortical loader." He turned the dial jammer up to its maximum setting. Apparently no topic they previously broached had been as offensive or as dangerous as the one they were getting into now, such that Geoff needed to block out the eyes and ears that had been blind and deaf to all of his other crimes. "This is the first I've heard of Townley, but I've heard a great deal about this painting." He checked the cortical loader sticking out of Alek's head. "Another minute left. You've got too much on your mind!"

"The painting?"

Geoff's dissipating smile turned over to a businesslike glower. "Big broadcast on that sale. Lot of interest from a lot of warring parties."

"Why's it so important?"

Geoff unplugged the cortical loader and pocketed it. "I dunno. It's got to have something to do with the patch or that union of yours. I mean, even the new commissar is hunting it down."

Alek leaned forward, mainly to be better heard over the hum of the Harpocrate jammer interfering with the scans of inquiring minds. "*I know where it is.*"

Geoff stared down at Alek without a coherent emotion to wrap his face around. He looked confused and hungry. "Piss off."

"Honest to God."

"Ha!" Geoff looked over to his packed bags and took a deep breath. He crossed his arms to stop himself from shaking with

144

excitement, and then freed one arm to point at the ceiling with a fleshy exclamation mark. "That's it, mate! That's our ticket out!"

"Yours, mine, Dan's, and Monica's."

Geoff winced. His mental dampener wasn't disabled like Alek's. *By choice.* The pain that kept everyone else passive and manipulable titillated him. After all, he believed that all of his pain was causally coupled to damage done to the regime. This contrarian masochism made him an intellectual, relatively speaking; not the other way around. And yet, Alek's invocation of his late wife really pushed Geoff past his acceptable pain threshold. "Dan, sure, but Monica? Monica's dead, mate. I think my resynch messed with your head a wee bit."

"No. She's alive. I know it. I saw it on the news. I saw *her* on the news. And my last client confirmed it."

Trying hard not to alienate his ticket to sanctuary, Geoff turned his wince into an elastic grin. "Right, right. Well, we can take the contract together. Sell the painting to the highest bidder. And split up our safe passage four ways."

"Five ways."

"Huh?"

"Danika has a plus one."

"Right..." Massaging his forehead, Geoff said staidly: "Just so you know, I don't plan on chasing ghosts with you."

"That's fine. I do need you to help me track down a man, though. We've got to pay Scott Townley a visit. No Townley, no painting."

"What? He have it or something?"

Alek tried to collect his thoughts and Green's. As for the latter, all that remained after the resynch were his own memories of having experienced her memories, which were far more incomplete secondhand. He could see the painting and where it was kept, and he knew that wherever Townley was, it wouldn't be far away and vice versa. "Yeah. Plus I have something for him."

Geoff hid his concern behind a sip of the residuals of Alek's moonshine. "Alright. Best crack on."

"Who do we sell to?"

The question seemed to barb Geoff. He put his hand on his chest and jutted his chin out. "Good question. I have a better one for you: *where is* the painting?"

Alek laughed. "You moron. I'm not going to betray a friend in the final hours."

Geoff scratched his belly as if it was essential to jogging his memory, and winced with pain once more. "I got a throwaway

145

connection to some foreign broad. Can only call her on the cable once, then her line reconfigures. Her name's Catharine or Castille or something."

"Cassandra," Alek murmured under his breath.

"Yeah. Maybe. Wait! *How'd yah know?* If it's the same person...This one deals in appropriated art. Sells the stuff to the Vatican museums over in Covington, Kentucky. Anyway, hers is the top bid. As a matter of fact, the only other big bid is actually just an EDS threat and demand. Cassandra offered me enough to buy my own Caribbean island the first time deals were making their rounds. That would have been a couple few years back now. Man, time flies."

Alek pushed away from Geoff, screeching his chair legs against the linoleum. He fought through a dizzy spell and stood up slowly. "I've got jigsaw memories from the trustworthee. I can see it. I know where it is, though only in relation to where Townley will be. I'm not trying to pull wool over your eyes."

The animal panic that had excited Geoff's nerves had passed, mainly on account of the moonshine. "I know and I know you well enough to know. Mate, we're going to get out of here! Maybe have a coffee for once instead of this eco-tea bullshit."

They shook hands to officiate their partnership.

"Coffee'd be great." Alek closed his eyes and imagined who or what besides Monica he would like to see again: "A steak, a bottle of wine, and a book!"

Geoff dragged the Harpocrate jammer back over to its cleared patch in the mess. "I've never had a steak. I think I'd start with a burger."

"Yeah? Fugitive's choice." Alek looked around the room and began to feel claustrophobic. He wanted to get a move on but every movement felt like the wrong one. He shook his head clear. "The painting—you don't really know what it does, eh?"

"What do you mean, *'what it does?'* It's a painting, mate. You look at it. You tell your friends you looked at it. And then the demsocks cut your brain out."

"Didn't occur to you that there might be something special about it? You said so yourself it has something to do with the Patch Over."

Geoff pulled a panel free from the wall. There were at least a dozen automatic rifles stacked together. He was more interested in the box full of grenades on the shelf above them, partly hidden by insulation. "It's a painting of some royal family, *apparently*. There's big money to be made off of nostalgia, especially when it comes to old-timey imagery."

146

Alek poured himself some moonshine and sat down. "The Family, eh?" The painting he had seen in Green's memories was that of an old man; a portrait; no family in it and certainly nothing special about him.

Agreeing with some internal directive, Geoff wandered off into the bedroom. He returned carrying an overstuffed crate of ammunition. He set it down and began sorting bullet types, all of which had been dumped into the same container. "Alright, Neuhaus." He handed Alek one of the rifles from his secret shelf, and gestured for him to load his own magazines. "Is Danika in? You talk to her already?"

"Sort of."

Geoff shook his head disapprovingly and handed Alek a high-capacity magazine.

"She has more to lose than either of us."

"Not true. But a friend in need..."

"A friend with a guardian van." Alek loaded the drum magazine and slid it into his rifle. "A *good* friend."

Geoff chuckled. "True. Very true." He set his own rifle down on the countertop, and began digging through his cache and stuffing his pockets full of explosives. He didn't have any armour stored away, as there would be no point in wearing it. EDS plasma could burn through anything that sold on the black market topside.

Alek scrutinized the ready rifle gifted him. Geoff had built a silencer into its barrel—that or its previous owner had. "The place will be jam-packed with guardians and the DSSP. They were always there, milling about in my memories—*her memories*—of the place. An army with these wouldn't pass go."

"Who needs an army when you work there?" Geoff's waist seemed to shrink as his confidence grew. Purpose transformed him into something besides a pitiful couch urchin; something passable, all depending on the test. He got on his computer and began programming them both identity chits.

"Wait, we go as ourselves?" Sneaking into bedrooms and flushing memories hardly seemed the necessary practice for breaking into a militarized state department. Alek's gut burbled. Geoff's approach seemed to matter less and their destination all the more.

"Like you said. An army won't pass go." Geoff summoned Alek over to his side with a wave, and wirelessly tethered him to the machine. There was a beep. "Alright. You are now Brant Czapran." He tethered himself, pulled up a different Reclamation-employee's file on his computer, and changed his own identity. "And I am Delilah Mortimer."

Alek shook his head. "Delilah Mortimer?"

"Don't judge." Geoff flexed his biceps. "I make a good Delilah."

The bravado turned Alek's stomach into another knot. He had seen men joke around before dying as someone else's punchline. "Alright, Delilah. Don't make me wish I hadn't put my faith in Geoff."

"Brant, babe, *I've got you*." Geoff grabbed the remaining explosives from the cubby hole including a handful of grenades. He armed two bricks with proximity triggers—enough to obliterate any intruders, but not enough to turn his neighbours to cinders—lay them by the door, and turned his projection spheres back on so that the mess disappeared and the apartment looked empty. "Now, how much do you have saved up?"

"Besides the cash I just gave you? Couple thousand greenback, few hundred quid..." While enumerating his wealth of currency backed by institutions in dubious shape and force, Alek affixed his gaze to one of the projection spheres Geoff had adjusted, or rather to where it had been before hiding itself in the illusion. He plucked and held it in his outstretched palm. "This have a built-in camera?"

Troubled by Alek's lack of focus, Geoff grunted. "Yeah, what of it?"

"I'm bringing it along. Just add it to my bill."

They locked the door on the boobytrapped apartment for the last time, and set downstairs to meet with a friend of Geoff's in the building's tertiary common room. Off in one corner, there were a dozen bicycles bolted down at the center of a screened-in simulation of a canyon meadow. Those early-risers active on the bikes barely peddled. The virtual grass and sunlight mediated by their actual eyes had them mesmerized. Between the bicycles and the square tables haphazardly arranged along the edge of a dry water fountain, there was a confession booth. It was ten feet tall with enough girth for an underprivileged obese person to cart into, and though made of glass, entirely blacked out. Inside, citizens could anonymously tattle on their neighbours for crimes against the state or conventional infractions, including aggressive speech and airs of superiority.

Geoff's friend nodded from afar, sat at a remote table blocked from view of the glassed-in monitoring station by the confession booth. Alek recognized him as an old client. *Lyndon Charest.*

Lyndon wore a non-regulation navy pea coat over his assigned clothing, which he kept bright-white and ironed. The jacket

148

sleeves were four inches too short so his gnarled hands stuck out like rusty hooks. They came to life when Alek presented a drive primed with his offering. Crypto signatures attached to ten years of savings were ready to be transferred for services yet-to-be rendered. Lyndon stuffed the drive into his jacket pocket. "What year is it?"

Alek massaged his implant site, still swollen, and sought out the meaning of what he took for a cryptic question. "Not year twenty-five like the EDS say, if that's what you're getting at."

"2060-something," answered Geoff. A look of self-doubt came over him. "2070?"

Lyndon became more animated. He looked over at the cyclists. "Ask them and you'd discover that civilization is, as your friend said, only in its twenties. Not the first time that liars have sought to call the preceding age of light *dark*." He reached down and produced a brown parcel. "Two Reclamation uniforms. They won't fit proper, but what do you expect given an hour's notice?" Lyndon was the deputy overseer in CBLOCK32's laundromat. He probably just grabbed the first two blue and white uniforms off the press.

While Geoff settled down beside Lyndon, Alek inspected the parcel. He undid the knot holding it together and tore into the packaging. "Nice work, old man."

Lyndon tilted his head as if pushed to the side by Geoff's praise. "Yes, well—like I said—they won't be a perfect fit, although if you're walking into a gov'ment department downtown, you've got bigger problems than hems."

"*Seems* that way," Geoff said with a big fat grin.

Alek reached down into his duffel bag, now packed and misshapen around guns and Geoff's explosives, and yanked out his scrubbing gear. One brief look around the room was enough to determine that anything extra to their present subversion would land them all in prison. "Where do you want to do your wipe?"

The question seemed to disgust the old man. "Wipe? I don't need to wipe," he said, easing back into his seat and into the realization that he had finally struck it rich. He may have been too old to enjoy the illegal services he now could afford, but he was certainly not too old for the satisfaction of buying power. "I'll be long gone before they realize those uniforms are missing."

Alek rolled his eyes and motioned to leave, but Geoff grabbed his arm and tried negotiating with the old man. "Neuhaus and I just don't want to be on your conscience when you get yourself caught."

"You said it yourself, Geoff," interjected Alek. "Everything is about to change and we've already assumed greater risk." Alek put the parcel into his duffel bag, now stretched to its limit, and stood,

149

this time pulling Geoff up along with him. "Forget it—let the codger remember with advantages."

Geoff rapped his knuckles on the table and quickly collected them with a smile. He shook Lyndon's hand. "I hope you find peace, L.C. Maybe we'll see each other soon. Who knows?"

Lyndon waved Geoff closer. His whisper carried so Alek could hear it plain. "They've flipped a few of our kind, Littlefield. Keep your wits about you." Without so much as an ounce of a care for subtlety, Lyndon leaned past Geoff's ear and gestured to Alek. "You sure he's not your Judas?"

Geoff grinned. "I'm sure. We'll be fine. As for you, get out of Blackpool before your next synch."

SIXTEEN

The General ordered everyone to arms and for the evacuation of the southern portion of Underpool. Noncombatants collected their belongings, and departed for the Sanctuary north of the underground city. The militants lined up along one side of the grotto for their turn inside the armoury, accessible via a torch-lit passageway stage right. Inside the armoury, Colonel Phan parceled out weapons and gear. This was no wartime socialism. It was transactional: soldiers were trading time and blood for capability and lead. In the end, they would be proprietors, either of headstones or of their own English gardens.

The case containing the nuclear mortars had been dragged up onto the stage and its contents divvied up. Two went to Miller, just in case he was feeling ambitious after securing The Family painting; two went to Zoya Khatri for an opportunistic strike; another two were reserved for McGregor's commandos who planned to assault the English Broadcast Station in Blackpool from the north; and the remaining four were given to the Engineer Corps whose orders were to strike relay stations in Lancaster and Southport. The presumption that no one would prematurely activate or drop the bombs was hopeful at best, even though great emphasis was placed on the weapons' volatility.

Stephen and Mirek sat on the empty case. There they eavesdropped on the officers' mission briefings. Still anchored to the podium, McGregor feverishly crystallized the plan in every squad commander's mind, and then handed each of them an untraceable ear piece to stay abreast of the race to the English Broadcasting Station and its relay stations in neighbouring divisions.

Once Wesley Miller had given McGregor his two cents and received a nickel in new information, he led Cassandra and Dax Thomar over to the back of the line. Their particular mission required the three of them—or at the very least Wes and Dax—to go in wearing exosuits. There was no point in testing bone against steel especially when there was so much steel in the streets of England designed to break bone. The exosuits would keep them moving until they gave up the ghost.

Through the slivers between the bodies in line, Stephen watched Wes get progressively more excited as he neared the armoury. Something about him had changed. He looked younger. He hadn't yet been fitted for his exosuit though he already stood

151

straighter, taller. Stephen wondered if it had merely been the presence of a beautiful woman that rejuvenated him, but looking closer when the shifting bodies made it possible, he saw that Miller barely paid Cassandra any mind. Brigadier Miller was afforded by fate and circumstance another shot at becoming consequential, and it showed.

"Some waste of time this is," said Mirek, head between his knees. "Everyone's going into battle and we're running away."

Stephen pried his eyes off of Wes and put his cap back on. "We're not running away, mate. We're going to die trapped over Continen'al Democratic Socialist waters in a Pingo jet with King Khatri's daughter."

Major Zoya Khatri surprised Stephen and Mirek from behind, and gave Stephen a good smack. "King Khatri's daughter doesn't need you chavs to tag along." She had in her hand a transponder given her by Colonel Phan, helpful only to the strategists helping monitor and coordinate the Resistance's progress in the field.

Blushing, Stephen tried to repair the damage done but could only stammer. "Wh-wha-what I meant..."

"Heya Major. Don't mind Stevie. He was just giving me morale a boost."

Zoya sat down between Stephen and Mirek, driving them to the edges of the case. She had already clipped her radio unit into her ear and was attuned to the crackling pulse of the Resistance. Something besides Stephen's excuse drove her to agreement. "Yeah. Sublevel fifteen. Make sure we've cleared everyone out." She looked to the young men seated on either side of her. "No more of that talk. No one's dying."

"Except for the soshies catching our ordnance," said one of two haggard soldiers schlepping up over from the radio room.

"Sure. Except for the soshies..." Zoya got up to greet the soldiers. "Lieutenant Lloyd Barnard, Corporal Jay Wu; meet privates Stephen Nowak and Mirek Dubchek."

Stephen and Mirek leapt to their feet. They attempted and aborted a syncopated salute, and awkwardly shook hands with Lloyd, a slab of northern granite with sledgehammers for arms, and Jay, a spry Hong Kongese dissident with a black mohawk raised above a scalp full of grey stubble.

Zoya tapped her ear piece. "You lads get your radios?"

Lloyd answered: "Yeah. Like having a beehive in your ear."

"We get 'em?" asked Mirek.

Ignoring Mirek, the Major prodded Jay. "Yeah? You get one?"

152

Jay nodded while sizing Stephen up. "Good work finding the nukes, Nowak."

"Yeah," grumbled Lloyd. "It'll be nice to give the enviromarxists a black eye for a change." Lloyd crouched down beside the case and ran his hand along its warm surface with religious intensity. "This it?" He looked up to Stephen. "This here?"

"Yeah. Or it was."

Zoya held one of the mortars up like a sacred idol. Lloyd slowly rose and marveled at the destructive ostrich egg. He recognized the warning label on its side. "Heh. We better all die today or we're going to die of cancer tomorrow."

"Cancer?" Mirek re-registered his body's bruises for symptoms of something far worse. He clenched his teeth and tried his best not to bug-out while subtly probing his body for tumours.

"Relax, mate." Stephen brushed shoulders with Mirek. "I'll personally print you replacement guts."

Mirek shoved Stephen back. "You slept with the confounded things in your room. You'll be the first to fall to pieces!"

"Alright, alright." Zoya looked each of the men up and down as if their costumes mattered. Like her father, she was a good judge of character. It wasn't merely an inherited compliment her brothers-in-arms paid her. She had never lost a man on a mission, and had been given enough missions to make that mean something. Part of her success was her ability to size up a soldier at first blush—to determine on the basis of how he held his head or stood at ease or spoke, abstractly or concretely, how he might perform under pressure. It was a family knack verging on pseudoscience, more voodoo than psychology, and she was good at it. "It's just the five of us headed west." Zoya gathered the men around her, pleased by what she had before her.

Jay Wu figured Zoya was joking. When she refused to parrot his smile, he took a step back. "A major should be commandin' a battalion, not running around with fewer than a dirty half-dozen."

If she hadn't already made her mind up about Wu, this may have been a disqualifier for a prospective teammate. After all, machismo contingent upon numbers and strength of force is a chemical consequence of certainty, not a product of conviction. Fortunately, Jay had both. He would now have to rely solely upon his conviction as the basis of any bravado moving forward.

"Shit, Major—Jay's right for once," Lloyd said, scrutinizing Stephen and Mirek even closer with the understanding that he might come to depend upon them.

153

"I requested a small team. Any bigger and we'll draw attention too early, and the success of our mission depends upon stealth."

Lloyd's eyes darted from Jay to the nuclear mortar. "Lot of eggs in just one basket is my only concern."

Zoya summoned Lloyd closer, and set one leg down on the case. She opened her hand and a holographic map manifested itself over her palm. It depicted the Irish coast. "Tearaght is where we're headed. S'a little island off County Kerry. Once airborne, we're going to have to move fast; first, south to Wexford, then west along the Irish Sea Wall. We have codes for Continental airspace, though it's anyone's guess if they'll still be good, so presume it'll be a wild ride. Jay—that means I expect you to take your tablets."

Jay made a mocking smile and rolled his eyes.

"Hold on one second," said Lloyd, setting a hand on Jay's shoulder. "A small team I can understand. But at least replace the kids with experienced killers."

"I thought we moved past that, Lieutenant." Zoya pointed at Mirek, mistaking him for the one with the experience trading with Carrella, the Preston tinkerer. "Brig Miller and the General say he knows the man with the jet." She oriented her point towards Stephen. "And he's glued to this one like a demsock to hypocrisy."

"Hey now," said Stephen. "I think you've gone cross-eyed."

Finished taking questions, Zoya posed her own: "Where's the jet?"

Stephen was quick to assert his knowledge: "In Preston near the Pingo black market. Y'know? Where the soshies run their side-hustles."

Jay piped in: "How're we getting there? By foot? House to house? Street to street?"

Stephen shrugged.

Lloyd, finally resigned to the team to which he had been assigned, nudged Zoya. "I have a buddy still tethered to the EDS programme. He drives trucks up and down the countryside. Does a job here and there for the triads, but he's on our list of friendly subversives. I reckon he could drive us just the same, unless you're set on a stroll through the brickworks."

"I'm taking the truck." Stephen was hasty in replying because it had been ages since he had been on a drive-along; not since driving through northern Germany. *Would be a lark this one last time.*

Zoya oriented Lloyd towards to the radio room. "The driver's name Byron Grimsby?"

154

"How did you know?" he said, looking back at the Major over his shoulder.

It was her job to know. The extent of her knowledge on her team would no doubt irk the four of them, Lloyd in particular, who she had selected not only because of his experience piloting drones—as close as most Underpoolians had come to flying—but also on account of his various questionable affiliations with subversives topside. "It's in your file courtesy of...*you!*" Zoya pushed him along. "Get someone on the comms team to package a transmission. We need a response within the hour or we'll have to dangle from carrier drones. Tell him where we're headed but nothing else."

"Yes sir." Lloyd marched over to the radio room. His voice boomed inside—the lieutenant on duty was an old friend.

Mirek pulled on Zoya's sleeve. "Eh, what're we doing after we drop 'em bombs?"

Zoya shrugged him off and chuckled. "Focus on what we do in the meantime."

"Fair enough," replied Mirek. He looked wild-eyed at Stephen. "I just wanna know whether t'make a parachute out Steve's panties."

Jay rolled his eyes. "Ah Lordy. You sure about these plonkers?"

"Oh, I'm sorry," said Zoya. She grabbed Jay by the fin of his Mohawk and rattled his brains. "Did I just lose your approval?" She released him and pinched his cheek. "If you and Barnard can't handle the job with the variables I've plugged in, I'll swap you both out for a more capable pair."

Jay was red with rage. The veins in his forehead looked ready to pop. He hated to be touched even more than he hated to be underestimated.

Stephen interrupted: "Corporal Wu seems better than a lot of the other screws around here."

Zoya and Jay smiled at one another, and then at Stephen. They had almost forgotten he was there and would otherwise have been content to rile each other up. It wasn't the first time, which is precisely how Zoya knew what buttons of Jay's to push.

"You heard the man," said Jay. He threw his arm around Stephen's neck, and shook him like an old chum. "Where this one goes, I follow."

Stephen, Mirek, Zoya, Lloyd, and Jay navigated a series of cramped tunnels towards the southernmost end of Underpool. Dressed in

155

Nephilim suits and helmets seized from failed raiders, they silently took in what on another day would have passed for banal. However, with the corridors now rigged with explosives, primed to blow at the first detection of EDS invaders, it was most likely their last time in Underpool, forcing them to appreciate all that they had taken for granted.

Still getting use to his spinal brace and added heft, Stephen tried to focus on movement alone but his mind strayed. He considered the General's strategy concerning the Irish bombing campaign. If the Continental Democratic Socialists' early-warning system was knocked out, the demsocks and the Chinese would undoubtedly send both an aerial and a naval fleet out to investigate the damage and reinforce against additional attacks. An American assault group could drop out of warp and handily destroy one wing of the Democratic Socialists' air force—and sink just as many boats—before ever making landfall. Perhaps the General was keeping his cards close to his chest. Perhaps the order he gave was to create a diversion as opposed to razing the foundation of the enemy's coastal prescience. Time would tell, but in the space in-between, the plan would remain the same.

"Boy, do you look like the dog's bollocks in that suit," Mirek said, holding his face mask up. "Pity the armoury kept your ball cap though."

Stephen slid his face mask up to showcase his displeasure at the loss of a good hat.

Mirek probed the gash in the torsal armour where a Resistance high-caliber round had punched through. "Mine's got a bleedin' hole in it."

"No one will pay it much notice," grumbled Lloyd. "And if they do, they'll be close enough to know to make another."

Mirek slapped his chest. "S'all good. Better for me circulation." Glancing at Stephen's unblemished armour, Mirek veered over. "C'mon. You're the more nimble one. How about we tradesies?"

"Piss off, will yah?!" Stephen yelled. He shoved Mirek into the tunnel wall, realizing only upon hearing a clink that he could have blown the two of them up and anyone else within a mile of them.

Zoya appropriated Mirek's satchel containing the warheads, and glowered at the both of them. "Enough."

"Reconsidering your squad, are yah now, Major?" asked Jay, smoking a Williams cigar and stomping along.

Zoya changed her pace to match Lloyd's and grabbed his forearm. "Your mate, the driver—"

156

"Ol' By-ron?"

"Byron Grimsby...He sounded whacked out on the radio."

"Sure did." Lloyd enjoyed the attention Zoya was paying him, and hammed it up accordingly. "Until he heard my soothing voice. We go way back..."

"How does he keep a radio if he's plugged in?"

"He's semi-annual for synchronization. Dumps bodies for the EDS wearing them brass nametags. They cut him 'nough slack for him to remain useful and for them to remain in power."

"And the Crossroads? Why can't he meet us on the shore?"

The more Lloyd spoke, the less self-conscious he became. His voice became less gravelly, which apparently was something of an affectation. "Crossroads used to be a rough neighbourhood, full of reds. Now it's just leftovers. S'where I used to trade ol' Grimsby booze for intel after Colonel Phan brought me in. It's as safe as demsock territory comes or goes. The soshies zoned it for new CBLOCKs that never came. Seems t'English population is always shrinking."

"You trust him?"

"Oh yeah. As much as you'd trust me."

Zoya nearly knocked herself out as she grabbed her face with an armoured hand. "For crying out loud!"

Lloyd looked to Jay for support.

"Grimsby will be fine," said Jay, expelling a plume of cedar-smelling smoke.

"It's Carrella I'm worried about," Lloyd opined.

Stephen glared at Lloyd. Lloyd was right to worry, but Stephen felt that this was more a criticism of him than the Preston tinkerer or anything else.

"The man lives by his lonesome, which means he's been cuttin' off helping hands along with demsock gauntlets. *But Byron?* I'd trust him with Jay's life."

Mirek spat and pointed two fingers in Lloyd's direction. "Grimsby can suck it." Unbeknownst to everyone else, this had become a competition of loyalties. "Carrella isn't half as crazy as my mate here, and Stephen's only half as crazy as the Major. So do the math!"

Stephen laughed. He was glad he had involved Mirek. He couldn't imagine the pressure of being the clumsiest fool in the pack. As he laughed he felt the bulge of the whisky bottle he was smuggling to Carrella to sweeten the deal, which somehow reminded him of the deal the Major had signed off on concerning Grimsby. "You've got Byron's wipe handy?" Stephen asked Zoya. Lloyd may have

157

forgotten, but it was clear from the radio call they all sat in on that Byron Grimsby would only drive them to Preston if they would clear his conscience as soon as they arrived at their destination. Though semi-annual, Grimsby couldn't risk walking into an unplanned synchronization with treason on his conscience.

"Yeah." Zoya opened one flap of her camo jacket. Neural net trodes dangled from an inner pocket. "A waste if you ask me, granted that by tomorrow he won't need it."

Dozens of heavily-armed Resistance fighters who were headed to protect the northern Sanctuary edged past Zoya's squad on the way. Those who weren't excited by the evacuation warning were alternatively motivated by Congress' plan to flood all of the southern tunnels, including the Resistance's subterranean farms. The days of eking out an existence on England's fringe were over, for better or for worse.

"Just look at all these able-bodied recruits, will yah?" Jay said to Lloyd, louder than necessary so Stephen and Mirek would overhear.

"Nah, mate." Lloyd clipped his rocket launcher to his chest plate to free up his hands to gesticulate wildly. "See, we need us some guys who ha'n't fired a weapon in order to convince the enemy to play nice for the sake of equity."

Jay spewed smoke and grinned. "Right, right. You're always right. S'why they made you lieutenant"

Growing impatient with the chuckleheads behind them, Stephen called out to Zoya. "Your da—he fought with Wes, yeah?"

"Until the end," Zoya replied. Whatever sentimentality she had brought onto the stage in the grotto she had left there. Her face and the look of focus on it were set in stone.

There was a flourish of colour down the way. A woman wearing a checkered blue-and-white dress and a pink bonnet led a single-file line of children at least fifteen deep, all similarly wearing their Sunday best.

Mirek nearly had a conniption. "Fiona!" he cried.

The young woman didn't recognize Mirek at first, and when she did—to Stephen's surprise—she lit up even brighter as red flooded her cheeks. "Merry!" She ordered the children to stand along the side to let passersby past, and threw her hands out in anticipation of a warm embrace.

Lloyd and Jay carried on while Zoya slowed to sate her own romantic voyeurism.

Mirek hugged Fiona tightly, and let her go to take in her attire. He took off his helmet. "You look lovely!"

"Burial clothes is all."

"Oh!" Mirek took offense to the notion that anything bad might happen to her. "Well then—bury me some're close and I'll rest happy."

Fiona waved coyly to Stephen, who she had taken for the guardian of Mirek's heart. She turned to Mirek with concern widening her eyes. "Where're you off to dressed like that?"

Mirek couldn't help but blush. He hid the gash in his armour and puffed his chest. "Top secret mission. Can't say much." He looked to the Major and then to Stephen, both of whom looked on with condoling smiles.

"Really?" Fiona's surprise may have confirmed Lloyd's and Jay's doubts about Mirek, but they had ambled a good ways ahead. She subtly glanced over at the Major who confirmed the statement with a grim nod.

"Well," she said, all of a sudden flustered, "I pray for your safe return."

Mirek looked back to Stephen nervously, and then quickly and awkwardly kissed Fiona on the cheek. She didn't seem bothered by it—if anything, a little remorseful that the gesture had come so late in the times and with such little time left for a follow up.

The children lined up behind her began to gossip and giggle. Fiona shushed them, and clasped Mirek's hands. "We'll be in the Sanctuary excitedly waiting for your return." She stepped aside so that her students and the orphans placed in her care could apprize their lowly champion. "Won't we?"

After much whispered deliberation, the children giggle-shouted: "Yes, Ms. Marsh."

Fiona squeezed Mirek's hands, nodded respectfully to the Major and Stephen both, and guided her lambs back to the heart of Underpool and beyond.

Once Mirek's crush had made it out of earshot, Stephen rushed him and slapped him on the back. "You scoundrel! Stealing a young girl's heart on the eve of war?!"

"Come on, you two. At this rate, the pheromones will beat us to Preston." Zoya resumed her default staidness and spurred them forward.

"We've always been at war," Mirek whispered back to Stephen. "But now I've something behind me worth fighting for."

159

The tunnel ended in the basement of a dilapidated post office. Zoya and her squad crept up two sets of creaky stairs. The large room—which had actually been two rooms before the wall separating customer from postal clerk had been torn down—and the old stone enclosing it, had been spared demolition on account of the fact that the pre-EDS revolutionaries had used it as a propaganda office.

The proto-demsocks' bloodthirsty posters and pamphlets gummed up the floor. "Bash the Fash...Feed the Rich to the Poor...Equity is a Riot Away...Guaranteed Minimum Income Is the Least We Can Do..." Ironically, the posters' black-masked designers likely ended up dangling by their necks in town squares or worked to death in EDS re-education camps on account of their supposed privilege and low trustvalue potential.

"You've been here before?" Jay asked Lloyd, who seemed to know his way around.

Lloyd nodded. He spotted Mirek digging around amidst the munged-up laminates and mulched paper on the floor. "Oi! Shit-for-brains! There's mines about. You be careful now!"

Mirek didn't give a damn. In fact, Lloyd's warning lent excitement to his curiosity. He stooped down to grab a button off the floor. He wiped it clean. There was a symbol printed on it depicting three black arrows inside a black circle. He turned it to show Stephen. "I told yah!" There had been an ongoing debate between the two of them over whether or not the four-arrow symbol that often appeared on high-ranking EDS officials' jackets had been a revision of some earlier design. Geezers in the Resistance recalled there only being three arrows signifying the revolutionary's tactics for change: violence, education, and elections. Sometime after the hardline socialists took power, the image was co-opted to mean something different altogether. The arrows were instead taken to represent the three enemies of the democratic socialists: the monarchy; so-called fascist organizations, which included any business or institution that turned a profit or wasn't committee-run; and finally the nuclear family. According to Wesley, the fourth arrow added struck at religion, the final enemy of the secular dogmatists—but of course they had weaponized certain radical religious groups to slay their opposition before turning, at last, upon those same useful idiots. "Count 'em, Stevie! Wes was right!"

Stephen rolled his eyes. "A misprint, probably."

"Quiet, *children*," said Jay, nosing over to a window greased with mud and exhaust. He looked out and up the street. "Eh, grumbler," he said to Lloyd. "That the Crossroads there, yeah?"

160

"Yeah," answered Lloyd, pulling the protective caps off of the rockets queued up in his gun's feed. "In all their glory."

The Crossroads, about which there was nothing glorious, weren't too far away; no more than a stone's throw from a good arm.

Zoya skulked around hoping not to find enemies laying in ambush while Stephen, Mirek, and Lloyd joined Jay at the east-facing window to survey their next steps.

The intersection was empty but for Byron Grimsby's truck. Knowing that he had a memory wipe coming his way, he had pulled out all the stops on all of his vices. He sat on the hood of the tan truck smoking a hand-rolled cigarette and drinking a bottle of vodka, kicking his heels into the grill and singing jollily.

Zoya handed the satchel containing the mortars to Stephen, and unfolded the stock on her submachine gun. "Wait for my all-clear."

"All due respect, Major, but Grimsby doesn't know you like he knows me." Lloyd peered back through the window. "He might just take off."

Shaking her head and making her way to the door, Zoya answered: "Give me a minute to size him up. If he takes off, he likely wouldn't have got us to Preston anyhow."

Stephen and Mirek took off their helmets, pressed their faces to the stained-brown window, and watched Zoya walk casually towards the truck with her submachine gun out. They couldn't make out what she yelled to Byron, although whatever it was elicited a friendly wave.

Before even engaging Bryon at the front of the truck, Zoya walked around the vehicle and inspected it for explosives and hidden killer drones. She pulled its tailgate down and peered inside. Once satisfied that Byron was *their kind* of subversive, she ambled over to meet him. He handed her his bottle, which she refused, then put it down to shake her hand.

After about a minute of what Stephen imagined consisted of some penetrating questions on Zoya's part, she waved them over.

"JW," Lloyd said with a sneer. "He tries anything funny, you blast him to kingdom come."

Jay switched off the safety on his repeater rifle. "I thought you said you two were mates."

Lloyd tilted his head and shrugged. "Better safe than gory."

They exited the post office. Stephen and Mirek followed behind cautiously at a distance.

"Lo-Bo, old boy!" Bryon yelled, sliding off of the hood. His excitement fizzled out a few steps towards his supposed friend. He

161

waited for Lloyd to reach him and grabbed him by his forearms, feigning to look him over for damage. "Wha' they been feeding yah? Cabbage and rat meat?"

"Been feeding myself, t'ank you very much!"

Jay walked up to meet his friend's acquaintance. "So you're the Grimsby I haven't heard much about."

"In the flesh." Byron saw Stephen eyeing his cigarette and offered him a drag. Stephen seized it and pulled overzealously. Mirek got in on the action and in three puffs, it was a smoldering butt. "Easy lads..." Byron shook Stephen and Mirek's hands. "So, this it?"

The sun was too much for Zoya—she wasn't accustomed to its brilliance—so she squinted in Byron's general direction, and deprived of one sense, played to her other senses and yelled her reply: "The five of us, as discussed."

Byron did another headcount, undermining everyone else's confidence in his abilities—especially in his ability to drive them safely. "Five...Right-o. Why the Preston RZ?"

Dead set against either of her juniors spilling details about the mission, Zoya intervened. "Scavenging. We need parts for our machines back home."

"Fun so long as you watch out for the Mountain League and the EDS killbots, eh?" Byron sighed. "I'd say the Preston Red Zone's a lot of trouble for scrap, but that's your business."

"Time will tell," Zoya said. She finally broke stone and smiled. "We'll give you a wipe once we arrive alive."

Bryon glimpsed Stephen's satchel. "That for me?"

Zoya patted Bryon on the shoulder. "Trust me. Nothing in there worth the wonder."

"Alright." Grimsby eyed Zoya's gun; he wouldn't dare ask if it was for him. "Now, let's get our little house on wheels in order. If we're pulled over for an inspection, I'm dead if you don't get us moving again. Do whatever it takes. I'm not opposed to you using force. The truck's not mine and they didn't see me grab it, which means two things: it'll be hot as soon as they take inventory tonight and you can drop me off anywhere with a clear head and that'll do me just fine."

Stephen pulled his visor up and adjusted the handgun tucked into the holster edging into his buttock. "Y'ever hear of old man Carrella?"

Zoya and Byron turned to Stephen slowly and disdainfully as if he was a child walking in on an adult conversation.

Byron broke into a nervous smile and then scratched his head. "Carrella. Carlo Carrella? Yeah. He's on our wanted list. The

162

EDS' I mean. You are too, by the way." He gestured to Zoya. "They've got faces of some of the Resistance playing on repeat over the state brain feed. 'Do Not Approach. Keep your eyes peeled and sentcom the Home Defence Department'." He laughed. "Screw 'em. You lot aren't winning, but the fact that the game is still afoot makes me shiver with delight."

Mirek was the first into the back of the truck. He shouted, indifferent to possible spies in the shambles encroaching on the Crossroads: "How long's the ride, mate?"

Zoya and Stephen joined him in the back with the answer following: "Twenty minutes unless we hit a checkpoint." Byron shut the tail gate and began closing the canvas curtain.

"How long if we hit a checkpoint?" asked Stephen, feeling more and more uncomfortable.

Byron panted. "A lifetime."

SEVENTEEN

Geoff wiped drool off of Danika's chin. He had blindfolded her so that the AI historians couldn't get an idea of what they were up to—so they couldn't reverse his handiwork. Taking a guardian offline and reintegrating her memories with her organic brain was no trifling matter.

"You realize," Danika said, slurring her words while propped up against the inner side panel of her guardian van, "That if you put this in pill form, the country would be hooked in no time." Although blindfolded, she knew to direct her comments to the heat emanating off of Geoff. "Shit's crazy, mate."

Alek was sitting in the driver's seat examining a three-dimensional blueprint of the Department of Reclamations. Even after downloading an architect and an engineer's experience files, he couldn't make heads or tails out of the building's security system. He was going so bleary-eyed trying to find a way to brain Scott Townley without getting Geoff or himself killed that the conversation aback the van barely registered. He did, however, know Danika well enough to register the tone and cadence she currently employed as unprecedented. She might have been at risk of good humour.

"Amphetamine of the masses," replied Geoff, wincing at the pain his mental dampeners put him through for manipulating the simple turn-of-phrase. He screwed a silencer onto his rifle to match Alek's so that their first few shots of the day might go unnoticed. "Why've you been helping Neuhaus all this time?" he asked Danika, who had his cortical loader blinking at the side of her head. Geoff hadn't seen any problem in taking advantage of Alek's cerebral vulnerability earlier and Alek was as close a friend as he ever had except for his late dog, so invading Danika's privacy just seemed par for the course. "What made you cross the thin blue line?"

"Lisa…" Danika sounded particularly groggy. She was taking the procedure harder than Alek on account of all of the useless data the EDS had dumped into her external brain. "When they found out I was with child, they put in an order to terminate my pregnancy. *My Patrick*—Sergeant Cornwall from my unit—took the call. He reported our baby stillborn and insisted that I'd been victimized by the whole experience. AI historians weren't active in your head 24/7 back then, so it was his word that counted and his word was enough. Spared me re-education. We didn't know about scrubbers or I guess we knew about 'em, but we didn't know any by name—certainly

164

didn't have anyone that'd help us out. The three of us wouldn't see the next cycle come memory review, so Patrick released a woman from holding that had been charged with neural tampering. Said it was a wrongful arrest. Granted she was a Neuhaus—Alek's wife no less—the truth was she was as guilty as sin, at least in the eyes of the EDS. The tit for her tat was a little more neural tampering. She returned the favour and cleared me and my guilt, but couldn't get to Patrick in time. He was brought into the DIHA early for erratic behaviour. He was a good man."

Sitting cross-legged in front of Danika, Geoff bowed his head. The story had moved him and stuck a frog in his throat. "Right. They didn't review his memories?"

Danika took her blindfold off and used it to wipe away a lone tear. "He didn't give them anything to review. He disarmed a guard on the line and that was it."

"Monica introduced me to Danika," said Alek. He slipped off of the front seat, and joined them in the back with the Reclamations blueprint oscillating above his cupped hands. "I told you. She's solid. A little greedy, but solid."

Danika threw two fingers up to Alek, then massaged her temples. "Is it done?"

Shaking his head, Geoff squeezed Danika's knees. "Give it another minute."

"Geoff and I are gonna walk in. He's already assigned us to Townley's team via their intranet, so we should be able to get up no problem. Getting out is going to be a doozy."

"Let us have a look." Geoff pulled the projection sphere out of Alek's hand and studied all of the possible exits marked in red. "Unless your van can sprout wings, there's no point looking at anything above the fourth floor." He intuited a command to the projection sphere and reset all of the higher exits to blue. "You've seen the painting. Is it in an office? Is it in a safe?"

Alek racked his mind for the answer. "It's on a wall. Between two doors."

"Hold up," Danika said, pulling out the cortical loader. She handed it back to Geoff. "There's not much in the way of art that's allowed up. Patterns maybe, but no graven images."

"I'm telling you. It's there. I'll know it when I see it."

"You're sure it's not in a safe or a vault?" asked Danika, finding her bearings and trying not to succumb to mania under the weight of all of her reintegrated experience.

165

"Yes," Alek replied with certainty. "Green and her co-conspirators wanted it handy so they could make off with it lickety-split once they had wiped their incriminating memories."

"A lot of unknown unknowns there mate." Geoff tapped his temple. "How bout we play it as it comes. Dan, we've got two reports automated. One at Reclamations you'll have to look into, and the next will be by CBLOCK40."

"Both are out of my jurisdiction."

Geoff threw up his hands signifying indifference. "Who cares? You're committing treason. You don't have to report in tomorrow. In fact," Geoff pointed to the cortical loader blinking at the side of Danika's head, "You can't. But if you want your spawn to reap the reward, Lisa's going to have to meet us at CBLOCK40."

Danika pushed Geoff and Alek out of the way, and rushed to the front of the van. She pulled a small comms device out from under the steering wheel. "Honey, baby, can you talk?...Yeah? Good...No, no, no. Everything's alright. Just listen very closely. CBLOCK40. I need you to get over there and hide out for a bit, okay?...When?" Danika turned to Geoff. "When?" she asked a second time.

Geoff checked the time and peeled off his shirt. He pulled the Reclamations uniform over his head. The shirt would have fit were it not for his bulge. "Ah merciful Lord!"

"What time should Lisa meet us?" Danika was losing her patience.

"Five. Six at the latest."

Alek repeated "Five!" in case Lisa missed the first answer on the other end.

"Five o'clock, baby. Alright...I love you too. Will see you soon." After hiding the comms device under the steering wheel, Danika turned to see Geoff all suited up with his hairy belly hanging out over his white-striped blue pants. She gripped her head. "We're screwed, aren't we?"

Alek slapped Geoff's gut. "Nah. He's big boned, but anyone who'd say so would be stitched up for prejudice."

Geoff sucked in his stomach enough that he could tuck in his shirt. "Feels just like my courting days."

"Now we know why you got a dog," Alek chided.

Turning red in the face, Geoff moved aback the van. "Shaddup. Going to call Cleopathrine and let her know the deal's on."

Alek corrected him: "Cassandra. Cassandra Doherty."

"I don't need her whole life's story." Geoff intuited the call and elected to vocalize for the benefit of his interested compatriots.

166

"Hello?...Yeah, Geoff Littlefield here with two of my mates. We know where the, uh—"

Alek mouthed, "The Family" with a look of great irritation knitting his eyebrows.

"*The Family* painting is," continued Geoff. "We're headed to get it this afternoon...No...There's four of us."

"Five," Alek interjected.

Danika and Geoff both did some quick arithmetic and looked at Alek dubiously.

"Monica's alive," Alek whispered.

Geoff bit his bottom lip. "Sorry, there're five of us...Names? Not a chance, lady. We just want out...Fine! Alright! Alek Neuhaus, Dan—Oy Dan, what's your last name?"

"Fyre."

"Danika Fyre, Lisa Fyre, Geoff Littlefield, and one Monica Neuhaus." Geoff turned white and looked morosely to Alek. He leaned over and whispered, even though his every vocalization could be picked up on the other end. "She says Monica Neuhaus works for the EDS."

"Bullshit!" shouted Alek. "You tell Cassandra—"

Geoff threw up a hand to silence Alek. "She says she can get the four of us out."

Alek sat back. He felt a cool sensation run under his skin. It occurred to him that to debate terms of exit would only doom his friends. If Monica was beyond his reach or beyond saving, he would at least get the man responsible. Right then and there Alek decided he would stay behind. He wouldn't surrender. He would fight. He wouldn't abandon Monica a second time, no matter what some American decided to label or libel her as. He nodded and perked up with the knowledge that at the very least his friends would get out. *At least someone would benefit from this nightmare.*

"It's a deal," said Geoff, elated. "CBLOCK40...Yes, alright. Tonight, say six?...Doesn't matter, to be honest. Just get us away from the EDS and the CDS and anything remotely resembling a demsock protectorate...Sure. Thanks, we'll need it." Geoff tapped his temple again and roared: "It's a deal!"

Danika started the van. "You two ready?"

Alek smiled at Geoff. His decision to stay behind calmed his nerves. "Always, Littlefield."

Geoff closed the Reclamations blueprint and shook Alek's hand enthusiastically. He turned to Danika. "Officer Frye, we're good to go."

167

Danika parked in an alley across the street from the Department of Reclamations. She prepared her own arsenal in the event that she would have to step into the fray. "I'd say good luck but—"

Alek interrupted Danika: "Just say a prayer."

"How will I know when you boys are headed back?"

"Something tells me you'll know," Geoff said, hiding his rifle in a cardboard box that wouldn't be out of place in a department where boxed goods were the currency.

As this wasn't the kind of answer that would satisfy Danika Frye, especially with lives on the line, she dug through the glove compartment. She pulled out a small transparent box containing two fingernail-sized sticky pads. "We use these to trail suspects without their knowing." She shuffled into the back of the van, and adhered one to Alek's neck and the other to Geoff's. "These are modded. No one but me will know where you are. With the blueprint, I'll be able to pinpoint your location."

"Great. Now you'll be able to know precisely when and where we get stitched up." Alek squeezed Danika's hand affectionately and jumped out of the back doors yanking along his own boxed rifle. He helped Geoff out in turn. Before closing the doors, Alek promised Danika: "We'll be free before the sun rises."

"Damned well better!" she said in reply.

Geoff and Alek crossed the empty street. The first and most crucial task was getting to the front door. Several machine guns positioned on the façade's plinths decloaked and pointed at their slow advance.

Alek's breathing became shallow and he faltered.

Geoff, impressed with a plastic smile, pressed him along. "Easy, Neuhaus. They'd have fired on us already were they certain we didn't belong."

They climbed the steps to the Department's heavy doors. On the threshold, they looked at each other with a kind of boyish thrill, and then continued in while a heavyset guardian barreled out.

At least two-hundred citizens were waiting to be called inside the reception area. Some were standing. Most were sitting on worn-out benches.

Walking past dozens of weary eyes and emaciated mugs, Geoff and Alek made their way to the front desk. Alek looked around for droids. There were no killbots or droids presently active, though the Shepherd Drone containment pods stationed like fire extinguishers around the floor were full—ready to deploy their dangerous contents at a second's notice.

168

"I'll deal with the front desk. You meet me at the elevators," said Geoff under his breath, barely moving his lips.

Alek nodded. He saw two elevator banks. From Green's memory he could only remember the one—the more decorative of the two. He set out for the familiar.

While Geoff tested the desk-clerk's patience and ability to flush out a fraud, Alek made his way to the second elevator bank. The floors and walls were marble. The elevator doors looked to be made of gold, and if not gold, then copper, not that Alek could tell the difference. Between the doors was a painting of some old yob. The very sight of it sent a chill throughout Alek. It was the painting for which he had come!

Alek set his cardboard box down carefully, looked around, and closely inspected the painting. Channeling Green's excitement, he ran his fingers down the sides and along the gilded baroque frame. There were no sensors or tripwires so far as he could tell. Still, he knew not to pull the painting down—it would be no good walking around in search of Townley with a gaudy golden frame under his arm. He looked around for a witness and saw no one. He could only hear Geoff talking to the clerk—who he kept calling "Dash"—about the weather. With a blade he had customarily used while working on rooftops, Alek made an incision along the top right-hand corner of the painting, intending to merely cut it free, but he stopped upon seeing something hidden behind the canvas. Contained within the frame and behind the image of the old man was a paper parcel. Alek tore the geezer's portrait a little more—just enough to yank out the parcel. He could tell right away from its weight and dimensions that it was not just another painting, but *the painting* he had come for and with which his friends would secure asylum.

That should have been it. The painting within the paper parcel, whatever its subject matter, was enough to satisfy the terms of the job Geoff and Danika had agreed to. Alek chastised himself silently with the parcel under his shirt and gun box back in his hands, ordering himself to do right by his friends—to cut them loose and to kill Scott Townley on his own. He was sweating profusely when Geoff finished flirting with Dash and made his way over.

"She can't give us the key because we're supposed to already have it, but said she'd give us time to find it before reporting us for having lost state property." Geoff called the elevator with a hard press. "Unlocked the elevator for just the one unauthorized ascent. Said Townley's on the fifty-fifth floor. Sweet bird that Dash." He looked back affectionately in the direction of the front desk.

169

"Mate," Alek said furtively. He stood close beside Geoff. "You can go." He unbuttoned his shirt and revealed one corner of the parcel. "Take it off me and go."

Geoff looked up at the numbers counting down to the elevator's arrival and then with a look of confusion at Alek. "What are you talking about?" He recoiled. "That it there? *Jeeze man*, so that's what the fuss is all about, eh?"

"Yeah." Alek motioned to hand the parcel off, but Geoff took another step back.

"And where you think you're headed?"

Gesturing upward, Alek replied: "Townley shot Monica. I'm going to return the favour."

Looking hungrily at the parcel offered him, Geoff closed his eyes and rocked his head. "They couldn't have made this easier...And yet you've found a way to make it next to impossible."

"Go. I'll catch up." He indicated the spot on his neck where Danika had put her tracker. "You can monitor my progress from the van."

The elevator chimed and the doors rolled open. Geoff looked at the torn painting on the wall and shook his head. "Do I look like a confounded admin? *In for a penny*," he pushed away Alek's offering, and cajoled him into the elevator. "*In for a pound*." He took a brick of plastic explosives out of his jacket and tucked into the hollow painting where The Family had been. "Monica didn't like me much, but I loved her like a sister. You know I did." Red-faced and angry with himself for becoming a better friend, Geoff got into the elevator compartment with Alek. "Besides, I remember what she did for me." He chuckled. "She wouldn't let me forget."

Brimming with incoherent emotion—one could call the sum of it gratitude—Alek trembled. His jaw locked. He fought to pry it open, and looked over to Geoff, towering beside him, and indicated the door, about to close. "Last chance, bruv."

"Then let me be counted."

The elevator doors slid shut on Geoff Littlefield and Alek Neuhaus.

The fifty-fifth floor was abuzz with bureaucrats virtually inspecting shipments with the help of AI sorters. It was important that potentially triggering or controversial materiel be scrutinized at a distance. After an incoming parcel was entered into inventory and scanned, the conclusions would be sorted and rubberstamped by an army of myopic desk jockeys.

No one seemed to notice the elevator doors roll open. If anyone had, they probably would have seen Alek and Geoff's designations and deemed them nonthreatening. There was fast enough turnover in the department that faces were rarely familiar. Familiarity was at best a liability—being known meant standing apart from the collective. Although not strangers to being overlooked, Alek and Geoff were surprised that, convention notwithstanding, they had not yet been molested by a helmeted brute or a Shepherd drone.

They exited the elevator feigning the kind of calm that only drugged outgoing cancer patients seem to exhibit, and made their way towards the room that their holographic blueprint had marked off as Scott Townley's office.

"I've got to say, Geoff, your tech is top notch," whispered Alek, matching Geoff's stride.

A frazzled man with eyes trained on his own feet hurried by, splitting the two subversives. "My apologies, comrades," he said breathlessly. He tried the door on the stairwell, but heard voices inside, and beelined it for the elevator.

Alek's ocular scan indicated the man was a demsock named Stuchberry. "There's a man afraid of his own shadow."

Closing the gap between Alek and himself, Geoff continued answering without paying Stuchberry any notice: "Tech's good yeah. What's not based on Monica's originals has been based on open-source designs *from abroad*." He winked and nearly dropped his cardboard rifle case while attempting to tap his nose.

This devious eye flicker drew Alek's attention to some greater meaning; what, he wasn't quite sure. "The cortical loader—the offlining you did for me and Danika..."

"Ah! That was largely Monica's again..." Geoff looked cockeyed at Alek. "Mate, they must've done a number on your head last synch, because I know you knew that."

Had Margaret Green's memories edged out room in his brain reserved for his own? The very thought made Alek's chest hurt. Though it may have been psychosomatic, the pain in his chest felt real, but not as real as the pain he meant to inflict upon Scott Townley—the demsock who had prevented him from creating new memories to replace those that had been damaged; from having another dance with Moni to the tune of one of their hummed duets.

Alek and Geoff made their way down a narrow hall lined on both sides by doors, some of which were open. Neither of them looked into any of the rooms. No one was owed any privacy, but a

171

passing glance might lock onto the wrong set of eyes. They marched on, past several Shepherd drone cabinets, to a set of three doors.

"Which one is it?" Geoff asked Alek as he tore open one side of his cardboard box so that he could get a handle on the rifle grip.

Alek put his box atop Geoff's and opened the middle door. "Keep an eye out for unwanted company. This should only take a minute." He lunged inside.

Seated at a plain, drawer-less desk in the windowless room was a large, black-haired man with a bristled Slavic jaw. He began to turn just as Alek landed on him. Before he could yelp or call out for help, Alek had driven Scott Townley's face into his desk and thrown an arm around his neck.

Geoff hurried into the room and closed the door behind him. He set the cardboard boxes down by the door and secured Townley's legs, bucking like those of a spooked stallion and making quite a ruckus.

Alek delivered Scott blow after blow to the face. Several thumps in, Townley managed to launch Alek off of him. Townley fell to the floor and crawled to a cabinet in one corner of the room. He got the middle drawer open when Alek dropped down on him again, this time kicking his arm just above the elbow and sending bone through the skin. Scott began to howl, but Alek punched him in the temple. Scott slumped onto the ground, barely conscious. He began sucking air through his mouth as he was unable to breathe through his collapsed nostrils.

Pre-empting a holler, Alek clasped Scott's mouth shut, suffocating him further. He turned Scott around, and pressed him against the wall by the cabinet.

Geoff inspected the middle drawer and brandished what Scott had attempted to get his hands on: a custom-printed single-shot handgun. "What 'ere you planning to do with this, eh?" Geoff hammered Scott on the forehead with the heavplast sidearm.

"Scott Townley?" Alek inquired, still gripping Scott's face, rapidly turning blue.

Scott nodded. He took his beating curiously well. He wasn't as brittle as the other bureaucrats. Most of them would faint at the sight of blood—but only their own blood.

"Scream, yell, try anything, then the next arm goes, and then your more prized extremities. You understand me?"

Scott nodded again.

Alek let go of the man's face. He stood up and crossed his arms, rustling Monica's memex. Geoff, who by now had figured out

172

how the custom print worked, stood beside Alek and took aim at Scott's head. "Why did you shoot her?"

Scott Townley was in a daze from the excruciating pain, yet able to cultivate the focus and cerebral alacrity to answer with a more pointed question: "Who the hell are you?"

"Monica Neuhaus. *My wife*. You shot her. Why?!"

Geoff nudged Alek hoping to keep his friend's volume from reaching gossip-worthy levels.

Scott spat blood and rested his head against the wall. "I don't know what you're talking about. You with the DSSP?"

Alek shared a look of disgust with Geoff. He wanted to do another number on Scott, but any more damage inflicted on the media might affect the message. "*I'm no secret police stooge.* I'm the Lancashire Lethe. I hate the EDS and all that you stand for." He balked at the notion of working for the regime. "You do it because she knew about the painting? *Is that it?* Why not just tell Green not to wipe?"

The mention of Margaret Green brightened up what of Scott's face wasn't obfuscated by welts or blood. "There were two of yah?" He smiled revealing the piano keys Alek had played with his knuckles. "Your bloody limey resistance is a joke. That painting was here the entire time and you sat on it, wasting the opportunity." Townley tried to wipe his face with his broken hand instinctively. Instead, he licked his mouth dry. "Now they will get it and burn it and we'll all die."

Geoff crouched down maintaining his aim at Townley's head. "You're not EDS?"

"*Nyet*, you stupid ox." Scott's answer was punctuated by pained inhales and wet exhales. "I've been working for four years on getting that painting to the Eastern Resistance—to Stroz and to people who'd know what to do with it. Not like you English. Your resistance is pitiful. In Poland, in Hungary, the battle is about to begin. Here, the war is already lost."

"We're not with the Resistance," Alek said, almost sorry that it was true. He remembered it didn't matter—not like Monica mattered. "Last chance, gazpacho. Why did you shoot my wife?"

Scott tried to sit up straight and ended sliding further down the wall, clutching his badly bleeding arm. "Green went to her—to both of you I suppose. Couldn't risk competition with the English Resistance over a weapon so powerful; over a weapon I knew they'd misuse. If word got out we had the painting, then—well, here we are. It was not out of hatred, *Lethe*. All is fair in—"

Alarms began to blare outside in the hallway.

"Oh Jesus!" Geoff groaned. He opened the door a slit and peered out. Shepherd drones ejected from their cabinets and congregated in the hall.

Townley shook his head, dribbling blood in an arc. "Now you've secured the fate of Europe just as your countrymen have secured the fate of England. I hope you're proud."

Alek hoofed Townley in the face. It may have been enough to kill him. Alek didn't care either way. The answer he wanted from the man was greed or hate or malice. Instead, the reason he got for his wife having been killed and turned into an EDS puppet was predicated upon hope and sacrifice. He equipped his rifle and leaned against Geoff. "Goddamned Eastern Resistance. *You ever hear of 'em?*"

"Doesn't matter now, does it?" said Geoff, distracted by and counting the drones he hadn't the munitions to destroy.

Alek scowled at Townley's crumpled form. "Broken communication and broken bones."

Over the intercom an androgynous voice announced: "The Department of Reclamations is now under lockdown. Please provide your identification for security officials. This is not a drill."

"Ah damn it." Alek gripped Geoff's shoulder. "Sorry mate."

Geoff shrugged off the hand. "Make it up to me by channeling the old Neuhaus."

"Deal." Alek closed the door, leaned his gun against it, and pulled out his projection sphere. "There're too many steel jobs out there. But I've got an idea."

Scott began snoring through his broken nose, one large bubble at a time. He half-consciously muttered an apology to Margaret Green who apparently was more to him than simply an accomplice.

"You going to finish 'em off first?" Geoff said, gesturing to Townley while intuiting specs to the projection sphere.

Alek looked down with disgust. "Y'ave one of them grenades handy?"

Geoff pointed his nose to his jacket pocket.

Alek took a grenade from Geoff and jammed it into Scott's good hand. He couldn't forgive the man for what he had done. Monica was life and Townley had snuffed it out. Nevertheless, she would never have forgiven Alek for leaving a Resistance fighter unarmed to face totalitarian evil alone. An explosive exclamation would do the trick.

"You're sick, mate." Geoff said, opening the door a slice and peering once more into the hall. "Just like me."

174

EIGHTEEN

The Reclamations Department operated within a sixty-storey black building that retained the brick and sandstone façade of the old Central Library as its street-level entrance. The Edwardian red and tan pillars supported a balustrade decorated with security cameras and proximity sensors. Before Jagjit had even exited his driverless limo, the same sensors and cameras had processed his personnel file and enabled him to enter freely without having to worry about the cloaked machinegun turrets set on the building's south-facing plinths.

Four of the Democratic Socialist Special Police (DSSP) officers that Jagjit had hand-selected to assist him in tracking down the cyber weapon were waiting for him on the front steps. They had with them a gangly middle-aged woman. The woman's sharp features stood out amongst the masked DSSP agents. In her hand was an orange clipboard.

The individual commanding the other three agents, already familiar to Jagjit, updated him via their mental intranet and explained where the DSSP was at with the pre-interrogations. "Commissar Hassan," said Major Poyraz Vola, whose thoughts were codified and transmitted direct to Jagjit's mind. "Poyraz here with Comrades-Select Second Lieutenant Roth, Sergeant Gaine, and Lieutenant Estra. We have in our care one Comrade Rose Denis. She is the shift supervisor for the first-order staff; oversees everyone but the department's top officials and security technicians."

Jagjit shut the door of his limo and waved to Allister, hovering low above the rooftops in his gunship. With his hand raised, he felt the weight of the sheathed knife strapped to the inner breast of his jacket. He brought the flaps of his jacket together and buttoned them, and intuited to Allister an order: "Fly a tight circuit. Notify me if you see anything peculiar. Fire on any unidentified personnel or vehicles."

"Commissar," Poyraz messaged again, uncertain if he was being ignored or if his mental note had missed its mark. "Comrade Rose Denis—"

"Yes, yes. I'll speak with her now," Jagjit replied. He approached the statuesque crew on the Reclamation steps. His leonine head seemed to grow the closer he got. "Execute order 1307 in precisely one minute."

175

"Yes, Comrade Commissar," Poyraz replied. He turned, gripping his head, and mumbled. He was one of the holdovers from bygone eras who still chattered their teeth and mashed their lips when speaking brain to brain. He might as well have been reading out loud.

Jagjit shook the hand of the Major whose voice was just in his head. He turned to Rose. "Comrade Denis…"

Rose stretched her arms out to Jagjit with trepidation and an offering: her orange clipboard with several pages attached. "Commissar, I have provided an offline list of staff as requested."

Jagjit nodded in lieu of any further pleasantries, and took the list. "Encounter any resistance? Any trouble at all?

"No, Commissar." The Department was staffed primarily by useless idiots whose purpose was merely to provide familiar faces—a sort of fleshy ambiance—for those with some modicum of real agency.

Jagjit flipped through the first three pages of idiots, and turned to the fourth page where the alphabetical list of agential officials began. Denis was high on the list with an "X" beside her name. She had requested a security evaluation for herself, unsure if she had unintentionally subverted the People's Will. The honesty impressed Jagjit. He cocked his head, looked at the uncertain woman in front of him, and then back at the list. He squinted as he scanned the remaining names for ones he might recognize. "Excellent," he replied without looking up again from the ink. "Thank you, Comrade Denis. You're free to go home." Allister's ship blustered by, completing his first circuit around the premises. Jagjit grinned at the sound of his own aerial superiority. "Don't dawdle, comrade. Lockdown is imminent."

Rose bowed at the waist, bid Poyraz and his men adieu, and hastily crossed the street. At a safe distance on the other side, she watched the Commissar enter the Department accompanied by his secret police, and the Reclamations door seal behind them. She saw the building's blast panels shutter all of its windows. She heard the groan of the Reduvius drones and Goliath mechs down the road that had been summoned to assist Allister in keeping the peace and in preventing the guilty from escaping. Sure she had seen enough, Rose slipped down an alley past an idling guardian van, and got as far away as she could from the fate set for the names on her list. Reclamations was about to be reclaimed for the Supreme Council.

The front room inside the Department had forty benches, each of which could sit five comfortably. Every one of the benches was packed with at least seven citizens, all waiting for their number

176

to be called so that they could petition the Department to reacquire personal effects that may have accidentally been seized. Although mental dampeners ensured the room had a stable average IQ of eighty-five, there were enough people in the room with high-enough value ratings to recognize that a visit from a commissar and the presence of the DSSP meant something was off.

It takes very little to spook a herd. An apex predator is a guarantee. As soon as Hassan made it to the front desk, the benches were cleared. Jagjit's agents unfolded the stocks on their machineguns, shouldered them, and took aim at the anxious mob, ensuring that no one would interfere with Supreme Council business. Someone closer to the street side announced that the doors were locked, and the whispering began.

To the tune of hushed concern, Jagjit rested his arms on the front desk. The woman behind the desk, a front-of-house clerk with the mononym Dash, oafishly sought out the correct keys for the elevators up to the top bureau, separate from the elevators that serviced the first fifty floors. As the whispers in the lobby turned to cries and gasps, Jagjit gnarred. Anyone who panicked around a high-ranking party member either had something to fear or fell short in their belief in *the cause*. He activated his crowd-control application, turned to face the two-hundred-or-so dispossessed citizens, and silenced them with a coordinated wave and thought. The room went still. The EDS could at any time and for whatever reason decrease bandwidth to a particular individual, group, or region, and simultaneously deluge him, them, or it with far more data-mining requests than could be reasonably entertained so as to halt any non-essential cognition. Utilizing this power, available in varying degrees to councilors, security forces, and commissars, Jagjit smothered the anxiety in the room. Everyone reseated him or herself or found space on the floor on which to lie down or crouch. With the Patch Over, this control wouldn't require physical mental dampening to work and would be total.

"Thank you for your cooperation." Jagjit said demurely. He couldn't tell if his agents similarly relished his ability and its immediate effect, but their recognition didn't mean a damn. He reset his elbows on the front counter. "Comrade, the key?"

The clerk, unaffected by the general pause, provided Jagjit with the security key to the restricted elevator bank. She opened a holographic window and pulled it into three dimensions. The whole of the Department of Reclamations shimmered between her and the Commissar, meta-tagged with several indications that order 1307 was underway. Every floor but the atrium and penthouse floors (the

177

latter where the shipping and receiving bay processed outgoing and incoming items transported by drones) were on total lockdown. The top floors, peopled mainly by officials, councilors, and trustworthees, had not been left in the dark and sealed, but nevertheless had been made aware that their mobility and communications privileges were temporarily suspended. If there was any question as to the necessity for compliance, the building's legion of centrally-managed security droids and Shepherd drones policing the halls would serve as a reminder.

"Commissar," Poyraz intuited to Jagjit. "The local guardians have dispatched six aerial units to assist Allister with monitoring the perimeter."

Jagjit fanned his hand in front of the clerk's face and the woman went slack on her feet. He looked over to Poyraz who was checking the action on his gun. "Splendid. Blockade all pedestrian avenues in the quadrant and have guardians sent to the whereabouts of everyone on this list presently outside of the Department of Reclamations." Jagjit handed Poyraz the clipboard. "Turn your privacy shields on. Your men too. We cannot risk any one of us being hacked." The privacy shields Jagjit was referring to—which required the permission from a commissar or higher-ranked EDS official to be activated or deactivated—prevented anyone from pulling live mental readouts from those behind them; not the AI historians in London, not England's best hackers, not Defence Minister Corven himself could examine their thoughts. With his own thoughts collected and temporarily private, Jagjit marched over to the secure elevator bank with the security key.

Poyraz studied the sheet, broadcasted the order over the Blackpool municipal channel, and regrouped with Jagjit and his men.

Unlike the ramshackle elevator bank that serviced the first fifty floors manned entirely by menial labourers and AI-dotters, the Department's elevator bank devoted to servicing the top floors was all veined white marble. A badly torn painting of the inventor of the technology responsible for the EDS' success and continued control was displayed in a gilded frame between two of the brass elevator doors. In a country with a universal prohibition on art, it was odd seeing graven images outside of the Supreme Council's mansions, and odder still to see anything from the old world let alone the Americas. Somehow the Outland Corporation's former chairman Niles Winchester's likeness seemed to avoid the contempt of even the most stringent censors who had made their late jihadist brothers-in-arms seem uncommitted to iconoclasm by comparison. In fairness, Winchester was said to have ushered in the final stage of capitalism and to have provided the means of neural collectivization. Jagjit appreciated the work of whoever had torn the painting from the top corner inward, revealing a hollow between the canvas and the frame. It may have been right to remember this personage from the past, but to rip it somewhat was a sign of continued commitment to the revolution. Despite being yanked forward from the frame, Winchester's soulless eyes still managed to follow the security key to the locking mechanism on the wall as well as to Poyraz's finger to the elevator call button.

While they waited, Poyraz studied the space for possible boobytraps or threats. Paranoia was in the job description, but the increasing rarity of regressive attacks made it largely unfounded. As he fussed about, he threw his voice in the Commissar's direction: "In case you were wondering, Councilor Bradley Miliband died slowly."

"I wasn't," replied Jagjit blithely, "Though I suppose that's good news."

The elevator chimed and the brass doors slid open. Inside was a disheveled man. He seemed absolutely surprised that the doors should ever open let alone open to the sight of the Supreme Council's foremost errand boy. His eyes widened at the sight of Commissar Hassan and grew even wider at the sight of the DSSP agents. He retreated into the corner of the compartment and rustled about in his pockets, eyes darting from Jagjit to Poyraz to the other three agents and back to Jagjit.

Right away, Jagjit identified the man via his implant's citizen registry. *Drew Stuchberry*. He was a station manager from the Ministry of Cultural Equity. "Comrade Stuchberry, are you not pleased to see me?"

Poyraz and his men looked to Jagjit, unsure of whether to treat the vertical gallivant in grey-trousers as a threat or not. "Comrade Commissar?"

Before Jagjit could calm the man's mind as he had those petitioners waiting in the front room, Stuchberry pulled a custom-print handgun out of his pocket and pressed it to the bottom of his jaw.

"Comrade! Drop the weapon!" Jagjit shouted.

It was too late. Stuchberry blew a hole through the top of his head. He dropped face-first in the way of the doors, which attempted to close but found his twitching mass and offered in turn a cautionary beep.

"That's one off your list," quipped Poyraz.

Jagjit sighed, entered the elevator, and knelt down in Stuchberry's blood. Pieces of implant metals cascaded like confetti

179

from the ceiling. He patted the body down for signs of a cause for such a hasty exit. There was a photograph in his trouser pocket—the same where he had kept a few rounds of ammunition for the single-shot pistol he had utilized to its fullest. The photograph appeared blurry to Jagjit. He couldn't make heads or tails of what it was supposed to be. All he could discern was that there were three or four figures under a blue sky. It must have been a copy of a painting; something from upstairs. He held the bloodied photo up for the benefit of his men. "What do you see?"

Poyraz's men shrugged. The Major at least attempted an answer: "Mountains or something. It's blurry."

It must be a prohibited image, Jagjit determined. Any image known to the EDS historians and archives was impossible to see, for an implanted Englander anyway. Jagjit held the picture up once more for inspection. This time he noticed some writing at the bottom left corner of the photograph's backside. It read: "THE FAMILY?" He lifted his mental shield just long enough for the AI historians to meta-tag the writing via his ocular implants. They pointed out that the penmanship was indeed Stuchberry's. Jagjit intuited a communique to Minister Corven requesting an insight as to the nature, meaning, and importance of the image. Only the most senior party members would have the trustvalue needed to view something apparently so egregious. As soon as he had sent in his request, he turned his mental shield back on. Surely not all the enemies nearby had the good sense to hollow out their heads.

Poyraz ordered around his men: "Comrade Sergeant Gaine! Comrade Lieutenant Estra! Clear the elevator, on the double. When back in, I want safeties off." He nudged his remaining underling, Comrade Second Lieutenant Roth, who was contently stamping boot prints in blood. Pointing back in the direction of the front desk, Poyraz shoved Roth out of the elevator compartment. "No one in or out! Do you understand?"

"Yes, Major." Roth shouldered his submachine gun and tracked Stuchberry's vitality out into the lobby while Gaine and Estra dumped his body out on the white marble. With two bodies cleared out, one living and one dead, there was far more room inside the elevator compartment.

"Major," said Gaine, unshaken but concerned, "You reckon they got more prints upstairs?" He had in his hand the coward Stuchberry's custom-printed handgun. It was a single shot self-defense weapon. Although it was made from heavplast and could withstand the heat and blast of repeated shots, the firing mechanism was only really good for a single hammer pull.

180

Jagjit stepped in between Gaine and Poyraz, and pressed the button for the Department's high-value reception. The doors slid shut and the elevator began to ascend. He interjected: "If so, today is the last day their triggers can be pulled. Count yourselves fortunate to be the last to risk all for the People."

Jagjit wiped Department Head Shrik Paradkar's viscera off his knife using her blouse. He sheathed it inside his jacket and looked out Paradkar's window. He spotted Allister's gunship as it passed in front of the neighbouring concrete monoliths. Its jets appeared like four-pointed stars mediated through the window on account of the thin layer of fog on the glass. Jagjit ran his finger down the window pane, leaving a watery trail that almost immediately resealed behind the motion.

Paradkar, still not finished dying, burbled and tried to turn onto her side in a desperate attempt to clear her flooded lungs. "Commissar...Please bury me in the forest..."

The top floor of Reclamations had a processing bay on its eastern face. There was a platform that stuck out five metres and a hangar-like structure built to receive and dispatch drones containing artifacts seized from the country's red zones and remaining dissidents. Behind the hangar, at the center of the building, there was a two-level hollow full of trees, broad-leaved plants, and a variety of colourful fungi. Paradkhar had successfully requisitioned the green space. She was owed a favour by the Ministry of Forestry and had made a compelling argument that a green installation down the hall from her office would remind workers of the EDS' goal—healing the planet—and would incentivize them to work harder for longer periods of time. The forest was responsible for the fog on the glass and probably for Comrade Denis' accusation of bourgeois extravagance.

"Commissar Hassan...Please!" Paradkhar propped herself up against the feet of her leather desk chair, and reached to Jagjit pleadingly.

"I think not," replied Jagjit. He summoned Major Poyraz Vola via the EDS neural intranet.

"Just lining up our suspects, Comrade Commissar," Poyraz replied instantaneously.

"I want you to put in a request. I would but I cannot risk lowering my shield." Jagjit now spoke aloud for Paradkhar's benefit. "To the Ministry of Forestry—I want the shrubbery creating all this damp torched. Also, tell Sergeant Gaine to de-cerebrate Comrade Paradkhar. She's been relieved of duty."

181

"Yes, Comrade Commissar."

Jagjit grabbed the orange clipboard off of Paradkhar's desk, wiped his shoes on moisture-rotted carpet, and emptied all of the air from his chest. A call came over the EDS intranet, tagged "HIGH PRIORITY". Jagjit intuited the connection. "Yes?"

Dr. Mallory Worthing's voice came across cleanly: "Commissar Hassan, I'm nearly there."

Jagjit turned and looked to the window where the line he had drawn was completely filled in. "I beg your pardon—*where* exactly?"

"Reclamations, of course. Have you apprehended Scott Townley?"

Grinding his molars, Jagjit's antipathy for the Doctor came back to him in full force. He checked the clipboard and reread Townley's name at the top of his list. "I do not see how that's any business of yours. You are supposed to be at the English Broadcast Station."

Mallory's voice had a certain playfulness about it. She seemed to be able to know when she had ruffled Jagjit's feathers and evidently enjoyed doing so. "As I have previously stated, the technology he is reported to have been in close proximity to—the same technology that is said to counter what I produced for the People's Government—poses a threat to the Patch Over. My team at the EBS has made all of the necessary preparations and I am ready to proceed tomorrow morning. If, however, Townley has any information that I should know, it is the expressed will of the Home Defence Minister that I be present to hear it firsthand."

"Yes. Unfortunately, the Department is presently under lockdown."

"Then you'll be sure to open the door to the processing bay in time for my arrival."

Had Paradkhar not already bled out, Jagjit may have used her as a voodoo doll to wreak havoc on Mallory's person. He stifled the acidic flow of cruel words along his tongue and smiled so to deprive the Doctor of the satisfaction of angering him. "I've sent the entry code for the receiving doors to you…and look forward to seeing you once again."

Jagjit terminated the call and exited Paradkhar's office wearing an angry expression that turned his black beard into an arrow head. Like any other period of revolutionary fervor, death and murder went unquestioned. He considered taking action now to ensure that all of his hard work wouldn't be eclipsed by a flipped subversive. Yes, he would kill Mallory Worthing once Townley spoke his piece. The Patch Over was ready, after all; the Doctor had said so herself. Even if Corven took issue with Jagjit's decisive action, he might overlook it to spare himself the trouble of finding another henchman with a comparable skillset in these final days.

Lieutenant Estra and Sergeant Gaine stood waiting between two rows of Reclamations officers and watching Poyraz beat an Artifact Registrar's face down his throat. (Any man over ten stone with any modicum of self-respect—the kind that triggers a weak man's insecurities—was getting a beating today.) Barring the Registrar and a few other truants, almost everyone on Jagjit's list of names was accounted for and on their knees. They held their arms above their heads so that their wrist stamps could be inspected without additional molestation.

Jagjit interrupted the beating by calling out to Estra. "Lieutenant, I want you to go and secure the Arts and Letters Vault. Shoot anyone who attempts to interfere."

Poyraz rolled the Artifact Registrar's body over and stood at attention beside Gaine. "*Commissar.*"

Jagjit nodded to Poyraz but focused on Gaine. "Doctor Worthing is on her way here. Wait for her in the processing bay and notify me once she's arrived."

Gaine looked puzzled. "But we're under lockdown."

"I am well aware. She has the door codes. Keep her there until we make our way up." Waving Gaine away, he looked to Estra who hadn't yet departed, and replicated the motion.

Estra licked his lips and ran around the corner, eager to find some sort of interference.

"Comrade Major," said Jagjit, focused on one name in particular printed on his orange-backed kill sheet.

"Yes, Comrade Commissar?" Poyraz was alert, though all emotion had vacated his face. He had steeled himself against caring about his victims. No aspect of his humanity would impair his ability to carry out the People's Will. He took one too many steps towards Jagjit so that they appeared attached at the hip.

"Townley. *Scott Townley*. He's our top priority. Locate him for me."

"Yes sir." While Poyraz devoted his thoughts to determining precisely where in the building Townley had hidden away, his body trudged along, leading the Commissar down the lane between the penitent Reclamatories.

A handsome young woman with chestnut hair and creamy skin made eye contact with Jagjit as he passed. The Commissar stopped, turned, and grabbed the woman by her wrists. A quick scan indicated she had an impeccable record. Worked hard. Never

183

complained. Believed in the Supreme Council and had never once been recommended for a post, meaning her placement in this moist and luxurious domain of influence had been the product of her persistent and joyful labour. She would have survived the purge unscathed had her name not been marked on Denis' list.

Jagjit did not know what the woman's crime was; whether she had a hand in the confiscation and movement of the Resistance's weapon of mass destruction or whether she had simply irritated Comrade Denis with her relatively superior beauty. Either way, in this small maze off the floor's larger maze of offices, store rooms, and vaults, all eyes were on Jagjit and he needed to be taken seriously—feared for proof, not just for context. He lifted the chin of the young woman. "Comrade Li, is it?"

"Yes, Commissar." Li closed her eyes and tried not to cry.

"Commissar—with regards to Scott Townley—" Poyraz was himself again and had finished his query.

Jagjit threw up his index finger, demanding that Poyraz shut up and wait his turn. "You know why your name is on this list?" Jagjit raised the orange clipboard as if to strike Li with it.

Li's chin began to tremble. She looked at the vague proof of guilt the Commissar was handling, and then side to side at her silent compeers. She nodded. "Yes, Comrade Commissar." She pointed to her work station, one chair at a long table crowded with screens and processing spheres.

Jagjit pulled her to her feet and threw her towards her station. "Go on! Show me!"

Both rows of penitent bureaucrats seemed to synchronously cave forward on their knees as if called to prayer.

Bleeding from her elbow gashed in the tumble Jagjit sent her on, Li approached her station. Every station had one drawer and she opened hers. Inside her drawer there were dotgrams neatly arranged on one side. On the other was a tuft of well-beaten paper. Closer examination revealed the prohibited paper to be coiled like pencil shavings—no! *Like a nest.* At its center was a tiny hedgehog working away on some fragments of an eMeal bar. Li carefully picked up her pet and turned slowly to Jagjit to showcase her animated transgression.

Jagjit grit his teeth so hard he nearly broke enamel. He was furious; not because Li had kept a pet or because Li was detracting from her effectiveness by sharing her allotted food with a rodent, but because of what she forced him to do—what the EDS demanded he do. Though he had his mental shield up, the AI historians were watching through the eyes of everyone else present. Corven would

184

review Jagjit's efficacy. He could not wait for the Patch Over to correct her. Jagjit had to enforce the rules today. He couldn't preserve Li. There was no drawer big enough or secret enough to keep her safe. *In the end all guilt is discovered and punished.*

Li probably felt the surprise hit her before the pain. Jagjit plunged his knife through the hedgehog and into Li's chest in one fluid movement. As she stood there hemorrhaging, rodent pinned to her heart, Jagjit took a step back. Had he not taken action against Li, action would have been taken against him and his men too.

Poyraz hurried over to watch the light leave Li's eyes. "Commissar—want the body, uh, reclaimed?" He set his hands on his hips, stared down at Li's surprised, final expression, and smiled.

Jagjit felt like mixing Poyraz's blood with Li's. Instead, he pointed to the stations on either side of Li's. "There's no way that her neighbours didn't know about her subversion. Have them report to DIHA. I want a full exam and re-education regardless of guilt. Ensure Comrade Li is de-cerebrated as well. I don't want any dead connections wasting bandwidth."

"Consider it done..." Poyraz pulled open a small hologram. "Comrade Commissar?"

Widening his eyes to adapt to the hologram's bright light, Jagjit grabbed Poyraz's arm and yanked the apparition closer. "Yes?

"Lieutenant Estra confirms that there are three individuals on the premises not currently at their posts."

"Townley!"

"Yes," answered Poyraz. "Along with two of his staffers."

"So where the hell are they?"

"Not going anywhere, I guarantee it."

Jagjit took a step back, seemingly repelled by his underling's confidence. "Where, Poyraz? Where?!"

Feeling the heat, now more intense with the Commissar scrutinizing him at a distance, Vola consulted the hologram and EDS intranet simultaneously. "Comrades Delilah Mortimer and Brant Czapran are his aides." Poyraz refreshed and reoriented the hologram so that Jagjit could glimpse their personnel files. "They are—*they were* logged not long before we arrived and were last synched in the north wing, fifty-fifth floor. Strangely, they weren't supposed to be here today at all—they were reassigned to Cultural Equity."

"And Townley?"

Poyraz rolled his head back and shook a new hologram into view. This time it was a rotating model of the suspect's face. "Uh...Cross-examiner from the Ministry of Cultural Equity...Uh, he

185

shares a temporary office with Margaret Green...Same zone; north on fifty-fifth."

"You finish up here. Home Defence Minister Corven wants anyone who mishandled artifacts brought in for questioning. Have all security drones on the fifty-fifth floor rendezvous with me at the elevator bank. Scott, Delilah, and Brant are guilty and guiltier for trying to evade us. I want them alive, Major. Broken is fine, but alive is essential."

"And this lot?" Poyraz pointed to the Reclamations staff on their knees.

"Anyone guilty of crimes against the People, no matter how big or small, shall be dealt with strictly in accordance with protocol."

He confirmed the order: "Yes, Comrade Commissar."

NINETEEN

Stephen had found a tear in the truck's canvas canopy and peered out. They were bustling down a maintenance road hemmed in by hedges that ran east along the River Ribble. Gargantuan supply ships pulsed in the sky above, carrying British production away to Beijing and Brussels. The supply ships looked like horseshoe crabs with thrusters in the place of legs. Apart from the horseshoe crabs' complement of security drones, flying around them in defensive formation, there were very few EDS machines out and about. Stephen figured that many of the drone patrols had been recalled to Blackpool—bad news for McGregor and Wes. Whatever the demsocks were planning—*the General had called it the Patch Over*—demanded a great deal of protection at the get go and just as many witnesses. Usually civic outreach was digitally and remotely experienced, but the EDS seemed set on leaving a firsthand impression on its citizenry.

They passed several work camps whose fenced-in yards were full of what appeared to be scarecrows. On passing the third camp of this kind, Stephen realized they weren't scarecrows at all but Englishmen. They must have been mentally dislocated to some virtual realm or the like while their bodies took in the vitamin D lacking in the gruel piped into their living quarters.

Near Clifton, they passed a work camp wholly unlike the others. This camp wasn't fenced in with steel and razor wire, though its perimeter was demarcated where the grass went from mowed to tall. At the center of the manicured field there was a large glass building shaped like a donut surrounding and surrounded by towering linden trees. Through the foliage, Stephen could make out people inside the building, staged on its multiple internal tiers, running what he imagined to be drills of some form or another. Interest piqued, he turned to Zoya for elucidation. "What's going on there?"

Zoya was monitoring the Underpool radio channel and didn't react at first. When Stephen prodded her, she turned to snap back. Instead, she followed his interest to the hole in the canvas. After watching the camp disappear behind them, she answered dispassionately: "Work camp. What about it?"

Stephen looked across to Mirek who appeared to be meditating. He turned back to Zoya. "The hell they doing?"

187

"S'for the government's science divisions. AI is amazing at predicting human behavior; really good at determining what a person's response will be to any normal stimuli. There's infinite stimuli; probably only a certain set of human responses. They want to archive all of them. They've been at this for years."

"So they're just running prisoners through simulations?"

"Prisoners from all species. They've been digitizing all possible variations for whales, octopi, rats, pigeons—you name it."

"Remember Moe?" asked Mirek, listening acutely despite looking entirely out to lunch. "The kid who lost his marbles? He was rescued from one of those places. The Major's right, but there's no words for what it's like—what they're calling *work*. Moe said that one minute they're making you build sand castles in your dreams. Next minute they're showing you colours they don't have words for. Mate, I tell yah: it's messed up."

Stephen felt sorry for the prisoners. He looked at Mirek sympathetically. "Why the need for the archive? I could understand the whales, but if you need a question answered, ask somebody."

Jay wasn't allowed to smoke inside the truck on orders from Zoya, so he had been biting away at a half-spent cigar. With the soggy head between his teeth, he answered curtly: "Them 'socks want to know every detail about what they will only permit to survive as virtual. London and Beijing are phasing out the flesh. That's why you don't see many kids nowadays—that and they think sex is intolerant and birth inequitable. We're all hardwired to reject socialism, you see. Hier'chies and the like are just part of being a human. So there's that. Plus we're bad for the environment."

Shaking his head in disbelief, Stephen first looked to Lloyd who nodded somberly, and then to Zoya who scoffed.

"Listen, Nowak," said Zoya, "That's why we do what we do. That's why we're going where we're going. And that's why we've got to win." Zoya put her finger to her ear and resumed listening for updates.

Stephen's blood ran cold. For once he envied his brothers. They didn't have to see what humanity had become—what they would put up with in order for the establishment to usher in their dubious dreams and nightmarish harmony. He pulled the gun out of his waistband and practiced holding it; first sideways because it was aesthetically pleasing, and then level, because he had been mocked in the past for caring about how he looked.

"Where's this Carrella at again?" Lloyd grumbled.

Having heard his neighbour regurgitate the answer so many times, Mirek replied: "St. George's." When it was clear his answer

188

didn't land, he elaborated further: "Yah know t'old mall they built up huge right before they scrapped cash 'n' profit?"

"I know the place," replied Lloyd. In his own travels to Preston, the Lieutenant had always avoided the areas dominated by the triads. "Know of it, anyway."

Jay saw Stephen fiddling with his handgun. "Oi, pass it here."

"All good, mate. I've got a handle."

"Well, you'll lose your fecking thumb handlin' it that way." Jay put away his cigar, squeezed his rifle between his knees, and reached over for Stephen's gun, which Stephen passed off reluctantly. "Toss me another round, will yah?"

Stephen fiddled around in his pockets. Someone in the armoury had given him a few handfuls of electric-grain handgun ammunition, effective on most unarmoured tech. He handed Jay a cartridge.

Jay chambered a round, took out the gun's magazine and fed it the extra cartridge. He smiled ear to ear. "That's one more round for—" He slid the magazine back into the well and the gun went off. No one was more surprised than Jay who had managed to keep a grip on the weapon but whose jaw had dropped.

The four men looked to Zoya who appeared ready to pop off herself. All of them leaned in have a look through the hole in the tarp the blast punched. There was no sky above. Just the belly of a supply ship.

Byron's fury penetrated the rear of the truck from his partitioned-off cabin. "What the hell was that?!"

There was a tiny splash hundreds of metres above them—a flourish of pink against the horseshoe crab's undershielding.

"Nice work, you festering pillock," Lloyd said, punching Jay in the shoulder.

"You've doomed us all" Zoya said with a pessimist's certainty. She grabbed her gun and knocked on the cabin wall. "Byron! You're going to have to go a whole lot faster!"

"Someone shooting at us?" he yelled back, speeding up to reach whatever limit the EDS' Mobility Bureau had imposed on the vehicle.

Stephen felt responsible, evidenced by his tomato-red cheeks. He remained transfixed on the view out of the new hole in the tarp. Red lights flicked-on one by one near the tail of the horseshoe crab. They formed a triangle and then dove. Drawing nearer, they came into focus: birds—*no*, Carrion Flies! At least twenty of the weaponized drones soared towards the truck. "Major!" Stephen yelled.

189

Zoya yanked open the rear curtain and kicked down the tailgate. Asphalt flowed past her. The yellow dividing line appeared unbroken. "How many?"

"Fifteen? I don't know. A tonne." Stephen pulled Mirek along, and perched by the rear of the truck. "We're jumping, yeah?"

Zoya pulled one of the mortars out. "*We* are splitting up." She handed the mortar to Stephen as if performing an egg toss, and tightened the strap on the satchel containing its twin. "Carlo Carrella?"

"In St. Georges mall...If you reach a Chinese bazaar, you've gone too far," Stephen said, fighting the stammer assured by his tensing jaw.

"I'll see you there," she said hotly, leaning out over the road in a squat. "Wu, you spastic—look alive! You're with me."

Jay returned Stephen his gun containing just as many rounds as it had originally. "My bad, bruv. That gun's total shite. Good luck, anyway. And watch your thumb!" He nodded to Lloyd and leapt out into the truck's dusty aftermath, protected from lameness by his armoured joints.

Zoya saw Jay get up and begin firing at the inbound drones. She winked at Stephen, and called out to Lloyd. "Barnard! If you get Carrella's ship first, don't wait around. Just get it done!" She let go of the truck and rolled off the road into a blur of green.

The first wave of Carrion Flies peeled after Zoya and Jay, who seemed to be able to decimate the flock with bursts of plasma and lead. Watching this, Mirek—dumbstruck and trembling—looked over to Stephen uneasily, phase-shifting on account of a poorly-timed drug flashback.

"That's that," said Lloyd. This time he didn't grumble. There was excitement in his voice. "If we're lucky, them bugs will leave us alone." He hurried to the truck's cabin wall and pounded furiously. "Oi! Byron! ETA?"

Byron didn't respond with words. He whooped and hollered. The truck jerked to one side and then to the other.

Barely in control of his own bladder, Stephen nevertheless firmed up. Seeing Mirek on his knees at the rear of the truck gaping at the fire show shrinking behind them, Stephen pulled him back to safety. "Guns up, Underpool!" He tore the hole in the ceiling open wider, and took aim with his handgun. Not only would he have not been able to hit anything, a barrage was entirely unnecessary. The drones seemed to universally decide on Zoya as their target and veered off. "They're going after the Major. I think we're in the clear!"

The truck rocked to the side again, but this time Byron's yells took on a different tenor and quickly became blood-curdling screams.

"Byron!" Lloyd shouted. He couldn't get through the cabin wall though struck at it as if there was a chance he might.

The bloody mandible of a Carrion Fly jabbed through the cabin partition wearing some of Byron's clothes. It nearly took off Lloyd's arm.

"Good God Almighty!" Lloyd roared as he fell back between Stephen and Mirek.

Stephen began blasting the cabin. In a flash, he had emptied his magazine and was left desirous of Jay's lost cartridge.

The Carrion Fly pulled its sensor-laden head through the cabin wall, accordioning the metal partition on either side of it as if it was aluminium foil. Its gun barrels were nearly through, after which point there would be no hope for the truck's passengers.

Mirek took aim at the drone with the plasma shotgun he had been awarded at the armoury. He fired a shot right into the bug's optical array as it was ready to descend on Lloyd. Blinded, it flailed wildly, trying to vivisect the Lieutenant where it had seen him last. However, Lloyd pulled himself to the side and up, unholstered his sidearm and corrupted whatever processers Mirek had missed with his first volley. The Carrion Fly flopped down, and Lloyd heaved it out of the truck.

"Nice shot, lad!" Lloyd said to Mirek, patting him on the shoulder.

Mirek normally would have loved some adulation, however he had gone pale. He pointed to the divot in the cabin wall at the unmanned steering wheel and the guts splayed over the dash. Before Lloyd could offer up any further blood-soused compliments, the truck wrenched to the right.

"Hold on!" Stephen bellowed. He braced himself and watched the world, framed by the truck's canvas, turn into a blurred disc. He was thrown from canopy to floor and into the benches, over and over.

There were radio squawks, beeps, and the sound of boasting. Stephen was on the asphalt, surrounded by splintered wood and glass. His hands were bloody. The wind had been knocked out of him. He could still feel all of his toes and that nothing was out of place, except for the bottle of booze he brought for Carrella, which was broken and dry nearby. Laying on the ground a few metres away

191

was Mirek's body. It was still. Lloyd was further away—on his knees before a committee of Nephilim soldiers near the smoldering wreck.

One of the EDS cyborg units overseeing his comrade interrogate Lloyd noticed that Stephen was still alive, and moseyed over. "This one's still kicking too." He put his foot on Stephen's back before he could roll over and laughed. "What's the sitch, Comrade Lieutenant? Did we find them dead or alive?"

The Nephilim interrogating Lloyd wasn't getting the answers he wanted. He put his gun to Lloyd's head. "That all depends," he said. "Where did you get those uniforms? And where were you heading?"

Lloyd had been significantly cut up in the crash. His bottom lip was split and he couldn't see through one eye on account of a broken nose that had jacked up his sinuses. Still, he was able to speak. "Manchester. Timbuktu ."

The roadside interrogator smashed Lloyd across the face with his gun. He turned to the cyborg pressing his boot into Stephen' back. "We'll do it here. On my command."

Stephen felt the bulge of the mortar Zoya had handed him. Under the weight of the Nephilim's boot, he tried to shift one arm under himself. The mortar hadn't gone off, likely because its fuse cap was still intact. Even with the cyborg crushing him, Stephen was able to get his fingers on the head of the mortar. He tried pulling the cap off to arm it. His death would result in instant karma for the EDS.

A few stray Carrion Flies were flying circuits around the scene, oblivious to the nuclear threat. One way or another they wouldn't be true to their namesake; Stephen and Mirek and Lloyd's bodies would be either be atomized or tossed in a bucket and reprocessed by low-level trustworthees into fertilizer.

"Three...Two..."

There came a far-off growl, robotic and bassy: "Fore!"

The Nephilim officer in charge dropped his gun. He staggered to one side and then to the other, and then fell back. The cyborg standing on Stephen similarly wobbled back. He collapsed beside Stephen with a smoking hole where his face had been.

Terror spread amongst the Nephilim. "Sniper!" one yelled before his stomach was turned inside out. Pieces of his spine and ribs shot out like wet confetti.

Three of the Nephilim began firing indiscriminately into the row of hedges along the road, pruning with plasma and lead. They would never know the inefficacy of their attempt because a launched IE (implode-explode) grenade pulled them into a molten slurry and sprayed their flesh and metal remains across the pavement.

"Good Lord!" Lloyd yelled, scrambling to his feet. He grabbed his would-be-executioner's gun and tried to pick a target, although all of the Nephilim and all but two of their aerial guardians had been destroyed.

Stephen smiled and in so doing realized he was missing a tooth or two. "Zoya and Jay came back for us!" he sputtered.

The remaining pair of red-eyed Carrion Flies ascended to determine where the incoming fire was coming from. They too were blown to pieces.

Stephen rolled over onto his back, and tucked the disarmed mortar back into the torn lining of his thinly-armoured Nephilim uniform. He fought to his feet. Something somewhere inside his body was broken, yet he was nevertheless able to make it over to Mirek.

Lloyd, meanwhile, covered Stephen, while also half-expecting Zoya to appear. "Major? Jay?!" he roared. "Get out here! You're giving me the jeebies!" Whoever had eviscerated the Nephilim early-response team was nowhere to be seen.

Checking for a pulse although untrained on how to do so, Stephen bleated: "Merry! Merry? Bruv, can you hear me?" He carefully turned Mirek over, took off his helmet, and immediately resented his younger-self's indolence, wishing he had paid attention when the elders were demonstrating CPR best-practices. Fortunately, he was spared a failing attempt. Mirek began to cough, and keeled forward. "Oh thank God!" said Stephen, looking up to Lloyd with tears in his eyes. "He's okay."

"Are we there yet?" Mirek said wearily, wiping blood off on his armoured torsal plate. He sat up and held his hand in front of his face. Two of his fingers were badly mangled. He instinctively snapped one back into place and the other back into the right shape, even though it was unlikely to ever function again.

Lloyd slowly inched towards Stephen while studying the countryside through the sights of his new rifle. "Get 'em up. We gotta go."

Stephen swished blood around in his mouth, and spat out broken enamel. "Who killed the screws?" He stood up on wobbly legs, and turned to help up Mirek. "Where's the Major?"

"Neither of you two move," said Lloyd, whose anxious mug was glued to his gun sights.

Several giants wearing thick, armoured exos that could have doubled as heavy naval diving suits emerged from the hedges on the right side of the road.

193

"Point that gun somewhere else!" said the leading tank man in a garbled voice, which was modulated by his green, double-steel-plated helmet.

With a great deal of reluctance, Lloyd lowered his weapon and stood protectively in front of Mirek and Stephen. "Resistance?"

The green-helmet nodded. "We haven't much time. They'll send the mechs in after us along with a Midge or two."

Stephen put Mirek's arm around his neck, and lifted him to his feet.

Although Mirek wasn't crippled, he was visibly shaken and still had not fully come to. "Oi, Lloyd! They Americans?"

The green-helmeted tank man chuckled, which sounded menacing mediated through his breathing apparatus. This modern-day John Bull pulled his helmet off, revealing a head of red hair and a pair of dark black eyes encircled by gold-rimmed spectacles. "Captain Bercilak Service with the 4th Battalion. Lucky for you we were scanning waves. Major Khatri sent an alert over the wire to be on the look-out for four n'er-do-wells disguised as Nephies."

The remains of the truck exploded in one final red-and-black tulip of fire.

Lloyd sighed. "Just the three of us."

"Yeah, well…" Bercilak beat his brows. "*Lucky you*. We were headed to Southport; gonna take out the English Broadcast Relay Station on orders from General McGregor."

Mirek's head snapped back. What captured his attention soon seized Stephen's also: another killer swarm dropping down from one of the horseshoe crabs above. "There's more coming!"

Bercilak put his helmet back on. "Stay close."

Mirek, Stephen, and Lloyd followed Bercilak off the road and through the hedges while members of the 4th Battalion lay two small automatic turrets to deal with the incoming drones. Once the guns were both firing and piling brass casings around the dead Nephilim, the 4th cleared out.

Bercilak brought the lot of them to an eight-by-four metre depression in a grassy field. He pressed a button on his stovepipe of an armoured wrist. The space above the depression began to glitter. A crystalline, fluid-like covering shrunk back like a magician's cape, revealing an armoured personnel carrier. The rear of the vehicle opened up and a ramp clanked to the ground. As the auto-turrets his troops had laid nearby continued firing on incoming drones, he ordered everybody inside.

Bercilak's soldiers clamoured into the red-lit steel box. Their suits didn't permit them to sit so they stood and held on to the straps

194

dangling from the ceiling. Lloyd helped Mirek into the back, and jumped in ahead of Stephen, who was intrigued by the APC's military innards.

"Awesome bullet magnet, this is," said Stephen as he squeezed between two oversized shoulders.

One of Bercilak's smaller soldiers, dressed all in yellow armour, took off her helmet and slotted it in the crotch of her arm. "Good t'ing it's bullet-proof then, huh?"

Even though Stephen knew that the little lady knew what he meant—that they were riding along in a tin can that a rail gun, plasma bolt, or a rocket could squash with ease—he appreciated her tenacity. After the accident, he needed all the assurance up for grabs.

Lloyd, alternatively, showed no sign of timidity or sorrow, which only meant he was expropriating that energy to suppress those very feelings. He had known Byron for years, and though he wouldn't admit it, Lloyd had caught a piece of truck between his ribs that had him bleeding internally. He caught Stephen staring at him through the throng of metal arms and metal legs. His face slackened and pooled into a smile. "How's Dubchek feeling?"

The ramp folded inward and the rear door closed.

Mirek pulled Stephen close and raised his voice over the sound of the gunfire back on the road: "What'd Lieutenant Barnard say?"

Stephen fired up the OK hand-sign for Lloyd's benefit, and spoke directly into Mirek's ear: "He said one more wreck might do your face some proper justice."

Bercilak gently pushed Stephen and Mirek aside with a muted, "Pardon," so that he could reset the cloak. It was deactivated by the button on his wrist and turned on by a switch at the front of the APC. One could blame the electrician responsible for this irresponsible design, but that would be speaking ill of the dead. Besides its poorly thought-through switch, there was nothing special about the APC's cloaking mechanism. It was a smart fluid that would keep their existence secret unless directly scrutinized by one of the EDS' scanners.

With the APC hidden from the drones pelting the corpses they left on the road with molten charges, Bercilak waved to the only person not wearing armour of any kind. A lanky young man with jaundiced eyes, seated furthest inside the vehicle with his back facing the front, nodded in reply. He grabbed a pair of goggles and wiped them clean, first on his sweat-stained boxer briefs, and then once more—just to be sure—on his Preston F.C. Lilywhite sleeveless shirt. He slid the goggles on and the APC's engine revved.

195

There was no front cabin to speak of; nothing resembling a traditional driver's seat. The APC had been an autonomous armoured troop transport, controlled remotely by some all-knowing machine or committee. Now, for lack of trust in AI, it was neutrally linked to the goggled waif, who had already begun to direct their movement with his eyes. The vehicle lurched forward.

Bercilak grabbed hold of a handle soldered to the wall beside Lloyd. "Khatri said the n'er-do-wells needed a lift to Preston city center. That about right?"

Lloyd nodded. "We're in the market for a puddle-jumper. Going about opening the doors for our friends to the West."

The details didn't concern Bercilak. He understood enough; that their mission was nominally important and they needed the lift. "Jeremy," Bercilak called up to the goggled man wearing only underwear. "Follow the trees until the 59 bridge. We'll let 'em out there, then double-back to our first waypoint."

"That's not city centre, is it?" Stephen piped up, familiar enough with the area to know that the bridge was too far or at the very least a dangerous trek away from their destination.

"No it's not," Bercilak said, raising his voice for Stephen's sake. "If we take the APC any deeper into the red zone, we'll draw enough attention to see that none of us completes our objectives."

Lloyd accepted the decision cooly. "Sure thing, Captain. We appreciate the help."

"Yeah! Thank you!" yelled Stephen, pulling shards of glass out of his cheek. "Thought we were goners."

Pulling his helmet up just enough to showcase his gracious smile, Bercilak answered: "We're all in this together, kid."

Gripping the ceiling strap like a chimp, Mirek swung into Stephen. "Oi, you have me gun?"

Stephen bunched up his face. His first inclination was to cuss out his neighbour, though there was a good chance Mirek had blood on the brain. He pulled out another shard of glass from below his eye and stared mercilessly at Mirek. "Should we ask 'em to go back, and pick through the flames for it?"

Mirek contemplated Stephen's suggestion. Finally he shook his head. "Say—want me to show yah how to load yours?"

Captain Bercilak Service knew enough not to ask specifically what needed doing in Preston. If anything, the greater context for the day might confuse his approach to his own assignment. Any gossip or unsolicited intel was a liability for all involved. Instead, he mainly talked about the splendor that would be their dawn attack on the

English Broadcast Relay Station in Southport. Some of his soldiers, including the yellow-suited Cecilia Thomas, were dubious of the plan's efficacy. That said, as was the case with the Welsh, Irish, and Underpoolian Resistance, their numbers were dwindling and hope was running out. If action was to be taken, it had to be taken before its effect could no longer be felt by the enemy.

Unlike Bercilak, Cecilia seemed interested in why a lackey from the Engineer Corps had dragged two twenty-somethings into the lion's den. "You wouldn't be the boys headed to Ireland, would yah?"

Stephen looked to Lloyd for permission to answer the question. Lloyd was busy bandaging his chest, more or less blinded by the armour lifted up over his head. Stephen turned to Cecilia and nodded.

"Well, I hate to be the one to tell yah, but you're headed in the wrong direction."

"We gotta grab an enemy jet."

"In Preston? Ah jeeze. I wish you luck." Cecilia had a soft face with softer features. Her big blue eyes produced in Stephen a kind of calm, like the first warm rays of sunshine after a long hard winter. She looked out of place in her yellow suit, although judging by the nicks and scarring on it, she was well-rooted. "Watch out for 'em triads."

Mirek had been gifted a new weapon—a small submachine gun. It was a plinker, the kind of gun that irritates more than exterminates, but a gun nonetheless. He swung into the conversation with the gun clipped to his chest plate, nearly chipping Stephen's remaining front teeth. "Triads, eh? Bloody hell. Why are they still here?"

Cecilia wiped her visor clean and answered: "The Pingos used the triads in Africa and South America for regime change. A clever way around violating the Armistice. In Preston, it's the Mountain League. They're more or less fixers for the PRC. England is where they come to rest and resupply for local missions."

"Mountain League...?" Stephen had seen the dragon-mountain symbol in the streets near Carrella's compound on his last foray into Preston, though he had had no idea as to its meaning.

Bercilak piped up: "They say they move mountains when in fact all they move are sex slaves and drugs."

Jeremy the driver whispered in Bercilak's general direction, blinded by the road ahead.

"Alright," said the Captain. "We're two minutes out. You three think you can manage?"

197

Lloyd pulled his armour down over his wound and readied the Nephilim rifle he had taken. "Can't thank you enough—all of you." He shook Bercilak's hand and nodded to the rest of the 4th Battalion, all hidden in their monstrous armoured suits.

"Our duty and pleasure," Bercilak answered. "As Cecilia was saying, you're not likely to find too many EDS screws around. It'll be triads. Do not let them capture you alive."

Mirek nudged Stephen. "Can't really capture a corpse, can yah?"

Stephen looked to Mirek morosely. "Prove us all wrong."

TWENTY

The elevator doors peeled back to the fifty-fifth floor. Several Shepherd drones rushed into formation beside and behind Commissar Jagjit Hassan as he rushed out. Although all operated by a single system, there was the appearance of competition between them—as if they were all vying for the Commissar's commendation.

Just as on the other floors, the English bureaucrats assigned to the fifth-fifth floor were all kneeling with their willpower overrun and fates left to capricious determinations. Jagjit swooped by, ignoring all of their exposed wrists. As he approached the north end of the floor, he began intuiting directions to his silvery entourage. The Shepherds busted into room after room in search of Scott Townley and his two aides, who had similarly gone astray.

Allister commed Jagjit: "Oi, Jag! A Londoner ship is trying to access the processing bay. I let it in? Or do you want me to shoot it down?"

Appreciative of Allister's loyalty—first to him, second to the EDS—Jagjit answered as if Corven was standing behind him and watching: "It's Dr. Worthing. Let her in, Al. But keep a watchful eye. We have three fugitives on the loose. Make sure my guest doesn't unwittingly let them out."

"Sure thing, boss!" Allister's speaker crackled as he fired his thrusters to meet and escort Dr. Mallory Worthing's jet to the processing bay.

Staring down a hallway where Shepherd drones mirrored one another's violent searches as if set to music, Jagjit shouted, "Find them!" The song and dance paused. All of the drones turned to face Jagjit, expecting an order or some elucidation. After a moment of silence, they proceeded to kick in more doors and terrorize more people. Jagjit meanwhile tensed his jaw so that his teeth clicked. The drones' discovery or lack thereof was translated into instant summaries and sent straight to the Commissar's implant. Sensing failure—as incompetency was hardly a trait ascribed to the selfless race—he pushed forward with the two Shepherds who had remained behind to guard him. Together they passed gutted rooms, some loud with sobbing, and others newly silent.

They came finally to a cul-de-sac where there were three doors that had not yet been busted down by the drones. With a slight tilt of the head imbued with all the meaning a drone could ask for, Jagjit ordered the two side doors knocked in. Both rooms were empty, leaving just the one. So full of curiosity and resentment was Jagjit that he ordered the Shepherds to stand down, and opened the third door himself. His eyes dilated. A yellow smile bulged his cheeks. "Comrade Townley! Looks like work has got you down."

Townley lay at the center of the room. He propped his head up with one arm, the hand on the end of which was obfuscated by his wet brown mop of hair. His other arm dangled across his chest. It looked formless, as if it had been deboned. Like his arm, his face too had been restructured. Purple and red blemishes covered his skin except where the skin had been torn. He could barely see through his swollen eyes, but knew enough that the EDS had finally caught up with him. "Khatri, you sonuvabitch."

The name Townley used to address him made Jagjit's skin tingle. It made all of the butterflies in his stomach whip up a corrosive hurricane. Jagjit Hassan took a step inside the room while his drone accompaniment stood shoulder-to-shoulder behind him, sealing the doorway. He crouched beside Townley and crossed out another name on his checklist. "I'm not sure who Khatri is, but I presume he's a damned-handsome socialist."

"*Damned* is right." Townley spat out a clot and a molar. "Go on, pinko. Do it! Kill me!"

Lifting and dropping Townley's broken arm gleefully, Jagjit shook his head. "We have much to discuss in advance of that, comrade. We can expedite much of this sanguinary process if you tell me exactly where your staffers Czapran and Mortimer are presently hiding."

Exhausted by the pain riddling his body, Townley slumped over. "Proshchay, Captain Khatri." As he lay flat on his back, the hand that propped up his head emerged from his tangle of wet hair. "I'll see you in Hell." In his hand was a primed grenade.

One of the Shepherd drones looming in the doorway pulled Jagjit back and out of the room, while the other standing next to it leapt forward onto Townley. The grenade went off. Pieces of drone and bone spat out of the room. Foam rained down from the ceiling tiles along the hall. Sprinklers went off and sirens began to blare.

The bang had left Jagjit momentarily deaf, although the signals transmitted directly to his auditory cortex provided him with all of the concerned voices and updates he might have otherwise missed. He pulled himself up with the help of the Shepherd drone that saved his life. The more scarred of his two hands began to shake. He had sustained no critical physical injury, but the shock burst memorial bubbles deep below the surface of his consciousness. "Two

200

suicides and no answers," he said to himself, although Officers Vola, Gaine, Roth, and Estra were listening carefully on the other end.

"Sir, Doctor Worthing is here—she wants to know if you are alright," said Gaine, whose subvocal mic was picking up some of Mallory's false concern and other blather.

Jagjit brushed dust off of his jacket and buttoned it up. He intuited a command to all non-human units inside the department: "Tear this place apart. I want every single employee accounted for. No one comes or goes until Czapran and Mortimer are located."

All of the Shepherds leapt into action.

"Gaine, keep the Doctor company until we've secured the building. Seal the processing bay until I give the all-clear. Major Vola?"

"Yes, Comrade Commissar?" replied Poyraz, breathless on another floor.

"Meet me in the lobby. I have a sneaking suspicion they're hiding among the hoi polloi."

"Yes, Commissar."

Returning to the elevator, already waiting for him, Jagjit dismissed his two new guards. He stepped inside the yellow compartment and pressed the button for the lobby. As the doors closed and the elevator car careened, Jagjit noticed a tooth stuck in his sleeve. It looked like a fish scale. He pulled it free, held it up to his eye, and scrutinized it. Dropping his mental shield and calling upon the historians at his disposal, he ordered a full psychological and DNA evaluation of Scott Townley: "I want to know where he is from; who beat him up; why he undermined us; and what he sought in return for his subversion."

The historians online ratified the Commissar's request.

In the peripherals of his third eye, all of the data his previous inquests had produced was ready for assimilation. Jagjit prepared to take it all in, and threw Townley's tooth to the floor. The elevator shook when the tooth hit the ground as if the enamel had grown in mass by an order of magnitude. The jolt slammed Jagjit into one wall, then to the ground. Debris peppered the elevator compartment's undercarriage, which sounded like pocket change tossed inside a clothes-dryer. Wires thrashed about in the bank, shaking not only the elevator but Jagjit's confidence. As new alarms began to ring and the elevator squealed to a halt, he picked up the tooth once more— examining it again to dispel any superstition that might fester. He got up, and called out to his men over the intercom: "Vola! Gaine?!"

Estra was the first to reply, still stationed in the Arts and Letters vault as ordered. "Roth just went offline. There's been an explosion in the elevator bank off the lobby."

Right away Jagjit knew what that meant—*why now and why here*: the painting was on the premises! *Townley had found it.* His staffers must be taking it out! "Get down there, now! Major Poyraz—I want a Goliath on the front steps right this second!"

As Jagjit had extended the broadcast to all available units in the area, there was in response a crispy chorus of "Copy-that's."

"They have a weapon of mass destruction and are trying to get out through the lobby! Stop them now!"

Poyraz chimed in: "On it, Commissar. We'll have you out of there in a jiffy. An engineer is coming down the shaft now."

"Good, Major. I want you downstairs as well—you'll be my eyes and ears," Jagjit roared.

"Yes, Commissar!" Poyraz said, embracing his responsibility and taking on a deeper voice.

As he swayed about in the dark, Jagjit pondered on Townley's misnomer. "Khatri." He had heard the name before—belonged to a terrorist Commissar Dorz had, despite himself, managed to eliminate. Jagjit queried the name. Surprisingly, nothing came up. No death warrant. No EBS broadcast celebrating the People's victory over hate. The only result that came up with any relevance was the file of an active terrorist, Zoya Khatri. Her photograph made Jagjit feel sick. Firming up, he attributed his reaction to his innate disgust for those who would put their own interests ahead of the collective.

It only took a few minutes for Reclamations engineers to cut the Commissar out of the compromised elevator compartment, and in that minute the lobby had become a forward operating base. It was full of Shepherd drones and security droids all with a vague sense of who constituted today's enemy. For starters, they killed nearly half of those citizens who had been waiting in the lobby. Estra searched the fresh bodies for the weapon of mass destruction—the so-called Family painting—and went around turning out pockets and opening mouths.

Major Poyraz Vola brought Jagjit behind the front kiosk where a physician stood expectantly to address his injuries. "Sir, there's been a firefight in the east stairwell."

"*They're still here...still alive?!*" Jagjit seethed. He grabbed Poyraz by the arm as the physician began to treat his shallow wounds. "How many combat personnel on site?"

202

Poyraz tilted his head for the answer his implant had ready: "Thirty-six. One-hundred and ten riot drones."

"Shepherds?"

"Yes, Comrade Commissar."

"Activate every last one of them and find these terrorists! Now! What they have in their possession is of great importance to the Supreme Council. See that it is not destroyed."

Poyraz patted the physician on the back as he would not dare be so chummy with his superior. "The People's Will be done." He ran off wearing a hot-eyed look of total focus.

Absent the Major beside him, Jagjit thought of the company he should presently have. He demanded Dr. Mallory Worthing's presence, for her own safety *of course*. He got in touch with Gaine.

Sergent Gaine answered uneasily: "Sir?"

"Tell Dr. Worthing I want her downstairs right this instant."

"She refuses to come. She says she's safer here."

Jagjit shoved his physician away and braced against the front desk. "You bring her down to the lobby via the west stairwell now or I will personally stamp your re-education request."

Gaine was clearly rattled. He swore to himself with Jagjit for an audience, having forgotten to turn off his subvocal mic. He petitioned Dr. Worthing to leave once more, and she refused, citing the pain of descending fifty-five storeys as reason enough to wait out the crisis.

"Sergeant?!" roared Jagjit. Those in the lobby who hadn't been killed or weren't preoccupied killing shunned their eyes from the sight of the enraged Commissar.

"Just one moment, Commissar."

"If I have to repeat myself one more time..."

There was some more negotiating on the other end followed by a scream and shouting.

"Sergeant Gaine, what's happening up there?"

"We've got a rogue Shepherd up in the processing bay."

Jagjit motioned towards the elevator bank, but stopped in his tracks on chewed-up marble. "Well, you have gun, don't you? Shoot it! Then get the Doctor out of there!"

Gaine made it to the lobby via the west stairwell from the processing bay looking like he had run a marathon. Worthing was better off, but just as winded.

All of the singed hair on the back of Jagjit's head stood on end at the sight of her. "Doctor, your timing leaves something to be desired."

"As is your handling of this situation," was her riposte. Mallory turned and silently thanked Gaine.

Jagjit raised his hand. He was on the verge on a venomous tirade when he received a transmission from Allister: "Oi Jag! Short and sweet, huh?"

"What? *Not now.*"

"Huh? Yeah, I'm looking at it now."

"At what?"

"Dr. Worthing—she's taking off. She need an escort or you figure she'll be fine?"

Jagjit looked over to Mallory. "Al, she's standing right in front of me."

"You serious, 'ssar? She wouldn't happen to have shared her ship and the door codes with anyone, eh?!"

"Allister—you shoot that jet down at once!"

Mallory looked puzzled. "What jet? *My jet?*" She scrambled over to Jagjit in a huff.

Jagjit grabbed Mallory by the throat and drove her into the nearest wall. "Who did you give the Reclamation door codes to?"

Unable to answer on account of his hand on her throat, Mallory mimed the words: "They were in the ship's security system."

Surrounded by witnesses and still hours shy of the Patch Over, Jagjit knew that the Doctor's hour had not yet come. He released Mallory, and wiped his hand off on his jacket as if she had sullied it with her very being. "All units!" he bellowed over the intercom, relayed into the surrounding streets. Jagjit felt like he was on fire—burning from the inside out. "Shoot down that jet!"

Poyraz re-equipped his rifle and regrouped with Gaine and Estra. "We're going hunting!" He whipped around to address Jagjit. "Comrade Commissar—permission to lift the lockdown and to pursue the terrorists?"

Jagjit nodded. "Send a Goliath to secure the crash site and call in a dozen Reds. Preserve the contents of Dr. Worthing's ship." He turned to Mallory, still recovering from near asphyxiation, and tightly gripped her hand. "Let's go recover the wreckage of your ship, *Doctor.*"

TWENTY-ONE

The Shepherd drones milled about like well-oiled tin men, escorting trustworthees out of their cubicles and offices, and down the hallway. They worked in simpatico with one another but out of synch with the EDS, as they were extremely efficient at not reduplicating one another's efforts. They clunked closer and closer to the room where Alek and Geoff resided along with the near-dead Russian spy, Scott Townley.

Geoff wasn't dumb, though he plainly figured their only remaining option was to fight their way over to the elevator. His index finger wavered above his rifle's trigger. "Here they come," he said, anxiously watching the drones draw ever nearer. "Ready up, Alek my boy. It's been a long time coming." He jutted his rifle barrel through the gap and honed in on the first of too many targets. "Ready up or spend the rest of your life ill-prepared."

Alek shook the projection sphere he had plucked from Geoff's apartment. "How do you adjust the resolution?"

Resting his scrunched-up face on his rifle, Geoff looked askew at Alek. "That's your great idea?" He scoffed.

"They're coming. One we could take down. Twenty? One hundred? Let's give them an empty room and pick a fight on a better stage."

"Like I said: a great idea!" Geoff withdrew from the gap in the door, slung his rifle over his shoulder, and grabbed the projection sphere. He tapped his temple and interfaced with the unit.

Scott groaned. "Don't leave me this way." He could barely hold the grenade Alek had gifted him, and had no idea what it was that he couldn't get a grip on.

With the projection sphere programmed in his hand, Geoff turned his back to Scott Townley. "Not in here. That pile of clothes will make 'em look everything over twice as hard."

After Alek agreed to leave the spy at the mercy of the EDS just as the spy had done to Monica, he sleuthed out of the room along with Geoff. Banking on progressive searches, they bolted into the first open door down the hall. This room was slightly smaller than Townley's office, similarly containing a small desk and chair below an anachronistic shelving unit that jutted out bare and cobwebbed. There was no room for them both behind the door, so they took a risk and moved to the opposite corner where they stood practically enmeshed. Geoff set the projection sphere at his feet and activated it.

A passing glance would see nothing awry in this small cubicle. The passerby would certainly not take notice of the two grown men dripping sweat in the corner, or at least Alek hoped.

Townley, still anchored to the room at the end of the hall, roared out: "Don't leave me this way!" The practised fearlessness that characterized his voice when feeding on Alek's punches had dissipated. It sounded like animal panic in the jungle; a sad whoop.

There was no blur of grey or silver; the yell hadn't been registered by the drones or, knowing the floorplan through and through, the Shepherd drones were saving the crier for last.

"How long've I got to suck in my gut?" Geoff whispered with his head wedged between Alek's and the corner slot.

"Until they've cleared this wing. Stairwell's our best bet."

They could both distinctly make out the chime of the elevator. Radio chirps and bureaucratic hails preceded an authoritative shout that filled the wing like a low church-organ chord.

"If anything so much as eyeballs us, you shoot your way to a clean death, yeah?"

"Yeah." Alek felt Geoff's heart race ahead of his own. "I owe you one."

Reflexively squeaking his lips, Geoff smiled benevolently: "We all owe someone."

A troop of Shepherds led by a heavy-bearded man—the commissar Alek had seen on the EBS News broadcast back at Green's CBLOCK—marched past the room containing Alek and Geoff. They slammed down a door or two and then there was a hesitation, a pause in the chaos. They had found Scott Townley just as Alek had left him.

Geoff began to twitch. "We should go now."

Noticing a little subdermal light flicker on the side of Geoff's head, Alek realized they had underutilized a precious ability. "Can you pull anything from their intranet? Anything on how many are in the lobby? How long this lockdown is supposed to last?"

"They may get a trace on me—on our location."

"Fire or frying pan..."

Geoff's eyes glazed over and his head buffeted back as if he was drifting off to sleep. "Shit, man. Lobby's crawling with screws and their toys..."

Alek cringed. They might make it to the stairwell, but after that, they had nowhere to go.

"Oh, hold on. "There's a ship—"

"In the lobby?"

"No, you knobend. In the processing bay."

"But the building is in lockdown."

"It landed *during* the lockdown."

Alek perked up. "Which means it has the door codes pre-loaded!"

Geoff leaned through the projection to get a sense of the goings-on in the hall. "Let's make for it."

"*Wait.*" Alek pinned Geoff in-place. "We'd be surrounded and I still hear more humming down the way. We've only got the one shot—don't want every gearbox in the department tooling us up."

There was a gasp and then a loud bang. Silt from the ceiling tiles took on multiple dimensions as they cascaded through the projection field concealing the two clandestine operatives from CBLOCK32. Sprinklers began spraying white foam to douse whatever fires were believed to have caught from Townley's final flame. Dozens of drones and men stampeded down the hall. Just as soon as they had rushed to the scene of the explosion, many of them had departed with a renewed resolve to make life unbearable for Alek and Geoff.

As he did his part in restoring the solidity of their disappearing act, Geoff pulled a transmitter from his jacket. "Ah crap, mate. That reminds me."

"What's that?"

"Fire in the hole!" Geoff winked and flipped a switch on the device. There was another tremendous bang, although this time far off and greatly muffled by the detritus padding all the various floors.

Whatever sprinklers hadn't been triggered by the grenade on the fifty-fifth floor and the explosives in the lobby began to spit more foam.

Alek was stunned for he wasn't sure precisely what Geoff had done—he was so preoccupied with the painting and his revenge that he had overlooked Geoff's boobytrapping efforts in the elevator bank. "What the hell was that?"

"We're headed upstairs, yeah? All t'more reason to draw them below."

Alek shook his face into a flabbergasted smile. "Quit it with the good ideas before I owe you too much."

There was a crunch in the doorway. A Shepherd drone strode inside, trailing white foam. Right away it struck the bureau desk with its machete, cutting it in half. The drone bent down to inspect the two spaces beneath the metal "M" it had created with its strike. Finding nothing worthwhile to report, the Shepherd's top section spun around, and then its hips followed.

207

The drone's machete was mere centimeters away from Alek and Geoff's noses, which they might have wished were several lies shorter or perhaps just flat on their faces. Alek's hand turned white, so tight was his grip on his weapon. Geoff clasped his mouth to minimize the volume of his excited wheezing. The slightest movement or interaction—a drop of sweat or an unintended implant resonance or a nasally breath—would have been enough to alert the killer drone. Alek and Geoff would both be halved, dissected, reanimated and then interrogated; only later they would be re-educated to death and then used as compost. But they were still as statues; concrete hardened around racing hearts.

The Shepherd strode out just as it had come inside, tracing lines through the foam mounting on the floor.

"They're looking for us," said Alek, "For Czapran and Mortimer."

"No kidding, Einstein." Geoff dug through his pouches, and pulled out a pair of what appeared to be haloes. "Yank your chit and throw on this choker." Whereas a halo highlights virtue, a choker conceals sin. These anti-surveillance devices would prevent any sensor from registering them as anything more than innocuous clumps of cells. "We just move up the hall with the projection sphere auto-populating. Anything that penetrates the field we'll kill."

After a uniquely bottom-heavy medical droid appeared and disappeared with Scott Townley's remains, Alek peeled into the hallway holding the projection sphere at arm's length and with his rifle slung behind him. Geoff followed close behind.

"Slowly, slowly," whispered Alek, creeping along the corridor with the projection fabricating an empty hall behind it.

There were several drones still searching for them ahead. One was inconveniently stationed just before the door to the stairwell. Alek pressed forward, dragging Geoff along. They could step aside into either of the rooms the drones had already rummaged through, but they would only be delaying the inevitable and a potentially less-manageable unknown.

"Damn. There's one behind us...Must've been picking through Townley's desk."

Alek didn't turn. He took Geoff's word for it. "There's another just by the door to the stairs."

Geoff took aim at the drone's midsection. As the Shepherd drones were headless and had a decentralized CPU, there was no guaranteed kill-shot—especially not with the caliber Geoff had loaded. "What do you want to do?"

"Are you still in their intranet?"

208

"Just tell me what to do, Neuhaus."

Alek would have been more prompt, though he hadn't any good ideas—certainly none that wouldn't make matters worse—but sometimes a bad idea is preferable to none at all. "Report activity in the elevator bank."

Geoff looked rearward and ahead. The drone behind them would race to the scene through their entrails while the drones further afield might all come running, close enough to see through the little sphere's illusion. "You're joking."

Committing to his bad idea, Alek gently elbowed Geoff. "Do it! *Now*, Geoff! *Now!*"

The EDS intranet was a good-neuralhacker's playground. The penalty for monkeying about was death, and as Geoff had warned, there were always bullies afoot. (Thankfully, he could retreat from it entirely or believed that to be the case.)

Seconds after Geoff's eyes glazed over once more, there was a flurry of activity. Drones and men alike motioned for the elevator. The drone nearest the stairwell leapt into action and was the first to the scene, prying the elevator doors open with its machete and club.

"Now!" Alek and Geoff jogged the remainder of the way to the stairwell door.

The drone sifting through Townley's material belatedly took to action just as Alek pulled Geoff into the stairwell and quietly shut the door. Alek waited a moment for a drone to bust through. When it was clear his bad idea had been worthwhile, he turned to console Geoff who seemed to be out of breath.

"Neuhaus, I swear I'm going to have a heart attack one of these days." Geoff leaned on the baluster and peered down at the fifty-five storeys of blue railing and white cement. "Good God, man."

Before Alek could respond, he saw two EDS shoulder patches appear at the top of the next flight of stairs. As their projection sphere was still activated, Alek hushed his partner and yanked him behind the false image of an empty stairwell.

Gripping his chest, Geoff clued in to the new threats. He re-equipped his rifle and took aim. He surprised Alek by not firing. His reason? Though his weapon was technically silenced, it wasn't truly silent; the gunshots would just be slightly dampened and might still rouse the attention of a dedicated drone or security official back in the hall. *A knife on the other hand?*

The masked security officials came down the flight of stairs, and walked right into Alek's projection, on the other side of which they fell to the ground with their throats slit.

Geoff tucked his blade away. "They'll be registered as dead in ten, twenty seconds."

Having stepped in the blood that Geoff had let flow, Alek was forced to take off his boots. It was one thing to leave bodies behind; a whole other thing to leave a trail of footprints.

Spurred to self-awareness by Alek's stripping, Geoff realized he too would make footprints, but of a different kind. They had both trampled enough foam to put out ever-shrinking fires en route to their exit. He took off his shoes and set them beside Alek's. "I don't give a shit. I'm keeping on me pants."

Alek pocketed the projection sphere and armed himself. "I think that's a good idea for everyone involved."

They ran up several flights of stairs where they came upon a guard overseeing a technician's repair of a Shepherd drone station. The drone station's occupant was stillborn—the Shepherd had not been fully released from its cabinet and was therefore unable to activate. The guard heard the buckle on Alek's strap clink against his rifle's magazine and turned around, startled. He reached for his sidearm, which his holster didn't seem ready to relinquish, and in that moment of confusion, Alek foolishly contemplated retroactively turning on the projection sphere; of letting both parties in the prospective melee save face and go about their business. However, the guard finally freed his gun and that sealed his fate. Geoff shot right through his mask while Alek confirmed the kill with a gut shot. The muffled blasts resounded throughout the stairwell.

The technician took a step back from the drone and raised his hands in surrender. While Geoff checked to make sure the drone was inert, Alek ordered the technician to turn around. As soon as the man was facing the wall, Alek clunked him where his head met his neck with the butt of his rifle.

"Merciful now, are yah?" Geoff kicked the unconscious technician in the groin to make sure that he wasn't faking. "Should start handing out prayer cards."

There was shouting downstairs—not in response to their most recent homicide but to the two bodies below. Alek ran past the guard's body to the door by the drone cabinet. "This is it!" He tapped on the stenciled letters, which read "PROCESSING BAY".

Geoff peered down and spied dozens of hands clutching railings on different floors. "Go on then."

A hiss and a whine of the Shepherd station's failing components gave both of them a stir. Alek examined the drone, half in and half out—frozen in a state of becoming. There was a tiny

210

portal on its chest plate spouting a couple thin diagnostic wires left dangling by the unconscious technician. "Hold on. Can you hijack it?"

"All I can do is remove friendly designations and prevent it from being remotely deactivated. It'll still come for us. Only difference is that it'll attack the demsocks too. Not worth the risk if you ask me."

Alek handed Geoff the projection sphere and opened the door behind him. "The greater risk is not to try." He held the door open.

"Piss off mate. What I said about people owing people...People can owe too much."

The ruckus below grew louder. It sounded like discordant choir coerced into song.

Alek looked past the door to the antechamber it swung into. It looked like a construction site; all bare, riveted steel and heavplast siding. Down the hall on one side, the ceiling grew higher. "Hangar's just around the bend."

"And you've got horseshoes up y'ar ass!" Geoff grumbled. Ever-so-reluctantly he trudged over, projection sparkling in front of him, and jammed the Shepherd's loose diagnostic wires into the side of his head. "It's not stuck. Just suffered a false start. Oi, you shoot this if it comes for me, because there's no starting sequence. It'll just go live, which means death for the two of us."

"Do it." Alek raised his rifle. A Shepherd couldn't so easily be destroyed, but Alek owed it to Geoff to at least try.

The voices down the stairs were close enough now for Alek to make out what was being said. The incoming demsocks had been put on to these latest two corpses by their security overseers.

Geoff's eyes glazed over. The Shepherd ceased to whine. There was a click. Geoff stumbled backwards. The cord didn't come out of his head naturally; instead, it snapped. The slight tug threw him off balance and shook surreality into the projection field. Alek rushed to catch him, and dragged Geoff out of the stairwell.

As the door swung shut, Alek and Geoff heard the Shepherd take its first steps. Alek ensured that the projection sphere was stable, and pressed Geoff along the hallway in direction of the processing bay. Behind them: muffled screams and grunts; gunfire; and the eerie scraping of metal against metal.

"How about you brush up on your hacking so the next time you're the one close and intimate with a killbot?" Geoff complained, just around the corner from the processing bay.

Alek, who had retaken control of the projection sphere, now made sure that the guardians filing into the stairwell behind them from the other end of the hallway were oblivious to the threat ahead. He checked the corner to see the fabled ship that had entered during lockdown: a streamlined teardrop with two fixed wings—one set stemming from the sides of the fuselage and the other set on its pointed tail—painted black with the Home Defence Department insignia on its sides.

Near the ship, a large Praetorian drone loomed over a DSSP officer and a petite bureaucrat wearing a beret. Alek heard the officer warn of trouble elsewhere and the bureaucrat answer back indifferently. It sounded like Monica. *It was Monica.*

Geoff tried to stop Alek from approaching her, but he was too late to do so quietly and too afeard of the Praetorian to attempt de-escalation loudly. "Mate! Mate!" He scurried to catch up with Alek, walking with the projection sphere displacing possible recognition.

The DSSP officer appeared frenzied: "Comrade Worthing, Comrade Commissar Hassan is presently dealing with two fugitive terrorists still believed to be on the grounds. With your permission, I'll be moving you to a secure location."

"Where, Comrade Gaine?" Monica replied contemptuously. "Wasn't this entire building supposed to be *secure*?"

The DSSP officer attempted to respond, but Monica cut him off.

"I believe I'll be safe with my protector." She patted the Praetorian drone's hulking metal forearm. "The Commissar can come find me here when he is ready."

It was Monica to be sure, though there was something off about her; something at odds with how Alek remembered her. Certainly a bullet could make a sizeable difference in one's appearance, but the changes Alek noticed in his wife could not have all been the result of Townley's attempted murder. Monica's hair was cropped back. She seemed to rest her jaw differently and to hold herself more confidently. The armband she wore was the same that used to give her nightmares. The nametag on her gaudy militarized medical uniform read "Dr. Mallory Worthing."

"Moni..." Alek said under his breath. He yanked at the thread around his neck on which Monica's memex was suspended, contemplating how he might replace this imposter's mind with the mind of the real Monica, and whether she too would be an imposter of another kind.

The Praetorian drone turned its horned head around and scanned for threats. Its eyes seemed to lock onto Alek, who froze and held his breath.

Geoff grinded his teeth. "I've paid my penny. Seems that monster will exact the pound."

"Quiet," said Alek, mortified by what he saw but elated to hear Monica's voice.

"I tell you what, comrade," said Monica, impressed by the officer's persistence. "You inform the Commissar that you'll be personally protecting me—that I don't feel like climbing fifty-five flights of stairs."

The DSSP officer relayed Monica's suggestion via his intranet comm. Clear from his bowed shoulders, he was being diminished on both ends. "Comrade, the threat—"

A bloody guardian slurped his way on hands and amputated legs around the corner. Before expiring just behind Alek and Geoff, he muttered: "Run!"

The Shepherd drone Geoff had sicced on their pursuers entered the hangar. Dark blood ran down its blade as well as along its baton. Evident from the radio chirps blaring from the stairwell, it had made mincemeat out of the first wave of demsocks ordered up the stairs. It focused on Monica and on the DSSP agent. The Praetorian didn't seem to attract its attention.

Alek and Geoff couldn't manage two false fronts. The Shepherd, on the projection sphere side of the illusion, noticed them too.

"Percy!" Monica called out to her Praetorian drone.

The Praetorian spun into action and charged the Shepherd before it could come for Alek and Geoff. As the giant humanoid adorned with razor-sharp edges, horns, and multiple layers of rolled homogenous steel plates ran towards the Shepherd, finally matched with a befitting foe, Alek circled around the action towards the jet and Monica.

Not willing to risk his neck despite the good Doctor's protest, the DSSP officer ordered to bring her to safety pulled Monica towards the rear stairwell.

Though Monica tried to call Percy to her aid, the Praetorian was preoccupied. It withstood the Shepherd's initial thwacking. The drone's blade bounced off Percy's armour plating like a flat stone along still water but without sinking. Before the sparks had gone out, the Praetorian grabbed the Shepherd by its midsection, lifted it over its head and yanked it apart. It threw the Shepherd's top section the length of the hangar, and smashed its twitching legs against the ground.

With Monica and her undesired escort avalanching down the stairs on the building's west side and the Praetorian smashing the

213

remaining vigor out of its ill-matched opponent, the way to the jet was clear. Alek and Geoff galloped over. The side door was open and the ramp extended. They hurried inside.

Right away Geoff checked the console to see if the codes were preloaded. Alek deflated behind him, clutching his breast, which seemed to be caving in. The painting's edges found his fingers under the fabric. He nearly had a conniption fit. *The painting!* He could have saved Monica then and there!

The Praetorian scanned the room for additional threats—thankfully not the jet—and ran after its master.

"I know what you're thinking," Geoff said, turning the jet on with a series of ham-fisted taps on the navigation panel.

Alek looked to his friend with tears in his eyes and Monica's memex in hand.

"And you're right. This jet will be shot down the second it leaves the building. So why not walk out the way we came?"

Alek resented Geoff for making light of the situation. This was no time for jokes. Then he saw through to Geoff's meaning. "AUTOPILOT" strobed on the jet's navigation console. The processing bay blast doors began to grind and squawk. They rolled to the sides, creating enough room for the jet to dart out.

Geoff shoved Alek out of the jet and hit the button for the door, which closed behind them as soon as the jet had swallowed up its ramp. "Time to find a new costume."

"Are you insane?" Alek grasped at the jet as it thrummed and began to levitate above the platform.

The jet turned in place, not far off the ground. Its rear thrusters lit up and, after some bluster, threw it out of the hangar in blink.

Geoff ran over to the stairwell they had just come from. "Get a hold of yourself, man." He stepped over the mutilated guardian who had crawled into the processing bay. "You're lucky by all accounts. Monica's still alive—which means you better get the painting to Cathandra."

"Cassandra..." Alek followed at a distance, sure that he had driven his friend to the brink of sanity.

Inside the stairwell, there were dozens of corpses. Wiser guardians had fallen back while Shepherds loyal to the EDS could be heard systematically making their way upstairs.

Geoff grabbed a helmet off of one of the fallen guardians. He lifted a leg here and an arm there in search of a suitable double. He found a torso with a chest to match his, and dragged it to the side and began stripping it. Cluing into this last-ditch survival effort, Alek similarly searched the carrion for a match.

The Shepherds weren't far off now. They were no doubt part of a universal effort to get to the processing bay, and for once they were exercising some sort of caution.

Alek turned out a pair of guardian leggings, and after watching a sluice of vitals spill out, put them on hastily.

"Now play dead, Romeo." Geoff slung intestine over his shoulder and threw himself upon a heap of other bodies. "Haven't a second to waste, mate. Find your place among the damned!"

They no longer had their stolen identity chits and were wearing their chokers, so if scanned they wouldn't register—definitely not as alive. Trusting Geoff as Geoff had trusted him, Alek complied. He slipped in between the fragments of his victims and calmed his chest, instructing it only to breathe shallowly.

No sooner had Alek embraced the role he might have to play forevermore than the Shepherd parade made its way by. The stairwell was so crowded with them, many of them ended up trampling the dead. Alek realized his leg was in the way of the procession, but there was nothing he could do about it. One Shepherd stepped on him baring its five-hundred pound load. Alek nearly bit his lip off trying to conceal his pain. Still, he did not move or cry. Another stepped on his ankle, busting what hadn't already been crushed. One Shepherd foot dragged across the pile of dead, striking Alek in the face. He didn't have to worry about reacting, for he was truly knocked out—not fully unconscious, but hoofed into that half-life between waking and sleep. An image of a young woman flashed before his eyes. Her face gained dimension and smiled. Behind Alek's mangled helmet and bruised eyes, she took on a body unblemished by EDS torture or bullets, and pulled him out of his pain and into their much-discussed cabin in the woods. *Moni...*

Monica sat on a loveseat across the room beneath a closed window. Sensing Alek there, lying prostrate with his hands clasped together, she smiled benevolently, and stood up. Turning slowly, she pulled apart the blue drapes obscuring the window's view, revealing a dense forest pricked by barbs of golden sunlight. She opened the window and turned, clutching her breast and breathing in the fresh air.

As the ambient light spilled into the tiny structure, it awoke a babe lain in a crib beside the loveseat. The child was good tempered. It began to coo and wave its pink little digits above its face. Gliding over the crib as by sheer will rather than by the movement of her

215

feet, Monica gently lifted the child and cradled it. She sat back down holding the child.

The drapes framing the window behind her picked up on a subtle breeze and began to grow longer and fuller. They seemed to envelop Monica; to run down her shoulders like a cape and over her head like veil. She rocked the smiling child in her arms, which reached for her flowing hair. "I told you: it's not just about our little family, but the whole human family. We're not meant to live like we have."

"I know. I've found something. I—I've found something that might make it better."

"I know, my love."

"But it won't be better without you."

"I am here with you, now and forever."

"I saw you, Monica. You're different now. They've turned you into one of them. They took you from me a second time." Alek found himself sinking; not onto his knees, but into the floor. The cabin fishbowled around him. He began to panic, and as he tried clawing his way out of the chasm swallowing him up, he heard the baby begin to cry. "Monica, don't leave me again."

"Have faith."

EDS physicians, secret police, and guardians picked through the blood and bone. The dead were carried downstairs. They would ultimately be carted to the nearest crematory.

Alek opened his eyes. He had been swept to the side like a pile of garbage. His ankle was mangled and he could see his own eyes reflected in the broken visor on the helmet he had stolen. Geoff wasn't where he had been. The demsocks had likely brought him downstairs.

A physician knelt down beside Alek and prepared his diagnostic wand to determine the identity of the corpse before him and its time of death. However, he was pushed aside by a guardian whose black dreadlocks jutted out under her helmet.

"Danny," Alek murmured.

"Comrade," said the guardian to the physician. "This one has classified intel on the brain. I'm going to take him directly to my superior this instant."

The physician shrugged his shoulders and moved onto the next body without argument.

Danika lifted Alek up. Her suit had basic exo-reinforcement ensuring she would never be outmatched by a suspect assuming he had no cybernetic upgrades. This same exo-reinforcement enabled her to carry Alek over her shoulder without slipping a disc. She began her descent with Alek's head bobbing between her armoured shoulder blades.

"Where's Geoff?"

As she passed a squad of Observers sent by the Supreme Council, Danika tucked her gaze into her sternum. When she had put enough room between herself and the Observers whose job it was to designate entire departments or regions for liquidation, she addressed Alek's fraternal concern: "He's already in the van."

Head still taking no small beating in the process of being carried down thousands of stairs, Alek wondered: "Put me down. I can walk."

"No," Danika said curtly. "You can't."

Pain slowly crept up Alek's leg, tensing his calf first, and then his thigh. Further down it felt like chaos—parts were certainly out of place. "Shit."

"Don't worry. In the van I've got another one of these—" She slapped her breast, indicating the guardian exo she was wearing; the kind that could have protected Alek's ankle as well as the guardians he had dispatched who had cheaper Reclamations-issued equipment.

The lobby was loud and busy. There were angry conversations, interrogations, and on-the-spot executions. The smoke from Geoff's bombs had settled, but there was still a cloud of fine dust in the air on which the various security lights, mainly reds and oranges, danced.

Danika carried Alek straight out the door, past the ambulatory drones hovering at the base of the stairs, and over to her van in the alley, idling with a very happy CBLOCK32-er aboard.

"Alek!" Geoff cried, opening the rear door of the van and helping his friend off of Danika's shoulders. "You're off your trolley! I tell yah! That was one hell of a gamble."

Settling into the driver's seat, Danika pulled off her helmet and beamed back at her compatriots. "Didja get it?"

Alek tapped his chest, and then gripped his shattered ankle. "Ah God."

"Mr. Neuhaus here also killed the man who shot Monica..."

Danika smiled nervously. "Oh yeah? Respect."

"Who—by the way!—isn't dead after all." Geoff passed Alek the guardian suit Danika had pulled out, and began dressing himself in the third such suit.

"Hold on," Danika said, throwing her elbow over her headrest. "Then where is she?"

217

Pulling his new leggings on, which came halfway to doing the job his tibia was no longer able to do, Alek intuited instructions to his implant to dampen the pain flooding his noggin. "They flipped her. She's a demsock." He reached for the thread around his neck but it wasn't there. He had taken the memex off. Alek bowled over. "Oh Jesus." Frantically he checked his person and probed around the back of the van. "Where is she?!"

Danika threw up her hands in surrender to nuptial troubles too big to troubleshoot on the fly, especially now when they had to get across town with everyone in the regime looking for her passengers. "Neuhaus—if you don't know, *I don't know.*"

"I gotta go back," said Alek, bleary-eyed. "I gotta find her!"

Geoff strong-armed Alek. "You go back in, that'll be the end of you Neuhauses. Take my word for it."

Danika shared a look of concern with Geoff and turned her sights to the way out. "Is he going to be a problem?"

Holding Alek in place, Geoff answered: "He's fine." Looking Alek dead in the eyes, he reiterated: "You're fine. We'll find her, but we won't find her here."

"Lock and load, and hold onto something!" Danika tightly gripped the wheel and flooded the engine with charge.

The van peeled down the alley and skidded onto the next street.

The acceleration threw the riders from side to side. Whatever wasn't fastened down tumbled about the compartment. Among the items that fell out of place, Geoff spotted a medical case. He had pilfered enough medical supplies over the years to know what the case contained. He stayed Alek's hand, once again pulling up his exosuit. Opening the case, Geoff combed over the devices inside. "Ah, here we are. Can't mend your broken heart, but sure as fire can fuse that bone back together."

Alek looked cynically at the clamp-like contraption in Geoff's clutches, and leaned back, pulling his leggings back down. "Go on then."

Geoff clamped the calcifier around Alek's broken ankle. Hundreds of little needles fired through the flesh, targeting out-of-place bone. The calcifier pulsated and squeezed tighter and tighter. Were it not for his pain dampeners, Alek would surely have passed out as the needles ruthlessly fused the bone together with artificial calcium deposits and a biodegradable spidersilk composite. Though his bones may not have been binded or reset properly, they were nevertheless reintegrated such that Alek could walk into a hospital for a more permanent solution.

218

"There," Geoff said, pulling the clamp off and away from Alek's horribly bruised, bloody, and needle-pricked ankle. "That'll last you a while. Exosuit will firm it up more."

"Thanks," Alek replied, having nearly forgotten losing Monica's memex.

"No problem, *Lethe*." Sitting back and looking up at the cityscape stretched around the windshield, Geoff muttered: "It's too bad you're not fit to race, because we're in one."

TWENTY-TWO

When the EDS moved the citizenry into the CBLOCKs, they left behind massive tracts of unattended land, both urban and rural. Although the regime's chief interest in this migration was centralizing the population to better manage its needs and control its behaviour, one lauded byproduct was the environmental reclamation that unwittingly took place in the aftermath. Whereas before the evacuation, there was the odd tree planted along every other street, Preston was now dominated by shrubbery, ivy, and other greenery. Flora flourished, covering brick, concrete, charred vehicles, and bones. Nature abhors a vacuum whereas human nature exploits one.

Although there were quarantine walls put up around the Preston Red Zone and security drones left to patrol the city proper, triads had nevertheless moved in. They weren't challenged by EDS forces because every gangster and his brother had a relative in the Chinese Communist Party, making them all virtually untouchable.

The principal syndicate—the Mountain League run by the cutthroat B. Lee Chan—had its dragon-mountain symbol stenciled on every structure in the area. It was also marked on the red flags that flapped over triad bases and storehouses. Lloyd was as careful to avoid these buildings as he was sure to avoid open areas, likely littered with anti-personnel mines and boobytraps.

When he spotted one such base up the road they were headed east in hopes of finding Carlo Carrella, Lloyd nearly bit through his tongue. Ten buildings down and on the north side, there was a three-storey brick building with concrete foam stuffed into all the gaps where the structure had been chewed up by gunfights and erosion. The first storey was gutted to make room for motorcycles. Where there had been stairs was now a pile of rubble and whorls of razor wire. Passage to the second floor was made possible by a heavplast gangway. It reached up to what had become the front door, clearly a window in ages past. The windows still true to their design on the third storey were lit with pale light and had their patchwork curtains closed. On the roof, bordered by a broken balustrade, there was a machine-gun nest left unattended. Vigilance may have been required to outlast other syndicates, but judging from the unpiloted gun on the roof, that vigilance was exhausted for the day.

As soon as he recognized the outpost for what it was, Lloyd pulled Stephen off the road and drove him aside into a burnt-out shop, completely black but for the white square on the counter where the cash register had been.

"What gives?" Stephen murmured in Lloyd's grips, feet barely touching the ground.

Planting Stephen safely out of the sight lines of the absentee-gangster's gun, Lloyd looked around for Mirek. "This is triad turf...Hey—where's your friend?" He joined Stephen in looking around for the third in their party.

Mirek had found a lone rose bush growing through the tiled sidewalk, and broke from cover to pluck a flower—a possible decendant from the Red Roses of the House of Lancashire.

"Merry! Merry!" As soon as he saw Mirek hunched over the red accent, Stephen waved his arms like an airport gate director.

Noticing the concern and commotion coming from the storefront, Mirek rushed to secure his delicate prize, crushing the rose and pricking his mangled fingers in the process. "Damn it," he muttered as he trotted to cover.

Lloyd throttled Mirek as he entered the shop. "What were you thinking?"

Stuffing the petals into his pocket, Mirek shrugged. "Something for the folks back home."

"Neither folks nor home will be there waiting 'less you smarten up." Lloyd looked to Stephen. "Mind your friend or we're toast. That's a Mountain League outpost you were just picking daisies in front of."

"A rose, actually," Mirek said, rubbing the residue between his fingers.

Stephen would have smacked Mirek but for the possibility that his yelp would alert the gangsters roosting in this English mausoleum. "Any word from Zoya?" he asked Lloyd, who still had a radio piece lodged in his ear. "Should warn her."

Lloyd shook his head. Even though Bercilak had intercepted a broadcast an hour earlier on the officer's channel, there had been no chatter since. Major Zoya Khatri was either keeping tight-lipped on account of nearby enemies or had been silenced for good. "She's no spring chicken. She'll be fine. Told us to keep on keeping on, and that's precisely what we'll do. Carrella's can't be far now."

"*It's not*," Stephen replied. The burnt-out shop they were gathered in resided on a corner bordering onto two streets, one of which snaked east past the old St. George's shopping centre. "Just up there on the left."

"North side?" Lloyd produced a small monocular and peeked outside of the storefront. He could make out one of several entrances

221

into the mall. The Mountain League's red flag was out of focus in his telescoped vision yet still in view. "We'll overshoot and come around the rear from the north."

Before questioning the Lieutenant's reasoning, Stephen and Mirek both leaned out behind Lloyd for a chance to see what they had missed when ducking into the shop.

"That the Pingo hideout there?" Stephen clicked his tongue against the roof of his mouth. "Looks pretty quiet."

"Aye. If they're anything like the gangs back in the day—*up north anyway*—that just means there's a lot going on out back." Mirek may have undermined his compatriot's faith in his present sensibilities with his sudden gardening interest, though his experience with seedy bars and their patrons was formidable.

Recognizing his neighbour's expertise, Stephen reflexively held his thumb over the back of his gun's slide but remembered Jay's advice. He corrected his error, and mentally prepared himself for another bout of violence. "The best way forward is straight."

Lloyd sighed and pinched his brow. "Right." Seeing that Mirek had gone back to obsessing over the flower in his pocket, Lloyd pulled him close. "So you figure they're active in the back?"

"Their getaway vehicles are out front. Their shipments are out back. I'll put money on the latter." Mirek pretended to dig into a different pocket for bullion.

Lloyd stayed Mirek's hand, and grabbed Stephen by the arm. "Hear me clear, you clowns. We're going to cross, and then hug them buildings there all the way to the mall. Stay close, move slow, and don't let 'em see you out the windows. I'll signal you over one by one. Alright?"

Mirek perked up. "Yes sir."

Stephen nodded.

Lloyd lifted his armour, tore a strip of fabric from his undershirt, and stuffed it into his gut wound to sop up some blood. Satisfied he had stopped the bleeding, he checked once more with his monocular to make sure the machine-gun nest was still unattended. Seeing that the coast was clear, he retreated into the shop. Popping shards of glass underfoot, he got a running start inside and practically lunged across the street. Once he had made it to the Mountain League's side of the rosebush, he equipped his rifle and waved over Stephen. Of course he hadn't explicitly specified Stephen in his instructions, so Mirek also ran across.

In their traversal, Stephen noticed a black-clad gangster peek his head out of the front door for a smoke. He tackled Mirek to the ground as the Mountaineer's furtive eyes scoured the street. Hidden

222

amongst the blades of grass that had cut up the asphalt, he whispered to Mirek: "Keep still, shit-for-brains!" He raised his head above the grass to see that Lloyd, finger on his trigger, had a bead on the nosy Mountaineer. A single shot would alert all of Preston to their location. That said, a witness could alert all of England. Submersing back into the green, Stephen scolded Mirek once more: "What the hell does 'one at a time' mean to you?"

Mirek, sweating and now taking matters seriously, shook apologetically, though he didn't shake loose his attitude. "Wee bit vague for an engineer."

From the shop nextdoor to the outpost emerged another triad sentry, this one carrying spacesuits up the stairs. The door opened for him, the building received him, and the smoking head slunk back into the triad base, sealing it and cutting the breath of smoke in half.

Lloyd summoned the lads to his side: "Oi, chuckleheads; on me." He didn't bother chastising them. He had more or less accepted the role of babysitter, even if his two unwanted children were pushing or dragging twenty-years-old.

They crept around the Mountain League's gangway, acutely aware of every move and sound that they each made. Relaxed conversations inside the outpost calmed their nerves as they passed. For a fleeting instant, Stephen thought he heard Cantonese, but realized his mistake—the Chinese communists had driven the dialect and all who had spoken it to extinction.

On the other side of the Mountain League base, an odd series of noises stopped Stephen and his ilk in their tracks. First there was a jostling sound like a rotary engine that wouldn't start. Then there were angry voices followed by feminine whimpers. Between the outpost and the next building on the block, there was an alley not wide enough for a fist to pass through. Stephen peered down the alley and saw labourers loading young English girls onto a truck. He turned to Lloyd who had also caught a glimpse. "Can't we do something?"

"We are." Lloyd was as torn up about the sight as his junior, but not ready to risk losing the war to win a quick battle. "Keep going," he ordered the two young men forced under his wing.

Mirek pointed out a badly-worn sign for the shopping centre. "I betcha Carrella can already smell that whisky."

Shoulders slumping under the weight of this reminder, Stephen turned to Mirek. "I don't have it."

"You what?!"

"It broke in the crash."

223

"What the hell! What're we gonna give him?"

Lloyd gently pushed the both of them along and grumbled: "An ultimatum."

St. George's Shopping Centre looked like it had succumbed to the dragon of legend. The easier way off the street was on the mall's west side, though Stephen had correctly remembered that it had been the more treacherous way inside. Carrella's massive curiosity shop was situated beneath the multistorey car park, which he had vented to permit aerial units to come and go. On foot, without having telegraphed their intention to drop by, getting inside was a wholly different matter than simply dropping in. To get to Carrella's without triggering any of the monstrosities he had pieced together for the sole purpose of eviscerating intruders, they had to retrace the steps Wesley had shown Stephen—much like a dance, but to be done in terrible silence.

In the side entrance Stephen took Lloyd and Mirek through, they discovered why the triads left Carrella alone. There was a pile of bloodied EDS uniforms and Mountain League costumes. *Trophies?* Stephen wondered. It was no secret that Carlo had lost his mind or at the very least had lost his way, but this ostentatious display had no precedent in the man's legend. Perhaps he had worn out his welcome. *No*, decided Stephen. They would have bombed the city into dust before admitting defeat to a lone lord of war. If this allusory mound of death had gone unpunished, then perhaps those who had ventured into Carrella's realm had done so against orders. *Yes*, perhaps the enemy's curiosity had them skinned like the proverbial cat.

There were fewer signs of mass murder deeper inside the mall, though the smell of death nevertheless hung heavy in the air. Each of the shops had been picked clean of anything of importance. Mannequins remained on their stages and hooks, although someone had dressed them up in the regalia of destroyed estates and classes. There were mannequins with bishops' mitres; bobby caps; tellers' visors; with goggles, lipstick, dentures, and other horrible additions that only a demented mind might find amusing or inviting, although neither was the intention behind them. They were scarecrows, and the piles of clothes nearer the entrance along with the ruddy streak marks up and down the consumer corridor were evidence that their omen was was legitimate.

In one of the shops they passed, there was a partially-burnt dress on display. Mirek fancied it or perhaps just the form of the mannequin it was pulled over. Stephen yanked him along and

224

repeated the warning Wesley had issued in that very hall: "Anything that draws the eye will draw blood."

"Stay there," ordered Lloyd upon reaching an atrium. He walked up to a railing and looked down, up, and around.

There was no glass left in the skylight separating the elements from the mall, which was a boon to the mold, moss, and flowers that had conquered the food stands and cafeteria below. Baubles and streamers danced on strings from the ceiling, gusted to life by a slight breeze through the skylight. Adjacent to Lloyd was an escalator wrapped with razor wire, which zagged down to the bottom floor. There were a number of clothed skeletons stuck in the wire. Clear from their placement and their pristine threads, they had been put there on display.

Although unnerved by the psychopathic decorations, Lloyd called up his reinforcements. "Alright...Where from here?"

It took Stephen another minute to reach the atrium as he was carefully plotting every step as Wesley had taught him—hoping they didn't have to rend their flesh to reach Carrella's shop. Mirek mimicked him, and in doing so, made it something of a game.

Feeling exposed with another floor above them and subtle movement—possibly just the wind moving kipple about in the various shops—Lloyd split the distance and accosted Stephen. "Where now, Nowak?!"

"There's a hole in a shop just over there." Stephen pointed out a shop crowded by silhouettes Lloyd had mistakenly thought to have belonged to mannequins. They were in fact four-armed Cymurai droids. Although menacing machines, the dormant droids were actually a hopeful sight. If the triads had killed Carrella, they would have dismantled the Cymurai as their Japanese-American design was an affront to Chinese sensibilities. Conversely, if the EDS had controlled the site, they would have destroyed the droids because they were not made by a Supreme-Council-approved manufacturer. Carrella was still the king of this hill. "A ladder goes down to a maintenance tunnel. There we announce our intentions and wait for Carrella."

Seeing the Cymurai and the four blades on each of them held high, Mirek gulped. "What about them then? I don't suppose there's another way down."

"To the maintenance tunnel? No." Tracking Mirek's focus to the droids, Stephen swatted away the danger. "Don't worry about them, Merry. If they were going to kill us, they would have done it already."

225

The three of them crept uneasily into the store. Stephen was the first to the center of the room where he had prophesized a hole and a ladder. Both were intact. The ladder went down to a scaffold stilted a few metres above the floor below, fastened to which was another ladder that extended into the murk plugging another hole.

"It better be easier getting out than it is getting in." Lloyd slung his rifle over his shoulder, and began down the ladder. "Like a bleeding corset this place is!"

Stephen watched Lloyd descend and then Mirek after him. He looked around nervously at the Cymurai before mounting the ladder. One of the droid's sensor arrays flickered—red lights behind its armoured mask flashed on and off, and it tilted its head. "Hiya," Stephen said, trying his best not to fall or wet himself.

The droid's head straightened out. As the Cymurai didn't cut Stephen to pieces on the spot, Stephen was encouraged, despite now being certain that they were being watched and judged by the madman himself. He slid down the ladder and smacked the scaffold, dusting Lloyd and Mirek below, and then shimmied down the second ladder into darkness.

Lloyd popped a flare and threw it as far down the maintenance tunnel as he could. "Through here, Nowak?"

Instead of answering, Stephen took the lead. The pinkish-red light of the flare drew him closer.

Mirek marveled at the boots that lined both sides of the tunnel, and considered swapping his own for a better pair. "You figure he's a collector?"

Lloyd crouched down and inspected a secret-police-issue jackboot. Inside of it was a brain implant. "Yeah. Not in the way you're thinking though."

Stephen reached the flare and pressed further along. At the tunnel's end, not far off from the car park's lower levels, there would be a counter. On that counter there would be a service bell. Although he couldn't see much besides what his shadow failed to occlude, Stephen could tell he was nearly there. The grit under his feet gave way to polished tile. A few steps across the smooth tile brought him to the counter. He waited for the sensation of Lloyd and Mirek's warmth behind him to ring the bell.

"Go on then," Lloyd said, gripping his gun tightly.

Mirek patted Stephen on the back. "For Underpool."

Stephen tapped the button on the bell, but the bell was muted. Nevertheless, somewhere off in the bowels of the mall, there was a penetrating screech. Once the screech died down, the sounds of a stampede shook the building's very foundations.

226

Mirek took aim rearward while Lloyd took aim at the darkness behind the counter.

"Put your guns down!" Stephen cried. "We're here as guests. You take aim, then you might as well take off your boots."

Mirek and Lloyd grumbled together, and reluctantly lowered their weapons.

The sound of the stampede preceded a metal creaking that emanated from beyond. It grew louder and closer, louder and closer. The last pinks and reds from Lloyd's flare hinted at its shape: it was bipedal, but not a man. It had a clownish face, though the similarity was accidental; in fact, its face belonged to another—it was a man's desiccated skin pulled over a Cymurai's metal skeleton. The droid's red eyes glowed through the embalmed dermis at Stephen, then at Mirek, then at Lloyd. Instead of blades for hands like its brothers upstairs, this Cymurai had hands—petrified human hands slipped on like gloves.

It was hard to make out the droid's unholy additions for the poor lighting, but Stephen was horrified even if he didn't know why. "Alright, maybe guns are a good idea!"

Lloyd raised his rifle.

A deep voice blasted from the Cymurai, mediated by lips that wouldn't move: "Who are you? And what do you want?"

Lloyd nudged Stephen.

"My name is Stephen Nowak. I have with me Lloyd Barnard and Mirek Dubchek from Underpool. I've been here before with Wesley Miller."

"Miller? Hmm. I don't recall a Wesley Miller." The Cymurai tilted its head and its human mask drooped.

Stephen gulped and firmed up. "The Resistance needs an aircraft. The Americans will soon be coming and we need to—"

The Cymurai tilted its head further so that it clanged against its shoulder and tore the human mask. "I don't recall a Wesley Miller."

Face half-red, half-shadow, Mirek looked pleadingly at Stephen. "Bruv! Refresh its memory!"

The Cymurai's head began to crush its shoulder while the exposed wires woven through its titanium neck began to spark. "I don't recall a Wesley Miller...I don't recall a Wesley Miller...I don't recall—"

Lloyd pushed Stephen to the side and unloaded a clip into the Cymurai's head and torsal panel. "Yeah? That jog your memory?"

Stephen stumbled back into the wall, his boots pressing others out of the way. "The hell did you just do?!"

227

Yanking the head free of the deactivated Cymurai, Lloyd inspected the machine's perforated transmitter. "That's what I thought."

"What?" yelled Mirek. He could barely even make out Lloyd let alone the droid on account of the flare having been reduced to a poof of pink.

Lloyd answered: "It's a local AI. Wasn't Carrella talking."

There was a click and then a hiss. Behind the desk, what had appeared like a concrete wall slid back on rails into a clean stone corridor lit by fluorescent bulbs.

"Splendid." Lloyd threw the Cymurai's head over his shoulder, reloaded his rifle, and circumnavigated the deposed concierge.

The corridor past the secret door was fairly tight. Piping ran along its ceiling and sides, running past the first of many plastic curtains. Lloyd led the way, cutting through the plastic curtains with the barrel of his gun. They proceeded along until they came to a particularly heavy and opaque curtain. Lloyd had Stephen hold his weapon while he tugged the weighted plastic drape to one side, and in so doing revealed Carrella's workshop. It was less a workshop and more a warehouse, although the warehouse like the preceding passageway was compartmentalized by plastic sheets.

There were oodles of android parts, decommissioned battle tanks, and gizmos from every corner of the country compressed and stored beneath the low ceiling; tables whereon skeletons lay alongside exosuits; shelves whose side panels were buckling; automobiles comprised of various makes and models like steel Frankenstein monsters; and vats of battery acid and silos full of grains of dubious origin. What Stephen could not see in the immediate vicinity was precisely what he promised the Resistance; what Zoya and Jay may have died for.

"Where's the jet?" Mirek wondered aloud.

"Never mind the jet right now. Where's Carrella?" Lloyd grumbled.

They passed through several more partitions of the warehouse without finding either a ship or a shipbuilder. Finally they entered a large room. Unlike the previous rooms, which had low ceilings, this hollow extended upwards through several floors of the mall's car park.

There was a work bench and a computer terminal at the centre of the room where the evening light touched down. Large shapes swaddled with linens and other covers were arranged around the work bench like standing stones. A metal walkway led

228

away from the room's center to a retractable staircase at the top of which was a riveted steel door with a porthole.

"It's got to be under one of these," said Stephen, lifting a corner of a cover concealing one of the cannibalized vehicles—a bulky hovercraft designed for swamp warfare.

Lloyd snapped his fingers and directed Mirek to the far side of the room. "On yah go! You said it's here. Find it! Quickly too. We're running out of time." Pulling up a blanket for the sake of his own disappointment, Lloyd added: "Just make sure to stay within earshot."

Mirek examined several possibilities up on jacks and bricks. One tarp-pull revealed a large polyhedron with dozens of tubes and vents exposed. "Not this one. It's some kind of life-support system." He left it exposed and kept looking.

"Nothing here either," Stephen rejoined, feeling the pressure mounting and more and more responsible for what he hoped was not originally a wishful thought. He ventured off to inspect a tarped vehicle on the other side of the room, opposite the retractable stairs. The first peek was promising. It bore a Chinese designation and had Mandarin characters stenciled along its side. Stephen jammed his gun beneath his belt, and began yanking the tarp with all his might. It wouldn't give, and Stephen didn't feel like committing to another wishful thought, so he pulled the tarp back just enough to gain access to the side door, and climbed inside.

Just then, incandescent light blasted through the porthole window on the riveted door at the top of the stairs. Mirek took aim at the sound unprompted by Lloyd, who was also ready to fire. Mechanisms behind the door jostled and clicked, and the door swung open.

Stephen heard the clamour. He had the door open and tarp partly up on what had turned out to be a defunct and plasma-bolt-ridden Chinese gunship. He could partly make out the workshop and the riveted steel door above it, and expected to see more or less what he had remembered: a man wearing an apron, but otherwise naked, with a long scraggly beard, and skin bronzed by engine oil. Instead of Carrella coming through the door, it was a triad gangster in full battle gear and a horned helmet: the head of the Mountain League himself, B. Lee Chan.

"Oh shit. It's a trap!" Lloyd yelled. He advanced, firing his weapon, but the gang leader's armour wouldn't yield.

Mirek joined in with his submachine gun. His barrage was equally ineffective. "What's the matter with these guns?" he roared indignantly as he fed his another magazine.

229

Unphased by their gunfire, B. Lee descended the steps while several more gangsters wearing variants of the same armour poured out of the door. One threw a stun grenade, which threw the Resistance fighters to the ground and temporarily paralyzed them.

B. Lee took off his helmet and set it down on the workbench at the centre of the room. He had wild eyebrows and a weak moustache that flapped over his steel, cybernetic jaw. Although the lower portion of his face was inorganic, his eyes still managed to communicate the elation that a smile alternatively would have conveyed. "So you are the ones who've been trying to get in touch with the Preston butcher."

Lloyd's nerves were shot, yet he still tried to grab his gun, dropped just out of reach.

B. Lee's men fanned out and explored the recesses of the room in search of additional intruders. One disarmed Mirek and put a blade under his chin.

B. Lee stepped on Lloyd's reaching hand. "Answer me!"

Mirek planted his hands in front of him to take his weight off of the cold steel pressed against his throat. "Kiss my ass," he said breathlessly.

Stephen, still hidden, looked on with baleful eyes.

"Wait!" said Lloyd. "Let the boy go and I'll talk."

"Boy? *Ha!* He's an old man on these streets," said B. Lee gruffly. He signaled his man to take a half measure, and the corresponding thug spilt a small rivulet of Mirek's blood.

Lloyd howled: "Stop it! I'll tell you everything!"

The gangster cutting Mirek released him. Mirek caved forward clutching his throat, unaware that he had only been nicked.

B. Lee lifted Lloyd up by his collar, and hurled him towards the work bench. "Go on! Talk!"

"Your government is going to unleash a plague upon the world to make the grass grow." Lloyd looked around for some implement he could use to bash in the brains belonging to the Mountain League leader, although his comment seemed to have done the trick.

Startled by the accusation or perhaps surprised that someone else was aware of the imminent global holocaust, B. Lee looked around the room at his equally-startled men. "You know about Kunlun?"

Lloyd nodded. In fact, he knew very little—nothing more than fragments of the gossip peddled around Mises Tavern and the snippets he had paid attention to in the intelligence briefings.

230

"And you thought the Preston butcher could do what? Give you the strength to sweep the tide back into the ocean?" In lieu of a tongue, the gang leader had a vox box set deep in his steel trap of a mouth that processed his linguistic intention and amplified it. "You see, we had a similar idea. We are not the joiners that the Chinese Communist Party wants us to be. We do not want to be cooped up in a computer stored underground, especially not with the likes of *your people*. We spoke to Mr. Carrella about helping us. He was not interested." He turned and directed his voice to the room at the top of the stairs: "Dai ta chuqu!"

From the room beyond the riveted door another armoured gangster appeared, dragging behind Carlo's mutilated corpse. He tossed the body down the steps haphazardly.

"You see," said B. Lee, gesturing to the disfigured body settling at the base of the stairs. "Mr. Carrella didn't want to choose a side. So I chose for him."

"All we need is a jet," said Lloyd glumly, visibly arriving at the conclusion that they had failed; that the Americans wouldn't come; that the Resistance and those whose minds they might liberate would be massacred in the streets. "Preferably a Chinese jet. One of yours will do."

Spotting the blood seeping out of Lloyd's uniform, B. Lee laughed.

Mirek began to shake with rage. "The Americans will send your lot packing."

B. Lee shouted out in Mandarin. One of his soldiers punched Mirek, rendering Mirek's entire body slack.

Lloyd, propped up against Carrella's workbench, couldn't see Mirek, but could tell he was in rough shape. He looked around for Stephen. When he didn't see him, he raised his voice: "Listen shithead! I've got a commando unit that's going to *track down objective Zoya*, and will get the job done no matter what happens here. Do you hear me?!"

Stephen heard him just fine, though he had something else in mind.

"Well," said B. Lee. His hand snapped back—apparently also a cybernetic upgrade—and a long blade fired out. "If they do, they're doing us a favour. But I will not repay that favour. Certainly not in advance." He raised his arm and with it half-meter of serrated steel. "Perhaps Mr. Carrella can make you a ship to take you back to the land of the living."

231

Lloyd heard an unmistakable click—one that had struck terror into him the last time he had heard it. This time it filled him with joy.

B. Lee saw the calm in his captive's eyes and turned around, arm still high in the air. He saw the source of the sound and with the sound came blinding light. B. Lee tried to drop his blade down on Lloyd anyway, but Lloyd kicked him back and lunged to safety as a stream of plasma flowed from the gunship aback the room.

B. Lee attempted to flee, but the toroid of excited matter found him and slipped effortlessly through his flesh. His petrified scream overloaded his vox box's amplifier so that when he fell in two pieces, the top half blasted dead-channel brown noise.

"Stay down, Dubcheck!" Lloyd yelled, as the plasma stream hit the far wall, leaving behind molten orange grooves.

The stream cut through tarped vehicles, and sent massive stacks of boxes and gear tumbling down. Finally, it blazed over to the gangster who punched Mirek. It melted off just his crown, then doubled back to slice through his breast.

Stephen's face was alight and crimped into a maniacal smile behind the plasma cutter—an anti-armour weapon jarring through the rear of the scrapped gunship. Since he couldn't pull the tarp off, he simply fired through it, setting the tarp ablaze. The fire had spread quickly and engulfed the oblong gunship.

The remaining gangsters tried for the stairs to the riveted door, but Stephen cut the stairs in half, and then liquefied those at its base. He stemmed the flow of plasma, and leaned forward on the gun, searching the room for another target. He saw Lloyd amble over to Mirek.

Lloyd pulled Mirek up gently. "Déjà vu, huh?"

Groaning and holding his jaw, Mirek nodded.

Stephen yelled out of the rear turret: "Is that all of them?"

Mirek counted the bodies. There was at least one missing. "No!"

Before Stephen could react, he felt a tug on his boot. Though he still had a good grip on the plasma gun, his attacker managed to pull him into the main fuselage and then out of the ship. It was an especially-angry gangster who had gotten ahold of Stephen, and thumped him repeatedly with a singed arm.

Mirek and Lloyd ran over to the sound of the scuffle. They froze at the sight of Stephen at gun point. This last gangster couldn't make his way out the way he came in on account of the melted step and couldn't leave the way Stephen had come in on account of the Cymurai. He was at a loss just as his foe had been only seconds prior.

"You will build a ramp out for me," said the gangster.

"A what?" asked Mirek, spying his submachine gun by the body of the gangster who had struck him.

"A ramp to the door. I will leave cleanly or I will make a mess of your friend!" he said, shaking Stephen about roughly.

There was a loud clang—the sound of metal striking metal. For a fleeting moment, the gangster looked around and in that moment lost track of where Stephen's head was. When Stephen saw the gangster's gun drift just slightly in front of his face, he threw his shoulder up and knocked the gun out of his captor's hand. Stephen swung his elbow back into the gangster's face, and thrusted his body backwards, sending B. Lee's last man to the ground.

Mirek and Lloyd scrambled for their weapons while Stephen contested the last gangster's attempts to secure his weapon.

Once the gun had been prodded out of reach by ten warring, long-stretched fingers, Stephen tore the horned helmet off of his foe and mounted him. Right away, Stephen locked both of his arms at right angles and began punching. Although the gangster managed to strike Stephen's sides, the effort was futile. Stephen had committed to the action—to pile-driving the gangster's cartilage into his sinuses—and had fully disassociated. Tears and snot ran down his face. His eyes appeared empty and reflected only the gangster's terror. Only when there was no face left to punch did he stop, and when he did, he vomited profusely.

"It's okay, mate," Lloyd said, putting his hand on Stephen's shoulder as he spat the last of his bile. "You did us all proud."

"What d'yah figure that sound was, huh?" Mirek asked, raising his gun and taking aim at tricks of the mind skirting through the dark.

"Sorry about that!" responded a feminine voice. "Got snagged on one of Carlo's contraptions. Didn't mean to keep you waiting."

"Major!" Stephen hollered, nearly choking on the flecks left over from his last purge. He wiped his mouth, got up, and staggered over to the sound of Zoya's voice.

Zoya didn't bother with words. She hugged Stephen, and waved behind his back at Lloyd and Mirek. "Where's Carrella?"

Lloyd pointed at Carrella's mutilated body, which had been mutilated again post-mortem by the staircase that had fallen.

"The tinkerer ambush you lads?" Zoya walked over with Stephen, and looked in amazement at all the dead bodies. "Was he working with the Chinese?"

"I'm under the impression that he said 'no' to the Mountain League..." Lloyd craned his neck to better imagine Carrella's previous

233

shape. "And that he would have said 'yes' to us. I think he was denied salvation at the last hour."

"Judgement's not ours," Zoya said, crouching to inspect the Mountain League insignia on B. Lee's armour. "Suppose that means the puddle jumper out in the street isn't a gift from a friend, but rather spoils of war?"

No one reacted to Zoya's mention of a ship outside. Stephen was still in a state of shock. Killing didn't live up to his subterranean fantasies, and he was trying to maintain dominion over his stomach.

Mirek was idly walking about and touching devices whose purposes he couldn't comprehend.

Lloyd for the moment wasn't concerned so much with the future as with the past. "Where's Jay?" he asked, already knowing the answer.

Zoya's eyes dipped. She walked very slowly to the work bench at the centre of the room, and sat on its edge. "Jay—" Looking up to Lloyd with wet, sympathetic eyes, she forced recent trauma into words: "When we were trying to lose our tail, we found our way inside a nursery."

Stephen knew all about the nurseries. They were something of a horror story in Underpool—one he figured had been embellished to incentivize fence-sitters to fight. The leading officials in the government had feared they might not live long enough to see the Mental Union, so it was deemed imperative that their health be maintained at all costs. The cost, in this case, was the lives of tens of thousands of clones whose organs and cells were far more effective in treating the officials' bodily degradation than the 3D-printed alternatives. Though there was a prohibition on procreation in England, the breeding centres allegedly weren't adding to the population but merely maintaining it, meaning no greater carbon footprint.

"We needed a distraction, and he wasn't going to leave that place standing."

Lloyd nodded. That was all he needed to hear. He had known Jay in the way that Stephen now knew Mirek. He would be surprised if Jay hadn't burnt the nursery to the ground. "You're certain he's gone?"

"Oh," Zoya scoffed. "*One-hundred percent.*" She took a breath and looked around the room. "Are you good to go?"

"Ask them," Lloyd replied, pointing to Stephen and Mirek.

"Pardon?" asked Mirek, realizing he had now lost as many if not more teeth than Stephen had himself relinquished over the course of the day. He looked at the parental admiration undergirding Zoya and Lloyd's eyes. "Oh, *good to go*? Hell yeah. Right Stevie boy?"

Stephen stood straight. "Go where? And how?! We haven't found a ship. Certainly not one that could stay airborne even if you took the ground away. I messed up, you guys... I remembered wrong. I condemned us." His jaw trembled despite his best efforts to lock his molars together.

"Clean out your ears, yah martyr! The triads have a ship outside."

Lloyd's eyes sparkled. "What kind of ship?"

"A small PRC transport ship."

"They don't put those down in Preston willy nilly. And if it was weapons they were hauling, they'd land one of those international cruisers. *Dubcheck*," said Lloyd in an accusatory tone. "You said you'd found a life-support system?"

Mirek nodded and pointed to the half-sheeted polyhedron.

Nodding in agreement with himself, Lloyd responded: "*Already chained up and ready to go*. That's why they were here. They had spacesuits over at the outpost. They're looking to get offworld, and Carrella was their golden ticket. Without life support, them locusts have to wait around for whatever the Pingos have in mind for the rest of us."

"Who gives a damn? A ship is a ship, regardless of why it's there," said Zoya, desperate for at least someone from her squad to share in her excitement.

"Unguarded?" asked Stephen, looking for a weapon with armour-piercing capability amongst the dead. "The ship, I mean. How many are out there?"

Zoya shook her head. "No idea."

Mirek rushed over to Stephen. "We've done it, bruv!"

Stephen tried pushing Mirek away, but his neighbour had too much momentum. The tackle turned into an excited hug and a slap on the back. "Alright, alright, Merry. Easy does it," he said, repressing his own enthusiasm and channeling his inner Wes. "We've found the starting line. Now we've got a marathon to run."

Lloyd spotted something off in the shadows. He disappeared and reappeared with a ladder over his shoulder. He lugged it over to the severed stairs and provided them with a way out. "Careful, now. There may be more lurking about."

As the Lieutenant staged the ladder, Stephen noticed B. Lee's helmet. He walked over, picked it up, and inspected it inside and out. "Oi—this one's identity chit's still locked in." Putting on the helmet, Stephen straightaway saw its value. A small heads-up-display

235

indicated the flatlines of all the men lying on the floor around him as well as a dated readout for a cargo ship. Carrella's jammers prevented the readout from updating.

Zoya summoned him over and confirmed the find. She returned the helmet to Stephen. "Good salvage, Private. Bring it to the ship."

Unable to climb with the helmet in hand, Stephen put it on and clambered after his squad.

They made their way out of Carrella's mausoleum, and passed several ruined Cymurais along the way. Carrella had not gone down without a fight. When he was captured, he had attempted to summon his creations to his aid. However, owing to one sort of malfunction or another, everything went haywire and his help never came. The same malfunction may have meant his death, but it also meant that the Cymurai Stephen and his squad passed when first arriving at the mall were inert despite being cognizant of their trespass.

Past the scene of what looked to have been a particularly ghastly albeit short-lived torture, Lloyd led Zoya, Stephen, and Mirek through a hallway of deactivated boobytraps and out the side of the carpark into twilight. What they had hoped to find inside had dropped down like manna from Heaven and awaited them in the street.

Given B. Lee and his Mountain League's misgotten presumption that their robbing and murdering of Carrella would go uncontested, there would have been no need for fleetness. Nevertheless, their cargo ship was ready and in position in the street outside the mall to make a quick getaway. It was buoyed on a magnetic cushion and its side thrusters were active, painting the nearby buildings sapphire blue and keeping its partly lowered rear ramp narrowly clear of the ground. On the side of the ship's vertical fin was a decal of the Chinese flag with its large party star and stellar subordinates strobed metronomically by a white navigation light.

Behind the cargo ship was a heavy lift drone hovering about seven metres off the ground, holding beneath it on four thick steel cables a platform large enough to carry a small car. If it was for the life-support system B. Lee had pursued, then this drone would have been perfect as a way of lifting it out of Carrella's lab. After all, the life-support system would not have fit through the twists in the corridors leading inside, and the cargo ship wouldn't have been able to fit through the portal in the roof of the carpark. Though the drone itself was unmanned, there was a guard keeping watch over it— likely waiting for orders to send it off or remote-control it over.

236

Zoya and Lloyd spotted the guard, and silently deliberated on how best to surprise him. They surveyed the area, ensuring additional Mountain League squads had not been called to reinforce their boss. Had the call been put in, it wouldn't have escaped Carrella's network of jammers.

Stephen squeezed between the Major and the Lieutenant, eager to share some of the messages he had received via B. Lee's helmet requiring immediate attention. "There's a group coming in from the northeast. Five minutes out." Stephen enjoyed the eerie depth of his modulated voice. "They know that something's happened at the mall. Some bugger named Zhaoping keeps asking if the Xiists know."

"Know what?" asked the Major.

Stephen shrugged.

"How many Pingos we looking at, Nowak?"

Appealing once again to the helmet's heads-up-display, Stephen tried to count how many units were inbound, but the red triangles denoting armed militants were more or less overlayed, creating one giant red triangle. "I dunno. A bunch."

With no time to spare, Lloyd quickly inspected the street and the windows above it for snipers down the sights of his newly acquired rifle, and then slowly made his way over to the guard.

Left behind with Zoya who anxiously watched Lloyd's back, Stephen leaned over and asked: "When you found this ship, why didn't you just go?"

She remained focused on the ship, the guard, and her man. "*Go?* You mean: why didn't I leave my squad behind?"

Stephen nodded.

"For starters, I no longer have a bomb."

"What do you mean?" Mirek interjected, crawling over from his lookout.

"When we were cornered—back in the nursery—Jay and I tried setting it off. Didn't work." Zoya gulped. She licked the sweat off her upper lip, and looked through her scope forlornly. "Was a dud."

There was a yelp and a gunshot. Stephen peered over the berm, and saw Lloyd firing a second round into the guard beside the drone. Lloyd stormed up the ramp and into the cargo jet. After a series of flashes and bangs, the Lieutenant reappeared, this time dragging behind him the body of a pilot wearing an elephantine mask.

"Coast is clear!" Lloyd announced, rolling the body down the ramp.

Mirek ran over to Lloyd. "Zoya's nuke was a dud."

"You're joking?!" Lloyd's face lost all expression. Under his breath he invoked the assistance of the Virgin, then asked Zoya as she neared the ramp: "*And ours*? The one Nowak has—is it a dud too?"

Zoya glared at Mirek as he disappeared into the ship, and then looked apologetically at Lloyd. "We can test it out if you'd like." She waved Stephen over and sought out the button for the ramp. "Sort of a one-time deal though."

"Hold up!" Stephen traded weapons with the guard, still breathing though unconscious. After yanking the gun free, he noticed a pop-up on his heads-up-display: a control option for the heavy lifting drone. He seized command and released the platform. Another simple eye-movement-triggered command permitted him to guide the drone back into the cargo ship. "Careful! Stand clear!"

The drone trundled inside the ship, nearly pinning Zoya against one side. Midway in the hold, a slim pedestal emerged from the floor to support the drone's tray while a magnetic hook suspended from the ceiling secured the drone itself.

"Entirely unnecessary, Nowak!" yelled the Major. "Just get in here!"

Stephen joined Lloyd and Zoya on the platform.

Zoya hit a button on a floor panel, and the three of them were quickly shoveled into the bowels of the jet. "We don't need more weight. If I ask you to do something, you do it. Leave the improvising to me."

"We could use it as a decoy," Stephen said in protest. Though the ramp was designed to drop quickly, it took its sweet time to close. "Speaking of improvising," he began, perplexed by the self-destructive reflex the Major seemed keen to downplay only a moment before, "Why did you and Jay try to off yourselves if there was clearly another way out?"

Lloyd gripped Stephen's shoulder. "There won't always be a Captain Bercilak or a Private Nowak to bail us out of trouble. Sometimes it's just a matter of evening the score and leaving the enemy without the satisfaction."

Zoya nodded knowingly.

"Damnation's quite the price to pay," Stephen said, recalling his own attempt to trigger a nuke. He took off B. Lee's helmet and handed it to the Lieutenant.

Somewhat hurt by the suggestion, Zoya threw her hands up. "So is slavery. So is letting the enemy know what we're up to and compromising the rest of the Resistance."

238

Catching a glimpse of the red triangle approach the epicenter of the map inside the helmet at Stephen's side, Lloyd spurred the others towards the cockpit. "A conversation for another time methinks."

TWENTY-THREE

After letting Dr. Mallory Worthing reprogram her Praetorian drone—which had busted into the lobby fit for war—Jagjit pulled her over to the Department of Reclamation's front doors. The blast shields reinforcing the doors rumbled along their tracks, yanked open by the Department of Reclamation's security system.

"Come along now, Doctor," said Jagjit. Blinding searchlights spilled into and overexposed the lobby to the point of making it feel like some ethereal nonspace. "We are in the midst of a revolution renewed. The future will not wait!"

As the external blast shields clinked back into place on either side of the front doors, Mallory broke free of Jagjit's grasp and corrected her garb. "Naturally," she said miffed and off-balance. In the fore, she could make out hundreds of shock troops, guardians, and drones. The penetrating searchlights hid all other details. Mallory blocked her eyes, attacked all of a sudden by stage fright. Although she had just rebuked Jagjit's unnecessary physicality, she took one step closer to him. Mallory was less likely to catch a stray bullet by the Commissar's side than she would be standing by her lonesome, unless of course there had been a coup she had not been aware of—*the inevitable revolution by tomorrow's leadership against today's; the tyranny of the new.*

"Comrade Commissar!" boomed a voice on a loudspeaker. "How many injured?"

Jagjit looked directly into the searchlights. He half-motioned to take inventory of the carnage behind him, but aborted the attempt and shrugged. It was below his station in the regime to answer questions posed by undesignated silhouettes. "Look for yourself. I expect the final tally sent to me in ten minutes." Jagjit received a neural-comm with a live stream of updates in the field. He minimized it from his attention and, behind glassy eyes, studied drone footage of the downed fugitive ship. "Doctor," he said, inviting Mallory this time to follow with an excited flourish. "Let's go have a conversation with with your ship's crew."

Mallory nodded, and nodded again indicating a shock trooper in a fully-armoured exosuit clinking up the stairs behind the Commissar.

The shock trooper stopped just short of Jagjit and threw up a salute. "The People's Army, Section 3, is on location, Commissar.

Lancashire is blockaded. Naval assets are in position. The Eastern Wall has been sealed and electrified."

"Excellent," Jagjit said, slapping the shock trooper on his polygonal pauldron. He began to circumnavigate the steel brute, but was inhibited by a garbled stutter.

"Com-comrade Commissar...Your orders?"

Jagjit clenched his jaw and looked back at the Department's whitewashed façade. "Tear this building apart. I want an inventory of everything—every shred of evidence, organic or inorganic."

Mallory pressed between them and added: "See if you can find and secure Margaret Green's processing sphere." On account of the hullabaloo, she couldn't whisper, so she barked her rationale to Jagjit: "If we can determine the source and nature of the weapon, perhaps we can go on the offense with its technology and its possible future iterations..."

The shock trooper's agreement fuzzed through his helmet's vocoder. He trudged up the steps, and was soon joined by the rest of his monstrofied ilk, who similarly saluted Jagjit as they passed him on the stairs.

Jagjit shooed away the ambulatory drones and guardian vans hedging in his limo as he crossed the sidewalk. The ambulances were remotely piloted by a separate EDS system over which Jagjit had no immediate control, so they remained in place and prepared to receive the bodies of the dead and wounded. The guardian vans, on the other hand, accommodated the Commissar's exit by finding better real estate where they offloaded armed herds that rushed up and into the gloomy lobby after the shock troopers.

A red band along the limo's side lit up as Jagjit neared the vehicle. As there were still vans and trucks clearing the way, Jagjit tamed his movement. He calmly opened the door. As Mallory ducked in, Jagjit halted her. "Margaret Green?"

Mallory sneered and ducked past Jagjit into the back of the limo "It's in the reports the DSSP sent over. Assimilate their alert regarding CBLOCK06. A Cultural Equity senior staffer on loan to Reclamations was found in an amnesiasic state. All signs point to implant tampering. She's no doubt involved. Her station was on the same floor as Townley's."

"Another confounded terrorist?!" Jagjit watched medical crews and guardians carry the dead out of the Department of Reclamations. "It's a bloody epidemic."

Lancashire seemed to have waited for Jagjit Hassan to take control before falling apart. The Supreme Council must have known it was bad, although they certainly failed to stress the true extent of

241

the social degradation. Did they send him, he wondered, to take the fall for their previous appointee's negligence and mismanagement? Or was he hand-picked because of his predilections and unorthodox methods? Was Corven aware of Jagjit's old-world sensibilities and keen to exploit them for the glorification of the People's Will? Whatever their reason, his being here was the result, and there was nothing else to do but nose into the fight.

Leaning on the side of the limo, Jagjit quickly ran through Green's file. "She'll be purged in the square at dawn with the rest of those destined to become the first memory of the final mind."

"Tell me," pleaded Mallory. "Is Townley still among our fugitives?"

Jagjit peered up at his drone entourage before jostling in and closing his door. The band around the car turned bright green. "Townley is among the dead. His disciples, if that's what they are, may have made off with The Family painting."

Mallory nearly choked on the dismal news. "Then we have to carry out the Patch Over now! Commissar Hassan, all of my work—*all of what we have accomplished*—will be for naught if they reproduce that painting or worse." She clasped her mouth and mumbled: "They could find a way to distribute it over the Net!"

Although he was in complete agreement—he couldn't possibly agree more—Jagjit still savoured the Doctor's unease. "If they make it go viral, we'll be erased from history long before the resultant sickness sets in." He double-checked that he was still blocking mental intrusion from AI historians and London snoops. Only Mallory could give him away. Sure not to self-incriminate, Jagjit settled into his chair and hailed Allister, who had shot down the fugitive vessel. "Allister? Have you secured Dr. Worthing's jet?"

The purr of Allister's minigun resounded over the transmission. He was strafing streets in the surrounding area to dissuade looky-loos from converging on the crash as well as to keep any unlikely survivor inside the ship from attempting to flee on foot. "Aye, Jag. It's down."

"Excellent! *Do not destroy it outright!*" Jagjit intuited the command for the limo to head over to the crash site in Carleton.

The limo's electric engine thrummed.

Seeing that Jagjit was no longer engaged in conversation with Allister, Mallory turned in her seat to address him: "Once we have the painting, I will have an offline computer process the code baked into it. We'll figure out precisely what we're up against, and can update all of our systems—neuter it outright. It's crucial that whatever system processes this cyber weapon is offline because there's no telling what affect it'll have on our machines, never mind the population." Mallory's eyes went pale, and she updated her team at the English Broadcast Station.

The Doctor's confidence and the presumption responsible for it—that the painting was now within reach—brought a smile to Jagjit's face. He tried to hide it by stroking his beard, but Mallory had already reciprocated, eyes now their original colour. "Good. And then I'll have everything I need to carry out the Patch Over without cause to worry?"

"Yes *we* will."

As the limo navigated the maze of ambulances and guardian vans, Jagjit saw something peculiar. Past Mallory's annoyed mug and out the window he spied one guardian carrying an injured fellow and helping him—not into an ambulance, but across the street, down an alley, and into a guardian van. Jagjit's ocular scan produced no personnel file on the injured guardian with the club foot, *no doubt damaged in the firefight.* The EDS employee assisting him, conversely, had her personnel file immediately available. Her implant wasn't scannable for some reason, though her uniform still carried her signature: Danika Frye—the erratic driver from earlier in the day in whose van Jagjit could have sworn he saw unidentifiable passengers. The report had been delivered him; Danika Frye's file was in his internal queue. Reminded that he had it available to him, Jagjit quickly assimilated all of the data the government had on Frye.

Danika Frye had once been accused of "enlarging the carbon footprint" and incarcerated, but only for a brief stint. However, during the time she underwent investigation by the DSSP, her sergeant was charged with subversion and convicted posthumously. (He had shot himself.) Frye was ultimately cleared of wrongdoing. *Enlarging the carbon footprint?*

"She got pregnant," Jagjit said aloud, stunned by his epiphany.

"I beg your pardon?" Mallory, still shaken by the shootout, was beginning to question the extent of the Commissar's insecurities and injuries.

Jagjit stopped the limo, and climbed over Mallory. "That's them! *She's* helping them!"

"Who?! Who's helping who?" Mallory bellowed, crushed by Jagjit's knee.

Opening the door, Jagjit convinced himself: "She must have kept the child." The Commissar saw what the AI historians and investigators had missed: *motive.*

243

Ever since the EDS ruled that motive was irrelevant when it came to judgment over criminal cases—the Party believed in group interests as opposed to individual intent—they stopped mining for answers in the way of *why*? They knew who Danika was in terms of her immutable characteristics, affiliations, and trustvalue, but that was also all they had recorded explaining her actions. Jagjit knew, however; the impending Patch Over had flushed her out and showed her to belong to one of the most ancient classes of subversives: she who puts family before the state.

"Where are you going?" Mallory yelled at Jagjit, barreling out the door.

"Poyraz!" Jagjit yelled over the internal comm as soon as his feet met the pavement.

"Yes Commissar!" replied the Major, already riding shotgun in a commandeered guardian van headed towards Dr. Worthing's downed jet. "Closing in on the wreck now."

"Change of plans." Jagjit watched the guardian van drive down the alley and away. "I've intuited an order for the DSSP to secure the crash and hold it for us with Allister's overwatch. I want you with me. Link up!" He keyed Poyraz into his discovery. "*Danika Frye.* Guardian with the Lancashire Constabulary. Pull up the coordinates on her dispatch vehicle. Track it down. Put it on bricks. Engage if engaged. Just try not to damage their cargo. *She has the painting.*"

According to the tracker on Frye's van, she was headed towards the coast.

Jagjit ran back to the limo, this time giving Mallory a moment to shift over. "We're going for a seaside pleasure drive."

Mallory secured her seatbelt. "That's a little bourgeois, don't you think?"

Slamming his hand on the vehicle's ceiling, mentally screaming for it to go, Jagjit turned and glared. "*I think* that's a little too much out of you!" He sent an order to the Lancashire overseers and to all security details in the region. He heightened the security level to maximum, enabling any and all nearby military assets to be deployed even in high-trustworthee zones. It was open season on anyone not penitent like all of the Reclamations bureaucrats Jagjit had and hadn't spared. The Supreme Council would approve. A timely purge eases congestion, lessens demands on scarce resources, and reduces England's ecological footprint. And Corven would demand such precautions be taken anyway, were he still permitted room in Jagjit's ear.

The limo pulled into the street abruptly. Although it was his initiative, Jagjit wasn't ready for the sudden acceleration. He fell between the seats and barked out in pain. The close-call in Townley's office had done more damage than he had originally surmised.

"As you did not direct that previous comment to a comrade, Comrade Commissar, may I just say—"

"Not now." Jagjit poured into his seat, and began pawing all the parts of his body that ached.

Mallory produced a healing wand from her jacket. It didn't so much heal as glue severed bits back together. She reached out to Jagjit, who was clutching himself as if sure he was disintegrating. "If we have even just a moment, I can mend what the previous physician failed to."

Jagjit's eyes fluttered with exhaustion and he waved away Mallory's sympathetic gesture. "Focus, Doctor. It's imperative that we get to the painting first."

"Why?" Mallory looked out her window at the blur of black and grey. She blinked through a series of implant menus and firewalled her thoughts. "So he doesn't kill you too?"

"Kill?" Jagjit's blood ran cold. "Who's going to kill you?"

"Corven. He pulled me from the morgue hoping I'd complete the Patch Over and for nothing else. The Council will have me re-educated into ash as soon as the broadcast is complete."

Tuning out the radio chatter and interdepartmental queries inundating his implant, Jagjit sat upright and gave Mallory his undivided attention. "Comrade Worthing, that's quite an accusation."

"You were right. I shouldn't have said anything."

"Doctor..." Jagjit moved his hands around as if trying to coax out of himself an apology, but surrendered the attempt.

"Well it's true, isn't it?" Mallory stared at the aggravation wrinkle between Jagjit's brows. "Even if he didn't explicitly tell you, you know it to be true because you're just like him. You don't want to share the credit and the acclaim. Only difference is that you'd do it yourself. I see it in you: that imperial hunger." Mallory put her wand away and straightened her garments, which had been tussled during Jagjit's unanticipated exit.

Jagjit's insecurity reached its zenith and then melted away. Mallory was not only a brilliant scientist. She was also an excellent judge of character. He may have proved her point right there, though it was still premature. Besides, Dr. Mallory Worthing's death now seemed eclipsed by his own; by the possibility he was to Corven what Mallory was to him: a means to an end.

245

Would Corven really kill him once Lancashire was patched over? Was that the reason for the regional focus? *So that the Home Defence Minister could update the rest of the nation by and for himself?* All of the questions that Jagjit began to ask himself centered on *his* wellbeing and he immediately realized this pattern. He was terrified on one level of analysis, though on a higher plane he found himself disgusted by his own self-obsession and ego. He had forgotten that he was serving the People, not securing a legacy for himself. He laughed. "I don't know about Home Defence Minister Corven...I confess there may have been a time where I wanted you atomized."

"Ah, *Comrade* Commissar, that's something besides this project and a short shelf life we share in common."

They sat in silence while the limo, cast in shade by the aerial drones keeping pace above, closed in on Danika Frye. They were speeding along the top tier of a four-tier superhighway, which connected every single one of the CBLOCKs northwest of Blackpool Central that were grouped in clusters of three, four, or six, along with their complement of lesser neighbours—storehouses, backup cypulchres, garrisons, and utility towers.

On the top tier, there was a seemingly endless juvenile forest planted along the median separating the nonexistent east and westbound traffic. Below, on the second tier, there were rapid rail lines—rarely used; a vestige from the great reorganization efforts that followed the EDS' initial seizure of power. The third tier sported another highway, this one used primarily by state officials in times of inclement weather and maintained in case there was ever need for a protected route from the sea to the military base east of the city. The bottom tier was populated by pipelines—one artery carrying the nutrients to every citizen's eMeal printer; one carrying and taking charge from each of the region's power stations; one carrying electric information; and dozens more bandying encrypted information and systems' signals. If the fugitives were wise, they would take the bottom tier to wherever they were headed.

"Deploy a platoon to every way station on alternating tiers of the A-Way in Blackpool—in fact, spread them from here to Lancaster," Jagjit ordered his deputy, Fik, who had begun chiming in his ear in an effort to appear involved.

"Comrade Commissar," answered Deputy Commissar Fik, "We're sending them now."

"Good. Keep this channel open. In the meantime, oversee the preparations for our public re-education and the Harmony Festival." Jagjit terminated the link and spotted a checkpoint ahead. The main checkpoint in line with the partition walls, where they would shake down interlopers passing between the trustvalue zones, was still ahead aways. This checkpoint was brand new. In fact, one of the magnetic anti-armour hedgehogs was still in the process of being deployed. When those who actualized his will threw salutes to the limo—pre-cleared and permitted to pass—Jagjit enthusiastically reciprocated. As Jagjit lowered his salute, he began to wonder if he would lose himself and his resolve if exposed to the painting—if he would lose himself at the hands of the coastal terrorists before losing himself in Kunlun. He nudged Mallory. "Are you familiar with any of the technology that went into making The Family painting? *The DDOS icon*? Is there any way of inoculating ourselves against its effect?"

Mallory hemmed and hawed. "There are too many unknown unknowns for me to say for certain. The Chinese records of its use in the War are, after all, incomplete. The damage may not be irreversible. If I'm not mistaken, it'll synchronize your exocortical data with a non-EDS server and restore all of your organic memory independent of your implant's mediation. EDS educational data may or may not be recoverable. If you are a true believer, which most with your title are and have been, you should be fine."

"And yourself? To put it bluntly: you're not a true believer. Much of your file is redacted, but it's clear that you were a subversive in another life."

"Is that why you hate me so?" Mallory crossed one leg over the other and folded her arms.

"Answer the question."

Mallory looked at her faint reflection in the window. "There is no telling what it will do to me. The same affect it will have on the rest of the population is my guess."

Jagjit cracked his knuckles. "Then you should stay far, far away from the painting, and have only the true believers on your team study it once I've locked it down. If your team's data is threatened, then we should take every possible measure to protect them."

"Very well then."

"I do not hate you." Jagjit reached into his jacket ran his fingers along the grips on his knife. "Hate is too strong an emotion and too powerful a word to explain how I've felt."

Mallory noticed Jagjit's hand, buried in his jacket. She shifted away on the bench. "How *did* you feel?"

Jagjit caught himself being himself and jolted up straight. "Are you broadcasting to London Central?"

247

"Not presently, no."

Taking his hand out of his jacket unarmed and turning it around for idle examination, Jagjit tongued his jumbled thoughts several times before giving them volume. "I believe in the revolution, in the Party, and in executing the will of the People, yet the work you've done and the work we're doing seems awfully counter-intuitive. Of course, reason and rationality are mechanisms of oppression..."

"It would seem that you are not a true believer after all." Mallory tapped Jagjit on the knee. "And you have no more business looking at that painting than I do." Her eyes glazed over and she winked, drawing Jagjit's attention to the fact that she was once again broadcasting her experience to the AI historians and to the Home Defence Department. "The painting is a threat to the nation and to all of those who wish to see it continue to succeed."

The panel in the front of the limo pulsed—an incoming transmission.

Jagjit sat up straight. "Yes?"

Corven's scowl filled the front of the limo. "That Hassan firewalled his cognition is questionable, but you too, Doctor Worthing?"

Mallory was quick with a lie: "Margaret Green and Scott Townley both had access to our systems and intranet. There is a remote possibility that we were being spied on by the very terrorists we are currently in pursuit of. I had to briefly break down precisely what and who had access to my implant."

"Well then! You should have notified me." Corven had received the answer he needed, but still had steam to blow off. "Especially if you've put me at risk!"

"Yes, Home Defence Minister," Mallory said apologetically.

"The cyber weapon of mass destruction—do you have it?!"

"We are on our way to retrieve it now, Home Defense Minister," Jagjit replied, glancing midway at Mallory for some sort of support. "It seems that they created a diversion. Fortunately, we saw right through it."

"Commissar Hassan, it is my understanding that anyone who looks upon what you're about to possess may be compromised—"

"Precisely why I've blocked direct neural transmissions to or from my exocortex and cordoned off my personal data." Jagjit breathed uneasily and loosened his collar. He was still disturbed by the Doctor's insinuation that his head was next on the chopping block.

248

Mallory leaned over so that Corven could better see her. "Home Defence Minister, the preparations Commissar Hassan has taken are sufficient. I would suggest, however, that you closely observe his behaviour both during and after his encounter with The Family painting via my experience. As per the Commissar's orders and owing to my troubled past, I will refrain from dealing directly with the cyber weapon, but will look on from a distance."

Corven stood up and out of frame, and walked over to the window behind his desk. "Problem is that we all have troubled pasts. Jagjit, I want that weapon of mass destruction delivered straight to my desk as soon as you get your hands on it. And I strongly advise you not to bother looking it over. I will take the Doctor's recommendation to heart. If I come to suspect that one hair on your head has been radicalized during your handling of the painting, I will have you arrested, re-educated, and—"

Having himself voiced and realized these threats on countless occasions, Jagjit interrupted, keen not to waste any more time: "Absolutely, Home Defence Minister. I'll update you once we have it."

"Commissar; Doctor; best of luck." The window closed and Corven disappeared along with it.

Aware that Corven could still look on through Mallory's eyes, Jagjit was careful not to emote or indicate any kind of derisive internal state. "You heard the Minister!"

Mallory was not too concerned with selling the dramatization. She raised her eyebrows and prepared to continue their conversation from before, but spotted something in her peripheral vision. Quickly, she leaned forward and pointed out the front of the limo window. "There! Is that them?!"

A guardian van zoomed up an onramp and merged a few metres ahead of the limo. Sparks sprinkled off the bumper as the van smacked the curb and rebounded. Its tires squealed. While the van's driver wrestled for stability, its rear doors swung open. Two men armed with assault rifles leaned out and began firing. The bullets smacked the limo's windshield, creating spiderweb-like marks. Although the limo was bulletproof, its window wouldn't remain so for long.

"Neutralize the threat!" roared the Commissar. "One of them has the painting—try not to damage it!"

Jagjit's entourage of aerial drones dove and began firing on the van. Smoke puffed and flame belched from the van's sides. It too was armoured somewhat; enough for its passengers to withstand this initial barrage.

249

The gunmen aback the van tossed explosive caltrops, which the limo's AI-driver handily maneuvered around. The gunmen fired a few more rounds and shuttered the van.

Again Jagjit's drones dove, this time mulching the rear left tire. The van dropped down onto the rim and began spewing sizeable flares.

Jagjit knelt at the front of the limo, face pressed to the webbed glass. "Where are you headed, Comrade Frye?"

The driver of the van leaned out her window holding a small grenade launcher. She took aim and fired—not at the limo, but ahead at a checkpoint marking the divide between trustworthee zones. The checkpoint consisted of two Mobility Department cruisers parked in a v-formation. The grenade hit its mark. There was a fiery burst and a visible shockwave that distorted the colours around it as it picked up and blew away stone, steel, wood, and flesh. Both cruisers were cast aside, trailing thick clouds of smoke. Still carving asphalt with its naked rim, Frye's van charged through the flaming remnants.

Examining a mental map of the road down which he chased the fugitives, Jagjit realized that unless Frye had somehow devised a way to get her van across the Irish Sea, she was headed to one of three CBLOCKs housing the worst of England's citizenry. CBLOCKs 39, 40, and 41, were each home to untrustworthees spared solely on account of protected flaws, and were no more than five minutes away. In fact, after minimizing his map, Jagjit could see them towering over the highway and blocking any complete view of the horizon. He figured CBLOCK39 wouldn't be the fugitives' destination, as there was a Nephilim garrison on its ground floor. CBLOCKs 40 and 41, on the other hand, he regarded as either homes to or launch pads for whatever the fugitives had in mind as they were slightly less militarized.

Although collateral damage at any of the projected destinations was more than acceptable, Jagjit wanted a clean capture. He ordered his small squadron of drones back and the specialist among them forward so that it could execute its sole function: to fire a focused EMP blast, which would take out the van's locomotion. Jagjit similarly intuited for the limo to fall back to a safe distance from the incoming blast. He and Mallory looked on as an owl-shaped drone swooped down and delivered its payload.

There were no flames; no explosion. The van's frame nearly went ahead of its axels, as the wheels locked up on account of the emergency brakes the power-down triggered. The vehicle skidded several metres before lurching into the median. It hammered against several trees in the highway forest, and tore up every sapling it came into contact with.

Unarmed save for his knife, Jagjit was hesitant to get out of the limo, which slowed down and stopped a safe distance away from the fuming van—hesitant especially after witnessing proof of the the fugitives' aptitude for gunplay. "Poyraz, ETA?"

"Two minutes. There's a dropship en route as well that'll pick you up. Word is your ride has taken substantial damage."

Staring through the white splashes on the windshield, Jagjit murmured: "Ah, yes. The sooner the better." Past the cracks, he saw the van doors open once again, and once again the fugitives began firing on the drones circling above like vultures. Once they had felled enough to even the odds for the moment, they fired at the limo.

One round penetrated the glass and struck the cushioning between Mallory and Jagjit. Mallory yelped and clutched her head as if struck.

Jagjit pulled Mallory onto the floor. "Don't fret. Reinforcements are on their way."

TWENTY-FOUR

"I keep telling you! It won't start!" Danika frantically toed the charge pedal. The van's electrical system had been sapped for good.

The three of them were stuck in a bullet-riddled van on the top tier of a four-tier highway that ran between minor EDS departments and giant CBLOCKs. They had already busted past the checkpoints between the westernmost trustvalue zone and Blackpool Central. Up ahead, connected over and under the highway by pedestrian bridges, piping, and access roads, stood CBLOCKs 37 and 38, each over one-hundred-and-fifty storeys a piece. Past them, there were some utilities buildings lined up to the next and final grouping of CBLOCKs before the Irish Sea. CBLOCK39 loomed on the south side where the highway began to curve north; 40 on the exterior of the curve; and 41 cozied up the inside of the curve. Their placement was unique owing to the placement of the highway as well as the topography of the shoreline. Rarely outside of the luxurious top-trustvalue zones were living complexes connected to one another in anything besides pairs. After all, separation assuaged fears about rebellions, not that the English had any fight left in them after their synchronizations. Since their inhabitants were so mentally dampened, however, 39, 40, and 41 were permitted to remain linked together by bridges, piping, and support.

"To hell with this!" Alek roared. "It's not far—I can see it from here! We'll make a go for it."

"Monica better appreciate the price of your revenge when all is said and done," said Geoff. He reloaded his rifle, and primed a smoke grenade. "Dan, you ready?"

Danika half-opened her door, smacking a tree trunk cracked in the crash, and peered out. She tightened her helmet and took aim at the growing specters on the horizon with her submachine gun. "Now?"

"Now!" Alek answered, burdened with the reminder that Geoff willingly linked his fate to his own. He kicked open the rear doors and leapt out, gun blazing.

After Alek's latest assault on their pursuers, the coloured band that ran along the trim of the EDS' chase-limo turned from green to orange. Armoured coverings dropped down overtop the wheels. The limo's reinforced windows, meanwhile, absorbed Alek's bullets without any sign of letting any pass through.

252

Geoff tried his hand at shooting down some of the remaining drones that corkscrewed overhead, each waiting to be ordered into the fray. He managed to knock out half the flock. While he tracked one of the flaming birds of prey to the ground, firing additional shots into it as it fell, he saw an incoming attack ship. *"Oh mercy!* Gunship inbound!"

Alek continued firing at the limo until he saw Geoff fall back. He caught up with him on the other side of the van where it was girdled by trees. Using both the van and the trees for cover, Danika racked her brain trying to plot a course forward.

Two of the drones dove and shredded the hood of the van, narrowly missing Alek, who hurled obscenities at them as they whisked back into the sky.

"We have to get to a lower level or they'll make minced meat out of us," Danika said, looking around for a viable way to the highways below.

"There!" Geoff cried. He didn't wait for a consensus. He mantled the median, cut through the thicket, and ran towards a way station on the far side.

"Wait! Littlefield! *Ah, damn it."* Danika popped off a few shots at the gunship, still out of range, and chased Geoff over. Alek followed closely behind.

The way station looked like a granite outhouse. It had a small green door with Mandarin characters stenciled in bold with English in smaller print underneath, which read: "PARADE LEVEL." There was a notice posted beneath the stencil that indicated the ladder inside the station was under repair and specified the EDS ministry assigned the task. It also suggested with a small marked-up map more ideal ways down to the "GROUND LEVEL".

Alek tried the door. "Locked."

"What are we going to do?!" Danika yelled, shrinking with fear.

"You've got the explosives from the van?" Geoff asked Alek, too shaken to comfort their getaway driver.

Alek looked back across the street at the van, barely visible through the trees. The gunship that had only a moment ago been nothing more than dark blip in the sky groaned by and pelted the van with concussion rockets. Didn't matter if the concussion rockets were intended to be non-lethal; the explosives inside the van reacted immediately. The van exploded, and as it bucked, exploded again, sending shrapnel whizzing every-which-way. *"Nope,"* Alek said, ducking to avoid metal fragments and splinters carried over on the shockwave. He turned his attention back to the way station door.

"Bollocks!" Geoff pushed Danika out of the way, and riddled the door's hinges with bullets. Once he had unmoored it, he kicked it open.

The gunship turned its gun on the way station as the fugitives rushed inside. Every projectile strike sounded like a thunderclap. The ground shook and the walls spilled their ingredients.

Alek began to slide down the ladder, which had rusted to the point of warranting the promised repairs. Danika grabbed the rickety rails next, and then Geoff.

Unable to hear anything, never mind his own voice, Alek nevertheless yelled up to Geoff: "I thought you were afraid of heights..."

"I'd rather fall to my death than into the hands of them soshies!" Geoff declared, trying not to look down.

The gunship razed the way station above them. Silt and pulverized rock rained down upon their heads. A piece of falling rebar missed all three of them before piercing one of the aluminum covers containing the ladder.

Danika looked up and saw that a boulder-sized portion of the way station had temporarily plugged the exit, but seemed poised to drop. "Faster, gentlemen!"

They sped up their descent, hoping the loose rock wouldn't intervene to help.

So corroded were the railings and so coated were they with dull grey thistles that Alek's hands began to bleed as he shuffled along. He looked up to Geoff to commiserate, but realized Geoff had on a pair of gloves as did Danika. Even if he was to die in good company, he still had to suffer alone.

There was no catwalk or place to climb off at the level directly below the street where they abandoned the van, as it was devoted solely to the trains that moved products to the coast and bodies back to the hinterland. This left the three of them exposed to adversaries approaching from the south for another few hundred rungs.

The threshing sound of the gunship's stabilizer jets drove Alek to abandon the climb and to attempt a controlled fall. He loosely gripped the rails with his hands and exerted pressure on their sides with his feet, and slid down with an excited wail, palming blood all the way.

Following Neuhaus' lead, Danika slid down rapidly after him.

Geoff saw the shadow of the gunship on the nearest government building. That was enough for him to abandon all apprehension and precaution. He might as well have jumped given how loosely he gripped the rails. He zipped down, speeding to the point of sounding like a train crossing a trestle bridge.

Even with the light exosuit supporting his brutalized ankle, Alek couldn't apply enough pressure to the sides of the ladder to slow down as much as what was needed for a safe landing. He struck the platform with enough force to leave a divot in the metal grid. He let go of the rails and staggered to the catwalk's railing, cursing and examining his lacerated hands. In the short time it took for Geoff and Danika to reach the platform, Alek managed to tear and wrap fabric around the gory trenches dug through his palms.

Geoff took a passing glance at Alek's ruddy rags, stepping just out of the way of a falling granite boulder that punched through the catwalk. "Now's no time for stigmata, mate."

Alek looked cockeyed at Geoff and was about to respond, but Danika yanked him forward. Whether her hearing was less damaged than her friends' or she was simply more perceptive, she had become wise to it first—the *brrrt* of the gunship's minigun. Her forceful shove spared Alek a mouthful of metal, and signaled Geoff to lunge forward.

They crossed the catwalk to where it met the stone of Tier 3. There was a slim set of stairs down two metres to the highway. They ran down, vaulting over multiple steps at a time, and hit the asphalt running. A stream of molten lead chewed up the concrete above them, and the preceding brrrt echoed in the subhighway.

"CBLOCK40 is just up there, but this road's about to see some serious traffic," Danika yelled, loosening the collar on her suit. "We've got to keep descending!"

Alek noticed a maintenance path that ran along the inside of the concrete walls hemming in the highway. These glorified troughs were exposed to the road every fifteen metres or so. Notwithstanding the incoming fire that managed to poke holes in the walls bordering the maintenance path, the path seemed a safer way west than by hitchhiking. Alek coerced his team over.

Danika mistook this first step as a half-measure. "This'll be the first place they look."

"We're not hiding. We just need to get to the next way station," Alek replied.

At least one-thousand bullets hammered the exterior of the path while the three of them hurried along the inside. Several of the rounds created portals allowing rays of early-evening light to pour in. When the barrage overshot their actual location, they took pause. Alek hurried to the nearest aperture and looked out, praying

255

lightning wouldn't strike the same spot twice. "There!" he said, excitedly. "There's a pedestrian bridge just up ahead." He traced the bridge through the wall to the subhighway. "It must run under us."

"That bridge runs to 39." Danika said, transfixed on the imaginary line Alek drew. She knew roughly the layout of the towers from her days as a junior guardian. If they made it all the way down to the ground, they could make a beeline for their destination. The pedestrian bridge, conversely, meant a detour and a possible confrontation with CBLOCK39's Nephilim security complement.

"It's a two-minute run, and another two minutes to tower forty. There's no other option." Geoff maintained his newfound faith in Alek, even if Alek was himself wholly uncertain.

The ground quaked. Alek presumed the gunship to have been responsible. He checked through his porthole. In fact, the ship had terminated its barrage and was hovering in place. "The hell was that?!"

Danika stood up slowly, looking eastward with her mouth open and jaw slack. "Pedestrian bridge sounds good..." She began to back pedal, and turned into a full-out sprint along the maintenance pathway.

Alek saw what had brought Danika onside: a Reduvius drone. The dog-like drone barely cleared the ceiling separating the train tracks from this highway. Marching along on either side of it were at least fifty Nephilim shock-troopers. "Oh damn." He turned to prod Geoff along, but saw that he too had taken off running.

In order to drop down to the covered pedestrian bridge, they had to leave the relative safety of the maintenance path and climb over the concrete wall. The added height of the wall meant a greater fall; even if successful in vaulting over, they might have to carry on more hobbled than before.

There was a burbling sound—like a spring waterfall. Alek looked over his shoulder and saw an orange light. *Oh damn.* A glowing orb glided up the highway and struck ground Alek had cleared not fifteen seconds earlier, consuming it in a matter-destroying implosion followed by an energetic blast. The Reduvius began probing the highway with more plasma bolts. It fired another and then another. Each shot found its way closer to Alek's crew, and each shot increased the local temperature by at least five degrees.

Alek caught up to Danika and Geoff, who had broken down sweating and whinging just above where the pedestrian bridge ran through Tier 3.

"I can't believe you forgot the explosives!" Geoff said, unclear whether or not he was chastising Alek or himself.

256

"Shut up! I can't hear myself think!" Danika said with her mask up, massaging the genius lurking behind her forehead.

Alek looked across the way. Just as there was a maintenance path on this side of the blockaded highway, owing to symmetry of design there was also a path on the far side. He knelt down and tightened the exoskeletal brace keeping his lower leg whole. "I'm going to get *our friends* to make us an exit."

Geoff shook his head. "You're what?!"

Tapping his real friends—for good luck more than anything—and raising his rifle, Alek climbed over the edge of the trough, and ran across six lanes of empty highway. The fast-approaching Reduvius spotted him and began to pummel the far side with plasma bolts. Each shot opened up the north side and sent chunks of rock hurtling through the windows of nearby buildings along the superhighway. Alek stumbled and fell into the trough as one plasma bolt tore through the asphalt itself, leaving a substantial, smoldering dimple. The gunship, too, got in on the action, and began unloading a firestorm onto the trench Alek had slipped into.

Alek dragged himself forward out of the way of the truckloads of debris that crumbled into the maintenance path. He hadn't properly thought through his plan. He had imagined the Reduvius and the AI piloting it would have been so kind as to blow a door into the far side through which his friends could gingerly exit. There were enough exits now for all of his friends, living and dead, to pass through, but a safe traversal of the highway was impossible.

Dead set on killing the fugitives ahead of the Reduvius drone, the overzealous pilot of the gunship switched from his minigun back to his rockets. Instead of concussion rockets, however, he opted for their lethal cousins. Without an active EDS implant to target—just as Geoff had deactivated Danika's, he had deactivated Alek's—the gunship had to rely upon trial and error when it came to destroying these latest targets. Its resultant imprecision was a godsend. Two of the gunship's rockets passed right through and struck the building on the other side of the highway. One rocket hammered into the far maintenance pathway, indirectly sending enough silica into its Alek's lungs to kill him with cancer years down the road. The last rocket in the sequence hit the near-side of the highway, nearly eviscerating Geoff and Danika, yet created an opening over the pedestrian walkway.

Though losing his remaining hearing with every additional thud and close-call, Alek nevertheless made out this duller boom. He pulled himself to his feet, and peeked over the edge of the trough. He saw Geoff and Geoff saw him.

Geoff waved him over, bellowing: "You did it!"

That would have been enough to die happy. Alek could have sat down and waited for the next volley of plasma or lead, content with the knowledge that he got his friends that much closer to redemption. "Damn it!" he muttered, realizing he still had The Family painting—that Monica was alive, and that without his help, she would remain enslaved in body and mind.

"Neuhaus!" Geoff yelled again.

"Go on! I'll catch up!" Alek yelled, hoping his friends could at the very least distract the gunship. He climbed out of the trough, and began his crossing attempt.

Danika looked out of the scorched opening, and saw where she might land on the pedestrian bridge below. For the most part, it was glassed-in with a riveted steel frame, appearing snakelike from the outside and intestinal on the inside. "I'm coming baby girl." She leapt and struck the steel spine of the bridge. With nothing on the smooth exterior to grip, she began to slip and slide. Fortunately, one glass panel couldn't support her weight, and as if being consumed feet first, she broke through the ceiling and collapsed onto a mosaic of broken glass. She lay prostrate, simultaneously waiting for a reaction from the gunship and determining if she had broken anything in the fall. When there was neither a reaction from above nor pain felt inside, she took off her dented helmet and began to crawl forward on the glass shards.

Within the second tier, the Reduvius and gunship's syncopated cannonade had produced enough dust and smoke to lend Alek some cover from the Nephilim rapidly advancing, though the Reduvius immediately spotted him with its infrared scanners. It fired one shot, which flew too high and likely carried on to the highway's curve where it would either strike CBLOCK40 or come damned close. Although the first shot-on was a miss, it still managed to trip Alek up. He stumbled at the middle of the highway and fell onto his face. He tried with all his might to get up, but his body knew what his mind would not recognize: *he was finished*.

The next plasma bulb glowed in the Reduvius' cannon well.

Alek closed his eyes. In that moment, he was convinced that he deserved to die. Scott Townley may have killed his wife, but by losing Monica's memex, he denied her an earthly resurrection. This was his comeuppance.

Geoff climbed out of the trough and ran over to Alek, firing erratically towards the Reduvius. "Come on, old man! To your feet!" Without missing a step, Geoff grabbed Alek by the arm and pulled him into the crater made by a previous plasma bolt. Unbeknownst to either of them, the crater was bottomless. The plasma had cut through the ground and the ceiling below it.

Alek watched a molten orb pass over the crater through which they fell, while Geoff saw the pedestrian bridge widening to catch them. As this portion of the bridge was inside the second tier, there was no canopy. Had there have been, there would be no telling whether they would have hit their mark. Canopyless, this stretch of the bridge received their bodies, which thwacked down right next to eachother. They both groused unintelligibly, and looked over and saw that the other was alright.

"Now *that's* the last time." Geoff said, sputtering some blood. He had sprained or broken something in the fall. He rolled onto his back, and pulled the gun strap off, realizing that his rifle barrel had been bent under his weight and from the force of the fall. "Damn it. Doesn't anyone make a quality firearm anymore?" He ejected the drum magazine, handed it to Alek, and threw his gun over the side.

Alek grabbed the magazine, and lifted Geoff to his feet. "Where's Dan?"

Geoff pointed over Alek's shoulder and Alek followed the gesture to the sight of Danika waving. She was still lying prone at the bend where the bridge skewed in the direction of CBLOCK39. "You know something? I think I'm beginning to like her—even if she is a guardian."

"*Was a guardian.* You saw to that."

They regrouped with Frye and advanced, keeping low along the first portion of the bridge so as not to trigger the gunship's portside motion sensors. It hovered in the air providing more clumsy overwatch for the Nephilim inspecting the Reduvius' spherical craters for biomatter.

Nearing the base of CBLOCK39, Geoff spied a platoon of Nephilim deploy onto the bridge. When he sighed, Alek and Danika took notice, and they too spotted the cyborgs, now splitting up, with one section marching their way towards them and the other section headed towards CBLOCK40.

Danika doubled-back to determine if they could possibly make a retreat, and saw that the Nephilim from the highway had discovered the portal down to the pedestrian bridge. She rejoined her compadres, dazed by their seemingly inevitable defeat. "What will happen to Lisa?" She began to whimper and collapsed into Geoff's arms. "What will they do to my little girl?"

Alek inspected the magazine gifted him by Geoff and jammed it into his rifle. "That's still up to you. One way or another, you'll see her again." Monica, as always was on his mind—her face

259

superimposed on his vision; her lips on his; her hands in his own. With the warmth of illegal love making him whole, Alek marched up the way, devoid of pain or doubt, curving nearer and nearer the firing squad. He raised his rifle and turned red with righteous fury. Howling, he began to run. But it was not just Alek running. Geoff, unarmed, and Danika, her daughter's champion, ran alongside him.

The covered bridge, now under the overhang of CBLOCK39, straightened with a dozen Nephilim in the fore, ready and loaded for bear. In tandem, Alek and Danika fired their weapons—the result of which stopped the enemy in their tracks. It was not this hail of bullets that stopped the Nephilim in their tracks, however.

A rocket screamed into the nearest Nephilim section, sending flaming cybernetic parts and human slush down the corridor. Those Nephilim not blown to pieces by the rocket were thrown over the sides of the bridge.

Geoff and Alek looked at each other in amazement. Awestruck and curious, Danika scouted ahead. She saw him first: a man in an exosuit many storeys above them on one of the bridges connecting CBLOCKs 39 and 40. She turned to Alek. "Friend of yours?"

Alek grinned such that his entire face wrinkled. "He is now."

The rocketeer, though sprinkled by pincers from the second section of Nephilim down below, reloaded his launcher and took aim. He fired another rocket, annihilating those who had the audacity to test either his mettle or his metal.

"We're not out of the frying pan quite yet," Geoff said, indicating the Nephilim gaining on them.

They ran through the marsh of the rocketed Nephilim, across the steps of CBLOCK39, and onto the pedestrian bridge routing to their destination—to the place where they hoped to meet Cassandra, or as Geoff might call her in his condition, *Catheter*.

The Nephilim from the highway may have picked up their trail—the rocketeer's handiwork no doubt having been a factor—but it was the gunship and the rolling sound of its reanimated minigun that forced the trio to keep running despite their shot nerves and injuries.

Above, their gracious welcome party of one took aim at the gunship and fired another rocket. The rocket splashed off of the enemy ship's aft jets just as its minigun began to spin, sparing the rocketeer from evisceration. The gunship spun wildly, and careened across the steel canyon and into the side of CBLOCK40.

Geoff took pause to wave thankfully up to their guardian angel. This show of thanks was the last thing the rocketeer saw for a plasma bolt rendered him nonexistent. Geoff looked for the source of the critical hit. "Reduvius drone!" he bellowed.

Another plasma bolt sparkled on by, smashing into CBLOCK40 and tearing right through its outer shell. There was much in the way between the Reduvius drone and its prey, so it abandoned its position and galloped towards a side ramp to the top tier from which it would have a view to a kill and dominion over the front of the housing complex.

"So much for our new friend, Neuhaus!" Geoff yelled, panting and regretting having fallen out of whatever shape it was that he figured he should still be in.

Alek looked back and saw more than just Geoff. The Nephilim had just about caught up to them. He took a knee, aimed down his sights, and fired a couple shots just to slow the enemy advance. Red splotches on the Nephilim-frontrunner's white armour indicated moderate success. Alek hurried towards CBLOCK40, lying to himself about Reduvius accuracy.

Pieces of the downed gunship were strewn all about CBLOCK40's platform. There was battery fluid leaking from the crushed fuselage, half-embedded in the side of the building. Its minigun was still spinning and clicking, linked to the ship only by a spent ammo belt and a power line.

Danika indicated a spot in the shadow of the gunship to avoid, and coaxed Alek and Geoff out of the way. Good thing too, as a flaming battery cell plunged to the pavement, spitting up its corrosive contents. A small splash landed on the toe of Geoff's boot. Though it burned through the material, it miraculously missed his toes. As they hurried up the steps to the front doors of the building, Geoff winked at the former guardian. He was quickly losing track of who owed who what. There would be a great deal of appreciation-accounting to do if they ever got out of Blackpool alive.

The doors burst open ahead of them. Five flash-blinded security agents flew out in a panic. They ran right past Alek, Danika, and Geoff, gripping their eyes and bawling. The reason for the EDS security agents' hysteria quickly became clear. There were corpses just inside. A lot of corpses. Corpses belonging to those the reaper chose not to spare.

Keen to avoid the Reduvius making its way over from the highway, Alek pressed inside CBLOCK40, half-expecting to find death. He saw instead something he thought had died—something he hadn't seen in a long time: the Union Jack. This Union Jack was duotone; just black and white and painted on a hulking armoured shoulder belonging to an equally hulking soldier in an exosuit with a bulbous satchel on his hip.

"You're late," said the soldier, shooting away groans amongst the bodies piled in the doorway. "That one with yah?"

Danika looked down the stairs at the threat indicated by the Union-Jacked soldier and saw the gunship's limpy pilot. The pilot tore off his helmet and produced a sidearm. Danika spared the pilot the energy required to lift his arm and shot it off. "No." The pilot collapsed behind her. "Just the three of us, plus one waiting upstairs."

"Good. Get inside," said the soldier. He shoved Geoff inside, let Danika through, and pulled the doors shut behind them. Having temporarily commandeered control over the building's security system, he initialized the closing of the blast doors. As they screamed into place, he turned to Danika. "You must be Ms. Frye. I met Lisa only briefly, but that's one tough little girl you've raised."

"She's here?"

"Waiting for us presently."

Danika cried happy tears. She bounded over and grabbed Alek's hand. Squeezing it, she thanked him repeatedly.

"Don't thank me yet. All of England is bearing down on us. I have no idea—" He threw his voice in the armoured soldier's direction. "No idea how we get out of here."

"Then come follow me. *This way.*"

The soldier's machine gun must have weighed at least two-hundred pounds. His exosuit made it look weightless as he waved it around and pointed to the elevator bank across the lobby, full of whimpering citizens, all cowering and scared. Even if those the soldier had spared couldn't remember, they were accustomed to seeing violence, just never directed towards the regime or its enforcers.

On reaching the elevator bank, the soldier hit the call button for the elevator. "Name's Wes Miller."

"Alek Neuhaus," Alek replied, spooked by the final crunch behind them made by the closing blast shields.

Geoff pinched one of his open wounds, and reflexively offered up his name: "Geoff Littlefield."

There was a chime corresponding to the opening of the doors at the end of the bank. Miller struggled inside, stepping in sideways and hunching over so that the spiky protrusions from his protective neck collar wouldn't catch on the ceiling. Alek and Geoff and Danika squeezed in around him.

"With Lisa, I count four," said Miller. "Who's the fifth?"

262

"My wife," Alek said solemnly as the elevator lurched upward. "Monica Neuhaus. *She's*—they poisoned her against us. She is with that bloody commissar and his ilk thinking she's something she's not. I'm hoping the painting does the trick."

Miller saw the parcel peeking out of Alek's mangled neckband. "That it there?" He smiled and took a deep breath.

Alek nodded.

"*It will.* I've been waiting a long time..." Miller's stared off into nothingness and his face went still. "I'm not just hoping—I am certain. And if one such miracle won't save England's ailing heart, then it's England no longer; just another nihilist shithole."

"This Cassandra lady," said Geoff, impressing Alek and Danika both with his pronunciation and recall. "She'll hold up her end of the bargain?"

"If you have what I t'ink you've got, then she'll bend over backwards."

"What's it do? *The painting*?" Danika asked, thumbing cartridges into a fresh magazine.

Alek looked at Danika with amazement. She had done incredible feats based on faith and trust alone.

Miller looked at the red numbers on the elevator's digital input panel counting up to the 150th floor. He had only enough time for the basics. "It's a painting with some seriously provocative subject matter—don't ask me what, because I don't know. As important as what's on the surface, if not more, is what's beneath it. There's machine-readable optical code baked into the painting. Was effective against Chinese cyborg units. We have a sense of what the code does but have no idea who put it there or when, and no one has been able to replicate it since."

"And the code—what's it do?"

"Ms. Doherty said it works along the lines of a banana DDOS attack."

Geoff looked to Alek and mimed saying the name, "Doherty", to which Alek mutely replied, "Cassandra."

"Like I said, we're not entirely sure, so this is speculation. If I'm right, this banana attack or *what have yah* reverses all the overstim and useless data they've been sticking in yar heads, and sends it back to Central, overwhelming their servers and oversaturating their bandwidth. All of the tech running on the EDS intranet will run stupid for a period. Also prevents 'em from checking inside your head long enough to get your head out of their system. That's step one—*the wrench in the gears*. Step two, and mind yah, this is all supposed to be near-instantaneous, you've got the organic restoration. S'what Doherty called it anyway. You get all of your old, deleted memories back."

"Like a systems-wide cortical loader with extras," Geoff said, trying to expound on Miller's explanation.

"Step three is—"

The elevator came to an abrupt stop. Red emergency lights came on and a warning bell started ringing. They had come just shy of the 141st floor, only ten away from the freedom they had been promised.

"Bollocks! They've regained control of the security system," Miller said glumly. He checked an oversimplified display of CBLOCK40's systems projected over his wrist. "They're inside the building." He slammed the elevator's input panel preventing a recall. "Careful, now. Watch the arms." He let the others crouch out of the way of his steel-embellished might and pried open the doors. They had been fortunate: the elevator had stopped only a few centimetres out of step with the 141st floor. Had they been trapped between floors, the security system could easily have flushed them out with an electric pulse. Holding the doors open for his fellow passengers, Miller waited for them to exit and then squeezed out of the compartment. "We've got to find the stairs," he said, looking around the landing for drones or signage.

Alek had had enough stairs for one day. "Any other way up?"

There was a security terminal right beside a Shepherd drone station. Geoff ran over, indifferent to the drone one command away from popping out and cutting him in twain. He interfaced with the terminal and mapped out the path of least resistance. He turned excitedly, and provided some much-needed guidance: "We can avoid the main stairwells if we cut through the Semiotics Common Lab. It's a self-contained subministry that occupies space from the 140th floor up to the 148th. There's an inner atrium with multiple ways up that we can take to..." Geoff looked back at the screen. "Screw it. I'll just show you. Follow me!"

The initiation light on the Shepherd drone behind Geoff flashed on. The cupboard expelled the drone, and straight away it raised its blade to flay Geoff. Miller leapt forward blocking the drone's swipe, and punched the drone back into its cupboard with his gauntlet. Although the drone resisted, Miller persisted, and punched it repeatedly until he had fractured its hull, after which he tore out its processor.

Geoff was shocked. He looked at the drone and then at Miller. "Whenever you're ready."

264

Another Shepherd popped out of its cupboard down the corridor.

Miller flipped the barrel on his gun and locked a variant barrel into place. He slipped a can-sized cartridge into the feed that jarred out the side and took the shot.

The Shepherd reeled back and burst into flame on account of the charged incendiary Miller had flung at it. Though an inferno, it tried to advance, but ran blindly into a wall, and then fell to the ground, bested.

"There'll be more," Geoff yelled, "Now that they're in control of the security system again."

"Crack on!" Miller replied. He pressed his temple and activated his communications device. "Dax! Dax? We're headed up now with or without you."

Alek took to Miller's side. "Dax was your friend with the rocket launcher?"

Miller's brow fell low over a rigid grimace. "He not make it?"

Alek shook his head gravely. "Saved us in the process."

Miller shrugged away his emotions and plugged another incendiary grenade into his alternate barrel. "Free men will remember him when they think on why they're free."

The Semiotics Common Lab, a universal feature of all housing complexes on the island, was comprised of two floors of cubicles where citizens had their linguistic abilities reigned in and their word-associations reprogrammed. The other six floors were full of exam rooms and offices where tests were run in an attempt to divorce symbols from their old-world meanings. With the building on high alert, the Common Lab was dead silent. Even without the intrusion of a few fugitives, it would likely have been empty, granted the Patch Over promised to render the lab's services redundant.

Once Alek and the crew had managed their way inside the first floor of the lab, Miller relieved Geoff as point-man. He called out to anyone waiting in ambush with words he knew would bring even the most stoic DSSP officer out of hiding: "Oi! The Supreme Councilors are all a bunch of fascists!" There wasn't a response, so he confidently led the fugitives through the maze of cubicles.

When he had been forced into the lab as a patient, Alek had found it difficult to ascertain the technician's objectives beyond what they had told him. It was now abundantly clear what they had been up to: eliminating English idioms, phrases, and virtually all metaphor that was not in keeping with EDS dogma. They had subjected him to this practice in CBLOCK32, but had always run a mental block on

265

their designs. Removed from the experience and looking on with an unpoliced mind, he could see the technicians' efforts plainly. "Two birds with one stone" became "Serve the People's Will twice with one concerted effort". There was no room for rock-throwing or violence to animals in the coming utopia. Other idioms were thrown out altogether, replaced by Party slogans with which Alek was well-familiar: "Power to the forest, not to lone trees; for the rogue wood stands against community." There was a naturalism inherent in most of the new expressions; one that seemed to conveniently discount humanity as a constituent. Alek gaped at one statement in particular: "Flesh divides us and holds us back from realizing unity." Quarrelsome voices yanked Alek's attention elsewhere.

"Yeah, but are you sure?" Miller questioned Geoff. He tried consulting the display on his wrist, but whoever had retaken control of the security system was also running a jam on all uncleared systems.

Geoff recalled: "There's an emergency landing pad on the 148th floor. On the exterior of the building, of course. We'll be able to get to the top from there."

Miller nodded, and waved the fugitives along and into the atrium—a dark, windowless hollow paneled on all sides with grey steel. At the centre was an elevator, locked as a result of the building-wide security alert. Off to the side, stairs zig-zagged all the way to the top.

They took the stairs to the top of the Semiotics Lab, and out the door to a triangular prism of a hallway. The inclined ceiling was all tinted glass, such that they could see CBLOCK39 and east into Blackpool. Alek looked out and was amazed by the number of troops funneling up the highway towards them. There were lorries trundling across the bridge to the front of the building loaded with support troops. Dropships were unloading men on the neighbouring rooftops—and no doubt on CBLOCK40's rooftop as well. They were surrounded.

At the end of the hallway was a secured door, marked "40LZ".

"That's it," Geoff declared. He hurried on ahead of the group. Though the door was locked and its panel bricked, Geoff had recognized the open/close mechanism as the same hydraulic system used across England. He yanked a wall panel near the door out of its place, and waved Alek over.

Alek, too, had long ago learned to trick the sensors on the hydraulic doors. Geoff created a gap in a snake pit of wires, and Alek unclipped the one responsible for maintaining pressure to the door. A cloud of steam shot out of the hole in the wall, sending Alek and

266

Geoff retreating. "Hey, Miller," Alek said, face burned by the steam. "Mind giving the door a little pry?"

Miller stepped forward and yanked the door open.

"Lovely," Alek said, queuing up to go through.

The emergency landing pad was empty. Whereas all the other CBLOCK rooftops were crowded with reinforcements, there wasn't a single white helmet or EDS patch to be seen.

Miller concluded aloud: "It's a trap."

Danika ran by him. "Lisa?! Lisa? Baby, you out here?"

"She won't be here," Miller said, chasing after Danika. "Dax settled her up on the roof with a projection sphere."

Miller's remarks did little to settle Danika, who took to the ladder to the top.

"If Cassandra's not here, we're toast," Alek said, brushing past Miller on his way to the ladder.

"Yeah—I realize..."

With wind gusting at them from all directions, this climb felt far more perilous than the way station ladder. It certainly didn't help that all of Blackpool now had a shot at them.

Geoff, no longer able to ignore his wounds, slowed to take a breath. He looked over to the other rooftops where enemy eyes returned his interest. "Why haven't they shot us? There's no way we're out of range."

"Don't look a gift horse in the mouth, mate," Alek yelled down, just as he mantled the edge of the top platform. He found Danika holding her daughter tight enough to break her in two.

"Lisa!" he yelled, happy to see his good deed half-grown-up.

"Mr. Neuhaus," she replied. She motioned to Alek, but Danika wouldn't dare terminate their hug.

Geoff made it up with a much-needed boost from Miller who could very well have raced to the top with a few choice leaps and bounds, but was sure not to leave anyone behind. "Where is she?" Geoff shouted, competing with the wind blasting off the sea.

Alek looked over at Miller. "Will Doherty risk it with them watching?" He pointed over at the ant-like bodies on CBLOCK39's rooftop, organizing themselves around a big mobile gun.

As the notion they had made their way through Hell and out only to find the Pearly Gates locked spread from Geoff to Alek to Danika, the air around them crackled. The five of them cowered, half-anticipating a plasma bolt or the like to swallow them up whole. Instead, a polygonal object distorted the light beside them. The illusion pulled back part-way along with the cloak on the rear of Cassandra's ship. A large plasmic shield fired out, providing cover for its eastern-facing side. Cassandra walked down its rear ramp. "Do you have it?"

Everyone looked to Alek.

"Yeah!" He said, carefully pulling The Family painting from under his jacket. "You can have it once we've all taken off together."

"Yes, yes, of course," Cassandra answered. She gestured to Miller, and he walked over to her. "Patch Over is happening ahead of schedule. They're planning on doing it at dawn. We need to move now! Get them inside."

Geoff slapped Alek on the shoulder. "For simplicity's sake, I'd say this makes us even." He made his way over to the ship and ran inside.

As soon as Geoff had entered, a shadow covered those still outside.

Miller raised his weapon but was smacked to the ground by a concussion rocket.

Another rocket threw Cassandra hurtling through the air and onto her face at the feet of Danika and Lisa.

Several more rockets flew into the partially-cloaked ship, tearing it apart with successive shockwaves.

Alek froze up. He watched Cassandra's jet torn to pieces and then blown back. "No!" he bellowed helplessly as Geoff disappeared in flame and over the side. He made a futile dash towards the ship as it scraped over the ledge, but was also knocked back and slapped against the ground by a shockwave.

Danika shrieked. She protected Lisa, balled in her arms.

Miller tried desperately to stand, though his exosuit had been disabled by the opening volley. All he could do was turn onto his back and watch the EDS dropship responsible for this mayhem land where Cassandra's ship only a moment ago had been perched.

The dropship's side bay opened up. Two Praetorian drones jumped out onto the fragments blown off of Cassandra's ship. One strode over to Miller and set its talons down on his armoured chest. The other took aim at Alek and his co-conspirators lumped together on the tarmac, all bewildered.

The dropship eased into park, and its thrusters went from red to a neutral blue.

A man—the same from the limo; the Commissar—exited, laughing to himself. Behind him came a woman—*Monica!*

"Oh dear God!" Alek muttered.

Seeing that the Praetorians under his command had disarmed his foes, the Commissar confidently walked over to Cassandra, who was bloodied and curled up on her side. "What good fortune! I have before me proof of American meddling in our affairs; the cyber weapon of mass destruction, *unless of course it went over the edge in that blaze*; and all of the principle traitors responsible for the last attack against the People."

"Jim?" asked Miller, reluctant to trust the truth his eyes reported back to him. "*Captain Khatri?*"

This invocation of another's name and title greatly irritated the Commissar. He walked over to Miller who was crushed under the weight of the Praetorian's foot. "You are mistaken. My name is Jagjit Hassan. I would say remember it, but only the living can remember."

"Says the man who can't remember his real name!" Cassandra yelled.

Commissar Hassan gestured to Monica, who took it as a sign. She walked up and kicked Cassandra in the face.

"So! Who has it? Who has *The Family*?" Hassan crouched down beside Miller. "Do *you* have it by chance?"

Miller spat into the Commissar's face. "Get stuffed. The Khatri I knew would have done himself in rather than put on that commie garb."

Hassan struck Miller, breaking his nose. "If you don't have it, then who does?" He stood upright and glared at Danika, who cried bitterly with Lisa buried in her arms.

Alek reached into his shirt and pulled out the parcel. He stood up, wobbly on account of his broken ankle, now just barely reinforced by its brace and calcium composite. This sudden movement attracted the attention of the second Praetorian, which took aim solely at him. Despite the threat of annihilation, Alek tore the brown paper and exposed the painting. He held it at arm's length and made it impossible for the Commissar not to see. "I've got it here, you son of a bitch."

Hassan smiled at Danika and turned his attention to Alek. His eyes tracked across the painting, widened for a second, and then wrinkled up along with the rest of his face into a smile. "*I see that.* I also see that—" he looked over at Monica whose eyes had momentarily glazed over, "Our fears have been misplaced."

Monica's eyes returned to their natural colour. She looked forlornly at the painting and at the man holding it up.

Hassan looked at Monica knowingly. "A lemon, so-to-speak; a counterfeit. Home Defence Minister Corven will be greatly pleased."

Alek held The Family painting on an angle to see for himself. The image—oil on canvas—was not, as he secretly suspected, that of the royal family who had been publicly executed by the EDS out front of Buckingham Palace. It didn't seem to be a royal family at all. In

269

fact, those depicted looked more like peasants of some bygone era. At the center of the painting was a veiled woman, dressed in blue and white. She held an infant who looked up at her lovingly. Beside the woman and child was a bearded man wearing a brown homespun cloak whose staff anchored the lot of them in the fore. The lines giving the figures definite shape were sharp; the shadows around them were especially dark; and all of the colours were faded, perhaps by age or as a result of the image's encoding. It was an illegal image to be sure. Any depiction of a family—especially that of a nuclear family—was forbidden in England. But a world-changing image?

Seeing that there was no reaction either from his wife or from the Commissar, Alek's heart sank. He looked past his shaky hands over to where Cassandra's ship had been shot into pieces and then blown over into oblivion. There was no consolation in knowing that Geoff died with hope in his heart, given that his hope was utterly misplaced and meaningless. Alek then looked over at his wife whose face, though agitated perhaps by the painting or by the ordeal of acquiring it, did not seem overly animated—certainly not as he expected it would be. Then again, all of his expectations seemed to have been incorrect.

Hassan intuited an order to the second Praetorian. The drone quickly stole the painting away from Alek, leaving the burglar swaying in the wind. Handed the painting, Hassan took another look and ran his fingers across the faces of the family depicted thereon. With The Family painting in hand, he walked amongst his captives. "The best kind of bad idea is the one that has no lasting impact."

Miller began to laugh morosely. "This was *your bad idea*, Jim."

Wincing at the sound of criticism, the Commissar left Alek standing bow-legged and dumbfounded. He rolled up the painting, tucked it away in his jacket, and took out a long, slender knife. He walked over to Miller. "We're not so different. I concede that you may think you are acting on behalf of the People—*in their best interest*. That is also what motivates me day to day. Only, I know—thanks to the wisdom and mediation of the *all-seeing* Supreme Council—what is truly in the People's best interest. I know what they need, what they want."

Miller squirmed and fought against the Praetorian's weight, but it was his own crippled exosuit that truly held him down. "Captain—don't do this."

Hassan ordered the Praetorian to peel back the armour protecting Miller's chest. The drone obliged and stood aside, allowing for the Commissar to bear down on the exposed soldier.

270

"Your heart was just in the wrong place," he said right before plunging his knife into the left side of Miller's chest.

Burbling, Miller tried to speak though the Commissar wouldn't hear him.

Danika cried out on Miller's behalf, and squeezed Lisa a little bit tighter.

When Alek foolhardily tried to intervene, he was smacked to the ground by the other Praetorian. He looked past Miller and saw Cassandra coming-to.

The Commissar cleaned off his knife and tucked it away. Still crouching next to Miller, he dug through the dying soldier's satchel. "Ah, what's this?" He turned around two egg-shaped mortars in his hands. He held them up to show Monica. "*Real weapons of mass destruction*. I appreciate you saving these for me."

Miller spat bloody bubbles in response.

"Hmm? Yes, I concur. Wouldn't want them to fall into the hands of someone who'd use them against the People." Standing and cradling the mortars in his hands, the Commissar ordered the drones: "I've called for a second ship to take them to the city square. Load them up as soon as it arrives. Dr. Worthing will be there to meet them—to oversee the re-education ceremony, won't you, Doctor?"

Monica looked at Alek with more depth than her eyes had admitted back at the Department of Reclamations. For a fleeting second, Alek recognized her again and felt his sadness reflected back to him. As she climbed back into the dropship, however, he realized once again that he had fooled himself, and rested his head against the tarmac. He knew for certain there would be no cabin in the woods; no children; no growing old with the last of the Warmington line; no song; no happy memory.

Out from the nearest Praetorian's gauntlet fired a sparking nub—a tazer. With it, the drone shocked and incapacitated Alek, and did the same with Cassandra, Danika, and Lisa. Miller was spared the electrocution on account of the fact that he was already immobile and dying. The Praetorians piled up the inert bodies. One joined the Commissar on his ship, and the other remained behind to load the fugitives onto the next, already taxiing around the tower.

271

TWENTY-FIVE

Lloyd took the helm. Zoya buckled-in beside him. Like twin pianists, they fussed over the control panel in a mad dash effort to familiarize themselves with their newly-acquired vessel.

Mirek and Stephen sat opposite one another on benches in the cargo hold, confounded by the realization of their dream—itself initially disproven in blood and then actualized by chance. Stephen figured the skirmish inside the mall that ultimately brought them this ship was Providence; Mirek, just good luck for a change.

"Wes is gonna be gobsmacked to find out we made good." Mirek toed the drone platform between them. "Yah think they'll have a song for us when we get home?"

Crow's feet framed Stephen's serious consideration. "The dead get first priority. Jay'll have a song, no doubt."

"What about Byron Grimsby?"

"What about him?"

Mirek struck his palm with a closed hand as if adjudicating. "He did well by the Resistance."

"Fair enough." A mischievous streak perked Stephen up. "Ah damn!" He attempted to maintain a straight face.

"Huh?"

"We forgot 'bout that dress in the mall. Fiona will be gutted that you went shopping and didn't get her something." Stephen's façade broke and he flashed his broken smile.

Mirek reciprocated and raised his voice: "I guess she'll have to settle for freedom."

There came an aggravated voice from the cockpit: "Pipe down back there and get ready for takeoff!"

After a few failed attempts to engage the navigation system, Lloyd discovered that B. Lee's helmet was sufficient to override the computer's locks. The radar system's interface materialized over a portion of the dashboard, indicating several supposed friendly units inbound. Of course, this having been a Mountain League ship disguised as a Chinese trade vessel, the friendly designations surely meant the converse.

"Does this tin can have any shielding?" Lloyd asked, busily flipping switches and doing his best to avoid any automated processes that might bring the ship back to the Mountain League.

Zoya studied the Mandarin characters. She had made the mistake of learning Cantonese before the second fall of Hong Kong (for a time, the English Resistance had enjoyed a contingent of Hong Kongese immigrants with whom she had consorted). It had done her very little good after the Battle of Camden Town, but now helped with pattern recognition. "Yeah—plasmic shielding underneath that shares a mini Moscovium reactor with the gravity cushion."

"Prioritize the shield so far as energy is concerned, but hold off until we're airborne."

From the cockpit, Zoya and Lloyd could see a dozen gangsters spilling into the street from an alley down the way.

"*Any time now*," Zoya said.

The jet jostled side to side as the main thrusters came on. Lloyd gave the engines some juice, and pulled back on the control wheel. "Alright! Shields up!"

Zoya triggered the plasmic shield and in the nick of time too—the Chinese gangsters had deduced that it wasn't their glorious commander taking off but someone else. They started firing on the cargo ship to no avail.

The overpowered takeoff caused the buildings on either side of the jet to collapse. Clouds of dust and debris enveloped the craft, and avalanched over the Mountain League militia still peppering the ship's plasmic shield with small-arms fire.

Zoya yelled back to Stephen and Mirek: "Hold on!"

Mirek got to his feet, and looked through the doorless opening to the cockpit window, outside which Preston gave way to evening sky. He muttered, "Hold onto this," making a lude gesture— to whom he was not sure; his contrarian verve, though not mute, was certainly dumb.

Stephen stuck his arms through the netting suspended from the inside of the hull and shook his head at Mirek. "Suit yourself."

The ship pitched upwards and its thrusters blared. For an instant, Mirek appeared fixed in place with the residue of his bawdy comment on his lips while the ship reoriented around him, though he soon dropped towards the rear of the jet like a ragdoll.

"Yahoo!" Lloyd bellowed, laughing madly as the ship accelerated and climbed higher and higher.

Even Zoya had seized on the fun in all of it. She roared and clapped excitedly as they powered away from all the death and ruin.

Stephen had shuttered his eyes and clenched his jaw, attempting to acclimatize to this new sensation. Though he had spent his youth imagining interstellar travel and aerial dogfights, he had never flown before, not including the several metres he was tossed from Grimsby's truck. The butterflies in his stomach had metamorphosed back into caterpillars which seemed to wriggle up

273

his throat. He swallowed them down, opened his eyes, and looked anxiously over at his friend, pinned down by gravity to where the ramp met the ceiling.

Mirek too had begun to laugh.

Stephen rolled his eyes. "You bloody fool!"

Despite all the forces exerted upon him, Mirek managed to climb back up the ramp and over to his seat on the bench, but noticing a bubble window behind the cockpit overlooking the stubby right wing, he kept on climbing. Once he reached the window, he stuck his head into the glass bubble. He felt like the cosmonauts in his neighbour's posters back home in Underpool. "S'too bad we don't have that whisky. This would be a prime time for a dram," Mirek said. He saw the Mandarin horseshoe crabs coming and going; Blackpool's energy lines and bridges pulsate; the CBLOCKs' lights twinkle; and the coastline beneath where he had spent his entire adult life. "Oi!" He smooshed his face against the glass hoping to improve his view, and recoiled as soon as he comprehended what he had seen. "The beaches are on fire!"

Stephen yanked his arms out of the netting and ran over to Mirek, easier now with the ship levelling out. He pushed Mirek out of his way and took his turn as cosmonaut. There were massive plumes of smoke and pillars of white water in and around the various entrances to Underpool. "Oh God...*Barnard! Khatri!* You guys seeing this?"

Zoya looked down to her right. She whispered to Lloyd: "They detonated the dams and blew the sea wall. Demsocks must have tried to get inside." She turned in her seat and yelled back, although she didn't have to raise her voice with the bubble window immediately behind her and the cockpit partition: "Don't fret, Private. That's our doing."

"A damned shame, either way," said Stephen mournfully.

"No fires up near the Sanctuary," Mirek said, pressing his index finger against the glass next to Stephen's face. "Fiona and the rest will be okay."

Focused on the dark and turbulent night sky ahead, Lloyd muttered: "*So long as we do our jobs.*" He turned up the opacity on his holographic map and overlaid it on the windscreen. "We're taking an indirect route, so it'll be about an hour before we reach our target, assuming they don't shoot us down."

"Big assumption," said Zoya. She managed to pull up the ship's log of past flights as well as a detailed aeronautical chart. "The closest the former crew got to Tearaght in their travels was

274

Killarney. Overshooting past routes will surely garner us some unwanted attention."

"Never mind that. You've got the security codes?"

Zoya took out a mobility chit and plugged it into the ship's communications dash. "Courtesy of the Irish Resistance...It's ready to go. Just hit 'TRANSMIT' or—" she paused and scanned the different Mandarin characters delineating each button's function. "'FASONG'. That one there."

"Here's hoping." Lloyd placed his fingers over the button, unwittingly leaving a blood splotch and saving the need to memorize its place on the panel.

Eying the bloody key, Zoya cringed. She motioned to inquire as to whether the crimson belonged to the Lieutenant or one of his victims, but stopped herself, seeing that Lloyd was preoccupied. "I'm going to check on our precious cargo." Zoya unbuckled her seatbelt, and joined Stephen and Mirek aback the ship. Once again she marveled at the warhead, and then began scheming ways of firing or releasing it.

After relaxing to the point of feeling like a stranger in his own scarred and bruised body, Stephen finally clued into the reason behind Zoya's kooky pantomime and joined in. He examined the symbols on the buttons for the rear ramp. "We could probably open this while in flight, yeah?"

Zoya pointed out the control panel responsible for opening the ramp.

Mirek sat down and looked on unamused. "Best bet is flying straight into the advanced-warning station."

"Bloody lunatic," Zoya replied, checking the rivets on the glass window.

Under his breath, Stephen said: "Look who's talkin'."

Mirek thought for a moment, and then said shrewdly: "We don't have to be in the jet. That's what auto-pilot is for."

Having overheard the majority of the conversation, Lloyd chimed in: "Nah. I deactivated the AI support system so that they couldn't recall us. We're running manual from here on out. Besides, it's an advanced-warning station. A flyover is already a longshot. A collision course will prompt them to shoot us down." He groaned and the ship juddered side to side.

Zoya handed Stephen the mortar, and rushed to the cockpit to find Lloyd clutching his ribs and wincing.

"How bad?"

275

"Take the helm." Lloyd swapped places with Zoya. "I plotted waypoints. Fly south then cut west. The codes yah plugged in seem only to be good for entering the airspace. There'll surely be demands for ancillary codes we don't have and can't fake. Never mind the collision course—my guess is they start firing missiles long before we can bomb the island." He gently pulled off his armour and piled it on the co-pilot's seat. After psyching himself up, Lloyd began peeling off his makeshift bandage, but stopped on account of the pain.

"That looks pretty serious, Lieutenant..." Zoya was preoccupied with keeping them airborne, but could tell just by the dark red in her peripheral vision and by the smell that Lloyd had been hiding the extent to which he had been hurt. "The triads?"

"No," he sighed. There was little to be done about the wound. He packed it with some more fabric and put his armour back on, grunting with every movement. "In the crash."

"I wish you'd said something sooner."

"Had I done, we wouldn't be mincing about it now."

"It'll take a little over twenty minutes before we reach the target taking your route. How about you relax a while. You'll need your energy for what comes next."

Lloyd smiled kindly and squeezed the Zoya's shoulder. "Sure thing, Major." He stumbled out of the cockpit, and walked past Stephen and Mirek, both puzzling over how to drop their warhead and still stay afloat. On the port side of the ship by the bench there were several lockers. Lloyd inspected one and found nothing except for a couple bottles of booze. The next in the lineup contained several automatic rifles. At the foot of the locker there were some low-grade mining explosives. "Some rice beer and guns in here should you need them. Might be a grenade or two on the bottom."

Stephen and Mirek bobbed their heads confirming that they had heard him.

Lloyd checked the last locker. Inside was an empty med kit. He grumbled, slammed the locker shut, and eased onto the bench. "Oi, Nowak—why bring in the drone if you weren't planning on using it?"

Rather than respond, Stephen examined the drone. "Is the helmet up front?"

"Hold off until you know what you're going to use it for. The drone won't be fast enough to hit the island before they can do something about it. This?" Lloyd indicated the ship holding them. "This just might make it." Lloyd rested his head down and crossed his hands over his chest, keeping pressure on his wound. "Jay would've agreed with Dubchek—he'd say fly the bloody thing straight into the station." Lloyd coughed and cleared his throat. "Me? I'd have to agree with yah—someone's got to be left to witness the glory."

Although no great sleuth, Stephen recognized something was wrong with the Lieutenant. He made sure that Mirek had a good handle on the bomb, and ambled over to Lloyd's side. "Nodding off, are yah?" Stephen noticed a pool of blood beneath Lloyd, and lowered his head. "Damn, sir—I didn't realize..."

Lloyd grabbed Stephen's hand and pulled him in for a whisper. "Buck up. It only grazed my soul." He spit up more blood, having made himself laugh. "Jay was right about you lads." His eyes wandered to implicate Mirek as well.

"There's got to be a med kit around here somewhere!" Stephen tried to wrench away from the Lieutenant, but couldn't break free. "What the hell, mate? I can patch yah up!"

"What's wrong with the Lieutenant?" Mirek asked, seated cross-legged with the mortar on his lap. He looked over his shoulder and saw that there was more to the conversation than simply his neighbour interrupting the Lieutenant's well-deserved rest.

Lloyd's grip was quickly losing its strength and hold on Stephen's hand. "Said t'ose two will wear our shoes when they come off.' Yeah?" He seemed to be carrying on a side conversation with someone or something in the ether. "*Yeah.*" His hand went limp.

"No!" Stephen checked for Lloyd's pulse and felt nothing. He tried to resuscitate him, but had no success. Frenzied, he called out to Zoya. "Major! Michael is—he's..."

"*Michael?*"

Stephen corrected himself and joined Zoya in the cockpit. Holding onto the back of the co-pilot's seat to keep from caving, he murmured: "Lieutenant Barnard is dead...I didn't know he was hurt that bad. I—*ah, damn it!*" He covered his mouth and closed his eyes.

Before setting out for Preston, Zoya had never lost a man on a mission. Now the bodies were stacking up. "He's in good company now; watching over us." She kept her focus on the southwestern Irish coast zig-zagging on the starboard side of the ship, and made sure not to fly directly into the range of the CDS anti-aircraft cannons and missile launchers. Throwing her comments out the side of her mouth to hit Stephen dead-on, she continued to console him: "We have an audience. It's time now to put on one hell of a show."

Stephen retreated into the cargo hold in a daze.

"What'd she say?" asked Mirek.

Stephen looked up at Mirek who was holding the nuclear mortar to his chest like a newborn. "Well..." He had already forgotten

277

the Major's exact words, but had a sense of what she meant to convey with them: "That the Lieutenant's in Heaven...And that we still have to earn our right-of-return." Stephen spied a tarp bundled up behind the side netting and yanked it out. Giving it a flick to throw off any debris, he laid the tarp over Lloyd's body.

Mirek stared at the covered form. "Wanna say a few words? *A prayer?*"

Stephen looked up with hot coals for eyes. "Don't mock me." He waited for Mirek to go back to mulling over the coded mechanisms littered throughout the hold, and quietly recited the words of a rite he heard whispered above men of conscience too many times before.

Hurtling through the air parallel to the emerald coast, the Mountain League's cargo ship had roused the interest of a CDS frigate anchored to a tower dock off the Sea Wall. The dashboard before Zoya, who had yet to wipe away the tears she loosed for the Lieutenant, was bright with a motley of blinking buttons and strobing warning signs. Although she ignored the alerts, Zoya knew she couldn't dismiss the incoming transmission from the CDSS Kiberd. She grabbed and put on B. Lee's helmet and took the call. Instead of savaging Mandarin tones and proving herself a fraud off the bat, she sat silent and waited for the pallid captain of the Kiberd to speak, whose face— similarly masked—was overlaid on the windscreen.

"To the commander of the ML427, this is your first and final warning: submit your mobility clearance code immediately." The Kiberd's captain repeated the warning in Mandarin.

Zoya quickly scanned the dash and saw the button Lloyd had bloodied. "As you wish." She smashed the button and prayed for results.

The Kiberd's captain looked down at his monitor and shook his head. "The legitimacy of your class-four mobility clearance is now under review. Until your review has been completed, we require that you land immediately at the coordinates I'm providing now or we will be forced to stall your movement."

Zoya nodded. "Very well," she said, voiced modified enough by her helmet to conceal her accent. She terminated the call, pulled off B. Lee's helmet, and sat there frozen by indecision. "We've got a big problem!"

Stephen ran into the cockpit. He saw nothing but the white and blue jigsaw pieces of the ocean below, the diffuse blues of the morningtime sky in front of the ship, and the last of the vanishing stars twinkling overhead. "What's the matter?" He looked out to the side and saw it: over ninety-metres long, adorned with railguns and plasma cannons, and rounded pewter edges—a demsock frigate. Stephen sat down in the co-pilot's chair and breathed uneasily. "What did they say? What do they want?"

"They want us to land. If we don't, they'll incinerate us."

Stephen put his head between his legs and racked his brain. "Can't outpace it?"

"No."

Sitting upright he looked up the stars and recalled the terms of the Armistice, as delineated to him by Wes. The Americans and Russians together ruled space; China kept its half of a damned world without fear of reprisal or contest. Unlike boundary lines drawn by conquerors in the past, the key line decided after the Sino-American War was just as invisible, but this time a horizontal line demarcating a vertical boundary between the stratosphere and the ionosphere: *the stratopause*. The Chinese and their subservient allies in Europe and Britain could not fly higher than fifty kilometers, with exception to the sphere directly over the Mandarin homeland and its protectorates in the Indian Ocean and South China Sea. Having always delighted in tales of space travel, Stephen was doubly excited over the notion of escaping the jaws of death and overstepping the realm of weather. "You think they'd violate the Armistice by shooting us out of republican space?"

Zoya had no better idea and Stephen's was better than nothing. "The stratopause..." The Major checked the altimeter. "Good thinking, Private. Buckle up!"

Stephen leaned over and looked back: "Merry! Get a grip on that mortar, and hold on tight this time. We're going—"

With a not-so-gentle pull on the wheel and a full-shift forward on the throttle, Zoya fired the three of them on a sixty degree climb through CDS-dominated airspace.

They all felt gravity's pull until it finally released them. Stephen's arms rose on their own volition. Garbage and baubles left behind by the previous crew rose from the ground and floated around the cockpit. Outside, the morning sky, all reds and oranges, tunneled around the ship until the colours looked compressed as one on the horizon. Above them were sheets of blue and above the blue, infinite darkness.

"Get our shields up!" Zoya ordered.

Although the button to activate the ship's plasmic shield was right in front of Stephen—and out of reach of Zoya—it was camped amongst dozens of others just like it, all with Mandarin symbols

279

equally meaningless to Stephen. He stared blankly at the dash, bobbing up and down in his seat. "Which one!"

"Uh..." Zoya looked over. "Third over from the left. Two rows down." Unnerved by her co-pilot's sluggishness, she conveyed a few more details: "With the symbol that looks like a picnic bench under the letter 'P' next to a Union Jack and hammer-and-sickle both wearing a hat."

That was enough. Stephen found and smacked the button. There was a thrum beneath their feet—the sound of the Moscovium reactor redirecting power to the shields.

"Perfect. Now, turn that green dial, and give us shielding on our underside."

"Aye, aye, Major."

Noticing the cargo ship powering up to the outer limits of their reach, the CDSS Kiberd took action. It nearly struck the rogue ship with a warning shot that blistered off into the stratosphere. Unable to spook Zoya into changing course with its cautionary volley, the frigate fired a dozen homing missiles. The first missile was deflected by the plasmic shield. The second had its warhead cooked to a dud by the shield again. The third struck the rear of the jet, crimping the ramp and blasting metal slivers into the hold. Keenly aware of the purpose of the cargo jet's ascent, the captain of the Kiberd fired another dozen missiles.

Stephen saw the missiles indicated on the radar, shredding ever closer through the space between them. He smacked away at the dashboard, hoping to find a magic button that might invigorate their shields. In midst of his panicked, celestial flailing, he saw the readout on the altimeter. The digital needle spun wildly under a numerical altitude-readout given in kilometres: *forty-seven...forty-eight...forty-nine...*

The missiles, although now impossible to see from the cockpit, were about to strike when—

Fifty! "We made it over!" Stephen exclaimed.

Avoiding a premature confrontation with the same enemy the Socialist Alliance intended to poison out of existence at a later time of their choosing, the CDSS Kiberd-sent missiles were remotely neutralized. They dropped away from their intended target back towards the earth. While the cargo ship's immolation had been temporarily postponed, it still had had a frigate on its tail, albeit far below with all of its guns aimed skywards.

"If I could, I'd kiss you!" Zoya said, levelling the ship just above the invisible border.

Stephen blushed and called back to his neighbour: "All good?"

Despite the damage to the ramp and hull inflicted by the third missile, the ship maintained the atmospheric pressure necessary to keep its remaining crew alive. The metal splinters in the cargo bay floated about aimlessly as did Lloyd's body. A sphere of blood ebbed across the hold wherein Mirek tried to station himself with the help of the side netting.

"Whosoever taught yahs to drive should be drawn and quartered!" Mirek piped back.

Checking the waypoints Lloyd had left for them, Zoya saw that Tearaght was close in a manner of speaking; one klick ahead, fifty-five down. In fact, were it not for the white carpet of clouds below, she might have been able to see it out the window—a grain of sand on blue marble. "We're closing in!" Zoya yelled for Mirek's benefit. "Here's where it gets tricky...If you haven't figured out how to deliver *our package,* we might have to take Dubchek's earlier suggestion to heart."

Stephen lurched up from his seat, grabbed B. Lee's helmet out of the air, and floated purposefully back towards the drone. He looked at Lloyd, suspended in the air above the bench, and settled down beside Mirek, who failed to mention or gripe about the metal splinter goring through his thigh.

"Feeling lightheaded, bruv?" kidded Mirek.

"Yeah, yeah." Stephen was too focused on the drone to play around despite the intense urge to savour every moment of this dream-come-true. "Merry, the Lieutenant gave me an idea. Or maybe it was his idea and—*doesn't matter.*" He looked over at Mirek's wound and gulped. Shaking away one concern in devotion to another, he pointed over to the lockers. "Lloyd mentioned there being explosives. See if you can boobytrap the mortar. Timed explosion in case the impact doesn't do it."

"Impact? Ha! *My plan it is.* At least now I won't need stitches." Mirek trailed gobs of blood over to the lockers. He pulled everything out, so that he was surrounded by loot. Among the items in his orbit were a few sticks of semtex and a timed charge. Very carefully he sandwiched the nuke in additional explosives, and threw a thumbs-up to Stephen, who—disguised as a triad kingpin—activated the heavy-lifting drone.

The pedestal lowered the drone's loading platform to the ground, while the magnetic hook released the drone itself so that it hovered in place. It had to be powered-on to compensate for re-entry, otherwise it would be thrown around as Mirek had.

281

Examining the drone readouts in B. Lee's helmet, Stephen noticed an important detail about the contraption. "The drone has a ten-second force field we can use. When we bail, the ship will be going hundreds-of-kilometres-an-hour. We'll be shredded by the difference unless the field gives us the opportunity to stabilize."

Mirek shrugged his shoulders. "Good. What yah telling me for?"

"How are we looking back there?" asked Zoya.

Stephen grabbed the nuclear mortar from Mirek, and carried it into the cockpit. From there he saw the shadow of the frigate on the clouds below. Disregarding the mammoth threat anticipating their return to CDS airspace, Stephen delineated his plan to the Major: "Line up with the target and then dive." He kept the mortar from floating away, and caught his breath. "It'll blow on impact or on discovery. *We* will dip out on the drone platform. Just think of the drone as one of those old weather balloons—only, all steel with a force field."

Zoya nodded even though she was still mulling over the plan. "If we drop out early, they'll catch us no problem."

"If we drop out late, we'll be atomized."

Mirek busted into the cockpit with a rifle slung over his shoulder. He had another in his hand, with which he pointed at the map. "That there—that's another island. Not far from Tearaght."

Stephen tightened the belts on the co-pilot's chair and strapped the mortar in. He grabbed Mirek's second gun. "Yeah, so what?"

"We've gotta put the drone down somewhere."

Zoya smiled. She had been with the pair long enough now to know that it wasn't naivety behind the question but faith and perseverance. "Water's a good place as any."

"Not the sea!" Mirek tightened up. "An island or a beach would be ideal."

Stephen almost had an aneurism. "Does it matter?"

Mirek whispered: "I can't swim."

"The hell you mean you can't swim?! You've lived by the shore your entire life!"

"Not all of us swam over from Poland, you clown. And I didn't spend any time poolside either."

Stephen shook his head. "Figured you might've learned to swim given how much you drink...What'd you think, Major?"

"Enough! Is the drone ready?" she replied, fed up with their trifles over where best to die.

"Yes," Mirek and Stephen answered in unison.

282

Eyes full of morning light, Zoya tittered. "Get on it and prepare to drop the ramp. We're over the target." She couldn't see Tearaght's jagged form through the clouds. She couldn't see that all-important armoured rock surrounded by lesser rocks in the North Atlantic, which had had its greenery and petrels replaced by satellite arrays, massive transmitter/receiver dishes, bunkers, and anti-space weaponry, and its shores crowded with water-borne garrisons and warships. But she didn't need to. She lined them up with the island in accordance with Lloyd's last waypoint and with some help from the ship's long-range sensors.

Instead of a holographic exclamation mark, now a pixelated skull rotated above the dash. The CDS forces below were preparing to take matters a little more seriously. According the cargo ship's sensors, the CDSS Kiberd was preparing to fire its ion-cannon. The Kiberd captain probably received the go-ahead from the CDS council.

"Nowak—redirect half-power from the shields to the gravity cushion. Re-entry at the intended speed will mash us otherwise. Focus remaining shields on the bow."

Stephen complied, reversing his earlier actions and turning the dial the other way round.

Though auto-pilot was deactivated, Zoya was nevertheless able to lock the steering wheel and force the nav system to maintain course. The horizon rose and the ship dipped. "Alright! Now or nothing."

Mirek, who had yet to return to the drone to bleed, checked the charges on the strapped-in mortar. There were three inserted into the plastic explosives. One was timed while the other two were to be remote-detonated. "How much time do you reckon?"

"Travelling at eight, nine hundred...? *Uh*..." Zoya racked her mind. The best she could come up with was a rough estimate. "Put seven minutes on the clock to be safe. If impact doesn't do the trick, then we might as well give ourselves some leeway until the timer does or we remote-detonate."

"Done," said Mirek, making his final tweaks to the demonic egg seated up front. He pushed himself aback the jet with Stephen in tow.

Zoya tapped the mortar on the side for good luck, and followed Stephen and Mirek into the cargo hold. Reaching the drone, already quivering with potential, she tapped Stephen. "Helmet please." He surrendered his trophy over willingly. Zoya interfaced with its heads-up-display and synchronized its readouts with the drone's own altimeter. She handed the helmet back, as Stephen

283

seemed the best acquainted with the technology among those present. "When the counter hits three-thousand metres, we bail."

Eying the damaged ramp that had inadvertently barbed him, Mirek turned pale. "We sure this'll open?" Answering his own question, he checked the panel. One of the pneumatic arms was inoperable. "Damn, bruv—it may not open."

"It will," Stephen answered back, lying flat on the platform with his rifle beneath him. Of course, it might not have opened, though there were other problems known only to Stephen that were equally as demoralizing. According to B. Lee's helmet, the CDSS Kiberd had just opened fire. As there was nothing for any of them to do, Stephen didn't share the news with his team. The ship might outrun the missiles, after all. Only then would the broken ramp matter, and even then, what was there to be done? All of the explosives had been committed to ensuring the mortar would go off.

Though its crew remained relatively weightless, the cargo ship itself felt gravity's pull. It began to rock about unsteadily. Its hull sounded like sheet metal punished by a hail storm.

Zoya lay down beside Stephen. Mirek, taking advantage of the gravity cushion's protection, knelt by the ramp's panel. He yanked the metal splinter out of his leg without complaint, and readied his hand over the button responsible for dropping the ramp.

More missiles fired by the Kiberd were fast approaching on an intercept course, however the cargo ship had exceeded speeds its designers thought possible. It veered perilously down—penetrating cloud and CDS airspace—towards Tearaght with all of the Resistance's hopes riding on it.

"Twenty klicks out," said Stephen, helmeted and still.

There was a whistling sound outside of the ship that stood out from the clamour made by the exterior tiles, which were peeling off one by one.

"What's that sound?" asked Mirek.

No sooner had Mirek asked the question then he was rewarded with an answer: a meaty thud. The ship and its contents jostled to and fro. Still, B. Lee's helmet reported they were on course and now going even faster.

More explosions, some distant and some dangerously close, went off, making the ship tremble more than its kamikaze descent had already allowed.

"That was a missile!" Zoya determined out loud. "*Nowak*— you keeping secrets?"

Stephen broke silence only to announce that they were now ten kilometers away from the island.

284

"Dubchek—cue the ramp and hold on next to me!" ordered the Major.

Mirek slammed the button and retreated to the security of his friends' warmth.

The ramp motors gasped for air as the crimped metal began to yawn open. Sparks fired where the ramp grinded against the ship's metal sides.

All three of them felt an instant chill and suction. They held on tightly to the drone platform while the Lieutenant's body flew past them along with anything else that wasn't fastened down, including Mirek's remote detonators.

"Mirek yelled, "Damn it all," though he was not heard.

"Five-thousand metres!"

Stephen glimpsed out the crack between the ceiling and the ramp, still labouring to open, and saw the Kiberd. *Maybe,* he thought, *they think we are crashing by accident.* His thought was interrupted by a screech and clunk just past his feet. The ramp opened all the way, and then broke free of the jet. Within an instant came another thud—some warhead had claimed the ramp as its prize.

Checking his helmet once more, Stephen saw that it was time. "Ready?"

Mirek shook his head, caving to animal panic.

Despite this protest, Stephen ordered the drone to split and engaged its temporary force field. It wrenched them out the rear of the cargo jet. As it couldn't match the jet's high speed, Stephen, Mirek, and Zoya all felt crushed by the quick deceleration—even with the force field's protection—and not just them; the cables fastening the platform to the drone similarly were drawn to their limit.

Even with his ribs broken by the sudden pull, Stephen at once felt a jolt of joviality and curiosity. Giggling to himself—which sounded morose when modulated by his helmet—he peered over the lip of the platform, and saw through the force field's blue hue the cargo ship whip towards Tearaght. In his survey, he also spotted another small island just to the southeast—Inishnabro—and ordered the drone to take them in its direction.

Groaning and bleeding profusely from his thigh, Mirek turned to Stephen. "Mate—a beach—somewhere nice."

"You got it, brother."

As Stephen steered the drone using B. Lee's helmet, the force field dissipated. A forceful gust of air barraged the drone and its carriage, nearly scraping Mirek off of the platform. The three of them clung on for dear life.

285

Puzzled over why she had not yet heard Tearaght's security forces fire their anti-aircraft guns—whether they feared detonating a massive payload over their heads, or were instead interested in preserving the ship's contents, or just averse to angering the Chinese even in self-defense—Zoya looked down at island. "God-damn-it," she muttered.

So focused was Stephen on getting them down to terra firma, that he disregarded the Major's fretting. Even if he wasn't distracted, it would have been near impossible to hear her without the insulation of the force field.

The CDS forces on Tearaght had caught the cargo ship in a tractor beam and were holding it at a distance, assuredly inspecting it with their sensors.

Several small autonomous fighter jets emerged from holes in the island's cliffs and rose to meet their would-be destroyer while a fleet of small hunter drones were dispatched, both from the island and from the Kiberd, to hunt down the heavy-lifting drone, just big enough to appear on their radars.

As the island of Inishnabro grew ahead of them, revealing itself to be more or less a beachless mountain, there was commotion around the captured cargo jet. The autonomous fighters attempted to flee. There was a last-ditch effort on the ground to throw up a plasmic shield around Tearaght, but all attempts at self-preservation were in vain.

There was a brilliant flash of light.

A leg of plasma fired down along the confines of the tractor beam, which—unable to contain the awesome power—lost its hold of the explosion, allowing a second sun to dawn over the sea. Spherical, the nuclear blast spread out in every direction. It engulfed Tearaght and threw up walls of steam wherever it met water. Massive waves formed a good distance away from the blast, and rolled out in every direction, preceded by an electromagnetic pulse. The pulse killed the heads-up-display in B. Lee's helmet and the electronics keeping the Resistance-manned drone airborne.

Stephen, Zoya, and Mirek fell the last hundred metres independent of their drone, and smacked into waves that felt as hard as concrete just before the shockwave travelled the four kilometres over from Tearaght to its neighbouring island Inishnabro. Stephen felt the initial impact against the brine, but that was the last of his sensation.

TWENTY-SIX

Jagjit and Mallory sat side by side in silence in the dropship bound for Blackpool Central. Without protest, Mallory had accepted the role of overseer of the mass execution of terrorists and subversives, some two-thousand souls. Deputy Commissar Fik had been cordial over the wire, though she was clearly miffed over being replaced in a visible posting so late in the game.

"We'll let you off at City Hall," Jagjit said, tired of hearing only the inner rumblings of the dropship and the occasional whine from the Praetorian's joints. He pointed to the drone. "Your Praetorian escort will be there waiting for you to arrive. I suggest that you ensure that no one has hacked it. As always, I hope it will defend you against all and any threats."

Mallory nodded heedfully. "And you? What will you do with the DDOS icon?"

"The *counterfeit painting*, you mean? I have a rapid carrier waiting for me at the EBS. I'll send it to the Home Defence Minister as soon as I land."

"Do let him know I had some hand in its acquisition and delivery."

Jagjit smiled. "You have my word."

"And you're certain you don't need my help in implementing the Patch Over?"

"That's right. I think it best that you are there when the fugitives are re-educated—to reap the fruits of your labour."

The Praetorian turned creakily to the side and interrupted: "Comrade Commissar, we are being asked to change our course." The drone was synchronized with the dropship; it might as well have been the ship itself communicating with the Commissar.

Jagjit and Mallory both shared a look of concern. "Why?" he inquired.

"There have been reports of gunfire and explosions in Preston and a small nuclear blast on a broadcast relay station in Lancaster." The drone's inability to emote or modulate its tone made the news it delivered seem rather lackluster despite its seriousness.

"A nuclear blast!" Jagjit nearly choked on the information, and glared at the bag containing the captured mortars.

Mallory unbuckled her seatbelt and clamored over to the ship's north-facing windows. The sun was not yet out so the only light visible came from the CBLOCK towers in the high-trustvalue

287

zones and—Mallory gasped—a massive column of smoke on the horizon above Lancaster. "The Resistance?" she wondered aloud.

"They're trying to stop the Patch Over. All the more reason to stick to our schedule and flight plan." Jagjit jabbed the Praetorian angrily. "Do not deviate or I'll have you turned into scrap."

"As you wish, Comrade Commissar." The Praetorian drone turned to face the front and regained its statuesque allure.

Jagjit intuited a command to Poyraz and Fik both: "Notify London we will be terminating all traffic between Lancashire County and its borders. My delivery to the Home Defence Department will be the last in or out. I want all forces to be tuned into the Patch Over, just in case the real Family painting is still out there. To ensure against possible resistance reinforcements from the east, I want the troops we currently have in the north redeployed to our eastern border. If possible, avoid engagements with the terrorists in the north. We need to reduce exposure until we have turned the page on Lancashire."

"But Commissar!?" Poyraz answered back, audibly perplexed.

"Notify me if anything changes! And Major, once you've seen these orders through, I want you to meet me at the EBS."

"Yes, Comrade Commissar."

Fik piped up: "Is Dr. Worthing with you?"

"Yes, of course." Jagjit looked over at Mallory and smiled. "Why?"

"She had quarantined her comms and is blocking AI support. I find it quite troubling."

"Comrade Worthing did so under my orders. We couldn't risk contamination by what could very well have been a dangerous memetic weapon."

"My apologies, Comrade Commissar. I look forward to seeing her on the dais and the parts of her report the Home Defence Office deems fit to declassify."

As Jagjit had been speaking out loud, Mallory couldn't help eavesdropping. She raised an eyebrow as the Commissar terminated his comm to Fik.

"The Deputy Commissar says hello."

"I'm sure she does."

Jagjit dropped Mallory off on the roof of City Hall, leaving her behind to oversee the first massacre hosted by patched-over Lancashire. She watched the Commissar' ship shimmer then disappear, and her gaze fell upon the city below, coloured carmine by the rising sun. Heavy

288

footsteps alerted her to her trusty escort, Percy the Praetorian drone.

From the rooftop lobby behind Percy sprang a porcine man. He approached Mallory rapidly—too quickly apparently for Percy, who quickly intercepted him and raised its arms as if to strike, hanging on its master's command.

"It's alright, Percy," said Mallory, setting her hand on the armoured-giant's hip. "This is—" She looked to the man for a reply.

"Ah yes," he said, tilting his head away from the drone. "Sam Mesk. Interim Head of the Blackpool Municipal Committee and Deputy Commissioner of the Harmony Festival."

"Well Comrade Mesk, we have an event to prepare for."

"Thanks to the glorious labour of members from the National Education Office, virtually everything is ready," Sam boasted. "If you'd be so kind and come with me." He turned and gestured toward the rooftop lobby.

Mallory brushed past and Percy followed.

Sam caught up, careful not to draw Percy's ire, and lead them through the rooftop lobby, and onto a funicular, which carted them down to the main hall along a very gradual track. The open funicular overlooked the city square on its left and vivisected City Hall on the right. As they descended on a spatially-wasteful diagonal, Mallory peered into the various activities on each floor. On one she glimpsed the manufacture and distribution of placards and signs all with the same slogan, "As One and One Together We Will Save the World." Those prospective audience members who had already received their signs were instructed how best to hold them.

"Normally, for the more populous re-educations," said Sam, attempting to direct Mallory's attention to her left, down upon the city square, "We watch from the balconies. Now of course, as per Deputy Commissar Fik's suggestions, we will all watch on the ground floor. Verticality suggests inequality, and that's just bad optics." As the funicular settled at its base, Sam trotted off, pointing out all of the details that had been delegated to municipal bureaucrats like him to oversee. Coming to the sudden realization that Mallory had remained on the funicular and was inspecting Percy's security protocols, he dug in his heels and fluttered his eyebrows. Whether out of compulsion or on account of insecurity, he found himself unable to halt his speech as he had his feet and continued his tour. "The Ministry of Plumbing will see to the irrigation of the square in the event that the phasers somehow make a mess."

289

"Yes, of course," Mallory said apathetically, locking Percy's control panel. "The prisoners—those we brought over from CBLOCK40—where are they now?"

Sam scratched his head. "Prisoners? Oh! Ha! Yes! Our new students..." He started see-sawing side to side in a more pronounced fashion that he had before. "They'll be arriving any minute now for enrollment and to be stripped down. Our phasers only deal with organic matter, after all."

"Naturally."

Sam giggled. "Precisely!"

Down a hall, perfectly symmetrical including the alignment of the Shepherd drones posted on either side at two-metre intervals, Sam brought Mallory all the way to a giant bronze door. A red light fired out of a button-sized disc mounted on the wall and targeted his eye. There was a click, and with that the door groaned open, allowing in a sewery smell.

Sam winced and visibly became self-aware of his judgmental expression. He quickly turned to Mallory with a smile. "Wonderful job the Supreme Council has done. After the final vote, Blackpool was a wreck; pulverized by the fighting and all around a place soured by past inequity." Waving his hand out as if conducting an invisible orchestra, he continued: "And now? What a difference!"

Blackpool City Hall was a three-winged building, bordering the square on all but one side where the parade route began and ended. Inside the square was the stage—a large area with four phaser generators in each corner. Unlike the sandstone floor surrounding it, the stage was situated on metal grates, which caught *students'* cybernetic elements but permitted for the instant disposal of their ash. On the edges of the stage's sandstone frame were amphitheatre seats, set in a semi-circle with a roped-off section midway up its radius designated for the Supreme Council, who would be watching from London.

Mallory took in the lackluster sight. Besides the banners draped below every window that could open, the scene was monochrome. Grey steel. Grey concrete. Grey lampposts. "I am surprised to hear you mention the final vote. How many cycles back do you have access to?"

Sam turned beet red. "I'm not sure I take your meaning."

"In my travels, the only citizens I have met with pre-calendar memory are revolutionaries and true believers." Eying Sam up and down, Mallory squinted. "I take it you belong to the latter of the two groups."

290

Taking this as a compliment, Sam let out a sigh of relief and wiggled his fingers. "Please, comrade, let me show you—"

Mallory focused on the roped-off section. "Where will I be seated?"

"Seated? Oh, well...Yes! Just one second, comrade." Sam opened a holographic seating chart and queried the Doctor's name while muttering, "Seated, seated, seat number..." He looked up nervously at Mallory and even more nervously at the hologram. "Oh..." He indicated the amphitheatre pressed up against the bosom of City Hall. "There—the front row of the second tier, just below the Supreme Council's platform."

"I'd prefer to be seated as close as possible," Mallory replied. "Standing room is alright as well; preferable, even." She walked over and inspected one of the phaser generators. Like the other three, it was adorned with spikes and set on a rail that led to the middle of the stage. All four of the generators, when activated, would slowly constrict the space and kill everything fenced inside of it. "I want to see the regret in their eyes—the realization that service to the collective is life-saving." She turned and smiled at Sam. "Chock it up to scientific curiosity."

Sam pulled at his collar, revealed to him to be too tight by his anxious gulping. "Yes, yes! The People's science! I do so appreciate the work that you do." He tapped on his holographic chart and made the necessary changes. "*Done!* First tier, first row." Although it had taken him very little time to accommodate Dr. Worthing and to see to the changes she wanted, in the meantime he had lost her to her fancy. She wandered over to the machinery cornering the stage. He nosily caught up to her and rushed into his explanation of the technology. "So the phaser generators—"

"The phaser generators will be activated before or after the Patch Over?" Mallory set her hands on her hips and browbeat Sam while Percy strode over to the generator, posturing as if to take it on as a threat to his charge. Mallory shooed away the drone, and silently bid Sam answer.

"After the Patch Over, comrade. It has been explained to me that this is to be a first memory, not the last of Lancashire's forgotten memories."

Mallory smiled. "Excellent work, Committee-Person Mesk. Please begin populating the amphitheatre as well as the—"

"Stage."

Mallory smiled without wrinkling her forehead or eyes. "For our audience, fetch a good mix of trustvalues. Ideally, in a place made ideal by cooperation by all, I would like to see a substantial number

291

of citizens with lower trustvalues. After all, they will need this first memory more than any else in the region; anything else would be inequitable."

Blushing at the thought of inequity, Sam stammered: "Yes, yes. Of course! I had originally figured a good mix from all over, up and down. I mean, there's no up and down, but, of course you understand! But yes, *lower trustvalues*. I will see to it and we will drive them in immediately."

"Within the hour. After all, the Patch Over will begin in two." Mallory turned slowly taking in the empty square and imagining the spectacle to come. "Comrade, I need to update my tablet. Where's the nearest garrison or armoury?"

"In the basement of City Hall. I can do it for you."

"No. You have much more important preparations to see to, Comrade Hesk." With an air of officialdom, Mallory clapped her hands. "This will be a brilliant display. And if the next time we meet we are not ourselves, I hope we get along just as swimmingly." Mallory left Sam stammering in the affirmative at the centre of the square.

TWENTY-SEVEN

Alek awoke to the sound of gnashing teeth, whimpering, and angry yelling. He sat up and rubbed his head, still full of all of his memories including the most recent underlying the present and verifying that this Hell was real—that Monica was truly dead and her body possessed by some demsock masquerader. Alek had been dumped down a steep slide into a white room lit by thousands of overpowered LEDs. The floor was a tarry black, textured and streaked with excrement and blood. He, like the thousands cramped together in the giant holding cell, had been stripped down to their underwear. Even their felt shoes had been taken away, perhaps to dissuade them from running anywhere, not that there was any place left to go.

Beside Alek, Cassandra was working tirelessly to stop Wesley Miller from bleeding out. She had already torn the portion of her knickers covering her thighs to plug the wound, and applied as much pressure as she had the energy still in her to exert. Although the Commissar's knife had miraculously missed Miller's heart, it had punctured his left lung. With blood pooling in his chest and his lung all but collapsed, Miller was running out of time. There was a good chance he might not even make it to his public execution.

Danika saw that Alek had arisen with great difficulty. His ankle had turned black and there were little harden bulbs of blood wherever the calcifier clamp had needled him. She walked Lisa—who was beyond rattled and wearing an expression signifying no inner state—over to Alek. She sat Lisa down next to Miller, and pulled Alek aside. "You told me it would work."

Alek lowered his head in defeat and shame. "It was supposed to."

"It didn't!" Danika had no more tears left and she knew full-well Alek stood to lose as much as her if he hadn't lost it already. "So what's the plan?"

Raising his head slowly, Alek furrowed his brow. "Plan?"

"Yeah. The painting didn't work. So what was your plan-b?"

Alek looked around at all of the misery and up at the ceiling. Below the grid of LEDs there were a number of dividing walls suspending on cables. Normally they would separate prisoners according to their trustvalue and where they resided on the intersectional matrix. It didn't matter now; such details would soon be forgotten. He looked back towards the slide. It had several rows of

293

lances pointed downwards. Bodies sliding into the room would not be barbed, but anyone with the fortitude and uncanny ability to climb up a fifty-five degree greased plane would impale themselves one way or another. The only way out was past a massive roller-shutter door on the other side of the room, above which was a catwalk patrolled by several guardians armed with flamethrowers. *The only way out of Blackpool will be as ashes on the wind.* "I'll figure something out. Now, you keep Lisa with you at all times. Wherever we go, we stay together. Yah?"

Danika didn't care much if Alek was projecting false strength and confidence or had it in him to fight the EDS army with his ass hanging out of tattered briefs. Despair was the final enemy, now the same as at any other time. "Yah." She pointed at Cassandra: "She's the reason we're in here! She lied to us..." Balling her fists, Danika motioned to strike, but Alek pulled her back.

"I don't think she'd be here if she was lying before." Alek nodded to Lisa. "Tend to your girl and be ready." Alek crouched down next to Miller, opposite Cassandra. He whispered: "It was supposed to work, yah? Because it sure as shit didn't."

Cassandra wore an out-of-place look of calm. "James didn't kill Brigadier Miller. Miller has a birth defect. His heart is on the right side. Khatri plunged his knife into his left..."

Alek looked dubiously at Miller's wound. "Is that supposed to mean something?"

"It may," Cassandra replied. "*That was The Family painting.* It wasn't a counterfeit."

"You know this how?" Alek's face went red. Doherty's certainty after having been proven wrong was more than he could take.

There was a ruckus across the room. A group of low-trustworthees charged the door. It didn't budge one iota. Nevertheless, the attempt was met with an extreme overreaction. The guardians on the catwalk above took aim with their flamethrowers, and torched those responsible for the charge. The resultant screams were harrowing and the smell of burnt hair and flesh overwhelming.

Cassandra grimaced and kept pressure on Miller's chest. "No one else knew that it depicted the Holy Family. Unless Townley made a replica—"

"Ah! Scott Townley! You realize he's the reason Monica's going around wearing commie garb and working for the evil empire?" Alek channeled the same rage he tried to quell in Danika. "Your man shot my wife!"

294

Such accusations fell on deaf ears in a room already loud with confused conversations and horrible pleading.

"He was one of many who promised to bring The Family painting to us so that we could give it to the Resistance. I had no idea how he planned to retrieve it, and it was late in the game when I realized he was a Russian mole in the EDS government. He intended to give it to the Resistance, just not England's."

"You didn't know who he worked for and you didn't know that he made a replicate?"

Miller opened his eyes and clutched his chest. Gurgling and desperately trying to breathe, he looked up at Alek. Very faintly he ordered him: "Chin up, boy. The cavalry's coming."

The heavy door rolled up and several droids entered to put out the flaming corpses. Once the fires were put out, the droids retreated into the hall on the other side of the door and Shepherd drones marched out to take their place. Over loudspeakers embedded in the walls came a nasally voice: "Line up, single file. Prepare your wrists for registration. The faster you are enrolled, the better chance you have of receiving a swift education."

Danika called over to Alek, pointing to her wrist. "We're not in the system!"

Alek stood up slowly and rolled his shoulders back. "Oh well. Not a whole lot more they can do to us."

Lisa broke away from her mother's protective hold. "Why don't they just burn us all here?"

The question stumped Alek. He looked over at the immolated remains. "They need to kill us publicly—to keep everyone in line and make them complicit."

Danika pulled Lisa back, and brushed her hair. "They'll try, anyhow."

"Help me get Miller to his feet," Cassandra implored Alek. She took one arm and Alek the other, and together they lifted the comatose soldier.

Alek groaned—his ankle had not been properly reset and it showed. There were now bulges and contours where there should not have been any. Notwithstanding his own instability, he helped Cassandra drag Miller to the rear of the herd of people trying to manage some semblance of a line. A line it was not; more of a fractal with the room's weakest inhabitants at its center, circling outwards and losing members to minor circles along its periphery.

A young man, bronzed by sweat and soot, saw Miller in the throng and beckoned to him: "Brigadier Miller! Wesley Miller! 'S'at'choo? G'd heavens!" He squeezed through the bodies in line, and stopped short of the bleeding soldier. Realizing Miller was not cognizant of his calls, the young man turned his attention to Alek and Cassandra. "Wot's done 'em in? One of them wankers fix 'em up? Bloody pricks."

"You with the Resistance, then?" Alek asked, securing Miller's limp arm around his neck.

"Private Yaxley, Engineer Corps. We were too early, t'others too late. Demsocks figgah'd us out and moved up whatever t'ey got planned." He wiped his face, only dirtying it more. "More lads in here puttering about—t'ones not barbequed, anyway."

Sensing Danika close behind him, Alek scrounged up the strength to peddle more bravado. "Tell your mates we're not going to go easily. Brigadier Miller here won't let you—certainly not when he comes to."

Private Yaxley looked Alek up and down then dismissed him with a smile. "Yah can be sure of it. After all, we've spent our lives not dying." Recognition yanked Yaxley's eyes open wide. He looked intensely at Cassandra. "Oi! Where are your Yanks? I ain't seen so much as a star or stripe, and we're 'bout at the wire."

Very curtly she answered: "Live a little longer, friend; trip the wire and earn those stripes."

With the line they proceeded out of the holding room and into a red-carpeted reception area, past a funicular, and down a gauntlet of Shepherd drones. None of the guardians seemed to mind that Wesley couldn't walk on his own volition never mind stay conscious for more than a minute at a time. Their focus was simply on getting their so-called students onto the stage at the centre of the city square.

The amphitheatre around the stage was packed full of people. Every second or third person held demsock propaganda over their heads. They hissed and jeered as the procession of deplorables made their way from the side wing of City Hall to the stage.

Danika indicated the generators at the four corners of the stage for Alek's benefit. "They'll demolecularize us. Does the *Lancashire Lethe* have a solution stowed away in a memory somewhere?"

Before he could answer, Alek saw Monica. She was seated in the first row. The Praetorian that had destroyed the hacked Shepherd drone at the Department of Reclamations towered behind her, head oscillating and vigilantly scouring the area for threats. *Screw it*, Alek determined. "Hey Moni!" he bellowed, shifting Miller's weight so he could throw up his hand. "Monica! Monica Warmington!" He waved wildly. For a second it seemed as though

296

she looked back at him. Alek's eyes were undoubtedly playing tricks on him, for he was convinced that she wore a look of sympathy. He called out again: "Monica!"

One of the guardians chaperoning the death march sought out the source of the agitation and struck Alek with his billy club. "Enough! No dilly dallying!"

Aware he wasn't a sheep for sheering but for slaughter, Alek spat at the guardian. "What does that even mean?!"

The guardian struck Alek again. Alek dropped Miller and fell onto his knees, cursing the EDS under his breath. Fighting through the pain of a broken or at the very least a bruised collar bone and with the help of Cassandra, Alek once again yoked the Brigadier's weight and continued to the stage.

Once the last of the prisoners had filed into the square, the generators turned on. There was a buzz followed by a crackle. Though barely visible, very real and very deadly phaser gates fired from generator to generator until there were four walls, each twenty feet high, and no way out.

A deep voice boomed over a loudspeaker: "Comrades! It is my distinct honour and privilege to welcome you and all united workers now looking on from across this great county, as well as those tuning-in on the continent and in the land of our liberators under the command of the most equitable and supreme of supreme councils, to the last moments of dependence on the past. In a few short moments, we together will pass from this age of enlightenment and into the sublime age of harmony. Our great revolutionary forerunners carried us out of the dark ages with this day in mind: that every democratic socialist will be a dependent part of the true body and the body dependent upon each true part, commanded by the dictatorship of the many, and directed towards a disembodiment into our truer shared self. Why?" There was a subtle beep that all heard, consciously or nay, and the voice continued with a prompt: "Because..."

The amphitheatre answered in resounding unison: "Because as one and one together, we will save the world!"

Since uproarious applause and clapping was considered too aggressive, those in the stands snapped their fingers or flailed their arms.

Alek motioned to Cassandra, and they gently let down Miller. Alek glanced up at the sky. The sun, mid-rise, hadn't yet passed over the rooftops. It occurred to him then that he might never see the sun again. As for Monica, he could see her clearly—standing and snapping her fingers—and wished for all the light to go out of the

297

world; for the sky to fall down on them or for the waters to rise and wash all participants in this cruel experiment out to sea.

Massive holographic projections flicked on. There were several iterations of the same video transmission thrown up so that everyone could see without exception. A tickertape graphic ran across the projection, now only depicting a black curtain with furtive shadows along the peripheries of the capture, which read: "COMMISSAR JAGJIT HASSAN'S MESSAGE TO LANCASHIRE WILL PREMIER MOMENTARILY. SYNCHRONIZE... SYCHRONIZE... SYNCHRONIZE..." This message played on repeat.

Miller spat blood, and lifted his head. He blinked spastically and chortled. Since his left lung had collapsed, his chortle came across as more of a death rattle. "It's been an honour, lads."

Private Yaxley threw up two fingers, and began cussing out the guardians stationed along the outside of the phasic walls.

Lisa burrowed into her mother's arms.

Cassandra looked to the skies for help that wasn't there.

Alek considered the grate beneath their feet and looked at all of the dentistry caught in its grooves. He shook his head. "We've got to do something." He hurried over to Miller and tried shaking some life into him. "C'mon, old man. There's got to be a way out of here."

One of Miller's eyes opened independent of the other, which seemed to have sealed shut. Recognizing Alek's voice and registering the shadow in front of him as Alek's form, Miller tried to whisper, though even that seemed to sap all of his remaining strength: "We have but one weapon left in our arsenal."

Eyes full and heart racing, Alek squeezed Miller's arm, trying to keep him conscious. "Yeah? *Come on*! Out with it then!" Alek looked up at the tickertape running along the bottom of the holographic screen, which indicated once more that the Patch Over was imminent. "Haven't much time. Tell me!"

"Call my men." Miller nearly keeled over. Cassandra buttressed him, locking her arms across his chest.

Alek pulled Yaxley out of the crowd. "The Brigadier's got orders for you and yours—get 'em over here right now."

"What? You havin' a laugh?" Happy to do anything besides wait for the inevitable and realizing then that Alek was dead serious, Yaxley called out the bodies around him: "Oi! Laura! Tommy! Saul! Adrian! Chang! Where's my Resistance at? On me now! Brigadier Miller's got a plan!"

Yaxley had a voice for public speaking. His call seemed to resound in the square, even managing to land outside of the stage where a few guardians with acute hearing began to laugh at their prisoners' prospect of having a plan. Everyone else within earshot—subversive, regressive, and citizen alike—similarly turned to the sound of this friendly authority. Several weary soldiers emerged from the thicket and met the young private, who led them over to Miller.

Yaxley pressed his ear to Miller's lips. The more the Brigadier seemed to say, the more baffled Yaxley appeared to be. He nodded soberly and cleared his throat.

"Well! What's the play?" Alek said frantically with his back turned to Danika who he would not dare approach now with anything less than a way out. His revenge, which had felt so hollow, had cost them all dearly and he couldn't admit that it was on his account they would all now have to pay.

Ignoring Alek's pestering, and pulling his compatriots over to him, Yaxley heeded Miller's order and raised his voice once more: "You all know it. T'ose that don't, never mind, though it's never too late to learn. Just find a hand 'n' hold it."

The soldiers fired mystified looks to one another, then joined all the others in fixing-in on Yaxley, who thundered: "Our Father who art in Heaven, hallowed be Thy name..."

Hands clasped hands throughout the fenced-in crowd, connecting like magnets. None of the non-Resistance subversives could have known the words or their meaning, though judging by the immediate outcry from the amphitheatre and the guardians outside the shield, it was a worthy petition.

Alek staggered backwards. He heard these words spoken in the memories he helped his clients forget. They had gotten his clients killed, and they didn't seem to be doing anything different for his friends now. While his own hope had finally been whittled down to nothing, the morale of the doomed boomed along with their voices.

"And forgive us our trespasses as we forgive those who trespass against us..."

The very idea of a bunch of hateful holdovers from the dark ages appealing to the Truth of those times seemed to vex the citizens outside the phaser gates. There was jeering and a futile attempt to overwhelm the prayer with EDS chants and slogans.

Concluding with a bittersweet "Amen," the impromptu congregation released one another's hands.

From the loudspeaker blared a deafening alarm—too late to interrupt the prayer although that wasn't its intended purpose. A hush fell over the square and all eyes darted up to the tickertape on the holographic projections, which had ended its crawl. The Patch Over was about to begin.

299

TWENTY-EIGHT

A long, black cloud hung in the air above the island of Tearaght. The CDS frigate Kiberd had narrowly avoided the blast, and now hovered a safe distance off the coast studying the damage and looking for survivors. Any other ship, whether it was naval or aerial, that had been in or just outside the blast radius had been vaporized, dashed against the rocks, or tossed into the sea.

The effects of the blast were felt kilometres away where massive waves slammed against the cliffs of Inishnabro. Flotsam and jetsam along with charred pieces of CDS ships were carried over and thrown against its fortress-like walls as well as into one particular cove facing the smoldering advance-warning station. That same cove had collected more than debris—there were several bodies that had been tossed onto the rocks. Among the bodies were CDS sailors and technicians, pilots and half-torched skeletons whose duties were theirs no longer. One body twitched—that belonging to Stephen Nowak.

Stephen's face was burnt. What bones had not been broken in the fall were broken in turn by the nuclear tide. He tried to move and was unable to do much more than blink and cringe. He tried to call out, but was similarly unable. If he could move, he would seek out Mirek and if he could call out, he would do the same.

Though unable to move or speak, his eyes had not failed him. Stephen looked up and saw the CDSS Kiberd lording over the havoc he had no small part in wreaking. He spat out sea water—the same that was exploring the cuts and scrapes along his extremities—and smiled. That was much better than just throwing another Molotov. Never mind England or the Resistance; Stephen had done his brothers proud.

In the cove with him, there was another survivor spitting up poisoned water. She was not so badly wounded as Stephen, though time would tell. Zoya Khatri sat akimbo, mesmerized by the facts that the mortar worked and had worked wonders. She broke her gaze and tried to pop her dislocated arm back into its socket. Though successful, it remained limp. She stood up and took stock of the carnage around her. Out in the bay she spotted something thrashing—too large to be a fish, too small to be a whale, and too frenetic to be mechanical. Despite her arm, she pressed into the shallow water, and vaulted off into the deep, spared the larger waves by the crescent of cliffs that sheltered the cove.

With her one good arm, she slapped against the water and pulled herself towards the excitement. Once she reached it, she immediately knew the cause.

Mirek, like his compatriots, had awoken on Ireland's edge, though was unable to stop the water from pulling him back out to sea. He held onto the body of a decapitated sailor, who had—for a period—kept him afloat. However, the dead sailor's partially-inflated jacket had been torn, and when he sank, Mirek was doomed to follow.

Zoya knew better than to compromise herself and Mirek both with just her one arm to bring them ashore. On her crippled swim over to her drowning subordinate, she caught hold of an empty munitions case, which kept her afloat. With some security in the choppy water, she paddled over to Mirek just in time to catch his stiffening hand. He had lost consciousness—perhaps faith too— when she found him, but by the time they made it back to shore, he was clearing his lungs in efforts to sing the Major's praises.

"An angel!" he cried.

This invocation caught Stephen's attention, lying paralyzed over on the other side of the cove. He tried again to cry out and was again unable.

Zoya grounded Mirek and straightaway began tearing fabric off of the dead to bind the massive wound on his thigh, which the fall had badly worsened. Mirek groaned and cursed her efforts, though had she not wrapped it, he would have bled out or been guaranteed to lose the leg.

"Where's Nowak?" she said, having grounded herself in reality after having succumbed to a dreamlike half-life in the wake of the explosion.

Mirek tried to stand. His leg wouldn't support him, so he sat back down and frantically looked around for his neighbour. "Stevie! Stevie boy?!"

They're okay, thought Stephen. *My friends are okay. It is done.* And with that realization, Stephen took his last breath and relaxed on the cold stone. As the light left his eyes, there was a sound like thunder if thunder was perpetual and knew no upward limit.

301

TWENTY-NINE

An English Broadcast Station producer named Nigel Dunthorp led Jagjit and Poyraz down a hall of windows looking into the various studios where news was routinely manufactured. Nigel indicated one of the studios, and had his followers press up to the glass. "We've been preparing citizens for the Patch Over around the clock. Not a single implant or screen in Lancashire County will miss the good news."

"I'm not here for the tour. Where is Doctor Worthing's team presently?"

"Ah," said Nigel with a grin. "Studio one, Comrade Commissar."

Jagjit looked for a reference point and saw "Studio 4" stenciled by the nearest door. He carried on without Nigel's directions.

Embarrassed over having his local authority usurped, Nigel rushed to Jagjit's side. "Everything is ready..."

"It better be," Jagjit replied, hastening his pace.

They entered the last room on the left. Poyraz went in first to clear it for possible threats. He popped out and gave the all-clear. Nigel squeezed in ahead of Jagjit, who shook his head at the producer's gall.

The studio was a high-ceilinged room with a small sound stage; almost too small, granted the importance of the coming broadcast. Jagjit ordered Poyraz to clear the rest of the floor, and after sending him out, locked the door behind him. He took off his jacket, careful not to reveal what its pockets contained, and folded it over his arm.

"I can take your jacket, Comrade Commissar," squeaked Nigel.

"No thank you."

Several EBS technicians rushed over to welcome Jagjit. One by one they bowed at the shoulders and shook his hand. As soon as he had paid them all a modicum of attention and boasted about the grandiosity of their work, they all went back to making their final adjustments to the cameras and microphones that would capture and convey Jagjit's catalytic broadcast to the people of Lancashire.

A projection sphere located stage left threw a living picture of members of the Supreme Council and Chinese dignitaries into one corner of the room. Captivated in anticipation of their great leap

302

forward, they sat at attention and watched Commissar Jagjit Hassan with an almost religious intensity. Corven was not among them. Perhaps he was waiting for the London Patch Over.

Jagjit addressed their projected likenesses. "Doctor Worthing will not be joining us. So certain is she of the great work we have done and are about to complete that she wishes to witness the result firsthand at Blackpool City Hall, where—as I'm sure you're aware—we're about to cut ties with the past and give the people a glorious first shared-memory."

Dozens of toothy smiles appeared in the audience and then vanished as the lights were brought down on them—done so as not to interfere with the lighting prepared for the Commissar's address.

Nigel scurried across the stage, ensuring everything was in place. Before cowering away, he tapped his foot on an "X" marked with black tape. "Here, Comrade Commissar. Please stand here."

Jagjit confidently took the stage and waved Nigel away.

The audio crew responsible for the array of microphones that surrounded the stage like willows adjusted their gear and similarly retreated into the shadow beyond the heavy-wattage lights already causing Jagjit to sweat. One of them piped up from the shadows: "Comrade Commissar Hassan, do you mind saying a few words so that we can make sure we've got the inputs properly calibrated?"

"Test, test," replied Jagjit, identifying each of the cameras and microphones pointed in his direction. "How's that?"

A technician in a black jumpsuit emerged to tighten one of the microphone stands. "Perfect. We should be ready."

"Should be?" Jagjit was being difficult for the fun of it.

Turning bright red, the technician stuttered, "Are! Are! We are ready on sound and picture!"

Jagjit nodded benevolently and straightened his shirt. He squinted and scanned the room for the senior scientists comprising Dr. Worthing's team. "Ah! Dr. Weil, is the Patch-Over program ready to deliver in full?"

Beside the stage, a few hundred heavy wires and cables were jammed into an obsidian sphere with a small interface. Manning the interface in Mallory's absence was the head of the Noospherics Department, Dr. Alfred Weil. "Ready, Commissar Hassan!"

Jagjit clasped his hands beneath the jacket folded over them and grinned. "Fantastic. I will give my opening statement and then cue you to begin. Do not begin before I cue you, is that understood? And cut me off or the broadcast at any point, and I will make you wish you hadn't."

The responsibility appeared to be crushing Dr. Weil. He hunched over and nodded. "Yes. Absolutely, Comrade Commissar."

Jagjit's implant warmed up with an incoming message from Home Defence Minister Corven. Jagjit accepted the call, which filled his head and glazed his eyes with a visual neural-link connection to London Central.

"Ah, Hassan. The time has come! I cannot emphasize how proud we are of the work you have done these past few days...and years!" Corven sat in his office with a contagious smile impressed upon his face. "Not only did you capture key elements of the regressive faction, but you got your hands on the cyber weapon before it did any damage. Truly outstanding! Job well done! Commander Xi Weihan is keen to meet you once you have carried out the first phase of the Patch Over in Lancashire County."

"I appreciate you saying so, Home Defence Minister, and I look forward to meeting the Commander...Are you not going to join the others in watching the broadcast?"

"I've elected to watch it from my office. I don't think I'd make it over in time, anyway."

Jagjit sighed and tried to nod a smile onto his face.

"Don't fret, comrade. It is only because I feel that I may become an emotional wreck hearing you deliver the Patch Over that I've chosen to watch it alone. And even then, millions in Lancashire will watch it with me, many of whom will also be crying tears of joy."

"I completely understand. *Now*, Home Defence Minister, I must reiterate what I've said in the report I transmitted on my way over: to ensure both the efficacy of the Patch Over and against possible sabotage here in Blackpool, I have sent the painting to you by carrier drone. It should find you within the hour. Furthermore, the EBS is now under total lockdown. No man, woman, drone, or force of nature can stop us now. If there is any trouble, only an official with top clearance will be able to enter."

Corven increased the field of view to include his desk on which sat a brown crate. "Phenomenal. Truly phenomenal. And yes, the Deputy Home Defence Minister just came by with the painting. In fact, I have it before me!"

Jagjit was so invested in his neural-link to London Central, that he nearly forgot he had a local audience of at least thirty-million souls. It would have been ideal to have patched over all of England at once, but that was not for him to decide. "Defence Minister, I am curious—"

"Yes, Hassan?" Corven stroked the case in front of him and filled his lungs with a satisfied breath.

304

"I could not make out the image on the painting. Whether it was the training you had me undertake or the AI historians assigned to protect me from perversion, I was unable to make out the image itself, its meaning, and its symbolism. Do you mind telling me what it was? Was it an image of some royal family? Of some notable capitalists or dead monarchs? Did it depict enemies of the Socialist Alliance?"

Corven's smile faded somewhat. Although his good spirit was unassailable, Jagjit's question piqued his own curiosity. "I don't think it'll do any harm for us to take a look together after the Patch Over. It didn't malign you the first time, so I expect additional scrutiny won't hurt."

"Forgive me—and I mean no disrespect or imposition—but I would love a hint at the very least. We have a few minutes left until we have the captive attention of the entire region, and afterwards it truly won't matter. While curiosity is the reflex of the dilettante, I cannot help but wonder how those regressives figured they might trip up our glorious leap forward."

"Fine! Yes!" answered Corven, caving to his own interest. He stood up so that his head was cropped out of the camera's field of view. He unlatched the four corners of the crate, and opened it slowly with a crazed look of excitement. "After all, mystery is a destructive force all its own, eh Hassan?" As Corven opened the crate the whole way, his look of excitement vanished and was quickly replaced by one of anger and fear. "Jagjit?!"

"As you well know, my name is James," intuited the former Resistance captain.

"Jagjit!" Corven screamed out in terror.

"And Monica Warmington also asked me to say hello."

There was a click and a hiss. The neural-camera feed to Corven's office went black and an error message popped up indicating: "USER CANNOT BE FOUND".

Captain James Khatri had replaced the painting with Brigadier Miller's nuclear mortars, and boobytrapped the case to blow when opened. It was a relief to have that monkey off of his back. James had to sell the lie until this very moment; to take advantage of his returned knowledge of Wes' dextrocardia to stab his old friend Wes in the chest without killing him as a means of convincing London he was still loyal to the EDS. He had to save, not kill, Dr. Worthing, having realized that she too was a good soul dispossessed of her body by bad spirits. He had to keep his horror at having been an instrument of socialist menace for years to himself— having fought for the same people who murdered his wife and son,

305

exiled him and sought to murder his daughter; the same ideology that had destroyed the country he loved—just long enough to find his way into this chamber of state propaganda.

James' eyes went clear and he raised his voice. "Let us begin. Dr. Weil, do not start the sequence until I have finished my opening statement."

Unaware of the Commissar's explosive change of mind, Weil engaged the black sphere, which began to pulse and thrum, and took several steps back.

One of the technicians knelt before James. He made one final adjustment on the primary camera, and gave the Commissar a thumbs-up and announced: "We're live!"

"O-right." James smiled. "Good evening, comrades." He reached into his jacket and pulled out a rolled-up canvas and a handgun, then threw his jacket off to the side. "Tonight marks the beginning of a new era. For the past twenty-five years we have struggled to eliminate dissent. We have struggled to combat our basest impulses. We have struggled with our humanity. Tonight, London wanted me to finally take away your remaining humanity..."

The Supreme Councilors, their guests, and the Chinese dignitaries—although shrouded in near darkness—still could be seen projected in the corner of the room turning to each other and moving about frantically.

"To rob you of your senses and to impede any attempt on your part to think for yourself, act locally, or to express an opinion contrary to the ones the Supreme Council have approved and proscribed. Tonight, I give you a do-over, not a patch-over. I return to you what is yours as opposed to taking what is God's alone...*To be born again.*" He tucked the handgun under his belt and began to unfurl the canvas.

The EBS technicians shared terrified glances and white-knuckled their arm rests. Dr. Weil, meanwhile, wasn't listening; he was instead focused on the obsidian sphere's interface, sending out preparatory packets to every mind wired in Lancashire but still withholding the prophesized Patch Over.

James turned the unfurled canvas to the cameras for all to see. Its effect and affect was immediate. Several electricians fell back. There was a surge of weeping and laughter and screams amongst the other onlookers in the room. The whole building seemed to resound with the sound of painful realization.

Someone began pounding on the window looking into the studio. It was Poyraz. His eyes looked like bonfires; his forehead covered in flop sweat. If he had seen the painting, it hadn't affected

306

him. He was likely a true believer—a totalitarian to the core; one whose angry yelps were muffled by the window and the wall; yelps that regardless would not have moved the Captain. Poyraz took out his rifle and began firing into the window. The bullets could pierce neither the window nor the door. Seeing that his weapon was ineffective, Poyraz resumed banging on the glass and screamed the Captain's false name over and over again.

Even if London had time to put out the fires downtown and ascertain that the epicenter of the small nuclear blast was Corven's office—or more importantly, that one of their own was responsible—it would have done them little good. They would simply discover the name of the man pulling the rug out from under their feet. Lancashire was virtually quarantined; by design, nothing could stop or straddle James Khatri's broadcast. London Central was as impotent as Poyraz. All they could do was watch and hope that The Family's effect was contained in Lancashire.

Holding the painting up, gesturing from camera to camera, James continued: "It is the second day of the cycle. In truth, it will be Sunday—the day of the seven-day week commemorating the Creator's stepping back from His creation and His declaration that it was good. He declared it was good; not toxic or parasitical or unnatural or viral, but good. He made individuals, man and woman, in His image. He did so and rested. But for you and for me—for those of us who forgot that this world and the people in it *are good*—there can be no rest. This Sunday will be a day of rectification; of renaissance; a rejuvenating reminder that we are individuals, not nodes in a collective. We are free Britons, all of us.

"Some of our fathers, mothers, sisters, and brothers chose slavery, leaving us no choice but to follow, bow, and obey. Today and for tomorrow, brave men and women have given us another choice. Do you want oblivion? Nirvana? Emptiness in a crowded room? A life delineated by zealots in London's ivory towers? A scorched earth for some bodiless, inhuman survivor? Or do you want to decide your own fate? Do you want to assume responsibility, and enter the world as sovereigns with infinite potential and infinite worth? Do you want your government to recognize that potential and that worth? Do you want to direct who forms that government despite the uneasiness that our decisions may cause this nation's insiders?"

Dr. Weil's eyes lit up with an incoming transmission. He looked at James and then lunged at the obsidian sphere. James drew his weapon, took aim, and blew the Doctor's stolen intelligence out the rear of his head. For good measure, he then riddled the obsidian

307

sphere with bullets—all carefully-loaded electric grain bullets that undid whatever Dr. Worthing had done.

Nigel made a run for the door and tried to unlock it. James shot him too.

James Khatri reloaded his weapon and tucked it back under his belt. He wiped his forehead dry. "I have heretofore heard and have myself spouted a great deal of nonsense about the EDS' commitment to democracy, but have you seen it? Have you ever made a free choice without immediately being punished or destroyed for it? Have you ever contradicted a state edict or denied an order from your councilor? Now that your memories have returned and are freed from EDS interference, think on it! Have you ever seen a Lutoner or a Blackpoolian or a Mancunian have their say in London? Never mind a vote, how about a say in your own life? Have you ever been free to choose a partner or start a family? You haven't because I made sure you couldn't. Men like me took your children and decerebrated them. Men like me sterilized those whose intersectional value was too low. Men like me, sent by the Supreme Council, didn't think you worthy of such choices or responsibilities. The Supreme Council thinks they know better, but all they know is submission and death."

No one dared interrupt James whose beard stabbed the air below his tensed jaw; whose unblinking eyes penetrated his captive audience and the walls behind them. For all the true believers amongst the EBS propagandists and technicians knew, this was part of some cunning strategy to destroy the old regime for once and for all. Nigel, the obsidian Patch Over sphere, and Dr. Weil may have just been subversives or sacrifices to and for the People.

James walked off stage and pushed aside Dr. Weil's corpse, which was blocking the data-delivery screen. He ran his finger along an unending list of critical-error messages and saw that the Holy Family painting had done the trick. "Wonderful!" Raising his hands and conducting out each syllable, James re-appeared on the stage replicated at Blackpool City Hall and all across the region. His voice boomed: "Your minds will no longer be policed by the state. Your memories are yours and yours alone, and they will never be tampered with again. The English Democratic Socialists may choose to kill you tomorrow, but now you can choose to fight back. You can choose because they can no longer suppress your faculties. They can no longer dictate who you were. They can longer tell you who you are. They can no longer hide the truth: that they hate you because they hate all of humanity. Like the PRC, they hate individuality. Like the CDS, they revile the little things that make each of us unique.

308

You've been little more than processing units these past few years. Now you are whatever it is that you will to be. My name is James Khatri, and I welcome you back to the land of St. George."

THIRTY

Pandemonium descended upon Blackpool City Hall. The sudden recollection of the cumulative history of thousands of years stolen from the thousands gathered around the stage sent many into apoplexy and hysteria. Whereas before, the state could deluge citizens' minds with mental white noise and hijack their thoughts, now they were left only with kinetic force.

Straight away there was an insurrection in the stands. Some took to fighting those with EDS patches on their uniforms as well as one another. Some wept. Others rushed the phaser generators in a vain attempt to disable the murderous gates that had begun to slide towards the very centre of the stage, crackling as they encroached on the flesh of those congregated within.

The true believers among the members of the municipal committee who had been seated directly below the vacant Supreme Council box tried desperately to make their way into the care of the Shepherd drones piling out of City Hall. Those not fast enough were walloped by those just reminded of what had been done at their request.

Even with the phaser gates closing in, Alek, Cassandra, Danika, Lisa, Yaxley, and the half-dead Brigadier Miller were over the moon. They screamed out for joy, hugged one another, cheered, and lost themselves in the bliss of saving not themselves but the day!

Alek saw the morning sun eclipse the buildings to the east and had the courage finally to look upon Danika. "I told you we had a plan!"

Danika pointed past him. Monica stood on the other side of the phaser gate with a case in one hand and a tablet in the other. The mob of confused English had ignored her, at least for the time being. Good thing too—with a piano stroke on the tablet, she powered down the phaser generators.

I should have known, thought Alek. *No bullet or demsock slogan could keep down a Warmington, and certainly not a Neuhaus.*

"Bricks!" Monica shouted.

Alek ran off the stage and embraced his wife. Amidst the chaos, they enjoyed what felt like a moment outside of time and space. It wasn't another bittersweet memory or a self-critical dream. It was real and it was theirs together. "I thought I'd lost you."

Yaxley motioned to intervene—to attack Mallory, who had been designated a high-priority target by certain Resistance groups.

310

Cassandra forsook Miller's side just long enough to dissuade the young private, saving him not only from misjudging his target's character but from her Praetorian guard, which appeared hell-bent on crushing skulls. "She's EDS scum!"

Cassandra corrected him, "Not any more. Save the fight for those who still want you dead." So stirred by the Neuhauses public reconciliation was the Resistance's resident CIA agent that she nearly forgot about her charge. Miller's groans reminded her, and she hurried back to his side.

After nearly suffocating her husband with kisses, Monica bent down and opened her case. "Don't jinx us!" She handed Alek a submachine gun and procured two handguns for herself. "Stopped by the armoury on the way...Ms. Frye!" she shouted.

Fearful of the Praetorian, Danika cautiously approached Monica. "Never thought I'd see you again, *Moni*. I take it the painting worked?"

"Yes...I got you something." She handed Danika one of her two handguns.

"Between the two of you, you were always my favourite," Danika said, checking the magazine to see that it was fully loaded.

"Dr. Worthing!" yelped Councilor Sam Mesk who ran into the fold. He looked at Danika, Alek, and the others with disgust. "We must leave at once! The regressive cancer is quickly spreading!" He tried to pull Monica way from Alek and her case, unaware that Percy, Monica's Praetorian escort, might perceive the attempt to be one of aggression.

Percy didn't wait for permission. The Praetorian drone tore Mesk's head off and threw his body into the stands.

Unperturbed by the impromptu beheading, Monica resumed rooting around in the case, and produced a healing wand. "For your new friend," she said, handing the wand to Alek, and indicating Miller bleeding at Cassandra's feet.

Alek ran against the flood of bodies and over to Miller. "Cassandra! Here!"

As soon as she had a grip on it, Cassandra jammed the device into the Brigadier's wound. It cauterized Miller's internal cuts and stopped his bleeding. Aware that it wouldn't be long before London or the commissar from a neighbouring region would send a drone army to kill anyone potentially infected by what they might call a memetic virus, Cassandra called on Alek to act: "We need to get these people off the streets."

Any building requiring a high-security clearance for entry would have been sealed off and locked down. The only places Alek

311

could think of that might have offered them respite from the coming storm were either too far away or guarded by drones unsusceptible to The Family painting. He turned to Monica. "What's around here without blast doors?"

Monica quickly consulted her tablet. "Signal-Repeater Station 214."

"Good. That's where we'll take our people."

The majority of Shepherd drones launched a full-out assault on City Hall, which they were programmed to keep secure for the EDS. Only a few dozen were permitted to hack and slash as required out in the square. Several of these unrestrained killbots began tearing through those distraught citizens in the stands who had been overwhelmed by their pasts. However, the killbots were quickly met by fierce opposition. Guardians, reminded of their true allegiances thanks to Khatri's broadcast, bravely attacked the drones, giving the reborn English an opportunity to flee.

Two Shepherds broke through the guardian line, and sped towards Cassandra whose face was now at the top of every EDS kill list.

"Percy!" Monica yelled, spotting the glint off of the drones' blades.

Percy, though no longer synchronized with Monica, knew precisely where its might would be best applied. It leapt in front of Cassandra and threw one of the attacking Shepherd drones towards the other. The second drone somehow managed to dodge the bipedal missile. It narrowly eked past a powerful jab from Percy's gauntlet, and thrust its blade into the Praetorian's side. The Praetorian raised one fist high like a hammer and dropped it onto the Shepherd's arm still penetrating its side. The Shepherd's arm broke like glass, and the drone careened backwards. Percy ripped the blade out of its side and with it swiped at the Shepherd until it was scrap.

Alek rounded up Danika and Lisa, and conferred with Yaxley, requesting that his compatriots help the guardians and steadfast English evacuate the citizens.

"What about Miller?" inquired Cassandra, having just completed closing the Brigadier's wounds.

Yaxley sought an answer from Alek who turned instead to Monica.

"Percy!" cried Monica. She pointed down at the unconscious Brigadier. "Carefully carry this man and follow me!"

While Monica was speaking only to Percy, all of the familiar faces in the vicinity complied and followed her.

As they broke out onto the head of the parade route, an explosion ripped through City Hall, shattering the majority of the windows and blowing glass out over the square. Although barely visible behind the roiling smoke, there were dozens of bureaucrats who had climbed atop the building's ramparts and as quick as they appeared, they disappeared—leaping down behind the amphitheatre to their deaths. Whether driven to despair by the truth of what they now knew they had done or perhaps by the prospect of being free, this suicidal tendency was replicated in various ways in the surrounding area, and although a minority reaction, was nevertheless harrowing.

Alek was dumbfounded by this orgy of blood. He tried to comprehend what it was that he had helped end as well as what he had started. Limping behind the Praetorian on whose hulking arms Miller's listless body now flailed, Alek watched cockeyed as another set of jumpers took their mark and dove into the city square head-first. *They must have been up to far worse than we thought.*

Lisa pulled on Alek's arm and alerted him to more pressing issues: "Mr. Neuhaus! Look out!"

A minority of guardians unaffected by the painting took aim at the mixed stampede of citizens and prisoners, and began firing indiscriminately.

In her effort to warn Alek and terrified of more violence, Lisa lost her footing and tumbled to the ground.

Confronted with the choice of firing back or lifting Lisa off the ground, Alek chose the latter and held the girl up behind Percy's armoured bulk for cover.

Pre-empting the Praetorian further monopolizing their retaliation and leaving those behind it exposed, Danika returned fire. She felt no shame in doming her former colleagues. After all, those true believers had been given a second chance and decided instead to double down on their failed first. Once she had put down the firing brigade, Danika took up the rear and steadied Alek's progress with a supportive hand.

"You alright?" she asked Lisa.

Lisa nodded miserably.

Alek squeezed the child. "Saved me's what she did."

With Miller folded over Percy's forearm and shielded by its other arm, the Praetorian followed Monica up a street adjacent to City Hall with Cassandra, the Fryes, and Alek running alongside it. Yaxley and the other Resistance fighters had scavenged the dead guardians for weapons, and provided covering-fire for the unarmed and half-naked prisoners still puttering about.

313

Monica consulted her tablet, which indicated a building ahead; a windowless, ten-storey black building jammed between two gargantuan towers. "There! Signal-Repeater Station 214."

Even with a compromised collar bone, poorly fused-together ankle, and a welt-covered body, Alek couldn't wipe the smile off his face.

The door to the station was locked. It wasn't a blast door, yet it was not an easy door to open. Percy gently placed Miller down on the stoop, and began to beat against the locking mechanism.

As Alek took to the steps outside Station 214 where his party had gathered and were now catching their breath, Cassandra stopped and asked him: "Where's Private Yaxley and the other Resistance fighters?"

Alek pointed past the bleary-eyed citizens stumbling about at a group of men busy quartering a Shepherd drone. "They'll be along in a moment."

Just then, there was the sound of threshing.

"What that sound?" Cassandra asked no one in particular.

Alek walked back out into the street and saw them: five EDS gunships flying in formation, coming in from the northeast. "Out of the street!" He roared. He grabbed one of the dazed citizens running aimlessly by, and redirected him towards Station 214. "Out of the street, now!"

Percy was making progress though not nearly enough or as fast as circumstance demanded.

The gunships began firing rockets and plasma bolts, filling the streets with flame and dust.

Danika ordered Lisa to wait at the safe-house door and ran out to reinforce Alek who had begun to shoot at the ships closing in. Having played this fruitless game before and nearly lost, she tucked her gun away and started directing the stream of bewildered citizens over to the locked doors. "We'll have the doors open in sec—just pull off to the side. Trust me!" Few seemed to trust her. It would be difficult to trust anyone or anything after waking up from a twenty-five-year ideology-induced coma. Nevertheless, Danika kept trying.

Alek fired his last round and clicked empty. He looked back at Monica—this time, *his Monica*—then back up at the gunships, now joined by hundreds of Midge drones, raking the streets around City Hall with explosive rounds. "Your tin man nearly got that door open?"

The locking mechanisms on the doors wouldn't give, so Percy had to punch a hole through and then pull the gap wider. The Praetorian finally managed a gap wide and high enough for people to

314

crawl through, albeit one at a time. There was no telling who or what lay on the other side, though it couldn't have been any worse than the inferno coming their way.

Lisa was the first through. She threw her hands out of the gap and seized upon Miller. Once the Brigadier was inside, the rest of those to whom Cassandra and Danika promised sanctuary began piling in. Every time someone crawled through, Percy pulled the gap wider, so that by the time it was Monica's turn, she could walk through.

"Go! Go!" Alek bellowed to Cassandra, now helping strangers through the breach. He looked back down the street where he half-expected to see Yaxley and the others. There was only flame. "Doherty! Get inside. I'll be right behind you!" The heat of the incoming fire and plasma was unbearable, such that it chased Alek through the gap.

As soon as Alek had made it inside, Monica ordered Percy to seal the gap with its body.

Outside there was a rapid succession of booms.

"You think the others got clear of the fire?" Lisa asked Danika.

Alek nodded to a speechless mother. "I'd say so."

THIRTY-ONE

From the west they came, colosses all; American dreadnaughts with a full complement of Valkyrie gunships and Marine transport vessels. Tailing them was a tubular anti-ballistic-missile ship capable of heading off thousands of demsock warheads, on either side of which flew forward-operating-bases packed to the brim with battle mechs. There were so many ships that together they appeared like storm clouds on the horizon.

Before the CDSS Kiberd could even react to this, the second major surprise of the day, it was split in half by a railgun round fired by the USS Matsui, a warship intended for interstellar travel and itself capable of destroying entire asteroids. The Kiberd fell to pieces and dropped into the brink while the spearhead of the United States Second Fleet powered on by.

Sobbing and cheering at the same time, Zoya waved on the liberators. Prioritizing her team over the historicity of the moment, she returned to mucking about the cove in search of Stephen. When she finally found him, opened eyed and motionless, she first checked for his pulse, then knelt down behind him and placed his head in her lap, sure to let what of him had yet to pass on hear and see the power of his perseverance.

Mirek saw that Zoya had stopped—that she had found something. "Is that Stephen there? How's he looking?" Mirek cried out, voice wavering and pitchy. When Zoya didn't respond, he crawled over, dragging his bum leg through the thicket of garbage and seared flesh. As he drew nearer, he began to slow his approach, unwilling to accept what he knew to be the case based on the Major's posture and silence. He locked his jaw, stiffened his upper lip, and closed the distance.

Zoya heard Mirek coming, and looked over with a tear-streaked face. She tried to smile. "He knew we won. He knew, Dubchek..." She sniffled. "He was ready."

"No, no, no!" Mirek sputtered. First he shook Stephen, as if trying to awake him from some fleeting stupor unrelated to a broken back or crushed chest. Then he held his neighbour's face, unwilling to concede the loss. "I'm not! Major, I'm not ready! Ah, damn it...Stevie!" He collapsed on Stephen, sobbing hard enough to be misconstrued as seizuring. The Major stroked Mirek's back sympathetically. After another failed attempt at resuscitating his friend, Mirek sat back and wiped his ruddy face dry. Pointing with

316

conviction at the body before him, he said with gritted teeth: "That there was the Pole holding up our English tent." He grabbed Stephen's hand, and tried to imagine what he might say or ask of him. Mirek jolted, having determined what Stephen would have wanted: "I'll say a prayer to the Good Lord for yah, brother." After doing so, Mirek recalled the rose he had plucked in Preston. He found the flattened petals in his pocket and rested them on Stephen's chest.

Zoya closed Stephen's lifeless eyes. She procured from her pocket the transponder Colonel Phan had given her back in Underpool and activated it. Tucking it back away, she put her hand on the back of Mirek's neck, pulling him towards her. "I'd say we all could use one."

THIRTY-TWO

Although the broadcast was finished and the Patch Over augmented to accomplish the reverse of what the Supreme Council was promised it would do, Poyraz remained committed to breaking into the studio and apprehending or perhaps even assassinating Captain James Khatri. He had gone and come back with a Shepherd drone, which had taken over his previous attempts to open the door. The drone was able to wedge the tip of its blade between the door and its frame, and began to lever it open.

James watched as the painting took effect on the technicians gathered around. They seemed horribly troubled by their memories. Many of them, after all, had been assigned different jobs by the central authority over the years, meaning that they might have been coming to terms with having committed murder, rape, torture, or any other variety of barbarity that the EDS had normalized. They squirmed and howled and puttered about. All of them were indifferent to James who rested next to the bullet-riddled obsidian sphere Dr. Worthing designed.

Once there was a sliver through which Major Poyraz could slip some venom, he began issuing demands and threats: "Open this door, Hassan! Your sentence may be lessened. Perhaps it is not your fault—perhaps the regressives got inside your head!"

The Shepherd drone was joined by another and then by another. Soon, there was a full platoon of trustworthee guardians and drones ready to eviscerate their former commissar.

James laughed, reminded of a cryptic revelation Rabbi Klotz had shared with him that hadn't made sense at the time. He muttered it aloud: "Though Moses could see the Promised Land, it was not for him to enter..."

"You will pay, Hassan! We will run your mind through every pain known to man in dilated time. You will regret even having been born!"

Taking aim at the door, now on the verge of bursting, James answered back: "I regret nothing."

Poyraz took a step back. The Shepherd drone compromised the hinges and bashed the door in.

"Now perhaps," said Poyraz, "but after a million years of virtual time, I wouldn't be so sure..."

James fired every round in his gun until there was no more, at which time he threw his gun at the first drone through the breach.

It leapt towards him, and knocked him down with its club arm. As James tried to pick himself up, the drone drove its blade into his side and pulled it through his stomach.

As Poyraz prepared to enter the studio, someone down the hall and out of sight grabbed his attention. "Oi, pinko!"

An EMP grenade burst midair, disabling all of the nearby electronics, including the drone preparing to behead James. Those guardians unaffected caught lead between their eyes and dropped without having put up so much as a fight.

General McGregor and a dozen of his men hurried down the hall, executing the disabled drones and double-tapping the guardians whose memories hadn't discouraged their party loyalty.

Poyraz had dodged the salvo by leaping into the room. Hearing the Resistance fighters close in on the studio, he crawled over to James who lay disemboweled beside the drone responsible. "Any regrets now, you traitor?"

James still had some light in him—enough to see that Poyraz had exposed his neck. He plunged his blade into Poyraz's neck, just below the skull. "You're the only one who deserved to feel the cold of this blade." James slumped down, pulling his guts over with him.

"There you are, you sunnuvabitch!" exclaimed McGregor. He ran over to Captain Khatri, and rushed to push his gut back into place. Realizing it was not a wound his old friend would recover from, he pressed his head against his captain's. "You did it, Jim! Took your sweet time, but you did it!"

"*Lieutenant*...? Is Zoya alright?"

Unsure himself though aware from CDS radio chatter that a nuke had gone off on Ireland's western coast, McGregor took a guess: "Absolutely. She shares this victory with you."

"And Sergeant Miller...?"

One of McGregor's men ran over with a med kit in hand.

Certain it would take more than a wand to work magic on James' stomach, McGregor turned away the offer with a slight shake of the head and gripped his old friend tighter. "*Wes too.* We're lucky our radiomen received your message when we did. Spared Blackpool a dozen or so mushroom clouds, though Lancaster's a different story."

James grinned. On his way back into the city, he had sent an encrypted transmission via an old Resistance frequency with access codes to the English Broadcast Station, sparing McGregor's forces the need to use the nuclear mortars on populated areas as well as the Herculean task of breaking into one of the most secure buildings in the country. James' eyes began to go dim. "There's a woman—her

319

real name is Monica Neuhaus...See to it that she has a place in the Resistance. Her insights into the enemy are invaluable."

"Yes, Captain."

"And Hugh..."

"Yes, sir?"

"N'one is free until all are free." With that, Captain James Khatri's body went limp.

McGregor lay the last commissar of Lancashire down on his back, and crossed his arms over his chest. He looked over at the cowering technicians and up at the cameras. "Those still on?"

"Y-yes!" stammered one technician who was soused in another's blood. The audio of James Khatri's last moments had been telecast across the region. "But it looks as if London is trying to terminate it. Can't though on account of the regional lockdown."

As any screen still operating had only one channel—that channel being the EBS—McGregor knew there might still be an audience; one comprised of uncertain and disoriented Britons with no idea as to what they could expect to happen next. He gestured to one of his men to guard the door and found his mark before the camera.

"Good mornin', Lancashire. I won't wax poetic because I couldn't possibly put it better than had done Captain James Khatri whom you just heard speak for the first and last time. Know this: with the help of our American and Russian allies, we will now begin to reclaim our island in defense not only of liberty but of humanity. The Chinese Communists and those godless, nihilist Europeans have a design to destroy all human life around the globe. We will not let them. Just as we will not let their cronies in London once again steal our souls, our memories, and our choices." He puffed his chest out and looked straight into the camera. "To all who fear the righteous anger of a spurned and enslaved people, know this: in victory, we will behave as Lincolns, not as Robespierres. Our enemies will have the rights they denied their victims and the victims will have the justice our forgotten laws promised."

320

THIRTY-THREE

As it was only a utility building, the lobby of Signal-Repeater Station 214 was far less open that the other EDS structures Alek had recently shot his way through. About ten paces inside the main lobby there was a kiosk around which a staircase was wrapped like a double-helix. There was a screen at the rear of the kiosk that would have normally depicted the EDS flag or some black-backgrounded slogan, but which now played a live-feed from the English Broadcast Station. Many of those half-naked citizens who Alek and his friends had channeled inside, clustered around the kiosk countertop and took to watching the live broadcast. Onscreen, a haggard middle-aged Scot with a large moustache accused the Communist Chinese and the Europeans of wanting to blow up the world.

"Is it true?" Lisa asked her mother, not part of the cluster but within earshot of the screen.

Though Danika hadn't an answer, she didn't want Lisa to fret so she suggested: "Mars, baby. They want to destroy all life on Mars."

The citizens gathered around the kiosk looked back to Danika and nodded, taking her reply as the God's-honest-truth. Their minds were still fresh and plastic. Although they had been gifted back their memories, for some there may have been too much to process to make additional sense out of what was presently happening, especially if it concerned leftist utopianism.

Alek groaned as he made his way through the gap in the door.

"Bricks, over here!" said Monica, mending cuts on one injured citizen with the healing wand she nicked from the City Hall armoury.

"There're still people out there," Alek said hectically, partly blinded by his own and other people's blood. "We've got to do something! The demsocks are gunning 'em down." He tried to peek back out, but Percy the Praetorian had wedged itself into the gap in order to prevent shrapnel and flame from blustering inside and harming its master.

"Catch your breath. Reinforcements are on their way," Cassandra said, more than content to repeat herself.

"Yeah?! When? If it wasn't for Monica, there'd be nothing left of us for *your reinforcements* to reinforce."

Cassandra turned bright red and threw her hands on her hips. "If you had met us at the specified time, we might have all been spared this slaughter—*including your friend on the roof.*"

321

Alek ground his teeth and stared berserk at Cassandra. Without unclenching his teeth, he fought himself, and choked finally as he swallowed his reaction.

Another EDS barrage shook the building; this time so violently that the marble floor in the lobby cracked in various places while the minimalist chandelier stranded overhead swung wildly.

"Neuhaus! Cool it!" Danika passed by Monica, who—although invested in the conversation—was still committed to closing her patient's deepest cut. "We're all just tired and hungry." Danika made slow, inoffensive gestures with both of her hands spread out wide. "Just relax!"

Looking past the former guardian, Alek admitted to Cassandra: "I just can't to wait for your reinforcements. I've seen too much death today to sit by and let more happen on my watch—especially not after *my friend from the rooftop* and I are largely responsible." Alek tried to nudge the Praetorian out of the way. Percy wouldn't move. He appealed to Monica for help: "Let me out! Let me out, Moni!"

"You'll get us all killed!" shouted Danika.

Cassandra shook her head and walked away.

Knowing him well enough to see that Alek was still consolable—and that any more yelling, and he might blow his lid and become useless to everyone including himself—Monica handed the wand to her patient for him to finish the job and rocketed to her feet. She pulled Alek aside and threw her arms around his bare body—hugs were always her quick fix for her partner's bad temper. He resisted at first because every part of him ached and he still doubted the reality of the woman embracing him. She kissed his neck. "C'mon..."

As soon as Monica's lips made their way to his and across the rest of his swollen face, Alek's chest seized up and he let out a soulful sigh. He put his arms around Monica and held her so tight that their bodies seemed to lose distinction.

"I know you want to do something." She brushed his greasy hair back. "We need to wait for a window."

Alek softened his voice and unclenched his teeth. "I have a window. Your tin man is blocking it."

With the authoritative style Mallory had left impressed upon her psyche, Monica replied: "We'll do something before the fires are out but not before the bombings are done."

Releasing another sigh, Alek staggered over to the staircase and sat on the steps. Monica followed him over, giving Cassandra and Danika both a sympathetic nod en route. As soon as she too had sat down, Alek attempted to put his arm over Monica's shoulders. Realizing he could no longer lift his arm past a certain point, he instead leaned into her. "For a moment—back at Reclamations—I saw you. Not that priss they'd reprogrammed you to be, but *you*. I saw my Monica." Happy tears rolled down Alek's marred cheeks. "I knew you weren't dead. And I knew you weren't theirs." He wiped his face on Monica's red-starred epaulette. "You've got to forgive me."

"*Forgive you?* What're you on about? You found me!"

Alek had done more than simply locate his wife, although now was no time to boast. "I was going to do what you told me never to do..."

Monica shifted away from Alek so she could better see him and read what of his mind his face could still communicate, which wasn't much given the beating it had taken. "What?"

"I found your memex. I was going to try to reset you."

Monica giggled. "Evaun gave it to you?"

Alek's eyebrows fired upwards. "Evaun? No! Your memex was in your sock drawer."

Pulling Alek back into her, Monica pressed her face into his neck, careful not to put weight on his broken bone, which he seemed to have already forgotten on account of all the dopamine coming his way. "In that case, I'm glad you didn't. That's my uncle's memex."

Embarrassed by how much importance he had placed on the little device and its loss, though thankful in hindsight that it wasn't so important, Alek smirked. "You mean it *was* your uncle's memex..."

Monica visibly considered giving Alek one of her patented punitive squeezes and decided against it. "He doesn't need it anymore."

Alek planted one more kiss on Monica's face, entirely missing her mouth. "I can't believe this is really happening. We can finally get out. Together!"

"Well..." Monica began to say.

"If you two are done canoodling, some of us would like to hear the General's speech!" griped Miller, no longer bleeding profusely from his chest and sitting up with a good view of the kiosk screen.

Unfortunately for Wesley Miller, the General had said his piece. A Resistance soldier appeared onscreen, pressed an eyeball to the camera, and then the feed went dark. The screen reset to an EDS poster, all black with white lettering: "From Each According To Their Guilt, To Each According To Their Oppression."

"You yapped right through it!" Miller shouted, genuinely upset with the reunited couple. He swatted at the air in front of him as if attempting to pull their stale words down. Recomposing himself, he pointed at the screen and said with pride in his voice and a lump in his throat: "He showed them though, didn't he? Old Khatri. I knew what they'd said about him was a lie. He proved them all wrong."

"Hold on—we talking about the bloke on the rooftop of CBLOCK40?" Danika asked. "I don't know precisely *who* they are and *what* they said about the Commissar, but if we're talking about the same man, he tried to stab you in the heart and killed a friend of mine."

Monica's ears perked up. She hadn't assimilated all of her memories and had yet to fully bridge all of Mallory Worthing's experiences over. "Geoff didn't make it?"

Alek locked eyes with Danika. "It was my fault."

"Enough of your martyrdom, Neuhaus." Danika pre-emptively dried her eyes. "Littlefield knew what he was doing and he did it well. This victory is his as much as it is ours."

The building quaked again, though this time the boom that lagged behind was unlike any that had been heard before. Then there was a screech! And a wah! Both penetrated Station 214's walls and the bodies of everyone inside.

Alek pulled himself to his feet with the help of the banister. "Sounds like a bloody volcano goin' off!"

Cassandra hammered the kiosk countertop with her fist. "They've arrived!"

Miller grabbed Alek's good ankle as he made his way over to the door. "Mate—let us up."

Alek lifted Miller to his feet, and helped him over to the door. Monica went with them and ordered Percy to clear the gap. However, the Praetorian failed to move.

Monica tried once more. She could reach its control panel through the gap, and when she did, saw that it was offline. "He's not responding."

Alek pulled Monica out of the gap, and tried shouldering the heavy drone out of the way. He was immediately sorry for trying. He yelped and retreated inside the lobby gripping his misshapen shoulder. "It won't budge."

A buzzing sound emanated from the kiosk. Everyone looked to the source: a mischievous looking adolescent stood at the desk with her hand on the terminal behind the countertop.

"Honey, what did you do?" Danika asked Lisa, gripped with terror.

The dead bolt cylinders that had originally prevented the Praetorian from opening the door withdrew against their springs. The slide barricade bar slid off to the side. And with that, the door opened, pushing the inoperative Praetorian drone out of the way and down the stairs.

Miller piped up: "Good one, scamp."

Having realized the extent to which Alek was injured, Danika helped Miller down the steps while Alek and Monica made their way to the street, joined in turn by Cassandra and some of the reborn English. The street was full of rubble, broken glass, pieces of melted plastic, and enduring flames. As for the people Alek had wished to save, they had cleared out—either by choice or by fire.

Percy had been peppered with most if not all of the above. The front panel of its rolled homogenous armour had nearly been split in two.

Alek shook the Praetorian's head, thinking maybe he could wake it up. After all, it had done a fine job looking after Monica, even if it knew its master by another name. "Like dogs, eh? Only as mean as its owner."

"Don't make excuses for it, mate," said Miller. "They're all bad."

Monica was nonplussed and far more focused on a fiery hulk in the distance. She prodded those in her company, bidding them consider the sight.

"A Goliath no less," stated Danika, recognizing the wreckage as having been one of the state's apparently invincible drones.

Alek muttered for anyone with an answer: "Did our people do that?"

High up above them, an EDS gunship made one last evasive maneuver and was blown to smithereens. A beleaguered squadron of Midges similarly began dodging incoming fire—from what it was not clear—and they too began dropping out of the sky like meteors.

Cassandra patted Alek on the back. "Your friend would be proud that you helped make this happen."

"Make what happen?"

The same sound he heard from inside the station—that titanic thud—once again resounded throughout Blackpool. Alek shook his head with disbelief and opened his eyes as wide as he could.

One of the Midges dropped to a low altitude, barely dashing against the Department of Genetic Levelling on the far side of

325

Blackpool City Hall. An American Hellion fighter screamed after it, pelting it with explosive rounds. A critical hit sent the Midge cartwheeling into the streets below. Yanking up some of the smoke of its most recent kill, the Hellion then began firing on an anti-personnel EDS cruiser.

"They actually sent someone to help..." Alek looked at Cassandra adoringly. He wouldn't apologize for doubting the reinforcements—after all, there was only the one—though he came close: "Good on yah."

Soon, another Hellion joined the first, and before the EDS cruiser was fully aflame, the two fighters pulled away and a railgun off an incoming American dreadnought finished the job. Each and every drone, gunship, and airship the EDS had dispatched to kill those Blackpoolians who had taken to the streets was felled in quick succession.

Among the liberation fleet were battle cruisers, frigates, and troop transports; THAAD flying fortresses to knock down ballistic missiles from the east; airborne aircraft carriers whose contents were sufficient to block out the sun; bombers and SEAL skiffs; and even an interstellar warbird. To have gotten this far, they would have had to cripple the Continental Democratic Socialist air defenses in Ireland as well knock out the Chinese naval forces in the Irish Sea.

This wasn't a police action or a mere rescue. This was an act of war; an invasion. Every town in Lancashire likely saw the same— this war in the air and on the streets—granted that wherever The Holy Family painting had been seen, its effects would have manifested and insurrection would be inevitable. It was even possible, notwithstanding the quarantine, that The Holy Family was seen outside of the northwest; that the rest of England may soon remember all that they had lost.

Admiring her countrymen's handiwork, Cassandra said: "It's a humanitarian mission, you see. Have you heard tell of Kunlun?"

Monica nodded.

Alek tilted his head in an effort to remember as if the memory itself were a ball in a maze. "Yeah," he replied, having found the maze's end.

"Chinese never were going to entomb British or European minds with their own in Kunlun. You'd have all died for nothing. Now, of course, the United States would be targeted by bio-weapons when and if the Chinese Communists ever got their shit together, so there's selfish motivation at work here as well. But my sense is—and I've been here working with your lot for over a decade—the English,

326

now that they have a choice, will choose life over death and liberty over slavery."

"You still think we'll form a democratic republic?" Miller asked Cassandra, now taking conversations he had overheard in Underpool more seriously.

Cassandra shrugged her shoulders. "All I can say is that if you choose state socialism again, I'd let the devil take every last one of you."

Alek had a good view of the future but he focused on the past. Examining the faint scar on the side of Monica's head out from the corner of his eye and unable to contain his curiosity, he interrupted this talk of politics: "The man who shot Monica was a Russian agent. Wanted the painting for some eastern resistance movement. *They with you?* I mean, are they with *us*?"

Cassandra looked around for spies, conditioned by years of unfortunate confirmations. "The Russians helping them certainly are. As for Stroz' Eastern Resistance, they're liberals for freedom, if that's what you mean. And we'd certainly like for them to succeed. As for lending them a hand..." Cassandra paused and crossed her arms. "It's important to recognize that England won't be an easy job, and the Chinese may full well decide this is where the war will be fought. If not, we may ultimately come to the aid of the Europeans. There's little worth saving between Calais and Prague, so if anything, we'd help the Resistance in the east with the help of the Ruskies."

A badly-damaged CDS troop transport, likely escaping from an aerial skirmish to the northwest, accidentally flew into the Blackpool fracas and was instantly obliterated. Pieces of it showered down over the city. Smaller, nonthreatening pieces peppered Alek and his posse.

Unphased by the shower of debris, Cassandra appeared rather intoxicated by their immediate good luck; so much so that she kissed Monica and Alek both, and then hugged Miller. "Today has taken a lifetime to bring about," she said with a cracking voice. She smiled even more intensely to keep from emoting in any other fashion, although at that point Monica picked up the slack.

"It's taken many lifetimes," Miller corrected her.

Lisa braved the residual heat from the flames that had scorched the street only moments before and exited Station 214. She regrouped with the rest of them. "Is it safe?"

"No," said Miller in response to the guileless voice of the generation that would inherit the fruit of innumerable sacrifices. "But what's safe?"

327

The talk of safety reminded Danika of the promise of being ferried up and away. "So are we getting out of here or what?"

"Of course." Cassandra firmed up and dropped the smile. "We'll get you and yours someplace secure. Then whoever's fit and willing to fight will be debriefed, armed, and sent south or east."

"To London?" asked Monica.

Alek grabbed Monica's hand. "That's where *they* are headed. You and I are going to go with Dan and Lisa—going to take a little holiday."

"You heard Jagjit—I mean, James." Monica looked at Alek askance. *"No one is free until all are free."*

"Oh hell," Alek blurted. He composed himself and whispered to Monica: "Perhaps a short break then."

Cassandra interjected: "This will be a marathon, not a sprint. England won't be taken easily. Even now with the might of our friends above us, it will take days, maybe even weeks, to fully secure western England. And when the principle gem is returned to old liberty's diadem—and only then—can we turn our attention elsewhere."

Alek breathed a sigh of relief. "A day or two without the EDS then."

Monica smiled kindly. "Fine. Afterwards, we'll consider putting the extensive knowledge of EDS technology possessed by Mallory Worthing into the service of the Resistance."

"Oh my dear lady," said Miller, seeming more and more spry. "It's no longer the Resistance. It's once again Her Majesty's Armed Forces."

Debating her response silently though nevertheless moving her lips, Cassandra finally committed to seeking elaboration: "Her Majesty?"

"You've seen her. The one from the painting. You might call her Lady Liberty. But Jag would have preferred I call her *Our Lady.*" Miller's eyes trailed off. "Queen not just of one island nation, but the world and Heaven above."

The Brigadier whispered to Cassandra, and she responded in her normal talking voice: "You'll know as soon as I know. If the air support is any indication, they made it."

A small white sphere dropped from the belly of a Hellion fighter. Spotting its shadow first and then seeing it descend, Alek drove Monica out of the street, mistaking it for a bomb.

Cassandra raised and flattened her hand, palm facing up, whereupon the sphere gently settled. Several blue lasers fired out of it, forming a line across her face. The line tracked up and down and up again. The sphere beeped, and then jetted back off.

"Mind telling us what that was?" asked Alek, still shielding Monica with his body.

"Resistance fighters carry their transponders in their pockets. I keep mine behind my eye. They know we're here." Cassandra turned to Danika and winked. "And they're going to find us some better real estate."

EPILOGUE

The thousands who had taken refuge inside the Resistance Sanctuary had received word from General McGregor that something miraculous had happened in Blackpool, which was already beginning to ramify throughout the northwest. Instead of providing them with a detailed explanation, the General simply had given them a set of coordinates and a rough idea of when they should reach them.

Assured that they would find protection as soon as they emerged from their subterrane (so long as they kept with them their Resistance transponders), they assembled their belongings and scoured the Sanctuary for stragglers. Once everything and everyone was accounted for, they journeyed en masse along twenty kilometres of meandering machine-bored tunnels all the way to the River Calder.

On the south side of the river was a derelict cottage conquered by weeds and saplings. In its yard was a mound and on the mound was an unlatched door. The cellar beyond the door and below the mound was featureless: a ten by ten metre stone box that could have made for a good cooler given a substantial block of ice. On the other side of the cellar's western wall was the end of the Resistance tunnel the Sanctuary had emptied into. The wall had never been knocked down for an earlier fear that the enemy might discover the route and harrow Underpool. Now, discovery didn't matter. A few of the soldiers assigned to protect the civilians hammered through the stone, creating a portal big enough for people to squeeze through single file.

Still uncertain over whether or not they could move about freely topside despite the General's assurances, the first few waves of Englanders from the Sanctuary took every precaution as they exited the cellar. They kept close to the trees lining the roads and scurried across clearings where there was little or no cover.

Though careful not to draw any unwanted attention, they were also careful not to take the gentle breeze for granted. Most heads were craned back to take in the afternoon sunlight, which threw the shadows of eastbound American vessels down upon Calder Vale's Victorian ruins and sedgy meadows.

Calder Vale, a small hamlet bisected by the river, had long ago been designated a red zone and in the time since had been left to rot. Even though there was nothing more than rubble and vacant stone frames to defend, there remained several Nephilim stationed on the little stone bridge that single-arched over the river, blanketed pink with cherry blossoms.

Spying them from afar, Commodore Dove displaced the younger Resistance soldiers at the front of the line and confronted the white-armoured demsocks bumbling about on the bridge. He lowered his shotgun, seeing that they were unarmed—that they had thrown their own weapons into the surging water below. Dove rushed the Nephilim. First, he demanded their surrender, and then, recognizing they would have been incapable of fighting regardless, he asked for directions. They answered in gibberish and conferred with one another in more gibberish—communicating little and comprehending nothing. It didn't take long for the Commodore to realize that if the Nephilim had been returned their minds, their minds were blank to begin with. Happy to have been spared the responsibility of spilling more English blood, Dove waved on the Resistance piling up on the south side of the river and instructed no one to molest those former enemies their victory had retarded.

Every book from Meyer's shop made it across the river under arm or on carts along with all of the art Underpool spared from the EDS censors' bonfires. More importantly, at least for Commodore Dove who paused the procession for a sample, Mises Tavern had survived the flood and the journey! Teresa Kaczynski had put her bar on wheels, and with the help of a handful of thirsty folk wheeled her new Flying Inn past their former foes.

Though the procession was long, the pace slow, and the distance to go something a timebound creature might wish to skip, the survivors were out of their skins with joy. They sang English songs the birds of Calder Vale and the surrounding area probably hadn't heard in decades. Though the survivors knew there had to have been losses—that some among them might soon be found out to be a widow, an orphan, or a piece of a forever-incomplete puzzle—in this moment there was only victory. Some laughed without hearing a joke while others cried happy tears hearing confidence in the children's' laughter and in the voices comprising the unmuted choir.

The children under Fiona's ever-vigilant care cut in and out of the exodus, chasing one another and the fresh air, unmediated by filter, brine, or stone. They shrieked wildly as if the open space had broken their minds, when in fact they had finally broken out of a closed space of mind.

Fiona, having been informed by a sympathetic radioman and friend of Lloyd Barnard that Mirek was coming home, picked the flowers along the way she would give him ahead of her heart in full.

She paused to reign in the kids, but was dissuaded from doing so again by Nurse Hobson, who indicated the allied ships above and suggested in so many words that there was enough positive authority to excuse a short bout of innocent recklessness. After all, who knew what news awaited them over the hill.

Their destination was atop a gradual hill that overlooked the surrounding wind-fanned knolls and forested plains, upon which several bell tents had been erected. The tents were trafficked and crowded inside and out by Resistance fighters. Some of the fighters had returned from Blackpool, while others were friendly strangers from the north who had fought in concert with the Resistance elsewhere, and been brought by fate and fortune to meet with the principle actors in this first act of a new war.

Off to one side of the marker to which the civilian resistance had been summoned, several droids assisted men in taking black crates out the back of a falcon-shaped VTOL aircraft. They lay these crates side by side and in rows of five, and sent back into the ship for more while Cardinal Nechtan and Rabbi Klotz went from crate to crate, moving their lips but saying nothing.

A troop-transport ship flew against the current of heavily-armed behemoths that were alternatively barreling eastward. It slowly descended until it touched down next to the VTOL. Its side door dematerialized and its ramp rolled out. Brigadier Wesley Miller, who had received some much-needed medical treatment aboard, slowly walked off on his own volition along with Alek and Monica Neuhaus, Cassandra Doherty, Danika and Lisa Frye, and dozens of other scarred and bloodied subversives.

A number of Resistance members coming from the Sanctuary rushed across the hill's flattop to greet their returning heroes along with their new allies. Miller detoured from the impending adulation, and limped over to the second ship, out front of which soldiers were consorting with Underpoolians and offloading heavplast coffins. Pibroch bagpipe music blared from the ship's loudspeaker. Miller spotted General McGregor among the men accompanying the droids from the troop transport to English soil, and hurried over as fast as he could. "Hugh!" he roared.

McGregor turned to the sound of an old friend's voice and lit up. "There you are!" He made sure that the coffin he had been chaperoning was lowered gently. As soon as it was settled, he ran over to Miller and hugged him.

Miller groaned on account of having been mended but not healed.

332

"You look horrible," McGregor said, inspecting his friend's face. "Ah!" He laughed ecstatically. "Magnificent job, old son."

"It worked," Miller replied uncertainly.

"You're damned right it did, though we're still not entirely sure how. If our scientists and engineers don't eventually come up with an answer, we'll have to defer to the understanding of theologians. It's really something, Wes. Not only has the EDS lost control of every mind in Lancashire, but they're also losing cognitive control throughout the rest of the country. I think that the liberation bug spread from London as well as from Blackpool, since members of the government, including elements of the Supreme Council, were streaming Jim's Patch-Over speech in London. I could be wrong, but so far, that explanation makes the most sense. Freedom's spreading like wildfire!" McGregor looked eastward with a wistful smile. "The Captain came through in the end."

"He always did." Miller could tell by the General's expression alone that James Khatri hadn't made it. "That him there?"

McGregor turned to the coffin beside him and ran his hand along the rough, freshly-printed plastic. "His daughter is on her way back from the Irish coast. She has already mourned him. Now she has only to bury him."

The very mention of Zoya first filled Miller with anxiety and then relief. "She made it?! Oh, thank God. Stephen Nowak and Mirek Dubchek are with her I presume."

The General's face cracked. He gripped Miller's shoulder. "They're both with her, though Private Nowak didn't make it."

Miller caved over. He sank to the ground, and leaned against Khatri's coffin.

The General knelt down beside Miller. "Without him, we'd have no victory today and no hope tomorrow." He shook the Brigadier and channeled some of his conviction over. "Wes, look at me. It's never really been about survival. It's been about living true and dying free. If even half of what Zoya relayed to me when they were picked up is true, that boy of yours died a free and honest man. You should be proud." Seeing Miller's eyelids turn purple, McGregor released him. "No one will fault you for missing him, but take heart; he's now with the ultimate proud Father."

"Wes! Hugh!" Cassandra strode over with a stalky man in tow, indifferent to what she was interrupting.

McGregor and Miller stood to greet the CIA agent. "Only took ten years."

Cassandra's smile pinched her cheeks. "Well, twenty-five, but who's counting? I want you to meet Wallace Forster."

333

The stocky man shook hands with the General and the Brigadier. "G'afternoon, gentlemen."

"Wallace is Commander of the United States Space Force SO Division."

"S-O?" asked Miller.

"Sub-orbit," answered Wallace.

Cassandra nodded and hurried to follow up: "We're able to provide the English Resistance suborbital support as well as weapons, mechs, and drones, but cannot commit many boots on the ground at this time, given Congress has not yet declared war. Commander Wallace will keep the skies clear in the meantime."

Wallace smiled. "We've already deployed a defensive shield in Leeds, which will protect the north from any English or Continental missiles. The USS Matsui has also been deploying jammer UAVs to make sure the enemy cannot directly or remotely control their military assets in Lancashire and mount a counter-assault. In the meantime, there's no telling how the Chinese will react; whether they'll try to keep the war abroad or draw us into their strongest sphere of influence and military might. Either way, now's the time to catch your breath, and I recommend you do so, because things are about to get mighty hectic."

McGregor looked to Miller, and with a confirmatory smile, agreed: "Sounds like a plan to me. Now, you mentioned weapons..."

Wallace threw his arm over the General's shoulder and took him aside. "Well! I'm glad you asked—and my sense is you'll need 'em to get your people out of the EDS concentration camps. You've no doubt heard of the THOR Cannon, but have you ever heard tell of the Titan Cracker R5?"

"Don't go far, Commander. In ten minutes we brief the President." Cassandra remained behind with Miller. "You going to be alright?"

"Not until I see the Supreme Council in the Thames floating facedown." He massaged the bio-laminate sealing his knife wound. "Now tell me: how yah figure we go about making that happen?"

Alek and Monica had both registered with the Marines as Resistance members—necessary not only because Monica was committed to continuing collaboration given what she knew of the regime, but because those not in the register would be treated with suspicion. They confirmed their allegiance with Colonel Phan who was tallying the names of those who had returned, alive or dead, in the largest tent atop the hill. Once their names were inscribed and their

334

intention to continue aiding the Resistance codified, the Neuhauses exited the tent and found a plot of green on which to unwind.

"I never thought I'd see the day—" Monica had kept a stiff upper-lip and her composure for longer than either of them could remember, even with memories restored. Finally, with the assurance of security overhead and her thoughts free from EDS scrutiny, she wept.

Though Alek was inflexible on account of the casts applied to his neck and shoulders, he kept his wife standing and inundated her with kisses. The past several months where he was alone seemed one long and horrible nightmare, no more surreal than this dreamlike freedom overlooking the liberated English countryside. Were it not for the pain still shooting up from his ankle, he might have asked for a pinch. Instead, he held Monica tightly. "Why did they let us off here?"

Monica wiped her face dry of Alek's kisses and her tears, and looked around. "Blackpool is still full of enemy drones and true believers. This is as safe a place as we're bound to find on the island." She saw Danika and Lisa exit the tent, having similarly put their names in the book of the saved. They waved as they passed and Monica reciprocated. "Before they masked me as Mallory Worthing, I was awake for a time on the operating table. That was the last time until last night that I was myself. And you know what I thought?"

"Before they flipped you?" Alek shook his head, pained with the knowledge of what the demsocks had done to his wife.

"I thought: Alek Cornelius Neuhaus will be furious when he finds out what happened, and he won't stop fighting until I'm free."

"I was...and I didn't."

"I know." She kissed Alek and smiled. "Thank God for that."

Thinking on those who hadn't made it this far, Alek felt Geoff's absence for the first time. "You were right back in Blackpool."

"What's that?"

"We can't stop until they're all free."

335

MORE FUN AND UNSETTLING READS:

CYPULCHRE

CLOUD technology has swept America's rich and willing into the Outland Corporation's virtual paradise, entombing their minds in server towers known as cypulchres. The CLOUD's inventor has lived in exile for a decade; feared, defamed, and despised by his former colleagues and estranged family. When he learns that the technology he created now threatens his family as well as the millions synchronized to it, he must take action. With the help of a gang of radical hacktivists led by another disgruntled Outland employee, he attempts to reverse the curse he has unleashed on humanity. Nothing is what it seems, especially in a war between realities.

ARCHETYPAL

The Outland Corporation's CLOUD, a much-loved and massively-popular virtual realm, has been destroyed in a suicide bombing, which has turned all of Los Angeles upside down. Millions of users who were in the CLOUD at the time of its destruction have had their data and electric selves corrupted, accidentally collectivized, and then dumbly redistributed. The fallout is catastrophic. While Outland's interim CEO Celeste Charming attempts to turn this tragedy into profit or worse, Dr. Oni Matsui sets out to free her captive friends and to prevent the forced evolution of humanity for which her good intentions have paved the way.

FAULTLINE 49

The harrowing account of American reporter David Danson's Gonzo-style trip through US-occupied Canada in search of the principal provocateur in the Canadian-American War: terrorist mastermind Bruce Kalnychuk. As Danson draws closer to the truth about the 2001 World Trade Center Bombing in Edmonton, Alberta, and the criminal war it propagated, his journalistic distance to the story collapses, rendering him not only a brutalized participant, but an enemy of the state. David's findings are as daunting as the personal price he's paid to make them available to the North American public.

NEWSREAL

Gruffington Buzz reporter Alecia Troust's hopes of promotion are dashed when she loses her make-it-or-break-it article. Instead of admitting her bad luck to her editor, Alecia fabricates a story about homegrown terrorism. Although she initially wins the admiration of her editor, Alecia's lie also goes viral, drawing the ire and interest of anarcho-communists, western chauvinists, jihadists, rogue intelligence agencies, the mainstream media, and other nefarious groups who seek to profit from maintaining the fake news' veracity. With the worst of the country desperate to exploit the story for political ends, Alecia must get the truth out before her fake news catalyzes a national descent into paranoia, war, and authoritarianism.

THE SAVAGE KINGDOM

WWI veteran Elijah Cooper searches for peace and solace on the African Savana. His pursuit is thwarted when he finds himself blackmailed into service by a Machiavellian aristocrat. Charged with the care of the aristocrat's petulant son, Cooper safaris into the Holy Mountains, only to be dislocated by a time fracture. With the aristocrat's son lost, and nothing familiar to orient him, Cooper must set out through perilous and lavish wilds, beset by war and with prehistoric monsters. Old foes resurface alongside Roman legions and Neanderthal hordes, prompting Cooper to lead by example and curb tyranny in all its unholy forms.

GET THESE TITLES AND MORE AT
GUYFAUXBOOKS.COM